THE BEOTHUK SAGA

THE BEOTHUK
SAGA

A Novel by Bernard Assiniwi

Translated by Wayne Grady

THOMAS DUNNE BOOKS

St. Martin's Press ✠ New York

THOMAS DUNNE BOOKS.
An imprint of St. Martin's Press.

www.stmartins.com

Library of Congress Cataloging-in-Publication Data

Assiniwi, Bernard.
    [Saga des Béothuks. English]
    The Beothuk saga : a novel / by Bernard Assiniwi; translated by Wayne Grady.
        p. cm.
    ISBN 0-312-28390-3
    1. Beothuk Indians—History—Fiction. 2. Vikings—New Foundland—Fiction.
3. New Foundland—History—Fiction. I. Grady, Wayne. II. Title.
PQ3919.2.A8 S1813 2002
843'.914—dc21   2001040860

Originally published as *La Saga des Béothuks* by Leméac
First published in Canada by McClelland & Stewart Ltd.

First U.S. Edition: January 2002

10   9   8   7   6   5   4   3   2   1

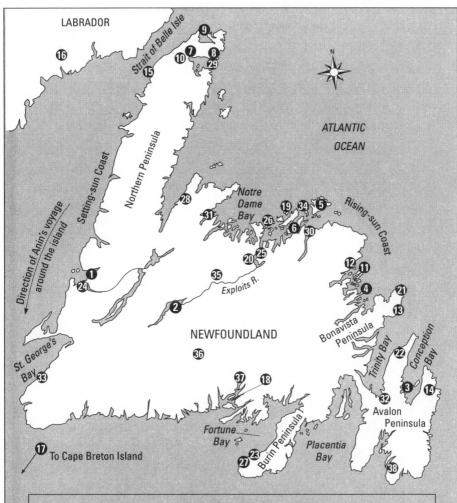

LABRADOR

Strait of Belle Isle

Northern Peninsula

Setting-sun Coast

Direction of Anin's voyage around the island

ATLANTIC OCEAN

Notre Dame Bay

Rising-sun Coast

Exploits R.

NEWFOUNDLAND

St. George's Bay

Bonavista Peninsula

Trinity Bay

Conception Bay

Avalon Peninsula

Fortune Bay

Burin Peninsula

Placentia Bay

To Cape Breton Island

N

Newfoundland Map Key

1 Baétha, village of the Addaboutik
2 Red Indian Lake
3 Site of first meeting with the Vikings
4 Site of Anin's second winter
5 Fogo Island
6 Site of meeting with Woasut
7 Winter site with Woasut
8 L'Anse aux Meadows
9 Pistolet Bay – occupied by the Vikings
10 Site of meeting with Scots and Viking fugitives
11 Site of John Cabot's landing
12 Site of Gaspar de Côrte Real's landing
13 Catalina
14 St. John's
15 Baie de la traversée (Ferry Bay)
16 Labrador – Land of the Sho-Undamung
17 Cape Breton Island – Land of the Shanung
18 Bay d'Espoir – Land of the Mixed Bloods
19 Twillingate

20 Botwood
21 Bonavista
22 Hant's Harbour
23 Grand Bank
24 Corner Brook
25 Exploits Bay
26 Exploits Islands
27 Fortune
28 Seal Cove
29 Hare Bay
30 Gander Bay
31 King's Cove
32 Dildo Run
33 Ship Cove
34 Change Island
35 Badger
36 Snowshoe Lake
37 Maelpaeg (village at Bay d'Espoir)
38 Peter's Arm

Contents

Part I   The Initiate   1
Part II   The Invaders   135
Part III   Genocide   217

Chronology of Events   323
A Beothuk Lexicon   331
Bibliography   340

I

THE INITIATE

About 1000 A.D.,
somewhere in the New World

I

ANIN PADDLED WITH all his strength. The sky was darkening and he wanted to be inside the line of reefs when the storm struck. He knew how fragile birchbark was, and that his tapatook would not survive if the rolling waves that were already blowing in from the open sea were to push him against the jagged rocks that lined the shore.

The wind rose. A wave came up suddenly, lifting the bow of his tapatook and throwing it towards the mouth of a narrow brook that emptied into the ocean between two cliffs. The reefs on either side were plainly visible, any one of them easily capable of tearing apart whatever the sea might throw its way. Anin steered away from the rocks and increased his stroke, pitting his tapatook against the strength of the sea. Could he make the brook without being thrown onto the rocks or against the cliff? If the storm was half as bad as he thought it would be, or if the creek turned out to be blocked, he would be paddling straight to his death. "I haven't made all of these discoveries over the past two cold seasons just to die such a stupid death now," he said to himself.

He turned the tapatook away from the brook and tried to paddle along the cliff face, but a second wave, larger than the first, lifted him again towards the shore. The raging water took the tapatook and sent it sideways towards the creek. Anin instinctively stretched his body along the length of the tapatook, reducing the chances of capsizing, and felt the craft race down the slope of the wave, then rise up another until he was almost level with the shore. He could not hear an undertow. "The brook must come from far inland," he told himself. "I might be able to touch bottom."

Gripping the sides of the tapatook, he raised himself to his knees and looked around. The brook forked away towards the setting sun, and he saw that he had to paddle quickly to keep from being flung on to the rocks. He grabbed his paddle from the bottom of the tapatook and plunged it deep into the water on the side opposite the shore, just in time to turn his craft towards the brook and away from the thundering boulders. Almost immediately he found himself gliding towards a sandy beach at the far end of a small, quiet pond. It felt like a place where waves came to die.

He lifted his paddle from the water. The pond was surrounded on three sides by high cliffs. On the side towards the setting sun there was a small stretch of red sand through which ran the brook he had seen from farther out, dropping down from inland in a necklace of silver cascades. Higher up, the gorge was flanked by vegetation, paler than usual because shaded by the cliffs. There was only one other living creature on the beach: Obseet the Cormorant, as astonished to see Anin as Anin was to be there.

A heavy rain began to pebble the surface of the pond. With a few strokes of his paddle, Anin ran the bow of his tapatook up onto the beach. He had spotted a break in the rock face, and removing his pack and dragging the tapatook high up onto the sand, he hurried to the shelter of the cleft. There he made a small pile of driftwood and dried spruce boughs, and using some of the birchbark he always carried for repairs, he lit a fire to dry his clothes. Then, worn out, his arms and legs leaden from many days of paddling, he unrolled his caribou skin near the fire and lay down. Within seconds, he was asleep.

While he slept, thunder rolled above him and lightning creased the sky. Gulls landed around his tapatook and walked stiffly towards the fire. Even Obseet the Cormorant, always a prey to curiosity, edged along the shoreline to cast a wary look at the intruder. None of this, however, disturbed the sleep of Anin the Initiate.

He was dreaming about the many things he had seen since he had left the village of his people. He had set out in the middle of one warm season, had travelled through two cold seasons, and was now nearing the end of his second season of thaw. At the feast held to mark his departure, he had said to his family: "I will return when I have seen all of our land. Not before."

He had often regretted his words. Many times he had wanted to end his voyage, but his pride had been stronger than his desire to return to his people. He could easily have travelled a few days' journey from his village, kept himself hidden for a time, and when he returned, told everyone that he had visited all the regions of their vast land. His uncle had tried that. But one day, fishermen from the village had ventured from their usual fishing grounds and discovered the trick: they had seen his uncle's camp and found several objects belonging to him. Being good hunters, they had also seen that the camp had been occupied for many seasons. When they returned to the village, they denounced his uncle as a liar, and his uncle, unable to live in disgrace, had killed himself by jumping from a high cliff.

Anin was neither a liar nor a trickster. He feared nothing and no one. At least he had never allowed himself to show fear. He had endured bitter storms at sea and had been stalked by a bear. The bear, smelling food in Anin's dwelling, had hung around his camp for six days; Anin had finally abandoned the camp and the food in it. Although his people had often told him that bears sleep during the season of cold and snow, Anin now knew that not all bears went into hibernation, or at least they did not go to sleep until they were no longer hungry.

In the course of his travels, Anin had had his tapatook torn on the sharp edges of coastal rocks and had himself been severely wounded. It had taken him more than one whole moon to mend his wounds and make a new tapatook out of birchbark. He had endured hunger and cold. He had been terrified by things whose very existence had been unknown to him until his voyage of initiation. During the two cold seasons he had spent alone, he had learned to take care of himself. Had he merely hidden near his people's village, he would not have lived through these dangers, and would have had to invent false exploits to relate to his kinsmen upon his return.

No, Anin was no liar. He had told his family he would return only when he had travelled around all their land. He had given his word, and once a word was given, it could not be taken back until either the task was complete or those to whom the word had been given requested that the task be abandoned. That was the law. Anin would travel to the ends of his people's land even if it meant never seeing his people again. But that, of course, was not possible. If the elders were right, the Earth had been made by Beaver in the image of his mamateek, and was therefore round. The male had built his mamateek below, and the female had built hers above, upside down, and the earth had grown between them, round as a rock but held aloft by the wind in the great realm of the spirits.

If he followed the edge of the round Earth, it was clear that he would end up at the place of his departure. And so Anin would return; older, certainly, perhaps too old to find a companion with whom he could add to the number of his people, but he would return. He might not be able to tell all the new things he had seen so that his people would learn from his adventures, but he would return with his experiences contained in his spirit, just as his food and weapons were contained in his pack. And he might not bring new and curious things back to show his people, but he would teach them the truth about the things that were out here. Even if there was nothing mysterious or magical about what he told them, he would tell them the truth. There is nothing mysterious or magical about the truth: it is simply the truth, and that is all one can say or do or tell or think or teach about it. It is not right to show a child how to make a whistle and then tell him that he will actually be whistling. But it is the truth to tell the child that by blowing his whistle, he will make sounds that otherwise he would hear only from birds. The truth alone exists: falsehoods kill. Lies kill those who tell them. Those who tell or pass on lies end up believing them to be truths, and they become snared in their own lies. The elders say that lies come from those who do not know the difference between their dreams and their desires. Between their dreams and their longings. Between their dreams and their ability to realize them.

Anin would return to his people. Perhaps by the end of the warm season, if he didn't waste too much time sleeping in one place.

He woke to the sound of footsteps. The sun was still up, but the sky was dark. Not a breath of wind. The rain had stopped. The only sounds were those of footsteps on wet sand. Even before he looked up he knew who was making them: Gashu-Uwith the Bear had finally caught up with him after all these moons.

Anin leapt to his feet to face the animal, which was coming directly towards him. The bear stopped dead in its tracks. He sniffed the air deeply with his wet muzzle and, despite his poor vision, sensed that he had found the food source from the previous cold season. Anin had no doubt that this was the same bear that had pestered him earlier. Gashu-Uwith was a great hunter. He had picked up Anin's scent when it was more than four moons cold. Anin had travelled by water while Gashu-Uwith had not left the land. The bear could not see very far, nor could he smell Anin when Anin was at sea, except when the wind was blowing in towards the land.

Gashu-Uwith was either Anin's enemy or his spirit protector; the problem was discerning the difference without making a mistake. Anin remained standing without showing his fear. Gashu-Uwith sat down on the red sand and, stretching his neck, sniffed the air. He stood up on his hind legs and sniffed again. Then he went down on all fours and walked slowly towards the brook, waded upstream, and disappeared over the lip of the first waterfall.

Anin remained on the beach for a long time, trying to decide whether or not the bear was his spirit protector. How else to explain why the bear had not tried to kill him last winter, even though he had been hungry, and hungry bears were known to stalk and attack solitary initiates? And this time, Gashu-Uwith had moved off as soon as he had sensed Anin's presence. By climbing to the top of the waterfall, had he been showing Anin a path? Often a spirit protector will lead an initiate along a certain path to avoid dangers that lay ahead.

Deep in thought, Anin stirred the embers of his fire and took a portion of dried meat from his pack. When he had eaten, he lay down on his caribou skin again and slept. When he woke up, his decision had been made. He went to his tapatook, secured his pack to the centre thwart, raised the tapatook to his head, and walked towards the brook. He climbed up on the less rocky side, and in a short time was at the top. He found himself standing on a rocky ridge that, on the left, became a tongue of land that ran down into the sea. Beyond the ridge he saw a magnificent bay, wider than he could see across. To reach this bay by water, around the tongue of land, would have taken him at least two suns. By this short climb he had been afforded a beautiful view, and had also been spared the dangers that always lurk beneath the dark surface of the great sea.

When Anin looked for a path that would take him down to the bay, he saw Gashu-Uwith sitting calmly at the base of a white spruce, as though waiting to guide him to a new discovery.

2
—

ANIN WALKED DOWN the hill towards the bay whose waters stretched as far as the sky. It was lined with a rim of sand that also ran off into the distance. Each time the waves retreated, he could see clams burying themselves in the wet sand; gathering them up, he thought, would be child's play. Anin lingered on this beach for many suns, well into the growing season, bathed by the sun's warm luminescence and nourished by the sea. When he was tired he stretched out on his caribou skin and slept. Finally, he woke early one morning and set out in the pale, predawn light, his tapatook on his shoulder, preferring to walk along the shore rather than paddle out to sea. He often thought of Gashu-Uwith. After showing him the path beside the waterfall, which had saved him from who knew what dangers and difficulties in his frail, one-man tapatook, the "lord of the land," as his people called the bear, had disappeared as suddenly as he had come. Anin walked for many days carrying his tapatook, sometimes setting it down in the shallow water and dragging it by means of a cord woven from caribou sinews.

One day he saw a flock of large, orange-beaked birds flying out towards an island on the horizon. He knew this bird. His people called them godets. It was a calm day, and Anin decided to paddle out to the island and kill a few godets for food for the next few days. He put his tapatook down in the water and paddled towards the distant island. He had almost reached it when the water beneath his tapatook erupted in an explosion of foam, almost capsizing him: a whale had suddenly surfaced, curious to see what strange creature was invading his water. When Anin reached the island, he pulled the tapatook far up onto the beach and lay down to rest. The island had been much farther out than it had appeared from the shore, and it had cost him much effort to reach it, despite the calmness of the water.

When he woke, he saw that the only place on the island where he could have landed was where he had, in fact, come ashore; the rest of it was nothing but sheer rock cliffs on which the godets made their nests. Armed with only his fish net, Anin climbed one of the cliff faces. The godets hardly took notice of him. They sat calmly on their nests, which they had constructed in shallow depressions in the thin soil at the top of the cliffs. Many nests contained young chicks, waiting for their parents to bring them food. When an adult puffin arrived with food, Anin snared it with his net, twisted its neck, and threw it down to the base of the cliff, near his tapatook. When he had killed ten, he climbed down again and spent the rest of the day skinning the birds so that he would not have to pluck them. Then he made a fire and hung them near the flames to dry and smoke. He soon had enough meat to see him through to the end of the warm season. He kept the fire going all night so that its warmth and smoke would penetrate deep into the birds' flesh.

The next morning, when the birds were sufficiently dried, he lay down and slept. When he woke, the sun was high in the sky and the wind was blowing sharply. High waves made the sea too rough for him to reach shore safely. He ate some smoked godet, then decided to investigate the rest of the rocky island. On the sunny side he saw a group of seals, females and their young, stretched out lazily on the warm, flat rocks. "I, too, should be with my people when the warm season is here," he told himself.

He spent the rest of the day on the island. From the top of its highest cliff he watched a pod of whales blowing very close to the island. Farther out, he saw a tapatook that seemed much larger than his own. "I have heard the Bouguishamesh also visit this land," he said aloud. "I'd best not show myself until I know what they're after." But the large tapatook, fitted with a sail, was too far out to sea for its paddlers to see Anin standing on the headland. That night, the initiate found a sheltered spot in which to spend the night, and slept like a child, feeling safe and confident.

In the morning he rose with the sun. After eating, he wrapped the rest of the smoked birds in his fish net, placed everything in the tapatook, and began the long paddle back to solid land. When he reached the shore, he walked for several suns along the beach, dragging the tapatook with the cord. One rain-drenched afternoon, Anin came to a rocky ridge that seemed to close off the beach. He told himself that it was time to launch his tapatook and continue his voyage by sea. His spirit had been decidedly low for the past two or three suns, and he knew that such feelings were significant. The last time he had felt like that, he had almost drowned, taken by surprise by a sudden squall. Such thoughts would continue to haunt him, he decided, unless he confronted the ridge of rock that had loomed up so suddenly before him.

When he reached the base of the ridge, he looked for a place to spend the night. The rain continued to fall heavily, colder now that the sun had gone down. "I must find a safe place," he told himself. "If I do not dry my clothes, I will never complete this voyage to my people."

As he followed the wall of rock towards the interior, he came to an immense pile of boulders stacked one on top of the other. One of the largest rocks in the middle formed a kind of roof. Rain poured down on either side of it. It was not the best spot to wait for the weather to change, but it was more comfortable than staying out in the rain. After lighting a fire and spreading his clothes out to dry, he rolled himself in his caribou skin and lay down near the flames, too tired to eat. The night seemed interminable. The dampness penetrated deep into his insides. He shivered. He felt the clammy cold of fear, the dread that one who lives close to nature feels when he senses that something is about to happen but is not sure what it is. Several times during the night he heard voices.

As soon as it was light enough to see, he got up, rolled his caribou skin and tied it tightly. The voices he heard must have been dreams, he thought, because he was certain he was alone in this strange land. He pulled on his leggings, threw the caribou skin over his shoulder, and walked back towards the beach, where he had left his tapatook and the rest of his provisions. Hunger gnawed at his belly. He had taken only a few steps, however, when he suddenly stopped. Directly ahead of him, a short distance from shore, was a huge Bouguishamesh tapatook with the head of a monster on the bow. Inside were many men running back and forth, their heads barely visible above the sides of the craft. He looked anxiously to where his own tapatook was hidden; it was still there, but two Bouguishamesh with hair the colour of dried grass were examining it, gesticulating and shouting to each other. Guttural sounds came from their mouths. Anin could not understand what they were saying. He stood stock still; it was as though his body and clothing had become the colour of rock, and he could blend into the landscape while observing these strange beings with their pale skin and grass-coloured hair. They were tall, at least a head taller than he was. Were the Bouguishamesh giants from another land? Or was it Anin who was from another land, and this was the homeland of these strange creatures? He wanted to show himself, to make their acquaintance, to try to communicate with them and learn more about them. But without really knowing why, he held back.

One of the beings walked towards the huge tapatook in the bay while the other one lifted Anin's, as if to see how heavy it was. Then he picked it up, placed it in the water, and climbed into it. Immediately the tapatook began to rock, and the Bouguishamesh fell into the water. He let out a terrible cry that made Anin tremble to hear it. The other being ran over, and seeing his companion in the water, began to laugh. Then the first man began to laugh, too, and pushed the tapatook back up onto the beach.

"They laugh like we do," thought Anin. "They do not become angry. They react as we would when something goes wrong. Perhaps they are friendly. But they are very big."

The two men with hair the colour of dried grass walked over to the large tapatook and began calling it. One of the men on board stopped moving about and answered in a loud voice, as though he were angry. Then the head of another man came out of the belly of the tapatook. His hair was the colour of fire, and he had a band of some soft material tied around his forehead. The man with the fire-red hair jumped into the water and began wading ashore towards Anin's tapatook. The two on shore ran behind him and had almost caught up with him when Anin heard a loud shout behind him. He jumped and turned around: a giant was running straight for him. Its hair was in braids, like those Anin had seen on the Ashwans when he was a youth, except these were the colour of dried grass. Anin ran to his tapatook to get his bow and arrows and his fish spear. He jumped to one side in time to evade a swipe from a grey club swung by the giant Bouguishamesh, but he slipped at the base of the cliff and a second blow from the bidissoni tore off a strip of skin as big as a hand from his right thigh. Pain seared up his leg, but the young initiate managed to grab his spear as he fell and jam its handle in the sandy soil. The giant ran at him like a bear charging to protect her cubs, and impaled himself on Anin's spear. He gave out another loud cry.

Without looking back, Anin clambered like a rabbit up the cliff, leaping from rock to rock. When he reached the top, he dashed into the woods and hid behind a fallen tree to see if any of the other Bouguishamesh were following him. Their tapatook looked empty. He heard loud voices calling out words that he could not understand. Silently, Anin stole back down to the beach. When he reached the body of the red-haired giant, he placed a foot on its chest and pulled out his spear. The voices were becoming louder, and Anin knew he had to act quickly: he could either run back into the woods or try to get his tapatook into the water and paddle out to sea. He did not like his chances on the water because the Bouguishamesh also had a tapatook, and so despite the pain in his leg he climbed back up the rock face and ran into the spruce forest. Once in the familiar labyrinth of trees, he circled back along the shore in order not to stray too far from his tapatook. He hoped to tire his pursuers, but he did not want to have to make another tapatook.

3

FOR THREE SUNS Anin ran through the forest, always in great pain. The trees here seemed to him much larger than those near the village of his people. The beings with the pale skin and hair the colour of dried grass were still following him, but he was young and agile, and his endurance allowed him to go many days without eating. If he were weaker, they would have caught him long ago. His thigh throbbed, causing him great suffering; the wound, which had bled freely as he ran, had turned an ugly, dark colour that worried him. At the setting of the third sun, he decided to stop and clean it despite the beings that were chasing him. He spent some time searching for the marsh plant that grew between the season of thaw and the season of cold and snow, and whose secret properties he had been taught. This plant, which had purplish leaves and looked like a man standing up, collected water in its base, and insects would drown in the water and the plant would feed on them to nourish itself. Anin finally found a slight depression in the ground with caribou moss growing in it, and the plant he was looking for grew there also, fertilized by the moss. He picked as many as he had fingers on one hand, because they were still quite young. Using a round stone, he crushed the plants in the hollow of a tree and made a paste. Then he applied the paste directly to the wound. At first he felt a coolness in his leg that soothed the pain, but then the wound began to sting until it became almost unbearable. He knew he had to endure this burning until the wound was cleansed and purified by the juices of the plant. The fever travelled up his body to his ears; he felt as though his face was on fire. Suddenly he felt weak and began to vomit until his stomach was completely empty. Then, exhausted, he lay down on the ground beneath a large white spruce and slept through the warm, humid night.

When he woke up, it was still dark and he was cold. He trembled like a leaf in the wind. He slapped himself all over to warm himself, then he got up and jumped from one foot to the other. His wounded leg was swollen, but the pain that had been so intense the day before was gone. But as soon as his body was warm, his hunger returned. It had now been three suns since he had had water or anything to eat but the shiny leaves of a plant with small red berries that gave strength but did not fill the belly.

The sky was bright with stars, and Anin could see his immediate surroundings. He was still in the small hollow; the ground beneath him, a thin layer of soil over rock, formed a kind of water reservoir, which was why he had found the purple plant growing here. At the edge of this depression, the white bark of the birch trees leapt brightly out of the darkness. Anin smiled: he could ease his hunger. He walked to the edge of the hollow and, using his flint knife, cut himself a large slice of birchbark. He scraped off the tender inside of the rind to make a sort of paste, which he chewed carefully, swallowing the juice and as little of the pulp as possible. His mouth felt coated, as it did when he ate the bitter acorns from the hardwood tree that looked like a man with many arms. He knew that he had to drink, and he found some rainwater that had been trapped in a small cavity in the rock.

By the time he had finished his meal, the sky had paled into morning. With his knife, he cut several young birch and oak shoots with which to make weapons for hunting. His bow and arrows were still in his tapatook, and he had nothing but his knife, a few thorns for fish hooks, and a length of cord made of braided grass. He had lost his caribou skin when the giant had attacked him. He had to get another one and he needed to find a sheltered spot before the season of cold and snow arrived. Somewhere close to the sea but still in the forest, where he would be protected from the wind but still able to find food and build himself another tapatook. A traveller without a tapatook was a poor traveller indeed, and had only clams and other castoffs from the sea to eat. When the cold hardened the beach sand and the sea covered itself to stay warm, the unprepared traveller died.

It took him longer than three suns to make a bow, and another three to make as many arrows as he had fingers on both hands. By then the cold had settled in. Already he had to get up several times during the night to put more wood on his fire in order to preserve what little warmth his body produced. Each morning he longed for the sun to warm him and let him accomplish the work necessary for his survival. To get food, he set rabbit snares and deadfalls for the larger animals. He caught suckers with a noose suspended from the end of a pole. He also fished in a nearby river, catching enough for his daily needs as well as for the cold season to come. He made flour from the inner rind of birchbark, which he dried on rocks placed near the fire, ground with a round stone on a flat stone, and then baked into bread. He also made frames for snowshoes, then began making a new tapatook with the bark left over from his bread-making.

He killed two wood caribou to give himself a cache of meat and also for their skins, to make clothing. With the hides from their legs he made leggings and sleeves for himself. He made a loincloth with skin from their backs, then sewed the remainder together to make a heavy blanket, softened, as was his clothing, with oil from the feet of the slaughtered animals. The oil also made them waterproof. Finally, Anin killed Mamchet the Beaver. He ate the meat and used the tendons to string his snowshoes. For nearly a whole moon he worked from sun up to sun down preparing himself for the cold season. Then the snow began to fall, heavy and quiet. The season of cold and snow arrived at about the same time that the wound on Anin's thigh shed its last scab.

It was time for Anin to go back to the great water, carrying the provisions he had accumulated over the past moon. The forest could provide him with some of his needs, but not all of them, and if he were to continue his voyage around his people's land, he could not leave the shores of this water, because it was only by following the shore that he could return to his point of departure. He began to portage his things to the great water, following the course of the brook that would lead him down to the shore of the sea. Since he knew he was in high country, and that the brook must therefore run swiftly to the sea, he did not drag his tapatook but carried it and his goods on his back. The descent took him two suns, carrying only his tapatook, his hunting weapons, and enough provisions for the return journey. When he came to the great water, he stopped and studied the horizon for a long time, making sure the big Bouguishamesh tapatook was nowhere in sight. When he was certain that he was alone, he continued down to the shore. The cold-season tide line was high, almost up to the trees at the edge of the valley. He could not waste much time finding a good spot to build his winter mamateek. He had to give up the idea of constructing a mamateek of birchbark, because it was already so cold that the bark would be frozen to the trunk of the trees and it would be difficult to cut off pieces large enough for a shelter. He therefore decided to make a different kind of shelter, leaning fallen spruce trees up against one another and interlacing their boughs to form a roof. With one of his snowshoes, he covered the whole shelter with a thick blanket of snow. Only the very top was left uncovered, to allow smoke to escape during the long, cold nights ahead. Two more suns passed while he worked on the shelter. Then he took as many suns as he had fingers to move the rest of his food and other items that he had made during his convalescence.

He had had to build a temporary shelter halfway between the shore camp and his forest camp, a place where he could spend the night during the two-sun portage. When he climbed back up to his forest camp, he carried nothing but food for four suns. But since it was uphill, he had to stop more often than when he came down. When the portages were finished, the snow had fallen as deep as his knees and the true cold had set in for the rest of the cold season.

Time passed slowly. The season was neither colder nor snowier than in preceding years. When his meat supply began to run low, he climbed back up to his forest camp, and for five suns hunted in the land of Kosweet the Caribou. When he found a whole family, he chose the youngest so there would be no meat left over to spoil when the season of thaw arrived. He took his time on this trip because, in the cold season, it was important to save his strength, so that when it was good hunting weather he would not be too sick or weak to take advantage of it. He also enjoyed the milder climate in the forest, sheltered from the wind and softened by the warmth of the trees.

One day, as he was descending towards the sea, dragging his provisions behind him on a large piece of birchbark, he saw Gashu-Uwith drinking calmly from a stream that ran near his midway camp. Anin stopped in his tracks, not wanting to startle or annoy the creature. Despite his growing suspicion that the bear was his spirit protector, Anin could not bring himself to trust it.

The bear raised his head and sniffed the air. He turned towards Anin and let out a low growl, then sat back on the ground, boldly blocking Anin's path. Gashu-Uwith was enormous. Since he was so close to Anin's temporary camp, Anin simply sat down in the snow too, and took out his bow and arrows, just in case.

The two beings remained in this position for a long time, watching each other closely and sniffing each other's scent. The bear particularly noticed the smell of fresh caribou meat. Neither of them moved, and the sun's light began to diminish rapidly. Anin did not like the idea of sitting there in the snow all night, wide awake, watching Gashu-Uwith sniffing the air, because the thought had come to him that Gashu-Uwith was probably still awake because he was hungry. He stood up slowly and, untying the caribou hide that was covering the meat, took out a large piece and walked with it towards Gashu-Uwith. The bear did not move. Anin stopped a few steps in front of him, tossed the piece of meat down, and backed away. Gashu-Uwith leaned over, picked up the meat in his teeth, then stood up and walked off along a path through the deep snow into the forest on the side of a steep hill. Anin watched him retreat. The bear stopped, turned towards Anin and growled softly before disappearing around the hill. Anin lit a fire, cooked himself a piece of caribou meat, then unrolled his new caribou skin and went to sleep. In the morning, he continued his journey down to his winter camp on the edge of the great water.

The rest of the cold season passed without incident, and the weather began to warm and the snow began to melt as the sun's strength returned. Only a few patches of snow remained here and there among the rocks and in the shadows of the trees. The largest pieces of ice, thrown high on the beach by waves, lingered in the shadow of the cliffs when the tide went out. Anin added to his store of dried meat, carved two new paddles, and tied his pack to the centre thwart of his new tapatook. One morning during the melting season, when the sun was just waking up, he left his cold-season camp and paddled into the setting sun. He continued in that direction for several suns, then turned his tapatook in the direction from which, every season-cycle, the coldness came.

4

PARTLY BECAUSE OF his heavy load, but mostly because of the strong current that came towards him from the direction of the cold, Anin's progress was slower than usual. He passed many islands of ice that floated into the sun and did not melt, and he was greatly impressed by them. "I would not like to live on an island that moved," he thought. "How would I know where the good fishing places were, if the island kept moving all the time?" And then he laughed as he realized that these islands probably shrank as the warm season advanced, getting smaller and smaller from bird-hatching time until they disappeared altogether.

Suddenly his attention was drawn to a large flock of gulls on the horizon, directly ahead of him and circling just above the land. He told himself that there must be a deep bay hidden behind the rocks that tumbled out into the sea. He must continue with caution. His experience with the belligerent Bouguishamesh had taught him a lesson. He angled in towards the shore and continued paddling closer to land. As soon as he rounded the first tongue of rock he saw a sort of inner bay, protected by a second point of land that was empty of trees but less rocky than the one he had just passed.

He slackened his rhythm and kept his paddle in the water in order to make as little noise as possible. From time to time he stopped paddling altogether and listened. He heard shouting and laughter that seemed to be coming from children or young girls. The closer he approached the point of land, the more clearly he could hear the voices. He tried to determine how many there were on the far side of the point: he counted all the fingers on both hands and thought that was about half the number.

He did not round the second point, but landed his tapatook on a small beach of coarse sand littered with algae and enormous fronds of seaweed. Bending down to make sure his knife was still fastened to his leg, he quietly took his spear from the bottom of the tapatook. His idea was to climb the low hill between himself and the voices to see what was on the other side, but first he glanced behind him, out to sea, to satisfy himself that the Bouguishamesh were not on his heels. Then he slowly made his way to the top of the embankment.

What he saw froze him in his tracks, and his skin became like the skin of a bird when it has been plucked ready for cooking. The scene before him was exactly like many he himself had partici-pated in when he was a child; it was as though he had returned to his own village as it had been many years before. Except that his own village had had nothing comparable to this calm, sheltered bay. Here, just below him, several youngsters were digging in the sand with sharpened sticks, turning up clams and other shellfish and tossing them into a basket. When the basket was full, one of the older children carried it to the head of the bay, where a group of adults was gathered around a fire. The adults were cooking the clams on piles of heated seaweed. Anin heard one of the older children shout something he almost understood, and the others dropped their sticks and ran toward the fire. Then the older child handed each of them an opened clam, and they all began to eat.

As their laughter mingled with shouts of pleasure, Anin knew that he was among people who lived as his people lived and spoke a language similar to his own. He wanted to stand up and show himself, to make their acquaintance, convinced now that these people were Addaboutik like himself. But he hesitated. Without knowing why, he did not dare to show himself to these people, no matter how friendly they appeared to be. None of them seemed to be armed. But he remembered that the Bouguishamesh had also been laughing delightedly when the giant attacked him from behind.

"Among themselves they are happy," he thought. "But would they be so with a stranger?"

He remained where he was, not moving, stretched out flat on his stomach, watching the others laughing and eating, talking and playing, just as he had as a child. He began to sense a large emptiness within himself. He could hardly restrain himself from jumping up and shouting, "Hey! I am alone and I miss my people, whom I left three warm seasons ago." But he did restrain himself. His emptiness was inside, and he kept it there. He was unable to reach a decision about it. The sun was high overhead, and the rocks around him were warm. He laid his head down on one of them and closed his eyes. He may even have fallen asleep, but only for a moment.

The next thing he knew he was on his feet: frightened cries from the children had roused him. Quickly he threw himself flat again. The children were running about in all directions, confused and shouting. He saw one fall face-down in the water, a long shaft protruding from his back – the shaft of a fishing spear. He recognized it at once: it was the kind used by the Ashwans, the people who came from the cold. He saw the adults, those who had been cooking the clams, lying on the ground, their backs, throats, and chests pierced by arrows. An old man, brandishing a knife, was struggling to get up despite the arrow in his chest, and one of the Ashwans amused himself by knocking him down with a long pole. Several times the old man tried to get at his attacker, but he never succeeded.

Anin saw two Ashwans come close to where he was hiding, chasing a young girl. Her face was contorted with terror as the two men gained on her. Anin looked behind him to check the distance between himself and his tapatook, and saw that it was too far away for him to reach it before the Ashwans reached him. He leapt to his feet and threw himself at the first of the Ashwans, dropping him with a single blow to the chest with the butt end of his lance and calling to the girl to launch the tapatook and wait for him offshore. Without hesitation the girl ran down the embankment, pushed Anin's tapatook into the water, and jumping into it, began paddling furiously out to sea. The second Ashwan, smaller than the first, rushed at Anin swinging high above his head a large knife blade lashed to a whale bone; before he could bring it down, however, Anin's spear pierced his body just below the throat. Anin raised his foot, pressed it against the small man's chest, and retrieved his weapon. The Ashwan immediately fell over backwards, dead.

By this time, the other Ashwans at the bay had become aware of the commotion above them. Anin spun around and ran down the embankment after the young woman. But when he reached the place where his tapatook had been, he saw the young woman still paddling in a panic towards the rising sun. She had already cleared the rough water close to the shore, where Anin remained stranded. Glancing about him, he saw that it was too late to escape from the Ashwans on land; his only hope was to dive into the water and swim to the first point of land, the one he had rounded before beaching his tapatook. He also realized that he must wait until the Ashwans were nearly upon him before he jumped, for if they saw what he intended to do they would simply run out onto the point to wait for him. He held himself ready, calculating the precise moment when he should make his move. In the corner of his eye he saw the tapatook rounding the point and heading for the first bay. Fully loaded as it was, he knew that the young woman would not be able to take it very far before he could reach her.

Then the Ashwans were scrambling down the embankment. There were three of them. Seeing that Anin was waiting for them, they stopped at the bottom and regarded him warily. They had seen their two dead companions, and perhaps suspected that there were more of Anin's people hidden behind the bluff. They hesitated long enough for Anin to take careful aim and hurl his spear into one of the Ashwans. Then, with a great shout of victory, he turned and plunged into the water and swam towards the point. The water was ice-cold, despite the lateness of the season, and Anin forced himself to swim quickly in order to keep his blood from thickening. When he reached the rocky promontory, he stood up and looked back. The two Ashwans were carrying their wounded companion up the embankment, apparently no longer interested in him. He let himself sink between two rocks, exhausted from his efforts and hidden from the view of the Ashwans. "They are savages," he thought. "They live only to kill."

He had often thought that luck was not travelling with him on his voyage around the world. Why, he asked himself, had he saved the young woman? She would certainly be as terrified of him as she had been of the Ashwans. Then he thought that he would once again have to make a new tapatook, and that this would take him a long time. He must not be discouraged. He stood up and, crossing the point, began to walk back along the shore, in the direction from which he had earlier come in his tapatook. Every so often he would stop and look back to see if the Ashwans had sent some of their number to follow him, then he would turn and continue his slow retreat. As the waves withdrew from the shoreline he walked on the wet sand, which was much easier on his feet than hopping from rock to rock. He could even run, and put a greater distance between himself and any eventual pursuers.

Towards nightfall, he began to look for a sheltered spot within the forest. All he saw, however, were isolated patches of stunted evergreens dotted here and there above the embankment. Then he stopped short: lying a short distance ahead of him on the sand was his tapatook. He slipped behind some large rocks and continued slowly, staying close to the cliff so as not to alert the young woman to his presence. He saw no sign of her near the tapatook, but when he was closer he saw footprints in the sand leading from the tapatook up to a small gorge cut into the embankment by a brook that emptied into the sea. Anin thought that the woman had been foolish to leave the tapatook out in the open, where an Ashwan could hardly miss it, and to show so plainly where she had fled. He dragged the tapatook higher up on the sand and hid it under some bushes above the tide line. Then he removed some dried meat from the pack that was still tied to the vessel's thwart, noting that the woman had taken nothing of his but his bow and a handful of arrows. When he had taken enough food for his meal, he decided to follow the woman's tracks at least until it was too dark to continue, and so he began following the brook inland, climbing over the many fallen trees that littered the ground. He did not have to go far. The woman's tracks soon revealed where she had left the path several times to investigate possible hiding places. Walking very lightly now, he searched each recess in the rocks that bordered the narrow canyon, and eventually came to a place where a dark cleft interrupted the smooth canyon wall. He made his way towards it, focusing all his concentration on the cavity, as though he were hungry and knew there was game in it. Slowly he drew his knife from the sheath attached to his leg, and stooping low, crept silently forward, stopping several times to listen. The only sound that reached him was that of water tumbling over the rocky stream-bed. Almost without moving he entered the cavern. Immediately his eyes made out the form of a young woman stretched out on the ground, her head resting on one arm. Exhausted from paddling, she had simply gone to sleep on the gravelly cavern floor. "If an Ashwan had found her like this," he thought, "she would be dead by now."

Quietly he approached and crouched down beside her. He wanted to study her. Her hair was the colour of the rich earth where plants grew between rocks. Her skin also was dark. There were still traces of ochre on her face. The Addaboutik coated themselves with this red powder in the season of plenty, when the mosquitoes were at their worst in the interior. She must therefore be from one of the inland clans. She was very young, hardly old enough to bear children. Her breathing became irregular; she had sensed his presence, but she did not move a muscle. Anin waited. He glanced away for a second, and she was on her feet before he could react, an arrow clenched in her fist. As she brought it down towards his face he rolled to one side, avoiding the blow, and sprang to his feet with his knife held at the ready. They stood facing each other, poised to attack. This is ridiculous, Anin thought: Here I am, standing before a woman whose life I have just saved, ready to kill her if she makes a sudden move.

"My name is Anin," he said aloud. "I am an Addaboutik, from Baétha, a village two cold seasons towards the setting sun, across the big water. I do not wish to harm you. I killed the

Ashwans who were chasing you. It was my tapatook that you used to get away."

Not since he had left Baétha had he said so many words at one time. She was the first other human he had spoken to at all; even when he had talked to himself he had not done so out loud. The young woman did not answer him. She was still frightened.

"I am Anin. I am an Addaboutik and I come from Baétha. Why did you take my tapatook and leave me alone to fight the Ashwans? I could have been killed."

The young woman seemed to have difficulty understanding him. Without relaxing her stance, and without taking her eyes from Anin's, she said:

"I am Woasut, Beothuk woman. I have heard of the Addaboutik. They are our cousins and live on the other side of the land, two moons towards the setting sun, along the rivers and lakes."

Anin was stunned by this intelligence. He had just learned that his own people, the Addaboutik, and this woman's people inhabited the same land. He had undergone the most severe dangers of the sea for nothing. Had he been fighting the Bouguishamesh and the Ashwans on his own land? How, after having travelled for two complete season-cycles, could he be only two moons from where he started? He could hardly believe his ears.

"Lower your weapon," he said to the woman. "I will not hurt you. I understand your words. Listen to me now, for you can understand my words too. Beothuk is also the name of my people's ancestors. We are related by our ancestors. Lower your weapon and I will lower mine. It would not be right for us to kill one another."

Woasut lowered her weapon and Anin returned his knife to its sheath. The two kept a wary eye on each other for a long time while they sat in the cavern, watching from the corners of their eyes, not sure what to expect. Night fell, and Woasut began to shiver with the cold. Anin stood up and left the cavern to find firewood and red evergreen boughs, which he brought back to make a fire. When Woasut was warming herself by the flames, he stood up again and told her he was going back to the tapatook to get some food. "I won't be long," he said to her, smiling broadly. "Watch out for Ashwans."

He had no trouble finding the tapatook in the dark. On his way back to the cavern, he thought to himself that all things considered it was good to have someone to talk to. When he entered the shelter, Woasut had not moved from the fire except to add more wood to it. Anin sat down before her and saw that tears were running down her cheeks. He did not interrupt her grief. They ate in silence, and tears continued to fill the young woman's eyes.

When it was time to sleep, they lay together under a single blanket, and Anin felt his manhood stiffen and his heart begin to beat strongly against his chest. Woasut pressed herself closer to him and did not move away when he let his hands explore her neck, her thighs, her chest. She even took his hand and placed it upon her breast, and then, without a word, she turned on her stomach, raised herself on her knees and loosened her dingiam, exposing herself to Anin, who moved behind her and loosened his own dingiam. With gentle insistence he entered her. Woasut received him with a small gasp and moved eagerly with his rhythm until, satisfied, he withdrew and lay down beside her again, holding her in his arms.

"I have given you my first time," she whispered into his ear, "because you saved my life." Then she slept.

When Anin awoke the next morning, Woasut was still curled peacefully in his arms. He felt boundlessly happy. Was it because of her, he asked himself? Was it the assuaging of his desire for a woman? Or was it because he knew he was not far from his own people? He did not know how to say what he felt. It was as though he were lighter. His arm under Woasut's head was tingling, but he did not want to move it for fear of disturbing her. She was smiling in her sleep. When she opened her eyes, she raised her head and looked at him. Lowering the blanket, she regarded his sex gravely, as though seeking confirmation of his strength and virility. Then she put his sex in her mouth and caressed it with her tongue until it was hard and almost on the point of bursting. Then she raised herself on her knees and invited Anin to repeat his act of the night before.

5

FOR THE FIRST time since he had set out on his journey of initiation, Anin was undecided. Should he cross the forest in the direction shown to him by Woasut, to rejoin his people, or should he continue and complete his circumnavigation of their land, as he had given his word he would do? If he crossed overland to his village, he would never know if the earth were round, like an island, or just a long, narrow spit of land that stretched endlessly out to sea. And he would be going back on his promise not to return until he had found out.

And what about the woman? Would she stay with him, to travel as his companion, or would she return to her own people? Had all her people been killed by the Ashwans, or had some of them escaped into the interior? Were the Bouguishamesh of this land, or had they come from some other, stranger, place? By continuing his journey, would he run the risk of encountering them again, or had they left this land forever? When the warm season was over, should he move inland to hunt, or stay close to the sea and survive the cold season by fishing?

All these questions must be answered before he could formulate a plan for the next several moons. Perhaps he should discuss them with Woasut? She knew the region well, and her knowledge would be useful to him. But she was a woman, and according to the elders women must not influence the decisions of men. He did not know what to do.

"If I decide to continue and she agrees to come with me," he thought, "she could sew my winter garments after scraping the skins. I must speak to her about it."

Woasut had gone to collect shellfish while the young Addaboutik gathered berries for the morning meal. While they ate, the woman seemed to rediscover her smile. She thought it likely that some of her people were still alive, all but the few adults and children at the bay. When Anin told her about the questions that were troubling him, her brow wrinkled. She did not know what she would do either. She thought she would first find out if her people were safe, and decide her own course after that. She asked Anin if he would help her find her people, but Anin refused.

"We must wait a few more suns," he said to her. "The Ashwans may not have left. They travel by land, following the rivers, with their sealskin boats well hidden and guarded. And they stay for the whole warm season. They go back to their own land only when it begins to grow cold here. We must wait."

Woasut said nothing for the rest of the day. When Anin told her he was going out to search the surrounding woods to see if there was enough game to support them, she lowered her head and still said nothing.

When he returned at nightfall, the fire in the cavern had gone out and the coals were not even warm. He knew that she had left. He quickly left the cavern and ran down the slope to the seashore: the tapatook was gone. All his belongings were there, strewn about on the beach. Filled with anger, he returned to the cavern, relit the fire, and lay down beside it without eating. It was a long time before he slept. He had refused to help the young Beothuk woman find her people, and so she had gone to find them herself, once again taking his tapatook and leaving him alone to face their enemies and the coming cold season. Without a tapatook he could not fish; he would have to enter the forest to survive. His indecision had allowed her to make this decision for him, and he promised himself that never again would he waver in his purpose. Then he slept.

At sunrise, he left the cavern, descended to the seashore, took some of the dried seabird meat from his pack, and began walking back along the beach to the bay where he had first seen Woasut. He walked swiftly, with determination, almost incautiously, like a man lost in his own thoughts. His heart was still filled with anger at the thought that perhaps he would now have to hide his tapa-took every night so that it would not be stolen by the very companion he had hoped would stay with him. When he reached the bay, he became more careful in his movements. He stopped and searched the whole area with his eyes. There was no sign of life. The bodies of the Beothuk were still lying where they had fallen, although the arrows that had killed them had been removed. The younger children, those who had been slain while they were gathering clams, had been washed out to sea with the tide. He picked his way cautiously to the head of the bay, avoiding the corpses. At the mouth of a brook that opened into the bay he discovered his tapatook, pulled up to high ground and resting upright. Checking the ground, he saw footsteps leading into the forest. Woasut had gone inland to look for her people.

He turned the tapatook over and hid it in the forest, then sat down on a large rock well out of sight. He ate some of the dried puffin, thinking about what he would do if the young woman came back. After a while, he lay down on the moss beside the rock and went to sleep. When he awoke, the sea was high on the shore and the sun had almost set behind the shadows of the forest. The air was cooler, and Anin felt himself shiver. He considered making a fire, wondering if it would attract his enemies, and decided to take the risk. But the wood in this place was difficult to light, and he had to blow for a long time before a tiny flame finally licked at the curls of bark. He waited beside the fire, then decided to spend the night there in the hope that the young Beothuk woman would return. Before very long it was completely dark, and once again he fell asleep.

By morning he had reached a decision. He ate another portion of dried meat, then retrieved his tapatook from its hiding place, dragged it down to the shore, and paddled back to where he had spent one night with Woasut and another night by himself. He would repack his belongings and continue his journey around the land, as he had set out to do. Nothing would prevent him from fulfilling his promise. Not even a beautiful young woman, no, not all the beautiful young women in the world. He would stay out of other people's affairs, never again would he interfere to save someone's life, unless of course they were Addaboutik. The reason he had lost all this time was that he had failed to keep his word. He should have watched the scene at the bay without getting involved in it, and told the story later to his own people, without allowing it to detain him on his journey. He should not have tried to help, no matter how pleasant it had been to spend that one night with the young woman. He arrived at the place where his tapatook was hidden, put his belongings back into his pack, tied the pack inside the tapatook, and pulled the tapatook high up into the forest, ready to be taken out at first light the next morning. Then he climbed up to the cavern, made a small fire, ate his evening meal, and went to sleep.

It was still dark when he opened his eyes: he felt uneasy, as though he could sense someone watching him. His eyes searched the cavern, but he could see nothing in the darkness. Quietly he raised himself to his feet and, without making a sound, took his knife out of its sheath. His eyes were becoming accustomed to the dark, and through the opening he could see a lightness where the sun was beginning to awaken. He left the cavern and returned to his tapatook. Suddenly he stopped. There on the beach before him was the dark shape of Woasut, lying curled up on the sand, shivering and crying silently. Anin felt no animosity towards her, despite the fact that she had taken his tapatook and the anxiety she had caused him the night before. He went up to her, bent down, and taking her by the shoulders, lifted her to her feet. He put his arms around her, placing her head on his shoulder, and held her close to his body. He felt the young Beothuk tremble against him like a small tree in the season of falling leaves shaken by a strong wind, and she began to cry aloud in great choking sobs.

They stood together for a long time without speaking, she trembling like a small, frightened child and he attempting to comfort her with his tenderness and his unspoken offer of protection. Slowly her sobs subsided, and he gently lowered her to the sand, retrieved his tapatook, placed it in the water, and lifted Woasut into it. Together they travelled towards the cold, still without having exchanged a single word. And yet they had reached an understanding.

6

GRADUALLY, WOASUT'S GRIEF subsided. It wasn't that she forgot what she had seen, but the pain of it lessened. She remembered her mother, her father, and all the young people of her village, not as she had last seen them, but as they had been when they were still alive. In this way the image of their death slowly faded. She still wept from time to time, when she recalled the sight of their bodies scattered about the village, all the people she had known and loved in her life, and realized with anguish that she would never see them again. And at times she was overcome by the thought that the same thing could happen to Anin. He too could die, killed by the bloodthirsty Ashwans, the people of the cold.

When this thought troubled her she pushed it away from her, like a beast that could not and must not touch her. She kept herself busy. She made their warm clothing for the cold season. Every time they landed the tapatook she insisted on helping Anin with the work of making camp. He no longer had to make a fire; that was now her task. He did not have to skin the animals he killed; she did it. She gathered firewood and kept the fire going. In this way, Anin could paddle for longer periods, even though the days were slowly becoming shorter.

One day, when Woasut and Anin were in the tapatook, she saw a long point of land stretching off into the distance in the direction of the cold. She explained to Anin that the point of land was not wide, that they could cross it on foot, and that this was less dangerous than paddling around it. To paddle around it would mean having to face the strong winds that blew up from his homeland. The sea on the other side of the point was always rough, and also it was from beyond the point that the Ashwans from the cold region came.

She told him about the time she had travelled to the end of the land with her father, and they had seen a large party of Ashwans landing in a shallow bay. They had been catching anawasuts, the large, flat fish with brown-and-white markings. Crossing the point, carrying the tapatook and packs, would be a matter of three or four suns; it took at least that long to paddle around it, she added, and the danger was far greater.

Anin thought about the promise he had made to travel around the world. Could he say that he had fulfilled the obligation of his initiation if he walked part of the way? It was already the falling-leaf season, and strong, cold winds were making the tapatook less responsive to the paddle. And having a second person and her belongings on board added greatly to its weight.

They found shelter that night in a small creek bed with a good supply of fresh water and well out of the wind. He told Woasut that they would stay there for several days while they considered their next move. They must have a complete understanding of their situation. The forest here was thinner, there was not much game and the trees were smaller. There was so little bark that they could not finish making their shelter the first night, and had to sleep under a cloudless sky filled with stars. It was the beginning of the cold season. In the morning, as soon as the sun rose, Anin left to investigate the area and to find more birchbark. The sun was high in the sky by the time he returned, carrying a large bundle of the rolled boyish, easily enough to finish the mamateek. While Woasut worked on the mamateek, Anin went out again, this time to a marsh where he had seen a number of mamchets, who built dams to create enough water for their houses. He had told Woasut that he would bring her the meat of this animal, and skins for making snowshoes. When he returned to the mamateek he had one beaver and two odusweets, rabbits with huge hind feet like snowshoes. Woasut had already finished

the mamateek, pushing the strips of bark into place on the framework of dead branches, and had started a fire inside, with enough
firewood to last several days. She was smiling, and when Anin
handed her the animals she began to skin them, quietly singing a
song she had learned during her childhood.

It was the first time Anin had heard her singing. She had a
sweet, calming voice. He was happy to see her coming back to
life: it made him feel useful. To be needed by someone else gave
his own life a new dimension. He was a helper. The thought of
perpetuating himself through others, in children perhaps, seemed
to grow out of this new feeling. That night, Woasut and Anin
both smiled in their sleep. They had tasted the sweetness of being
two in a world that seemed to them filled with misery and suffering, in which every stranger seemed hostile and evil.

Anin awoke at daybreak. Woasut was already outside, reviving
the previous night's fire. Suddenly she cried out:

"Anin! Come quickly! A vessel out at sea!"

Anin joined her and saw one of the strangers' boats passing
some distance offshore. He put out the fire so it would not
attract the attention of these warlike men with hair the colour
of dried grass.

"Fortunately our tapatook is well hidden in the trees," he said.

They waited until the strange craft passed completely out of
sight, towards the cold end of the land, before relighting the fire.

"You were right to advise me to cross the land here rather than
paddle around the point," he said to Woasut. "We would surely
have been attacked by those murderers with their cutting sticks.
It was they who wounded me before I met you."

Anin had not mentioned his encounter with the Bouguishamesh before, and so he told her the story of his brief battle
with the infuriated giant.

"I have never seen such a large tapatook," Woasut said when he
had finished.

"It takes them wherever they want to go," said Anin. "They
use the wind to make it go, and only need to paddle when there
is no wind. I have seen one at close hand – there were more

people on it than I have fingers. And they were bigger than the Addaboutik, at least the one who tried to kill me was. I am hungry, Woasut."

"I have gathered sea cucumbers. Would Anin like some, if I cooked them on a stone in the middle of the fire?"

"Hmmm . . . yes."

The young Beothuk spread the sea cucumbers on the fire-stone, sprinkled them with saltwater and some berries that were in season. While they ate, Woasut showed Anin the two pairs of leggings she had made, which they would wear when the weather turned colder. She had made them from the skin of the legs of a caribou Anin had killed ten suns before. She had turned the skins inside out, carefully scraped them, and then softened the leather by pounding it on a birch log from which she had first removed the bark. With the caribou hair turned in, the leggings would hold in the body's own heat. Anin told Woasut he was pleased by her handiwork. After the meal, he said, he would go back into the woods to hunt Mamchet the Beaver, so that she would have fur to make shirts. The fur of the beaver was softer than that of Appawet the Seal, but it was also heavier and lasted longer. To make two shirts she would need at least twenty furs. Higher up, there was a marshy creek that fed the brook where they had built their mamateek, and he had counted more than a dozen beaver there, including adults and a litter of young that had been born that spring. In one or two suns he would easily have enough furs for their needs.

Taking his bow and several arrows, he set off in the direction of the marsh. Before he had taken a hundred steps, however, he found himself face to face with Gashu-Uwith the Bear. He had run into him often during his two season-cycles. Now he stood motionless so as not to alarm the beast, who was grunting and stretching himself. Eventually, Gashu-Uwith took a path that led to the top of the tongue of land that separated Anin and Woasut from the windy sea, and which they would soon have to cross if they were to reach Baétha, the village of the Addaboutik. Once again, thought Anin, the bear was showing him the way. Without the bear's guidance, Anin would have had to spend several suns finding a path wide enough to allow them to carry the tapatook and their heavy packs to a more sheltered place, where they could safely spend the cold season. The path followed by Gashu-Uwith even went close to the marsh where Anin had seen the beaver family. Anin decided to explore no further; he would take these beaver pelts and then continue his voyage by crossing the land. He waited patiently beside the marsh, and before long had killed four young mamchets with his arrows. To catch the rest, he made several balance-traps, using large logs weighted with heavy rocks and baited with sweet, young birch branches. He would return the next day to check his traps, and to find another family of mamchets in another marsh or in the deeper water before a dam.

Back at the mamateek, he told Woasut about his encounter with Gashu-Uwith, and explained to her that he now knew that the bear was his spirit protector. Woasut did not laugh at his belief; her own people believed in such things, she started to tell him, and then stopped. At the mention of her people, her face contorted and tears formed in her eyes. She could not forget. It seemed to her impossible that she ever would, and she cried for a short time. Anin allowed her to cry. Our memories are our own, he thought, and no one has the right to even ask us about them. If we choose to talk about them, then others will understand what we are feeling. But if not, that is our own business, and others must learn to respect that decision. If we do not want to hear lies, then we must not ask questions.

The next morning, while Woasut worked on the skins, Anin returned to the forest for more mamchets. At the marsh, he found three of his traps had fallen but only two mamchets had been caught. The third had apparently managed to work itself free and escape. He hung the two on a spruce tree and then decided to explore farther into the bush along the path shown to him by the bear. When the sun was at its highest, he found himself at the junction of three different paths. He thought the one heading into the wind would be the right one to take across the tongue of land, but just as he was about to set off on it he heard

Gashu-Uwith growling on the path that led into the cold, towards the end of the point of land. He decided to follow that path, despite the fear that the bear's presence stirred within him.

"If she was going to eat me," he reasoned, "she would have done so long before now. Still, I can never be entirely certain of her intentions."

He slowed his pace so as not to come upon Gashu-Uwith unexpectedly. As the sun was beginning to set, he suddenly entered a magnificent clearing, a sunny meadow nestled at the edge of a small lake fed by a sparkling stream. The lake's outlet was the same creek that he had been following the day before, when hunting for mamchets.

"This is a good place to spend the cold season," he thought. He climbed a ridge, and from its top he could see three coastlines in the distance: one towards the cold, another towards the wind, and a third towards the setting sun. All three were less than a day's portage from the clearing. Woasut would be happy to spend the cold season in such a sheltered place, protected from the wind and with a good lookout for enemies. That alone made it worth while bringing her here for her opinion.

He hurried back to the mamateek, almost running down the path. If he had not hung the beavers close to the path, he might easily have forgotten them in his haste to reach Woasut and tell her about the discovery Gashu-Uwith had shown him.

But Woasut was not pleased by the prospect of spending the cold season so close to the sea. She was afraid of the Bouguishamesh. The strangers they had seen had greatly unsettled her, and she wanted to cross the point of land and return to Anin's village before the coming cold season. Only then would she feel safe, she told him. Anin reminded her that, even if the village was as close as she said it was, they would have to cache most of their provisions, including their warm clothing, and live on short rations if they were to get there in time. Even at that, they would need to begin paddling before the sun rose and continue long after it had set. They would exhaust themselves, and very likely arrive at the village in bad health, just before the onset of the cold season. She knew how important it was to build up their strength and their provisions during the warm season if they were to survive the cold until thawing time. Woasut asked for more time to think before making a decision. Anin replied that the last time he had taken too long to think he had almost lost her. But he gave her until the next sun to tell him what she wanted to do.

"But if I decide to spend the winter here, what other choice will you have?"

They thought about it for a long time, lying on their comfortable sleeping couch in the mamateek. When morning came they were sound asleep, and the sun was high in the sky before the two young lovers emerged from their caribou blankets, still quiet and thoughtful.

"I will make the portage up to your clearing," Woasut said, "with our provisions. I will decide when I see it whether or not I will stay there for the cold season. If I decide to continue, my own belongings will be there and I will not have to return to the sea except to gather more clams."

Anin smiled and told her that he would help her with the portage, even though it meant losing several days of preparation for the cold season.

7

WOASUT WAS STRONG and did not seem to tire. She carried the mamchets killed by Anin the previous suns, as well as the two pairs of leggings and the mitts she had made for herself and Anin, in preparation for the season of cold and snow. All this she loaded on her back and carried to the clearing discovered by her man, without once stopping or resting along the way. Anin carried the store of clams Woasut had gathered from the beach, the hides from the other animals he had killed, his hunting weapons – spear, bow, and arrows – his paddle and the tapatook, which he lifted over his head. He wanted to see if there were fish in this lake. The two were young and in good health and would survive the cold season as long as they had enough provisions. Anin smiled as he walked. He was thinking that once Woasut saw the clearing, she would also see the wisdom of his arguments for remaining there through the cold season. Deep down, he knew he would not change his decision to stay, and he also knew that Woasut would bend to his will. On the other hand, she had been right to counsel him to cross the point of land rather than risk the strong winds by trying to paddle around it during the leaf-falling season. By stopping to consider their plans, they had avoided being captured by the Bouguishamesh in the large tapatook that was moved by the wind.

When they arrived at the small clearing, Woasut could not contain her delight. How beautiful was the little valley, and how magnificent the view! Anin took her to the top of the ridge and showed her how far they could see.

"You knew I would like this place, did you not?" she said to him. "Does my response please you?"

Anin smiled. Yes, he had known that she would like this place. Not only because it was beautiful, but also because it was well hidden and far from the places frequented by the Bouguishamesh and the Ashwans. Everything they needed for the cold season was close at hand: they were surrounded by evergreens and birch, there was the lake, the little brook that fed into it, and there was easily enough game to feed them. There might even be fish in the lake. Anin put his tapatook in the water, and, taking out his fishing net, tied a small piece of beaver meat to it and paddled out, keeping close to the shore. He had not gone far before he felt something tugging at the bait. It was Dattomesh the Trout. After the melting season the fish must have swum up the stream from the sea to spawn, only to be trapped in the lake when the water went down. This was good; it meant they would be able to vary their diet from time to time. As soon as he caught a second dattomesh he returned to shore and handed them to Woasut, who had already started a fire. She stuck two green birch wands in the ground so that their tips were above the flames, and on these she laid the fish. Soon the flesh was cooked and they ate. When they finished their meal, they stretched out on the soft ground. Woasut took off her dingiam so that Anin could see her sex, and Anin felt his male strength surge through him. He was like a thirsty animal scenting water, and he rolled onto Woasut, who remained lying on her back. Anin was surprised that she did not turn and raise herself on her knees.

"Do you not want to?" he asked her.

"Yes, I want to," she said. "But I also want to watch you. Come into me like this; I will raise my legs."

Uncertain of the way, Anin knelt before his mate and positioned himself between her legs. There were some awkward moments as he tried to find her sex, but once he was inside her he found their movements so pleasurable, and the smile on her face so delightful, that his satisfaction was very soon complete. But when he began to withdraw from her, she held him: "No, don't stop," she urged him. "I don't want to stop yet."

When she would not let him go, Anin tried to tell her that he was finished.

"But I am not," she said. "Please don't stop. It feels so good."

From this Anin realized that his happiness did not guarantee her happiness, and he continued until she was satisfied even though his own passion had been all but spent by his ejaculation. Then the two lovers lay back on the grass and slept, each dreaming of the contentment that grew stronger within them with each sun. When they again stirred themselves, it was time to return to the mamateek. First they were careful to hide the food under piles of rocks to keep it from predators. Then, leaving the tapatook beside the lake with the paddle in it, they took the path back down to the seashore. At the first bend in the path they heard snorting and saw Gashu-Uwith watching them from the direction of the cold. Anin smiled and said to Woasut:

"Look, my spirit protector. He must have been a member of my family when he was an Addaboutik."

Woasut let out a loud shriek of laughter that seemed to frighten Gashu-Uwith, and he ran off in the direction of the cold.

"Your family frightens easily," she said to Anin. "He's not very brave for a spirit protector."

As they passed the pond created by a beaver dam, Anin saw a mamchet gnawing at the base of a birch. Taking his bow, he put an arrow through it and watched as the animal fell over backwards and then tried to run back into the safety of the pond. But death came to him too quickly, and he stopped some distance from the water. One more skin to make jackets, and more meat for the cold season. He picked up the dead animal and slung it over his shoulder, holding it by its scaly tail. Then he continued down the path behind Woasut.

Just as they reached the mamateek, Anin smelled an unfamiliar odour and stopped, signalling to Woasut to remain still. They waited a long time, every sense alert. Something was happening, and Anin could not see what it was. The mamateek was not visible from the bay, which gave them an advantage over intruders. The odour was becoming stronger. Anin still could not identify it, but he knew that it was not normal. His eyes swept along the coastline below them, and eventually he discerned the outline of a sealskin boat pulled up at the base of a cliff. Ashwans! And very close, although they apparently had not found the mamateek. Before deciding what to do, Anin had to know how many of them there were. He waited patiently for what seemed a long time. The sun had now circled behind them, and the bay was in the shadow of the cliffs. Soon they would not be able to see their enemies if they came up towards the mamateek. Still they waited, crouched behind a fallen log a dozen or more steps from the mamateek. Night fell and darkness surrounded them, but there was no sound, no stirring of the wind, no rustling of nocturnal birds; it was as though they, too, feared the Ashwans.

Anin felt his heart pounding against his breast and thought it was so loud it was drowning out all other natural sounds of the night. Of course there was no question of sleeping with the enemy so near, perhaps ready to strike. Time passed in an endless and agonizing wait. Woasut moved very slightly to prevent herself from becoming numb, and Anin cautioned her not to make a sound. But there was no one else about that night. Night is for resting, for Ashwans as well as for other men. Ashwans have to sleep. Where else would they be? Why didn't they return to their boat? What were they up to? Unable to wait any longer, Anin signalled to Woasut to stay where she was, and stood up. He waited until his blood began circulating properly in his veins again, chasing the numbness away, and then, with infinite caution, moved forward very slowly without stepping on twigs that would snap and give him away. His goal was the sealskin boat that was pulled up to the trees, well above the shoreline. It took him forever to reach a place in the bush from which he could see the boat clearly. Then he stopped and listened, assuring himself that there was no one nearby. The odour that had warned him of the Ashwans' presence was stronger here, and at last he could identify it: it was Gashu-Uwith's excrement. And it smelled fresh. But why had Gashu-Uwith been down here with the Ashwans? Before going out to take a closer look at the sealskin boat, Anin moved further along the shore in the shelter of the trees. The smell of bear scat grew stronger. There was something about it that made it smell like that of Anin's own people. Anin knelt down to get a better view of the ground. The moon had appeared and a soft glow illumined the night. Very near him, Anin saw two human shapes lying on the ground. One was on its stomach, the other on its back, its throat torn open. On the corpse with the ragged throat was a pile of Gashu-Uwith's excrement. The bear had obviously surprised the two Ashwans, and killed the first by grabbing him by the throat, and the second by completely eviscerating him. What surprised Anin most was that the bear had not eaten the bodies. Never in living memory had a bear attacked a human except when it was starving or wounded and incapable of hunting. But never at this time of the season-cycle, when there was plenty of fresh fruit, fish, and an abundance of small animals. Gashu-Uwith was fat and obviously not starving. A bear would attack a human to protect its young, but again, by the falling-leaf season their young no longer needed protection. Anin could only conclude that the bear had attacked the Ashwans out of anger.

"Is he really my spirit protector?" Anin wondered. "Or should I be worried for myself and Woasut? When we met him on the path, Woasut had frightened him off with her laughter. Was he trying to tell us what he had been doing here?"

Still being careful not to make a sound, Anin returned to Woasut and told her quietly what he had seen, and suggested that they take turns sleeping to ensure that they were not attacked during the night. Woasut could sleep first watch and then Anin. They would decide what to do in the morning.

When the sun was in the sky, Woasut awakened Anin and they went down to the Ashwan bodies. They dragged the corpses to the sealskin boat, lifted them inside, and when the tide was at its highest, pushed the boat as far as possible out to sea, so far that it would not wash up again in the bay. Then they quickly dismantled the mamateek, rolling the poles and bark into two large bundles, which they carried up to their clearing by the lake. Then they returned to the bay and removed every trace of their presence. Marks in the ground that they could not erase they covered with heavy stones. Then, when they were satisfied, they left the bay, telling themselves they would never return to it unless it was absolutely necessary. They must not attract the attention of anyone who might come looking for the dead Ashwans.

8

THE CALM LIFE of sedentary people reigned in the little valley where the Addaboutik and the Beothuk were preparing for the cold season. Their daily routines filled their entire waking time, despite the rain that often marked this part of the falling-leaf season. Anin hunted Mamchet the Beaver, Kosweet the Caribou, and Odusweet the Rabbit, and set snares and nets for Zoozoot the Hare and the fish in the lake. Woasut skinned the game, dried and smoked the meat, stored it in bark containers, made warm clothing from the hides, and insulated the mamateek with dried moss. She worked hard to make their dwelling as comfortable as possible for the time of snow and deep cold. Just before nightfall she also collected armloads of dead wood and stacked it close to their dwelling. Some of it she would use to dry and smoke the meat, the rest she would use later to warm the mamateek.

One morning Woasut suggested to Anin that he hunt a bear, because she would need grease for the cold season. For the first time, Anin erupted into anger, to the great astonishment of his companion.

"Do you want me to kill my brother as well?" he demanded. "Gashu-Uwith saved you from the Ashwans, and now you want to make bear grease out of him?"

Woasut said nothing, understanding her error. She had forgotten that Anin thought of Gashu-Uwith as his spirit protector, which made the bear a member of his immediate family, equal in status to his brothers and sisters, uncles and cousins. She did not dare to suggest another fat-laden animal, such as Appawet the Seal, for fear of re-igniting Anin's anger. She did not even venture to change the subject by telling him that she was carrying Meseeliguet, and that he would be a father when the snow melted and the first flowers began to appear. She feared Anin's anger in the same way she feared the Ashwans who had slain her people. She could not explain this sense of fear; she felt her heart tremble in its presence. She remembered the words of her mother: "You must never provoke those who provide food for the clan."

That morning Anin left without saying another word to her. He took his spear and his fishing net, his bow and quiver of arrows, tied them to the centre thwart of his tapatook and carried it on his shoulders along the path that led down to the seashore. Woasut was sorry she had asked him to kill Gashu-Uwith. Now he was going to hunt where there was the risk of encountering Ashwans or the Bouguishamesh, and not coming back. She understood that when a man is angry he is less careful than when he is calm, and places himself in greater danger. She also knew that a momentary lapse of caution or a misplaced step could result in her being alone to face the cold season, the birth of her child, and all the dangers of the world that surrounded her. Suddenly she felt as afraid as when the Ashwans were chasing her, trying to kill her. She was as afraid as she had been the first time she heard Washi Weuth, the night spirit, the god of thunderstorms. Washi Weuth the unknown one, the mysterious one, he without body who could smother thought on long, sleepless nights. Washi Weuth, the enemy of female Beothuk children, whom even the male children hated. Washi Weuth, whose name no one dared say aloud for fear of calling forth his dreaded apparition. Now Woasut regretted her words so much that she could not sit passively by the mamateek waiting for Anin to return. Seizing her own fishing spear, she ran down the path towards the seashore. She must go to Anin and soothe his anger before something bad happened to him. She must find him and help him to fulfill the task he set himself when he left in the direction of the sea. She knew she could overtake him, because he was carrying the tapatook on his shoulders. Even though it was not heavy, it was awkward on the path and would slow him down. It was always getting caught in branches and bumping against trees, and Anin would have to cross the stream many times, hopping from rock to rock. Woasut walked quickly, sometimes running to catch up with the only other human being left in her life. She ran to meet the father of her child, who would be born from their chance union, to rejoin the man who had saved her from the Ashwans. She ran to be with the man she had come to respect. She was almost at the seashore and yet she had not caught up with him. She was suddenly afraid again. Rushing out onto the beach, she saw Anin untying his weapons from the tapatook's thwart, preparing to launch the craft into the water. She shouted to him:

"Wait for me! I am coming with you!"

Anin stopped what he was doing and stood up, surprised to see his companion running towards him. When she reached him she stopped and stood directly before him.

"I will paddle while you hunt. It will be easier that way."

She knew that he was intending to hunt for a seal in order to provide her with the fat she needed to cook and preserve the fresh meat. For the whole of that sun they paddled among the rocks of the bay, searching for basking seals and not finding a single one. When darkness came, they landed, made a fire, and then sat looking blankly at each other before bursting into laughter. Neither of them had thought to bring food. Woasut took a burning branch from the fire and searched for the breathing holes of clams in the sand, and Anin, using another branch, dug them up when she pointed to the right spots. They completed their evening meal with a few sea cucumbers. Then they lay down to sleep, but without blankets they awoke frequently to put more wood on the fire. Still they were cold. There was a hard frost that night, and even though they were sheltered from the wind, the first cold night of the season is always the hardest to bear.

In the morning they returned to the water and searched the bays. This time they found many seals stretched out lazily on the rocks where the waves foamed over them. Some of the younger animals, curious to see what strange new creature had entered their territory, swam out and rubbed against the tapatook. Woasut paddled in the stern while Anin, braced on his knees in the narrow bow, waited for the right moment to strike with his amina. Suddenly, the head of a young seal appeared above the surface of the water, and at the same moment the spear plunged into its throat. As it dove, Anin let the cord attached to the spear's shaft float freely so that the panicked seal would not capsize the tapatook. When a blossom of blood rose to the surface, Anin knew that he would not have to wait long before pulling in the line. Gradually the seal stopped struggling, and Anin hauled it over the side of the tapatook. He made an incision in the animal's lower jaw and passed the free end of the amina's cord through it. Then he untied the amina and tossed the cord to Woasut, who caught it and tied it to the tapatook's stern thwart so that they could drag the seal to the bay at the base of the path that led to their mamateek. Slowly they paddled together. They were both much more tired than they realized, and the return journey took a long time. They paddled in silence.

When they arrived at the bay, the wind had come up and snow began to fall in large flakes. It was the first snowfall of the cold season. When they landed, Anin tied his weapons to the centre thwart and lifted the tapatook onto Woasut's back. He carried the seal. Woasut reached the winter camp before him, having the lighter load, and had already begun to prepare their first and only meal of that sun when Anin arrived. After eating the dried meat and drinking the sweet water, Anin gutted the seal and hung it from a stout tree branch so that Woasut could drain the oil from it the next sun. Then they slept, exhausted from the sun's hunting and the long portage. That night they were not cold, wrapped as they were in their warm caribou blankets and huddled close together in the mamateek.

9

THE SNOW HAD covered the ground since the time of the full moon, but it was still not very cold. The white mantle that blanketed the earth each season-cycle was not yet thick enough to make their snowshoes necessary. Anin began to be worried that he had not seen Kosweet the Caribou in these parts. He knew that the caribou took to the forests and the mountain valleys for food as soon as the snow became so deep that it covered the moss on the plateaux. Their winter camp was in a perfect spot for Odusweet, which Anin found in abundance, but it was not good to eat too much rabbit, since there was not enough fat in the meat to provide protection from the cold. Too much rabbit also caused an ache in the stomach, and made you empty yourself too often. It also made pregnant women sick, so that they would often lose their babies.

Ptarmigan was also plentiful in their area and partly made up for the lack of red meat. Aoujet the Ptarmigan was so unafraid of the Addaboutik that Anin could almost catch him with his bare hands. But Anin was fully aware of how wise he had been to choose a winter camp close to a lake, for Dattomesh the Trout gave Woasut the nourishment she needed for the baby she was carrying. But to get him she had to prevent the hole in the lake's winter covering from freezing over; a single sun's inattention and the ice would be too thick for her to break. They would have to use large, pointed rocks tied to handles made from the wood of the softwood trees that lost their needles in the cold season. This tamarack wood is very heavy, and makes for hard work.

The time had come to increase the size of the territory they hunted. They would have to risk encroaching on land occupied by other inhabitants if they were to procure a greater variety of game. Woasut now spent her suns maintaining the fire, keeping the fishing hole free of ice, making regular trips to the permanently installed net to remove any trout that became caught in it, and completing the warm clothing she had been making from animal skins. She also softened the fur blankets that would keep her child warm when it was born in the growing season.

Anin finished the front curve on the snowsled he was making from the wood of the by-yeetch, or birch tree. This wood bent easily even in the cold season; no matter how roughly cut the strips were, the snowsled was strong and easy to pull. He tied a cord to it made from plant roots oiled and braided by Woasut before the first snowfall. Now he was ready for his journey of exploration. He told Woasut that he would leave the next morning at sunrise, and that he would be gone for several suns. She would have to keep an eye on the provisions to keep scavengers away from the meat.

"I see you are making clothes for a baby," he said to her with a smile. "Is your sister pregnant?"

"You were so angry I did not dare to tell you," she said quietly.

Anin did not say another word, but went outside to rub the snowsled with seal fat. The first thing next morning, after placing some provisions in a sack, the Addaboutik left. He carried his snowshoes over his shoulder in case more snow should fall, and his bow and quiver across his chest. With his hunting spear in his hand, he set off along the path that headed into the wind and towards the cold. When the sun was at its highest above the horizon, Anin found himself in a place where the trees had become much smaller and seemed to bend down to let the wind blow over them. There was less soil, and the ptarmigan flocked together more. He saw fewer tracks of fur-bearing animals, such as the marten, and by the end of that sun they had stopped altogether. From these signs Anin concluded that there was no forest at the end of the point of land. He had truly entered the land of cold and snow, where the wind was master of everything when it chose to blow.

That night the young initiate built a temporary shelter using snow and the few evergreen branches he could find. Even though he had kept his fire-making sticks well wrapped and dry, he had difficulty starting a fire. He ate a small portion of dried meat and then rolled himself up in his caribou blanket. He told himself that it was fortunate he had killed the caribou as soon as they had arrived at the wind-storm coast, also called by his people the sunrising coast. And then he slept.

He rose with the sun, ate some smoked fish and began walking towards the sun-setting coast. More snow began to fall, slowly but heavily, in large, wet flakes, and it stayed with him throughout the entire sun. He passed only a few clumps of stunted trees and an occasional tamarack, which stood straight up as though defying the wind to knock it down. Then he saw something move in the distance, a black mass that was drifting slowly down from the direction of the cold. He lay down flat on the ground and watched. It was a herd of caribou. The animals would stop often, scrape the snow from the soil with their hooves, and eat the moss beneath it; then they would continue their migration towards the sun-setting coast. "They are heading for the high mountains where there is better forest cover," thought Anin. "They are late leaving. This heavy snowfall must have told them it was time, since it will make the snow too deep for them to survive down here. If I remain where I am, out of sight, they will pass close by me, and I may be able to take one or two of them."

He waited a long time. The snow had buried him so completely that he was part of the white landscape by the time the caribou drifted within range of his arrows. He was well prepared for them, and chose one of the first animals at the head of the herd, a large male whose antlers had already dropped. Although he was numbed by the long wait, Anin's arrow went straight to the animal's heart. The caribou staggered on for several more paces, then crashed to the snow-covered ground. Anin leapt to his feet and sent a second and then a third arrow at a female that still carried her antlers, and she too fell heavily to the ground, struck in the shoulder and in the heart. At the sight of him, the rest of the animals turned and fled, and his hunting was over. The herd veered off in the direction of the cold.

Anin spent the rest of that sun gutting the two animals, skinning them, and rolling up the hides before they could freeze. He stored their hearts, livers, kidneys, and tongues in his food bag. Then he cut up the carcasses so that they would take up as little space as possible on his snowsled. The lower legs and feet he discarded, but he kept the hooves for making knife blades and skin scrapers. He also kept the female's antlers for harpoon tips and arrowheads. He squeezed out the contents of the intestines and rolled up the casings, which would be used to make thread for sewing garments. Splitting open the skulls, he removed the brains and placed them, too, in his food bag. Then he arranged all the meat on the sled, securing it with strips cut from the ends of the rolled hides.

When he was satisfied that everything was well packed and ready for the long haul back to the mamateek, he lit a fire and cooked a piece of caribou liver that he had already begun to chew while it was still warm and raw from the animal. Then, scooping a sheltered hollow in the snow, he rolled himself in his hide blanket and fell asleep almost immediately.

The snow continued to fall throughout the night, and in the morning when he awoke it was up to his knees. He had to walk with snowshoes for the first time that season. He knew that the real cold had not yet arrived, because the snow he had heaped up the night before with his snowshoes had been enough to keep him warm while he slept. The sled was heavy with fresh meat and it would take him longer to return than it had to come. It had taken him two suns to get to this place; it took him four to get back.

When he arrived within sight of the mamateek, he called to Woasut, who came running out of the dwelling, crying with happiness at the return of her man. She had been very afraid for him, she said, and for herself as well. She had imagined terrible things happening to him in the six suns he had been away. She herself had been frightened by Gashu-Uwith, whom she had heard prowling near the mamateek at night, and whose tracks she had seen in the snow in the mornings. For two nights, she had also heard wolves howling nearby, and had slept with her hunting spear close by her side. She had convinced herself that she would be alone forever.

Anin tried not to let her see how her complaints disturbed him. He believed that such dark thoughts were preludes to defeat, and he had been taught to turn them away before they could lodge in his mind and weaken him. But his face betrayed his true feelings: his jaw muscles tightened, and he knit his eyebrows. Woasut realized that she must not express her fears to the only human she could count on to protect her from them. Instead, she helped him cut up the frozen caribou meat and hang it in skin bags from trees nearest the mamateek, high enough to be out of the reach of predators, especially Gashu-Uwith, whom she feared most of all. But Anin decided to leave a large piece of meat on the path, just where it entered their clearing, as a gift for the animal he thought of as his spirit protector. If Gashu-Uwith had once been an Addaboutik like him, Anin was obliged to share the spoils of his hunt with his kin. Woasut disagreed with him – she was afraid that if they fed the bear, it would stay with them for the entire cold season – but she dared not breathe a word for fear of angering her man again.

When the work was finished, Anin took the cooked liver from his food bag and handed it to Woasut, as his gift to her. They ate together and talked about what had happened during his absence. The young woman told him that she had taken only three trout from the hole in the ice. Anin replied that, from the place where he had killed the caribou, he had seen a large bay cut into the windward side of the point of land. He also described the country, with its flat, treeless plateaux and no animals except caribou. That night, the two young lovers repeated their ritual of affection for one another many times before falling asleep in each other's arms.

10

THE SEASON OF cold and snow was showing signs of weakening. The snow retreated a bit more with each sun, and longer sunlight allowed Anin and Woasut to do more work outside the mamateek. Provisions were getting low; very little of the caribou meat was left. They ate more fish than red meat. The young woman avoided eating rabbit because she did not want to empty herself too often and risk losing the baby that was growing within her. Her belly had become steadily rounder during the past two moons, and she was starting to find certain movements difficult. Walking in deep, soft snow caused pain in her thighs, and she felt a sharp pain whenever her harness cut into her waist, as it did when she went out to gather firewood.

Her fear of the bear, however, seemed to have been without cause. The animal had indeed taken the meat Anin left for it at the head of the path, but it had carried it off deep into the woods and had not returned for more. Anin explained to her that fear was called Geswat, and that Geswat was born of not knowing what will happen. "When you do not know what an animal is going to do in certain circumstances," he said, "you fear that animal. But if you allow Geswat to control you, to determine your daily actions necessary for survival, she will slowly rob you of your reason. And when there is no more reason in your head, your life is at risk every second: you do thoughtless things, you act foolishly, you lose control of your mind, and you also put others in danger. That is why we must teach our children to know all the beings that live around us, to observe their habits and know how they behave. And if you ever feel Geswat getting hold of you, Woasut, you must fight her off immediately by remembering all the things you know about whatever it is that is causing that fear. For example, if you fear Kobshuneesamut the Creator, the All Powerful, that is not good: it means you do not trust him. If you are afraid of him, it must be because you have committed a reprehensible act. You have behaved badly. You must therefore go back and undo that act. Kobshuneesamut wants nothing from us but that we act correctly. If we do, then there is no need for fear. Fear will not exist. If the child you are carrying is a male child, then he must not even be allowed to speak of such a thing as fear. He must not breathe a word about it. Geswat exists only in females, who are the cause of her spreading, because females speak of their weakness born of ignorance of the things that surround them. That is why Anin was angry when Woasut said she felt fear. Anin must be strong and invincible when he faces life. He must always force himself to make the right movement, through his knowledge of the world around him. In fact, he must undergo the initiation exactly for that reason: so that he will learn all about the world and therefore never experience fear. Anin can be cautious of the world, he can be careful not to make a false step, but he cannot be afraid of it if he learns from his experiences."

Woasut spent the rest of the cold season repeating Anin's words over and over, so that she could raise her child according to his beliefs. She also promised herself that if she had a daughter, she would teach her not to express the fear she herself had felt so often since her own childhood. The panic she had felt in the presence of the Ashwans, when the warriors from the cold came down and killed her people, betrayed the Beothuk's ignorance of who the Ashwans were. Since they had been surprised by the warriors, they must have been unaware that they could be attacked by them. Since they had been unarmed when the attack occurred, it followed that they had been negligent, had failed to take proper care of their children who were gathering clams. Therefore, it was the Beothuk's own fault that they had been killed. Such a horror need not be visited upon the children she would bring into the world in her lifetime. All she had to do was teach them to be always alert, prepared for the worst, ever conscious of their surroundings. She would never need to be afraid for them . . . never.

Anin watched the melting snow and felt a strong desire to take the path to Baétha, his people's village, but they would have to wait where they were until Woasut's child was born. Woasut could not undertake a long portage, with their heavy provisions and the tapatook, so close to her time. He must fortify himself with patience and await the birth.

Meanwhile, as the weather became milder, he could explore the area surrounding their clearing more thoroughly. In fact it had been a relatively mild winter; very little snow had fallen since the sun when Anin had killed the two caribou, two suns' walk in the direction of the cold. They had had only two snowfalls, and not heavy ones, and the cold periods had never settled in for very long.

One morning as he was leaving on one of these explorations, he told Woasut not to worry if he did not return that evening. He wanted to go as far as the bay he had seen across the snowfields when he had killed the caribou. He left without taking the sled, walking on snowshoes and carrying his hunting weapons and his fishing spear. After one sun he found that the snow was nearly all melted, and he took off his snowshoes and slung them across his back. His moosins were well enough rubbed with caribou oil and insulated with moss to protect his feet from the wet ground.

In the distance he could already see the temporary shelter he had made for himself on the first night of his hunting trip. Now there was so little snow that he had to cut boughs to make it habitable for the night. When he was sitting comfortably by his fire, he thought about all that had befallen him since he had set out on his voyage of initiation, and he realized how lucky he had been to meet Woasut. She had brought a new level of meaning to his life. He no longer thought only of himself, of his own difficulties and happiness. He now took into consideration the difficulties and happiness of Woasut and her child. "Her child, my child," he thought, then: "No, our child." He smiled. The words made him feel happy.

Suddenly he heard voices, the sound of people shouting. Quickly putting out his fire, he strained his ears to listen. They were men's voices, and they were arguing. He remained per-fectly still in the darkness, then after a short time decided to hide behind a nearby rock that was a hundred paces from his shelter. He stayed there for a good part of the night, but heard nothing more. Returning to his shelter, he relit the fire, then lay down on the ground and slept, his hand gripping the shaft of his fishing spear. He slept lightly, waking several times during the night. Each time he listened until he was certain nothing was happening before going back to sleep.

In the morning his body ached everywhere. He ate only a few mouthfuls of food and then hastily broke camp. This time he could see the large bay long before he arrived at the spot where he had killed the two caribou. He also saw green grass covering the land as it spread out before him, which surprised him, as did the stands of trees on the edge of the bay. Not big trees, but trees just the same. The snow must have been gone from the area for at least one moon, since the grass had had time to turn green and wave in the wind. Or perhaps the grass had never dried out in these parts? Had it been an exceptionally cold season here, too, with little snow and only short periods of intense cold? Was it perhaps always this warm?

He decided he would walk as far as the bay, but because of the voices he had heard during the night he moved with increased caution, looking about him in all directions and constantly checking the horizon. He did not want to be taken by surprise by the Bouguishamesh, as he had been in the evergreen forest on the rising-sun coast behind him. Now he could see the bay quite clearly, and one of the large Bouguishamesh tapatooks pulled high up on the sand. "Better not get too close," he thought; "these belligerent strangers do not like company."

This is where the shouting he had heard must have come from, carried all the way to his ears by the wind that blew from the setting sun. He angled to his right and walked directly towards the cold. By the end of that sun he had seen two more boats and a kind of mamateek covered with clumps of earth, surrounded by a fence made from woven sticks. Within the compound were a number of strange beasts that he had never seen before. Three were horned, and others had long, thick hair cascading down the backs of their necks and covering their entire bodies. "Beasts from another world," Anin said to himself. The three horned animals were huge, much bigger than caribou, but the others were smaller. Like bears, he thought, only lighter in colour. Except for one, which was all black.

"It is very good that we did not paddle around the point of land," he thought, not neglecting to thank Woasut for influencing his decision. "We would surely have encountered these strangers, and who knows what would have happened." He sensed that it was not good for him to remain long in one place, and, moving quickly, he returned to his shelter. He travelled much of the way in the dark, and had some trouble finding the spot. When he finally found it he was exhausted, and immediately stretched out on his hide blanket without even bothering to light a fire. Now that he knew there were Bouguishamesh nearby, he did not want to attract their attention. He slept.

He rose with the sun and began his trek back to the mamateek and Woasut. As he passed a clump of stunted evergreens, he saw the shadow beneath them move. He stopped and held his breath.

His spear was in his throwing hand, ready to be launched at the first hint of danger. He crept forward, slowly closing in on the shadow. He sensed a presence behind the trees, and in two quick leaps he was there: it was a woman. Her hair was the colour of dried grass. A Bouguishamesh woman, her eyes opened wide in terror, awaiting death. Anin looked quickly about and saw that she was alone. He squatted on his haunches and she recoiled further under the tree; Anin held out his hand and smiled to reassure her.

"I am Anin, the Addaboutik from Baétha. I will not harm you."

She did not seem to understand. He repeated his words, keeping his hand out and still smiling. The woman stood: she was pregnant, like Woasut, and very near her time. At the nape of her neck was a large gash, the blood in it beginning to thicken. It looked to Anin very like the gash he had received from the Bouguishamesh's cutting stick. He pointed to the wound and told the woman through gestures that it needed to be seen to. She nodded but did not move. He held out his hand again, inviting her to follow him, gesturing that he would take her to his mama-teek. The woman held back for a moment, then followed him from a distance.

Just as the sun reached its highest point in the sky, Anin and the woman emerged from the forest into the mamateek clearing. Woasut was very surprised to see the strange woman with hair the colour of dried grass. At first she was angry, but when Anin explained what had happened she agreed to care for the woman's neck wound. She took dried herbs from her medicine pouch, melted some snow, and mixed a paste in a wooden bowl. This she applied to the woman's wound. The woman's belly was almost completely exposed, and Woasut could see that her skin was extremely pale compared to her own. Her nipples were pink, not brown, and the aureole around each one was paler yet. Woasut opened her own clothing and compared the colour of her breasts to those of this pale woman. She was astonished at the difference. She turned to Anin.

"Are you sure she's not sick as well as wounded?" she asked. "I've never seen anyone as light-skinned as this one."

Anin smiled.

"I have seen many Bouguishamesh," he said, "and they are all like this woman. She is going to have her baby very soon, too. If we don't send her back to her own people, she could travel with us. She could help you work."

Woasut said nothing, but her face hardened. Anin had decided to take a second wife, and that did not please her. Normally when a man took a second wife he chose one of his first wife's sisters, so that there would be no arguing. Woasut regarded this strange woman critically. She was not bad-looking, but she was as pale as a trout's belly. What man would want to sleep with a woman who looked like a fish? And if they had a child together, what colour would it be? Woasut gave the woman some trout and a piece of dried meat, which the woman accepted, smiling often as she ate.

The couple then began teaching the stranger a few words of the Addaboutik and Beothuk language. By nightfall, the woman could say several necessary words, such as meat, caribou, fish, fire, medicine, water, breast, legs and arms, hands and head, eyes and mouth, nose and cheek. Then Anin lay down between the women, beneath the caribou skin blankets, and Woasut immediately placed herself on her knees so that Anin would enter her, in case he entertained thoughts of the woman with the pale skin and hair the colour of dried grass. When he was satisfied, Woasut asked him to continue rocking until she was satisfied too, conscious that the stranger was watching them curiously. Woasut kept up a steady flow of low cries of pleasure and moans of contentment, to let the woman know that she was happy and could make her man happy all by herself. That way, if Anin coupled with the stranger without satisfying her, the woman would know she was not his favourite wife.

THE SNOW HAD completely melted and new growth was beginning to show green through the yellow moss. Although the
nights were still cool, the sun in the season of new growth
warmed the mamateek for the three sheltering in it. The
Bouguishamesh woman, whose name was Gudruide, had learned
the Addaboutik-Beothuk language fairly well, and could make
herself understood in it. Her irrepressible laughter made her
presence almost tolerable to Woasut, who nonetheless continued
to treat the woman like a slave in order to maintain her own
status as first wife. Anin had yet to show the slightest inclination
to couple with the newcomer, but still Woasut never let the two
of them out of her sight when they were together. She was afraid
she would be reduced to begging for her turn with Anin if he
decided to take up with this fish-skinned woman from another
world. She was as strong as Woasut, and equally experienced in
the ways of the world, and often took the initiative when they
were performing their daily tasks.

For example, Woasut did not have to tell her when it was time
to check the fishing line. When the ice on the lake began to melt,
each time she ventured out onto it she came back with wet feet,
and had to dry her strange foot-coverings by the fire. These foot-
coverings, she said, were made from the skin of an animal that had
two horns. The skin was wrapped around the foot, and then a rigid
pad was placed beneath the foot and secured to the leg by means of
strings cut from the same skin. Unlike Anin and Woasut, she did
not stuff her foot-coverings with moss to keep out the cold. And
her clothing was made from the hair of yet another strange animal,
smaller than the two-horned kind; this one's hair was woven
together by the Bouguishamesh to form a different sort of skin.
Anin described as best he could the two new kinds of animals he
had seen in the enclosure surrounding the Bouguishamesh's mamateek. Woasut was astonished to learn that, with these strange

beasts, it was not necessary to kill them in order to take their skins, because each season-cycle their skins grew back and could be taken again and again. According to Anin, that discovery alone was worth the three season-cycles he had spent away from his people, and the many hardships he had endured.

Woasut considered that it was better, after all, that Anin had returned with a female rather than with another male. Two men and one woman in camp would have caused competition for the woman. Beothuk women had long ago learned to accept one another and to share their men; between men, however, there was always rivalry and conflict over women. That is why there were more Beothuk men than women. Woasut still resented the presence of this strange woman, but she knew better than to let Anin see it. She also knew that it was good to have a female to help with the birthing – as long as the two of them did not give birth at the same time.

Anin finished readying the tapatook for the growing season. He had made new arrows, changed the sinew on his bow, and made three more spears so that the women could help with the fishing. He helped the women gather armloads of moss and dried them near the fire, to be used when the birthings started. And he collected what remained of the dried meat and placed it in bark baskets, which he buried near the mamateek under a pile of stones to keep them away from wolves and bears. A permanent fire was also kept burning near the pile, to keep other possible thieves away.

One morning, Woasut announced that her child was coming. Anin made a smaller shelter for himself, outside the mamateek, so that Woasut and Gudruide would have more room. He asked Gudruide if she would help with the birthing. That evening, Woasut refused to eat. Her contractions had begun and she wanted to lie down to conserve her strength. She would not sleep, however, for fear of robbing her child of its vigour. This was a Beothuk tradition, and she would follow it even though all her people were dead. She wanted this child to survive and to per-petuate her race. She had learned the birthing tradition from her mother and she knew what had to be done. She made a cushion of dried moss with which to receive the newborn, so that it would not hurt itself when it fell from her; she wanted its first experience of the world to be as soft as possible. Between contractions she rested, lying in the mamateek and waiting, and then pushing to help the baby along its passage from the internal to the external world. Above all, she did not want the pale-skinned woman to touch her until it was absolutely necessary.

Gudruide remained outside the mamateek, sitting with Anin, who was looking at her curiously. She had a certain attraction, he decided, despite the distasteful pallor of her skin. Could such a skin be as soft as Woasut's? He moved towards her and held his fingers to her face. She smiled. He looked down at her round belly, and touched it, too, through her strange garment, which was tied with cords cut from the skin of that odd, two-horned animal. Slowly she untied the cords and lifted her dress, disclosing her naked skin, and gently took Anin's hand and placed it on her stomach. It felt taut, as though on the point of bursting. He caressed it, feeling his desire rise for this woman for the first time since he had brought her to the mamateek. He realized he had been regarding her as a kind of wounded animal. "When she has learned more of the Addaboutik language," he thought, "I will ask her why she left her people." He saw the tuft of hair above her sex, darker than the hair on her head. Fascinated, he placed his hand on it. Woasut did not have such a tuft. No sooner had he touched her there than he felt her tremble, and her skin bunched like the skin of the ptarmigan when it has been plucked. She swallowed with difficulty, clutching at the remaining cords binding her garment, and suddenly the entire front of her dress was open, and she lay down on Anin's caribou blankets. Despite the coolness of the night air, sweat trickled down from her temples. Anin found himself caressing her pale breasts, running his hands from them to the tuft of hair above her sex, then behind her to her firm buttocks. The strength of his desire for her mounted rapidly. When his own sex was hard, he signalled to the woman to turn over and raise herself on her knees, which she did without hesitation. Although his caresses to this point had been gentle, he now thrust himself almost brutally into the Bouguishamesh woman and threw himself into the rocking motion that leads quickly to a man's satisfaction. She took the assault without a murmur of protest, even quickening its pace by raising and lowering her backside ever more rapidly until he was finished. When he tried to slide out of her she grabbed him and held him to her, letting him know that she wanted him to continue. Anin re-entered her and resumed the rocking motion, and again she increased the rhythm, emitting small sounds of pleasure that quickly built to a loud, sharp cry that sounded almost like pain. At that moment, Woasut stuck her head out of the mama-teek in time to see Anin withdraw from the fish-bellied woman, and Gudruide turn from her kneeling posture to kiss Anin's sex. Then, seized by a violent contraction, she barely had time to return to her moss bed before the child began to come.

Squatting on her haunches, she pushed as hard as she could with each new contraction. The baby's head was almost out. When its body was fully engaged in the passageway, she could no longer hold in her own cries. When the woman with hair the colour of dead grass hurried into the mamateek, still naked, the baby was already born. It was lying on the moss bed, and Woasut had fallen over backwards, exhausted from her exertions. But she looked up and smiled at Gudruide, showing teeth as white as cold-season snow.

"I was able to stay on my feet the whole time," she said proudly. "The baby will be healthy and strong. What kind is it?"

"A male," Gudruide told her. "Do you feel strong enough to bite off the cord yourself?"

Woasut nodded and sat up, and Gudruide placed the male child in the new mother's arms. Woasut held him lovingly, then took the natal cord between her teeth and bit through it. She licked the child thoroughly from head to toe, after which Gudruide took him and wrapped him in a soft caribou blanket to keep him warm. Then she returned him to Woasut, who lay down with him and held him tightly in her arms.

"It's a male," she called out happily to Anin.

12

ON THE SUN after her confinement, Woasut was up fulfilling her daily tasks as usual, and ordering Gudruide about when Anin was away from the mamateek. She wondered when the woman with hair the colour of dead grass was going to deliver her own child. She sent her out to check the fishing line, convinced that the ice on the lake was about to break, and watched carefully as the woman waded out to the hole through the water that covered the thin ice. Then she saw the woman return to the mamateek with a beautiful trout, the fishing line rolled neatly around the birch stick that kept it from being pulled through the hole by the fish. As always, Gudruide removed her wet foot-coverings and draped them over a branch near the outside fire to dry.

The sun was warm and pleasant, and Anin had gone down towards the bay to hunt game. Woasut was already carrying her child on her back, strapped to a wooden board that Anin had made for him. Anin had bent a birch bar across the top of the board to protect the baby's head should the board slip from Woasut's back when she was standing up. They had not yet given the child a name. They wanted to wait until the child's character became apparent. Privately, Woasut thought they should call it "The Child Born While Anin Was Coupling with the Fish-Woman," but she dared not express her thoughts openly.

It was the custom of her people that, when there were more women in a village than men, a man could have more than one wife. And if a man had two wives, it was expected that both would be equally satisfied! Usually the second wife was known to the first, but if there was no other woman in the village a strange woman could become a second wife. And it was important that disputes and bad feelings be avoided in a village. Woasut was therefore confused. Was it right for her to feel such animosity towards Gudruide? Certainly it was not. Her duty was clear: she must follow tradition. What was more, Gudruide had made herself extremely useful, helping with the newborn child since the night of his birthing. Why, then, was she complaining? But she could not help wondering what would happen when both women were available for coupling, and both wanted to couple at the same time?

Suddenly the women heard voices coming from the direction of the wind. They sat still, listening carefully. Two males, speaking a language Woasut did not know. Gudruide sprang up in terror and ran towards the path leading down to the bay, calling to Woasut to follow her quickly.

"Hurry! Take the baby and run with me. They are Vikings! They will kill you!"

With that, Gudruide set off as fast as a woman on the point of giving birth could run. Woasut, no less mindful of her previous experience with the Ashwans, tried to run after her, but she was still weak from childbirth and could not move as quickly as Gudruide. The Bouguishamesh did not seem to be aware of them, despite Gudruide's loud cries. The women had no sooner disappeared down the path than the two Vikings emerged into the clearing and saw the mamateek. Each of them was carrying a cutting stick, which they thrust again and again through the bark covering of the mamateek. After wrecking the empty dwelling, they tore off down the path to the bay, in the same direction taken by the women.

The destruction of the mamateek had taken only a few moments, but it was enough to give the women a small lead. The men were quick and strong, however, and were gaining rapidly. The women ran as fast as they could; even though heavy with child, Gudruide was running faster than Woasut, who was carrying her baby. At a sharp turn in the path, Gudruide almost collided with Anin, who was returning with a beaver slung over his back. The pale woman was trying to tell Anin about the danger behind them when Woasut caught up with them. Anin could see that the women had left their weapons at the mamateek, and so he threw the beaver into the woods and told the women to hide behind a large rock. He took a long cord that had been looped through his belt and quickly tied it to two trees, across the path just below knee height. Then he stepped off the path just as the two Bouguishamesh came hurtling along it. Both tripped over the cord. Before they could get up, Anin's harpoon plunged into the back of one of them, and Anin grabbed the second one's hair with one hand and thrust an arrow into his throat with the other. The first one tried to get up, the harpoon still protruding from his back, but the shaft caught in a tree and the man fell forward, uttering a strangled cry. The second man was clutching the arrow in his throat with both hands, unable to move. Blood flowed from his mouth and from the throat wound made by the arrowhead. Anin left them and joined the women.

"We must break camp immediately and go towards the wind," he said. "Other strangers will come to look for these two, and we will have no end of battles. A pregnant woman and another who has just given birth cannot put up much of a fight. We must go."

Before leaving, Anin retrieved his harpoon from the back of the first Bouguishamesh, and tore his arrow from the neck of the second, who gurgled in agony and then fell face forward to the ground. Then Anin took up the strangers' cutting sticks and their long knives and gave them to the women for safekeeping. They took the path back to the camp, taking every precaution to make no sound. There could easily be other Vikings on the path or at the camp. When Gudruide tried to tell Anin how many Vikings there were in the land, Anin told her to be quiet: no talking until he gave the order. When they arrived at the camp they soon saw how much damage had been caused by the strangers. The bark covering the mamateek was completely cut through and would never keep out the rain. Gudruide found her foot-coverings some distance from the fire where they had been drying. The dried meat was untouched, hidden in baskets under the pile of stones. Anin asked the women to take only what was absolutely necessary – blankets, food, clothing – and to make three tightly tied bundles. They would carry their weapons in their hands, ready for use.

"Do not weigh yourselves down," he advised them. "We have to walk fast, and we have to walk a long time if we are to keep ahead of these strangers. We must reach the setting-sun coast, where the wind comes from, as quickly as possible."

Working together, the three soon had the provisions packed and tied to the portage straps. They put the bundles on their backs and Anin hoisted the tapatook upside down on his head above his pack, and the three were ready to set off on their journey by the time the sun was at its highest point in the sky. Woasut carried her bundle on her back with her child strapped to her chest. Although Gudruide, too, was heavy with child, she was still strong, and her pack was slightly larger than Woasut's. All three walked swiftly, with Anin in the lead. They would not even stop to rest until it was dark.

The sky became cloudier as they walked, and towards nightfall it began to rain, lightly at first, then gradually with more and more intensity. A snow-melting rain, cold and steady. Anin called a halt to the march and told the women to put down their bundles and gather material to make a temporary shelter. They had forgotten to wrap the firewood in waterproof skins, and so that first night they had to rely on their blankets for warmth. The women found a few small pieces of birchbark, which they leaned against the overturned tapatook to provide some protection from the rain. The child was safe and warm. Anin circled the area carefully to make sure the tapatook was well hidden from the path. Then they ate a bit of dried meat. Wrapped warmly in their caribou blankets and huddled on either side of the baby, the two women slept under the tapatook while Anin, also covered by a blanket, sat outside and kept watch. He listened to the rain. He dropped off to sleep from time to time, but always awoke with a start, thinking he had heard voices drifting through the rain. Then he would sleep again. His dreams were strange and vivid.

He was up before the sun. Stiff and aching from the night, he awakened the women, who were even more tired than he was. The child was already showing signs of hunger, and Woasut put him to her breast before eating her own meagre meal. While the women were repacking the bundles, Anin went off to a large rock that he could see towards the region of cold. He had an uneasy feeling that the voices he had heard during the night had come from there. When he was close, he approached the rock carefully from the wind side and stopped. He could hear the sounds of heavy breathing. A hunter now fully alert, he stole a quick glance around the rock and saw three figures stretched out on the ground beneath an overhanging portion. Two women and a man. He noted with astonishment that they seemed to be unarmed. He would take a chance, he decided, and wake them up and bring them to Gudruide, who might understand their language and tell him who they were. He leapt towards the man, jabbed him with his fishing spear, and retreated. The man jumped to his feet and pressed himself against the rock, while the women woke up screaming and crying out.

Anin told them to walk ahead of him, using eloquent gestures to make the Bouguishamesh obey. Instead, both women sank to their knees, crying and wringing their hands. One of them wore a dress similar to Gudruide's, but the other was clothed in skins sewn loosely together about her legs, with a kind of apron covering her sex, while around her shoulders was a blanket made from the skin of those animals whose hair returns each season-cycle. The man remained on his feet. His hair was the colour of the wildflowers that filled the clearings at the height of the warm season. He was wearing skins wrapped around his legs to the tops of his thighs, held in place by cords. The poorly dressed woman had hair the colour of red ochre, the powdered stone with which the Addaboutik covered their bodies in the warm season to protect themselves from biting insects. All three strangers were bigger than Anin, but he was the stronger because of his spear and his bow and arrows, which he carried over his shoulder. He gestured to them again to get up and walk towards his temporary camp, where his own women were waiting.

The man seemed resigned to his fate, but the women were visibly terrified. As they neared the camp, the tallest of them saw Gudruide, who was coming to meet them, spear in hand. She seemed to recognize her as one of her own, and threw herself into Gudruide's arms, crying and laughing at the same time. The two women babbled in their throaty Bouguishamesh tongue while the second woman and the man stood back and looked on without smiling, remaining wary. Anin, always on his guard, prodded them with his harpoon. Gudruide pushed herself away from the woman she had been embracing and spoke to Anin in the Addaboutik language:

"This is my younger sister," she said. "The Vikings tried to kill her, too, just as they tried to kill me. She ran away with these two Scottish slaves, escaping from the two men you killed on the path to the bay. They are not dangerous to us. They have nowhere to go. They will be killed if they return. May we keep them with us?"

Anin did not reply at once. Three more people to feed. Two more pale-skinned women. A man who might be of some help.

"This man," he said to Gudruide. "Can he hunt?"

Gudruide spoke to the man in Bouguishamesh and waited for his reply before turning back to Anin.

"He says he will quickly learn if he is given a weapon to hunt with. He also says he can run faster than the wind."

Anin smiled at this phrase. He lowered his spear and poked it in the back of the Scottish slave. Could he trust these three new-comers? Gudruide he trusted. Her younger sister seemed hardy, as did the other woman, able to carry the packs while Gudruide and Woasut rested. The man could carry Anin's pack, leaving him only the tapatook.

"We will take them with us," he told Gudruide. "But they must work hard. Each must take a load."

Gudruide was happy. She translated Anin's decision and her happiness spread to the three new faces. The Scottish slaves threw

themselves to their knees to thank Anin for his mercy, which made
Anin furious with them. He ordered them to stand up on their feet.

"The Addaboutik hate weak people who spend their lives
begging. This is now the second time these people have gone
down on their knees before me. I will not tolerate weakness. I
would rather kill them."

Gudruide tried to explain that their kneeling was a gesture of
gratitude, not weakness, that the two people were slaves. Anin
understood none of this. Kneeling was a woman's gesture, and was
undignified in a man. It showed feminine fear. The woman must
also learn not to feel fear, and above all not to show fear if she felt
it. Otherwise he would kill her with his own hands. He would kill
the man, too, if he showed any more signs of weakness.

"They are in the land of the Addaboutik now," he said, "and
they must live like the Addaboutik or else die. They must also
speak the Addaboutik language. They must learn it so that I may
understand them. I do not want to hear the Bouguishamesh language again. I must understand what everyone is saying. The man
is not yet ready to learn how to hunt. He will be given a weapon
when he is truly a man."

When he had finished speaking he seemed perfectly calm. He
looked at Gudruide: "What does this mean, Scottish slave?"

Gudruide explained that the two had been captured on an
island in the Irish Sea. That meant they had been forced to serve
the people who had captured them, and these masters had the
power of life and death over them. She added that the word
Scottish meant that they came from a country other than the one
she and her sister came from. Anin seemed satisfied by this
answer, and remained silent while he considered it. Then he told
Gudruide to tell them what he was about to say.

"In this country there are no slaves. There are only males and
females. Males are stronger than females, but females are very
useful and good companions. No one gets down on their knees to
beg. Knees are for coupling, or for wrestling, for satisfying our
needs among ourselves. Tell them that here, Anin gives the

orders because he knows the country better than the others. And tell them that they must learn to speak Addaboutik."

While Gudruide relayed his words to the newcomers, Anin went to join Woasut and the child who had been with them for barely two suns.

13

THE SIX MEMBERS of the clan were standing at the top of a cliff overlooking the windy coast at the edge of the long tongue of land they had just crossed. There had been no further incidents during their trek towards the wind. Gwenid had easily carried her older sister's pack; Della, the Scottish woman, had taken Woasut's so that the Beothuk could better look after her baby. Robb, the slave, was given Anin's heavier load. They had had to make a detour towards the cold region to get around a chain of high mountains, and so crossing the tongue of land had taken them seven suns. Anin considered that there had not been seven suns, but rather seven periods of wan light, since the sun had not once shown itself.

Robb carried Anin's heavy pack without complaint, a broad smile never leaving his lips. Della, whose load was as heavy as Robb's, removed her leg coverings and put them on only at night, despite the thorny bushes and sharp branches they had to walk through. Her legs were strong and shapely, Anin did not fail to notice. Well muscled. She, like Robb, smiled a great deal of the time, and talked almost incessantly. She repeated the Beothuk and Addaboutik words that Woasut and Gudruide had taught her over and over, and so was soon able to express at least her simpler daily needs. Robb was less quick to learn than Della, partly because Anin spoke to him hardly at all while they were walking, and not at all when they took turns beating a path for the others.

Now, at the top of the cliff, they decided to take shelter from the wind near a brook that fell sharply down towards the sea at the head of a long bay. Water from melting snow had formed a natural, sloping path down to the shore, but Anin chose to make camp at the top rather than expose the clan unnecessarily at the bottom. He also thought there would be less wind at the top, and they would be close to the forest, where they would find firewood and bark, of which there was none at the level of the bay. He set the three women to gather firewood and start a fire. They also collected moss, still dry from the recent season of cold and snow. Then they cut evergreen boughs to carve out a place that would be protected from the wind and the damp.

Meanwhile, Anin and Robb went off in search of birch trees big enough to provide bark for a mamateek. Armed with sharp cutting stones and short clubs, they set off into the bush. When they found a suitably sized tree, they made a long, vertical incision on one side of its trunk, and two circular incisions at the base and higher up. Then, more slowly, they peeled the bark from the trunk, tapping the sharp stones with the wooden clubs. To make the top incision, Anin stood on Robb's shoulders while the slave moved around the tree. It took them a whole sun to gather enough bark to make a mamateek large enough to hold six adults and two babies, since Gudruide must surely be approaching the time of her confinement.

The two men also marked the position of an immense birch tree from which they would later take bark for the second tapatook they would need when they were ready to begin their sea voyage in the warm season. They did not take the bark now, because tapatook bark must be in prime condition. The bark they had taken, they rolled and tied into loose bundles so that it would not be difficult to stretch over the framework of the mamateek. When they returned to camp with their first load, they found that the women had already cut and positioned the poles for the framework, and had traced a circle in the centre for the firepit, which would be made with stones the women had also gathered. Anin was astonished. How had the women cut the poles so quickly? Della raised her robe and showed him a large, iron axe tucked into the belt of her undergarment, and broke out into loud, sonorous laughter that was pleasant to hear. The three other women also began to laugh. They were proud of the good work they had done. Soon all four of them were doubled up with laughter, which the two men found so infectious that they, too, began to laugh without quite knowing what they were laughing at. It was as though their exhaustion from the long journey was being evaporated by cascades of pure joy and relief.

It took them several suns to settle into their new camp and to be rested. The women made plans to gather clams and sea cucumbers, and Woasut promised to show the others how to catch squid. The mamateek was completed during the first sun, just after nightfall, the women having no trouble putting the last of the bark in place and leaning heavy poles on the covered framework to secure it. Anin lit the fire and the clan ate the last of the dried and smoked meat.

That night, Gudruide spoke in Addaboutik about her life in the cold country, which she called "the North." She came from an island called Ice-land, she said, and had emigrated to another place called Green-land. Her parents were fishers and farmers, planting seeds in the earth and raising the two-horned beasts and also sheep. She spoke about animals they called horses, on which they rode and which they also used to pull heavy loads on large sleds with wheels, runners that moved in circles. The men from Green-land would often go off in search of new lands that were good for farming, she told them. The men would spend months at sea without seeing land, and often they would drown when there were storms. Gudruide told how she had come to the land of the Addaboutik and the Beothuk. They had almost been killed by waves higher than five men. The waves had swamped their drakkar, which was a tapatook big enough to hold them as well as three two-horns and ten sheep. Anin and Woasut marvelled at her stories. Anin wanted to know why her own people had tried to kill her and her sister and the two slaves.

"My husband was a close friend of two brother merchants," she replied. "Finnbogi and Helgi. The brothers had entered into an agreement with a warrior, a woman named Freydis, who became Finnbogi's mistress. When she was pregnant by him, she told him he must give her half of all the goods covered by their agreement. Since he already shared the ownership of the goods with his brother Helgi, Finnbogi told Freydis that he could not give her what he did not rightfully own. Freydis then had the brothers killed by the two men that you killed on the path, Anin. My husband knew about this, and told Freydis that when they returned to Green-land he would denounce her. So she had him killed, as well. My sister and I also knew about this, of course, so she also tried to silence us. But we fled, each going in a different direction. I went alone, and Gwenid took the two Scottish slaves with her. The rest you know."

Anin pondered Gudruide's tale. What a strange life these Bouguishamesh lived. In order to gain possession of a few goods, a female warrior would kill three men and attempt to kill two women and the slave couple. Among the Addaboutik, a murderer was punished by death or banishment from the community. These people were greedy, and he and Woasut had been lucky to have come across only three of them, and to have killed all three. The two women from the North could not be blamed for the bad conduct of the others, of course. Still, the strange customs of the people Gudruide had described made him realize he must remain on guard, so that nothing of the sort would happen to him and Woasut. As for the two Scottish slaves, they must be greatly relieved at no longer having to serve such people.

That night, with the fire burning and the six adults and the child adding the warmth of their bodies, it was very warm in the mamateek. They lay almost naked on the evergreen boughs covered with caribou blankets, and in the soft light of the fire Anin contemplated the skin of the four strangers. He saw Gudruide's round, white belly, which seemed ready to burst, and the dark thatch between her legs. He looked at her sister's long-limbed body, and at Della's fiery red pubic hair. Woasut's sex was completely hairless. Anin wondered how it was possible that there were so many differences between people. Their skin colour, their hair colour, the rich growth of hair between the legs of these pale people, and the absence of such hair among the Addaboutik and Beothuk. He determined to ask the purpose of this nether hair the next time they were all talking together, as they had been this night. Then he lay down beside Gudruide, enfolded her in his arms, and went almost immediately to sleep.

14

THE WOMEN HAD been awake all night. Gudruide's baby had arrived – a beautiful girl.

Plump, healthy, pink, her skin paler even than that of the other new members of Anin's clan, she was so big that for a while it seemed she would never come out. Gudruide spent most of the night in labour; it was nearly dawn when the baby's head finally appeared in the passage. It was Gwenid's first birthing, and she had been quite unnerved. Della, the Scottish slave, seemed to have had more experience; still, as the night wore on, she had said they would have to sacrifice the child to save the mother. Although Woasut could not understand what the two other women were saying in that guttural language of theirs, she knew that Gudruide's situation was serious. At the critical moment, she ordered the other women out of the mamateek and melted some of the seal fat that she had been carefully conserving since the previous leaf-falling season. She coated her hands with the warm oil, inserted one deep into Gudruide's birth passage and slowly withdrew it, pulling the baby with it. Then she inserted her other hand, and urged Gudruide to push with each new contraction. Before long the baby's head was out, and the child was born with no further difficulty. But Woasut knew that it would never be as strong and resilient as her male child, because Gudruide had been lying down when she delivered it. Also because the female child had waited so long to come out. That was always a bad sign in a newborn.

Woasut prepared a bed of dried moss and, since Gudruide was too weak to do it herself, licked the baby until it was completely clean. She also had to cut the cord with her teeth. Gudruide was all but unconscious. "Without me," thought Woasut, "this baby would be dead. These people know nothing about birthing. What did they learn from their own mothers?" She covered the mother and her baby with a caribou blanket and went outside to inform the others that the newborn was a female and apparently in good health. The news was joyfully received, and despite their fatigue after a long, sleepless night, everyone went off to perform their daily tasks.

The two men went hunting. Anin thought it was time for Robb to learn how to hunt the game of this country. He took a length of cord, gave a spear to the Scotsman, and carried his own bow and arrows. He also brought a net for catching fish. He would take Robb up to the high marshlands at the top of the plateaux. While they were gone, Woasut taught the two women to plait and oil dried plant strips, and to fashion them into snares for trapping rabbits. She also showed them how to set the snares. When all the snares were properly set, the women descended the path to the shore of the bay, where they gathered clams and sea cucumbers. At the foot of the waterfall there was a small tidal pool, where they found a salmon that had been trapped there by the receding waters. They quickly surrounded it and caught it with their bare hands. They were completely soaked after their adventure, but very happy, and when they returned to the mamateek they took off their wet clothes, spread them near the fire to dry, and were sitting naked, talking and laughing amongst themselves and Gudruide when the men returned. There was no shyness among the women, and they did not attempt to cover themselves when the men entered the mamateek. They went on cooking clams and sea cucumbers on the flat stone set in the middle of the firepit. During the meal, the men's eyes never left the women's glistening bodies. Woasut was wearing a strip of caribou skin between her legs, held in place by a thin cord tied around her waist; she still flowed with the aftereffects of childbirth, and she had placed a lining of dried moss under the caribou skin. As long as she was nursing her child, there could be no question of coupling with Anin. Still, she understood that men wanted women, and she smiled when she saw Anin and Robb admiring the naked bodies displayed so temptingly before them. She was curious to see who would couple with whom. She hoped Anin would honour Gwenid, the sister of the woman to whom she had developed a strong attachment since their shared birthings. She thought the two slaves would choose each other. But she was wrong: it was Della who drew Anin's gaze. Her dark red hair seemed to have a powerful attraction for him, and as head male of the clan he signalled to Robb that the latter was to have Gwenid. Then he lowered himself to his knees and told the Scottish woman to come to him. Della looked shyly at Woasut, who turned away quickly so as not to seem to be consenting to their union. How could she? She was first wife, but Anin was the provider, the man who had saved her life, and the chief of this clan of pale-skinned strangers. When Della turned and presented herself to Anin, he first caressed her from shoulder to rump, then nibbled playfully at her neck, and then entered her brusquely. When he was satisfied, he withdrew, and the young woman did not insist that he continue, as his first two wives had done. Robb, perhaps being shy, covered himself and Gwenid with a caribou blanket, under which he caressed her ardently. Just as he was about to enter her, however, she turned to him and raised her legs, so that he was obliged to take her face to face. The movement pushed aside the blanket, and the eyes of all the others in the mamateek were drawn to their coupling. It was only the third time Anin had seen this new position – once when Woasut had turned spontaneously to him, again with Gudruide, and now with Robb and Gwenid, the sister of his second wife. He was intrigued by it. When the couple were finished, he could not help asking Gudruide what it was that women saw in it.

But it was Woasut who answered. "It is good to see the man's face during the act," she said. "Good for the woman, at least."

Gudruide agreed. "In Green-land, the females prefer it this way, but men who think only of their own pleasure always do it from behind."

Anin did not reply to this, but he felt the rebuke. By even asking about matters related to coupling, he had broken an unspoken rule of his people, for whom discretion was an important virtue. Before setting out on his long voyage around the earth, he had seen clan members performing the act when others in the mamateek were awake, but it was customary to wait until the others were asleep, when the fire was reduced to a heap of glowing embers that cast a filtered light. But here, Anin's clan performed the act of satisfaction openly, without shyness or shame. Although this was new to him, he did not think it disagreeable. That night, everyone slept soundly, except for the two babies, who woke several times demanding to be fed.

Woasut would soon feel desire for her man reawaken within her. She told herself that having several wives was good for the man, a way of ensuring that he was always in good spirits. But for a woman it was a perpetual source of anxiety, envy, and jealousy. And of frustration, which ensured that she was often in bad spirits. Woasut accepted the situation, since it was as natural to her as living and breathing. Gudruide thought that she herself would have been less jealous of her sister, Gwenid, than she was of the Scottish slave, Della. But she also told herself that it would not be a bad thing for women if they were able to depend on more than one husband.

"In our land," she thought, "a man can have only one wife when he is at home, but when he is voyaging he takes mistresses. The woman Freydis, who tried to have us killed, was the bastard daughter of Erik the Red, and the illegitimate sister of Lief, Erik's son. Our men behave much like the Addaboutik, but they are hypocritical about it. They do not act openly, and they are often jealous of their women. I prefer the way things are done here. And Anin is much more agreeable to look at than the Skraelings, whom Woasut calls Ashwans."

As a slave, Della had been forced to submit to every imaginable whim of the Viking men. She, too, thought it was better to live freely here, among these people. It had been terrifying to be caught between the jealousy of the Viking wives and the brutality of the Viking men. But she felt that if she could have Anin to herself, she would teach him to be less rough with her than he had been that first time. She had had enough experience among mariners to know how to make a good man like this Addaboutik think about the woman during the act of satisfaction. She could speak about this with the other women, now that she was no longer a slave. She thought she could make allies of them, that their lives would be better here than it had been for her in Green-land.

Gwenid thought that Anin ought to have chosen her for his third wife. In Ice-land, a husband could kill a male slave if his wife were impregnated by him. But this was hypocrisy, because often the male slave had been seduced by the wife, who was frustrated from having been left so long alone by her husband when he was away voyaging with his mistresses. Gwenid believed that Anin would make a wonderful lover once he had learned how to please a woman. When she watched him coupling with the Scottish slave, she had marvelled at his strength, his passion, his rhythm! She had been very jealous. She told herself that she would have him before long.

For Robb, possessing a woman who was bigger and more robust than his Scottish companion was not a bad bargain: "This Gwenid is more pliable than Della," he thought. "She is less disdainful of me now that I am no longer a slave among her people. But she coupled with me only because she did not know how else to behave in front of Anin. Woasut would be a very interesting challenge, once she has recovered from having her baby. She has a beautiful body, and her dark skin is as soft as duck down. Would Anin be jealous? Is everything as free and easy here as it seems? How pleasant it would be to rise from being a lowly slave, without rights, to a lord and master of my own clan! But I must tread carefully for fear of angering Anin. When I know more of the Addaboutik tongue, I will ask him about the proper way of behaving here, and among the Addaboutik people. Are there many women in his village? Will they be available to us, or will we have to share these four women with other men? How agreeable it is to be no longer a slave! Life here is so much more worth living than it was when I was condemned to serve the people of Green-land."

These thoughts distracted him from his work, but only for a few moments.

15

ANIN AND ROBB returned to the enormous birch from which they planned to take the bark for the second tapatook, which would allow the entire clan to get to the Addaboutik village of Baétha. It took them one whole sun to find it again. Anin first drew lines where the incisions were to be made, using a piece of red ochre rock. Since Robb was not tall enough to allow Anin to reach the top of the trunk by standing on his shoulders, Anin tied a stone to one end of a long cord and tossed it over the lowest branch of the tree; he then looped the end around his waist and cinched it tightly. Robb took the other end of the cord and, with Anin's help, pulled until he had hoisted Anin to the first branch.

With Anin thus suspended, Robb wrapped his end of the cord three times around a nearby tree; when Anin was ready to be lowered slowly to make the vertical cut, all Robb had to do was slacken the cord slightly. When all three cuts were made, Anin began separating the bark from the trunk. This was a painstaking operation, because even a small split in the bark would render it useless for a tapatook. But the work went well. It was the season when the sap was rising within the tree, and the bark was moist and pliable.

When they had completely removed it they spread it out in the sun, and before long it was lying flat and uncurled. Then they rolled it up again, this time with the inside facing out. It was light enough for one of them to carry; indeed, the finished tapatook would not weigh more than a child of five season-cycles.

Back at camp, the men decided to make the tapatook close to the waterfall, since they would need plenty of water to bend the ribs and bark into the proper shape that would allow it to float. There were hundreds of rocks near the waterfall as well, which they carried to the mamateek. They then began the process of shaping the bark. Even though it was freshly cut and still filled with sap, they had to soften it still more by immersing it in the stream for two whole suns, held down with the rocks. Then they very carefully fitted it between two rows of sharpened stakes pounded into the ground in the shape of the eventual tapatook. Its central form would be determined by a thin, bent piece of birch inserted across the bottom and up the sides. To give the hull greater strength, long, thin strips of pine, dried at the fire, would then be laid lengthways along the bottom, under the central rib, and other ribs of birch would be tied in place, equally spaced along the tapatook's length to give it its final shape and rigidity. The curved gunwales were also to be of birch. Anin explained to Robb that the entire process would take at least one moon. The bark and ribs had to be woven to the gunwales with thin pine roots, boiled and split down the middle, and every joint would be sealed with a mixture of pine gum and beaver fat. This was the method that the Addaboutik and Beothuk had followed to make their tapatooks since the first birch tree provided the bark for the first tapatook, and this was the method Anin's clan would use now. The only innovation in this case was Della's cutting tool, which she had stolen from the Bouguishamesh, and which would make the work go faster. Since Robb and Della were equally accustomed to wielding the strange axe, both would be allowed to work on the tapatook.

Woasut and Gwenid augmented the clan's food stores with shellfish from the bay and small game from the forest. Gudruide looked after the babies, except during feeding time, when each mother continued to feed her own child. Woasut's son was already eating cooked meat; Woasut chewed it for him first, to make it easier for him to digest, then placed it in his mouth.

Gudruide was recovering slowly from her birthing and would still need many suns' rest before her strength returned to her. She was excused from the heavier chores about the camp. Anin suggested to Woasut that she wade out into the bay with fishing lines to catch various kinds of fish. It was nearing the time when the small fish the Addaboutik called shamut would wash up onto the beach in waves. They ought not to miss this seasonal gift from the sea.

One morning, Anin witnessed a scene that rarely occurred among the Addaboutik, and which Woasut said she had also never heard of among the Beothuk. Gwenid gave an order to Della, who refused it, saying she was no longer Gwenid's slave. The two women began shouting at each other in the Viking language, hard words spat out furiously. Before long they were hitting each other with their fists. Gwenid was the bigger of the two, but the Scotswoman was stronger, quicker, and much more enraged. There was much kicking, punching, and pulling of hair. Anin stepped in only when Della reached for her axe and was about to bring it down on Gwenid's dried-grass-coloured head.

"If you kill her," he said to Della, "then you must either submit to the same treatment, or be banished from the clan. That is the law of the Addaboutik. There is nothing I can do to save you. We do not kill members of our own clan here."

The slave lowered her weapon, visibly calmed herself, and returned to splitting pine roots. Anin took Gwenid by the shoulders and marched her into the woods. He explained to her at length that the women must get along with each other if the clan

were to survive. There was the matter of presenting a united front
to their enemies; they must forget about such things as social
levels that prevailed among the Bouguishamesh. All people were
treated the same by the Addaboutik. All women were equal, and
all men were superior to them, because the men provided the
clan's food and weapons. Gwenid seemed to understand, but she
was still angry enough to explain that she had been jealous of
Della ever since the clan leader had shown her preference.

Anin smiled and said that such preference was not necessarily
a permanent mark of favour, but was rather the expression of a
momentary need.

"A clan chief may chose one woman one sun and another the
next. Only the first wife is given preference, according to our
custom. If the number of women becomes less than the number
of men, then the first wife would be the only wife. And second
and third wives must also attend to the needs of other men, so
that there will be no disputes among brothers or other male
members of the clan."

The young woman met Anin's gaze directly. "Then I can hope
that in time you will choose me?" she said.

Anin was embarrassed. "You may hope that I will take you, yes."

Without taking her eyes from Anin's, Gwenid untied the cords
of her dress. "Take me now, then," she said to him.

When the two returned to the camp, the others pretended not
to notice that Gwenid's dress was spotted with mud, and that dead
leaves from the previous season of cold and snow clung to it, sug-
gesting that she had been lying on her back on the ground. Only
Della responded by splitting pine roots with an angry vigour.
Woasut smiled inwardly: Anin seemed to have chosen Gwenid as
his third wife. This would bring the three women closer together.
Gudruide was uneasy, however, even though she, too, had secretly
hoped that Anin would favour her sister when they had been
together in the mamateek. Now she was not concerned that the
clan chief had taken her sister, only that he had done so away from
the eyes of the other members of the clan. She hoped that this
would not cause jealousy among the others. She had to admit that

she herself was envious of her younger sister for having succeeded in getting Anin alone, where she could have him to herself.

Robb was also discontented, but he did not let it show. He thought that if Anin was permitted to take Gwenid, there was no reason why he, Robb, could not do the same with Woasut and Gudruide. He was not particularly fond of Gwenid, and he had had Della many times already. Sometimes he had even coupled with her to please the sailors on the Viking drakkar. What a show they had put on! He was rather proud of his feats of endurance with her. As slaves, they had been obliged to obey or else risk losing their heads. He told himself that his situation here among the Addaboutik was much better than it had been with the Vikings, and he went back to work on the new tapatook.

16

WHEN THE TAPATOOK was finished, Anin and Robb looked upon it with pride. Della, too, was happy that she had been allowed to work on it. It was almost as though she were considered a man, able to wield an axe like anyone else. She had shown Anin how to sharpen its cutting edge with a fine-grained stone. And then she had split the roots of the white pine to make the cords with which the bark and ribs were sewn to the tapatook's gunwales. Anin marvelled at the knowledge acquired by this woman from a country he probably would never see in his life. She lifted the new tapatook onto her shoulders and began carrying it down the path: it was time to see if the craft was solid, watertight, and easy to handle. Anin picked up the two paddles from the old tapatook and, signalling Robb to follow, set off down the path to the shore of the bay.

It had taken the better part of a moon to complete the construction. Gudruide was now completely recovered and working alongside the other women as usual. Her daughter was now also old enough to eat meat, and Woasut showed her how to prepare it. The three women were on the shore gathering shellfish when Della appeared with the tapatook and placed one end of it in the water with the other end still on the beach. Anin told her that a tapatook must always be boarded parallel to the shoreline, never with one end up on the sand where it could be broken or torn on a sharp rock. Della had placed the tapatook as she had seen the Vikings place their drakkars, which they always left pointed into the water, ready to be shoved off in a hurry if the need arose. Drakkars, he said, were made of stout planks, and could not easily be damaged by rocks, even though such construction made them too heavy to be carried like a tapatook. The three women stopped collecting shellfish and helped launch the new craft. Anin boarded first and sat in the stern. He invited Robb in next, to occupy the centre, and gave the second paddle to Della, asking her to help him paddle. The others pushed them out into deeper water.

Della knew how to row with an oar, but this was the first time she had used a paddle. She had to turn around often to observe the strokes that Anin used to control the tapatook. She was amazed at how easily the craft moved through the water, and how responsive it was to the paddle. When Robb tried to stand up, she also came very close to learning how easily a tapatook could be capsized. Anin barely had time to yell at him to sit down: never stand up in a tapatook, he told him. Robb understood immediately. Returning to shore was more complicated than leaving it had been. They had to arrive side-on, not bow-first. But the former slaves were intelligent and learned quickly.

That evening there was a celebration in the camp. Everyone told stories from their respective cultures, and Woasut sang lullabies to put her child to sleep. Then Gudruide sang lullabies in her own tongue, and for once Anin did not reprimand her for not speaking Addaboutik. The strangest singing was Della's; she sang Celtic ballads with a soft, sweet voice, and her gentleness surprised those who had watched her wield the axe like a man.

When the song was over, everyone noticed Gwenid, who was rubbing her breasts.

"Why are you doing that?" Anin asked her.

"Because Della's song was very moving, and it made me feel like caressing myself. It is something I often saw women do when their husbands were a long time at sea and they had no slaves to comfort them. That was before the people in my country became Christians; now they have been told that such gestures are sinful. But it feels good."

Anin asked Della to sing another song, and told Gwenid she might continue rubbing herself.

"I want everyone to enjoy themselves tonight," he said. "We are now ready to begin our voyage to Baétha. Perhaps we will have something to teach my family and friends whom I will be seeing again for the first time in three seasons of cold and snow!"

That night a new atmosphere of peace settled into the mamateek. Gone was the tension that jealousy and envy had created. Woasut sensed this change, and watched and listened with the eagerness of one who wanted to learn everything. She no longer guarded her position as first wife, no longer felt anger at being neglected. She felt again what it was like to belong to a family. The three other women did not seem to her to be rivals, but were more like sisters with whom she could share, learn, and understand her life. Her zest for living had returned. No more would she mourn her lost people, killed by the Ashwans who came down from the cold regions for no other reason. No more would she dream only of vengeance, as she had since she had seen their corpses. No more would she blame the males of her clan for their carelessness in exposing themselves and their children to attacks from such a well-known enemy as the Ashwans. She let herself be gently rocked by the rhythms of Della's singing, which spoke to her of tenderness and friendship, words she had not known until someone had explained them to her in her own language. She felt love for these strangers who had come from another world. They were not like her, but still she might learn from them much of what she needed to know about life.

Anin, too, thought that meeting up with these strangers had been good. He could now be the leader of a clan, which he had dreamed of becoming since his childhood. He remembered stories about voyages told by the elders, in which the marvellous melded with the mundane. From now on, it would be he who told such stories, and his children would draw lessons about life from his own experiences, heard from his own lips. They would learn that the Addaboutik are not the only people in the world, and that Ashwans are not the only dangerous enemies.

In the mamateek's half light, cast by coals that glowed softly at the centre, eight people slept happily. When the sun returned, they would begin the final stage of Anin's voyage around the world. A voyage that had taught him the serenity of being part of a clan.

17

AS SOON AS the sun returned they ate a hasty meal and broke camp. They packed everything into small parcels, so that the weight could be evenly distributed in the tapatooks. Then they carried it down to the shore. The tide was at its highest, and so the portage was shorter. They stood about while Anin arranged the packing and determined who would travel in each tapatook. Two new paddles, finished the previous sun and made of birch, would also serve as poles. Anin placed himself in the new tapatook, which was bigger and able to carry more weight, along with the two mothers and their infants. He fastened the children's carrying boards to the central thwart, back to back. Gudruide took her position in the middle and Woasut climbed into the bow. The larger portion of the baggage was also stowed in this tapatook. The three remaining clan members and the rest of the parcels occupied the smaller tapatook, with Della at the stern, Robb in the bow, and Gwenid balancing them in the middle.

Both tapatooks set out together, entering the sea from the small brook and rounding several small, rocky islands at its mouth. As soon as they were in open water they felt the force of the wind against the tapatooks, and before they could get their sterns lined up with the wind the smaller of the two craft nearly capsized three times, largely due to the inexperience of its paddlers and to Gwenid's nervousness at the centre. But once the wind was behind them the tapatooks picked up speed. The shoreline on this windy side of the land was made up of ever higher cliffs. Anin began to recognize some of them as places where his people sometimes came to catch halibut. He knew from this that they were no more than five or six suns from Baétha, and the knowledge made his heart sing with joy as he entered this final stage of his long journey.

The coast was dangerous, with numerous foaming rocks and off-shore reefs to negotiate. Despite the heavy load it carried, Anin's tapatook was of lighter construction, and he was able to keep the lead. He often turned to see how his three companions were faring, and slowed his rhythm several times to allow them to catch up. When the sun was near its highest, he looked ashore and saw Gashu-Uwith, his head pointing straight up, sniffing the air. This made him feel that something was about to happen, and he decided to turn into a small, rock-strewn bay that was close by. When he twisted to look behind him, he saw that the second tapatook was well back. He shouted to them to hurry, but the wind was blowing towards him and his companions heard nothing. But they had seen Anin's tapatook turn towards the land, and they knew enough to follow him, despite the risk of being swept onto one of the sharp rocks that filled the bay like so many miniature islands. By the time they saw the huge, dark clouds rolling in above the cliffs, it was too late. The storm broke, the wind whipped at them from all directions, and it became almost impossible for them to control the tapatook. Despite their mightiest efforts, their lack of skill was pushing them directly towards the cluster of jagged rocks.

Anin, meanwhile, had already entered the small bay and seen a sandy beach at the end of it. He and Woasut doubled their paddle rhythm in order to reach it as quickly as possible. They had just managed to land when the storm broke. They swiftly untied the two children from the thwart, unloaded the packs, and, leaving Gudruide to set up a shelter, relaunched the tapa-took and paddled out to help their companions. As soon as they left the shelter of the bay they were hit by a gale that nearly over-turned them. By paddling as hard as they could on the leeward side, however, they managed to turn the tapatook into the wind. They could see their three companions clinging to a large rock and trying to keep their heads above water. Their tapatook was still upright, riding on the crest of a huge wave, but it was being pushed by the wind towards the cliffs. Anin and Woasut paddled after the tapatook, intending to save it and return it to the three castaways. Barely managing to avoid the rocks, they finally reached the tapatook, and Woasut held on to it long enough for Anin to attach a cord to its bow. Then they towed it towards their companions, who did not see them until they were almost upon them. At the sight of the great tapatook coming to their rescue, however, they let out great shouts of joy.

Climbing back into such a slight craft is not easy. Each time they tried, the little tapatook would capsize and the three would be thrown back into the water. Finally, Della, who was more agile and less panicked than the others, managed to pull herself up on the stern of the large tapatook, and Anin gripped her clothing and pulled her aboard. Robb and Gwenid decided to hang on to the sides of the small tapatook while Anin and Woasut towed them towards the shallow bay, again with great difficulty. Once they were sheltered from the fierce wind, it was an easier matter to make it to the small beach, where Gudruide and the children awaited them. When Robb and Gwenid were able to touch bottom, Woasut and Della waded out to help them ashore while Anin secured the two tapatooks, hauling them high up on the sand. Then he, too, came to help the swimmers.

While Woasut lit a fire to dry their clothing, Anin built a make-shift shelter by leaning the tapatooks together before a small indentation in the cliff face and covering them with caribou skins. The weapons had been tied to the ribs of the small tapa-took and had not been lost, but all the small packs and much of their dried and smoked meat had gone down. Fortunately, Della's axe was still attached to the centre thwart. Gwenid and Robb shivered before the fire, wrapped in caribou blankets, and Gudruide fed the two babies while Woasut helped Anin complete the shelter. Dazed and exhausted, but still showing her bravery and strength of will, Della had not got out of her sodden clothes. When she finally did so, she burst into tears and wept in Woasut's arms. Woasut did not know what to say to comfort her. Della blamed herself for the accident that almost cost them their lives, including those of Woasut and Anin. They ate very little that night, and no one thought about coupling. Anin did, however, recount to them how he had decided to turn his tapa-took towards dry land.

"When I saw Gashu-Uwith the Bear," he said, "I knew that there was a place of safety nearby. I also knew that there was a storm approaching. But because it was coming from the direction of sunrise, we could not see it behind the high mountains. We were very lucky that my spirit protector was able to warn us in time."

Anin told them how, in the course of his long voyage, the bear had often helped him by showing him the right way, and that once the bear had saved him and Woasut from the Ashwans. Although they might be uncomfortable this night, he said, they must thank their gods for saving their lives.

18

THE WEATHER HAD not improved by morning. It was still raining, although the bark baskets they had set out the night before to catch the water were not yet full. They had to lay out a caribou skin to catch enough rainwater to allow them all to drink. There was no spring or river emptying into this bay, and there could be no question of going in search of one. They were camped on a narrow beach at the foot of steep, cliff-like hills. It was not a very comfortable situation, but Anin decided they would stay there until the weather was safer for paddling. He stood on the shore and looked attentively out to sea. The tide was coming in, and in the distance he discerned a strange, white cloud hanging just above the surface of the water. He ran to awaken the others.

"Get up!" he shouted to them. "The shamut are running!"

Everyone came hurrying out to see the seasonal phenomenon repeat itself once again. The women from the North knew the season when this small fish threw itself upon the shore to lay its eggs and then die. Every summer they would gather huge quantities of them and spread them on their fields to fertilize the soil. But the season here among the Addaboutik was much earlier. It was still the moon when the seabirds finished laying their eggs. Everyone grabbed baskets and packs, anything with which to collect this new gift from the sea. Anin took his fishing net and met the first wave, and when he returned to shore he was carrying a load of fish, each no thicker than two fingers and about as long as a woman's hand. Della, Gwenid, and Robb, completely naked, filled their containers, and Anin, Woasut, and Gudruide continued working with the net. They soon had enough fish to eat for several days; only fresh water would be scarce, if the rain stopped. When they had caught enough caplin, the women rebuilt the fire from the previous night, placed a large, flat rock in its centre, and proceeded to cook and distribute the fish. What a delicacy these small fish were! Anin suggested they cook the rest until they were dry and crusty, so that they would have food for the next few days of their voyage.

"There are not many more beaches like this one down this coast," he said. "No telling how often we will be able to stop. This fish is nourishing and will allow us to keep up our paddle rhythm."

Cooking was women's work, so the two men set about examining the short stretch of beach carefully, partly to pass time, partly because it was always important to know as much about their surroundings as possible. The rain increased in intensity. Anin, dressed in a caribou robe and his short dingiam, kept close to the shelter of the cliff and climbed partway up the bluff, while Robb, naked as a worm, remained out on the beach. He was heading towards a large rock when a huge, black bear came out from behind it. Robb ran back to Anin, calling out that they must fetch their weapons to defend themselves against Gashu-Uwith. Anin laughed at him.

"Gashu-Uwith saved your life yesterday, and today you want to kill him?"

Robb was surprised. He looked at Anin questioningly.

"This bear is your spirit protector?" he said.

Anin gestured to Robb to take a look at the bear. Robb turned and saw that Gashu-Uwith, too, was gathering caplin.

"You're certain he isn't dangerous?" Robb asked.

The two men returned to the camp. Gudruide was exhausted from her recent childbirth and the long paddle, and would need several suns' rest before she could continue the journey. She was excused from most of the daily tasks in camp. Anin also suggested that Woasut set floating nets in the bay, to catch more fish.

One morning, Anin witnessed a scene that was rare among the Addaboutik. Robb came to him.

"As the clan chief, which woman do you prefer?"

Anin was surprised by the question. He thought for a long time before answering. Then he looked the Scotsman straight in the eye.

"As a member of the clan, do you have a preference?"

Robb hesitated. He had not expected Anin to turn the question back on him. He, too, thought before answering.

"I like them all," he said. "They are all good to look at, and I would take any of them."

"Well, then," said Anin. "Ask the one you want most. If she accepts you, you may take her. But if she refuses you, you must not take her. If she decides not to be your coupling partner, then she is a free woman."

There was a long period of silence between the two men. Finally it was Robb who broke it.

"But if there is one that you prefer, I would not ask her. You are the chief, after all."

Anin looked at Robb, and Robb could see that he was grateful. Anin was astonished that this stranger had enough respect to know his place in the clan, and also to speak directly about it.

"I love Woasut very much," he said. "She is the first woman who gave herself to me, and the first woman I served. But now I am not certain if I ought to consider her mine. She is free to choose whomever she wants. It has been two moons now since she bore her child, and I am the father of that child. But some-times I feel as though I am the father of the whole clan, and that I could be the father of all the children born to it. My father told me that the chief of the clan must above all ensure that the other members are content, satisfied, and safe. He must establish the life rules and see that harmony reigns among the people. But my father did not tell me which woman I must choose. He did not say if that woman would then belong only to the chief, or if she belonged to the community. He said nothing to me on that subject, and I do not know if a woman belongs to me as my bow and arrows, which I have made with my own hands, belong to me, or if she is like my fishing spear, or my bird net. And even if my bow and arrows belong to me, another man may use them if he has need of them. If you need my spear, I do not see how I could prevent you from using it. And my bird net is for anyone to use who needs to catch a bird so that he may eat. I do not now know if I must consider Woasut as belonging to me alone, or whether she is a free member of the clan."

Upon delivering himself of these reflections, Anin lay down and went to sleep, leaving Robb to ponder the meaning of his words – words that did not, to Robb's thinking, answer the ques-tion he had asked. He was even more confused than he had been; Anin had left him free to make his own decision about whether he would couple with Woasut, Della, Gudruide, or Gwenid. He was no further ahead than before, except in his growing desire to have a wife. Finally he, too, ended his reflections by lying down and going to sleep.

The women, meanwhile, had been holding a similar discussion, and were laughing merrily amongst themselves. They had learned to live together without rivalry. The events of the past few days had reknitted their bonds. Woasut had not hesitated to go with Anin to save Della's and Gwenid's lives, which at least proved that she wished them to go on living. Gwenid, who until that moment had been jealous not only of her sister, but also of Della and even Woasut, could no longer admit to that sentiment. She did not want to have Anin all to herself now; trying to entrap him would seem to her to be an act of betrayal against the other women. Gudruide, thinking about the night that Woasut gave birth to her son, was sorry that she had seduced Anin. Della could never forget what Woasut had done for her. The four women talked for a long time about their unusual situation, in which one man was wanted by all of them. As Gudruide explained, in her country men fought over the possession of a single woman, and women were capable of equally barbarous acts to secure the man they loved. She asked Woasut if she still resented what had happened on the night of her childbirth. Woasut smiled and explained that at the time she had felt pain.

"But according to our tradition, a man must have more than one wife if there are more women in the clan than men."

She explained that the laws of her people were not well defined in these matters, and custom was a more useful guide. She also told Gudruide that the most important thing was Anin's decision. He was chief of the clan, and the other members owed him respect.

"The worst thing is to see your man coupling with a stranger," she said. "But when the other woman is a member of the clan, we understand the man's need, and no longer think only of our own."

"If we all wanted to couple with the same man," said Gwenid, "would the other clan members not feel frustrated?"

Woasut laughed along with the other two women.

"That's why we must not argue among ourselves," she said. "We will ask Anin to advise us. He will know what we should do."

19

IT DID NOT take the women long to repack the parcels. When all the packs were safely stowed in the tapatooks, Anin told Della that she would paddle in the bow of the large tapatook, and Woasut would take the stern of the smaller vessel with Robb in the bow. Woasut's male child was tied to the centre thwart of the small tapatook, and Gudruide and her female child were settled in the centre of the larger one. The remaining caplin were then evenly divided between the two crews and stowed in the respective tapatooks.

The weather was promising when they pushed off from the shore of the bay and paddled towards the warmth of Baétha. This time the two tapatooks remained close. Woasut was an experienced stern paddler, and Robb had learned how to manage the bow, and so the rhythm in the smaller craft was smoother and the tapatook went more quickly. Gwenid kept time with songs from her native country, and Robb sang Scottish songs. When it was time to eat, they paddled a short way up a shallow brook to where the water was calm, and ate without getting out of their tapatooks. Then they left the brook and continued working up the coast.

Their drinking water ran out that evening, and so they were forced to find a freshwater stream where they could make their camp. The sun had barely begun to set when Anin signalled to the others that he had seen the place where they would spend the night. He had noticed a small waterfall dropping into the sea, close to a strip of land long enough for there to be room to camp as well as to catch more caplin. The tapatooks turned towards it.

It was a beautiful spot, and everyone was glad to step onto firm ground. The paddlers' legs were stiff and their knees ached. It was time to rest. Woasut's child had been crying for some time, but Woasut had been too busy to answer his repeated demands for her breast, since she did not want to risk falling too far behind Anin.

Camp was set up quickly by those not attending to the needs of the infants. When Woasut finished nursing her child, Anin took him and held him in his arms for the first time since he had been born. How frail he felt in his tiny clothes! How handsome he will be, thought Anin; his coppery skin had the slightly pinkish tinge of the Addaboutik. He was the first to be born to the Bear Clan, Anin's clan, the first son of the first Addaboutik to travel completely around the world, or at least around this immense island that they thought of as the world. He would name his son Buh-Bosha-Yesh, the first male. Anin announced the news to the other clan members.

"Buh-Bosha-Yesh is the name of the first male born to the Bear Clan."

Woasut was happy. By bestowing a name, Anin was acknowledging the child as his own. From now on he would not simply be his mother's child, but Buh-Bosha-Yesh, first son of the Bear Clan, the child among children who lived to protect the members of his new family.

"Tonight, Anin will couple with Woasut to confirm that she is the first wife of the chief of the Bear Clan and the mother of the first male child born to this new family. But this does not mean that Woasut is a prize, or a possession. She remains a free woman. Anin possesses nothing but his duty to the clan to ensure its welfare. What belongs to Anin also belongs to the clan. And Anin must belong only to the clan, not to any one person."

Everyone ate their fill in order to build up strength for the final stretch of the voyage. After they had eaten, Anin asked Della to sing her Scottish songs while he honoured Woasut with his caresses, his tenderness, showing her the friendship that every member of the clan should show to every other member.

When the chief entered the first mother of the Bear Clan, he did so facing her so that she could see him. And when his body shuddered with the fulfilment of his pleasure, Woasut's face lit up with acknowledgement and pride. There was no need for Anin to continue rocking after he had spent himself, for the Beothuk woman he had encountered on his journey around the world was already satisfied. Happy to have given pleasure, content with the decisions that he had communicated to the other members of the clan, Anin slid under the caribou blanket, but not before he noticed that Robb and Gwenid were coupling in imitation of himself and Woasut, and that Gudruide and Della were lying in each other's arms, a sign of their friendship and of their clan solidarity. Seeing that the women were no longer jealous warmed the heart of the very first chief of the Bear Clan.

That night he slept as soundly as a hibernating bear, and his dreams were full of joy and optimism. He dreamed of bounty and peace. He dreamed of expanding the clan, of the creation of new villages in order to take better advantage of the resources of the island. He saw people living again on the coast of the rising sun, where there was plenty of game and berries. He imagined whole villages of happy people living a life of great ease. He saw many children playing with bear cubs. And women and men living together everywhere in harmony and solidarity.

Gwenid no longer found it humiliating to couple with a former slave. She even took a certain amount of pride in it. She was glad to have assuaged this desire that had been mounting within her for so long: to have satisfied her appetite for pleasure that her senses created in her. She had seen too many women left alone when their husbands travelled to distant lands, who were obliged to seek out slaves when the fire that burned within them threatened to consume them. She was happy not to be among such women. She thought of the bitter conflicts that took place when their wayfaring husbands returned, of the possessiveness to which the women were forced to submit by their egotistical partners. Never again would she live through such scenes. The respect Robb showed her increased her pleasure. She was satisfied with this taste of a different world, a world she could never have imagined before meeting him. A world in which she had to make her own way, but where there was no jealousy, no rights of possession. She thought of the conflicts this new religion would create in her old country, and she was glad she would never have to witness it. And Robb had been so attentive to her needs, so gentle in his caresses. He had learned quickly how to live like a free man, by watching and imitating Anin. She liked him very much in this new role.

Her arms around Woasut, Gudruide whispered in her ear: "I envy you, yes, but I am not jealous. You are truly the clan mother. But I long for the day when I will couple again."

Della was sad. She kissed Woasut, and then began to tell her of her sadness. She did not feel as much of a woman as she would like. She wielded the axe and the spear like a man, she did men's jobs, and as a result she felt she was less desired by the men.

"No, I am not jealous of you and Gwenid," she said. "It is simply that I am sad to find that I am not desired. Only once has Anin looked upon me as a woman. Robb used to treat me like a woman often, but now he no longer looks at me at all. Perhaps I am more man than woman."

Woasut held Della in her arms to console her, and Della sobbed like a child, crying softly to herself while the Beothuk gently stroked her strange, red hair. Then she slept.

20

NOW THAT THEY had embarked upon the final phase of his voyage, Anin was no longer trying to discover what the world was like. The very fact that he knew this coast so well proved that he had been travelling around an island. In fact, he had known this since the day he saved Woasut from the Ashwans, but he would have known it by now anyway by the familiarity of these bays and inlets; he had set off towards the region of warmth, and now he was approaching his own village from the region of cold. Being close to Baétha again made him want to paddle faster, but he knew it was dangerous to hurry. He could hardly wait to see his father, his mother, and the other members of his former clan, the clan of Edruh the Otter, so anxious was he to tell them that he was now the chief of the clan of Gashu-Uwith the Bear, his spirit protector. As he paddled, he looked forward to the evening when he would introduce the members of his new clan, his new family, to all his old friends. He would tell the village children about his adventures, and hold his son up to show his father. He would tell them how he had discovered that their world was an island, and he would present his wife to his mother. "This is Woasut, a Beothuk woman from the outside world but who is nonetheless kin to the Addaboutik." He could already see the curious stares the newcomers would attract, with their pale skin and hair the colour of dried grass.

For several moons now he had been the centre of his clan, and he had enjoyed the attention. Circling the world in three season-cycles was no small accomplishment, and he knew the status it would give him in the eyes of the Addaboutik community. Thinking of it made his paddle slide ever more smoothly through the cold water.

Woasut knew that Anin's people would want to know how her people had lived before they were killed, that they would question her, watch her every movement, and that some of them would not like her as much as they would like the other members of the Bear Clan. She had seen this happen in her own village. She dreaded the moment when she would meet Anin's parents. She did not know how Anin's mother would like losing their son. Gudruide wondered how these black-haired, dark-skinned people would respond to someone with her milk-white complexion. How welcome would she and the Scottish slaves be? Perhaps they wouldn't be welcome at all? Gwenid hoped that there would be young men in the village who would be interested in her body, and that she would be able to feel better about herself. Robb hoped there would be new territories to discover, and new friends who would teach him about this world that he was beginning to like so much.

As for Della, ever since Woasut had taken her into her arms and comforted her, she had thought of nothing but the warmth of Woasut's body and the smell of her hair. She longed to have Woasut as a close friend, and wanted nothing more than that the young Beothuk woman would hold her again and bring comfort and solace to her, so that she would no longer feel a neglected woman. Neither Anin nor Robb had shown the slightest interest in her since that first and only time with Anin. But her friendship with Woasut had grown, as had her relationship with Gudruide. She would do anything to preserve these bonds, which had perhaps already gone beyond friendship. She was not concerned about her reception among the people of Baétha. She had encountered many different people, and they had always treated her like a slave, a servant, or an amusement. She was happy now in her new position as a free woman, although the men's lack of interest in her saddened her greatly. She thought she was pretty enough. Perhaps Woasut or Gudruide would find her attractive some day?

When the tapatooks rounded a rocky promontory, Anin saw three vessels much like their own in the choppy water. He called out to the occupants, who appeared to be fishing. One of the new tapatooks came towards Anin's, and its paddlers recognized him immediately. They called out joyfully and waved to the members of the new Bear Clan.

"There are four paddlers in our tapatook," the bowman called to Anin. "We will go on ahead and tell the others you have arrived. You are only one sun away from Baétha."

Anin raised his hand to stop them.

"I do not wish to arrive until tomorrow. I need to prepare myself first. Is there a good spot near here where we can set up our last camp before returning to the village?"

The fishermen told him that there was an island halfway to the village with a mamateek on it. "It is big enough for all of you, and you will be comfortable there this night. There is firewood and dried fish as well. We will see you tomorrow."

The Addaboutik fishermen turned their tapatook about and paddled back to join their companions. A short while later all three tapatooks disappeared from the Bear Clan's view. The island with the mamateek was where they had said it would be, and the eight members of the Bear Clan landed and prepared to spend a comfortable night in the birchbark dwelling. There were no birch trees on the island, so Anin guessed that the men had brought the bark over from the mainland. He could see the shore-line of the mainland; it was less precipitous, and there were many birch trees, the tree of life to the Addaboutik, growing there.

The mamateek was easily big enough for twelve people. The floor was covered with evergreen branches and sealskins. A few steps from the entrance there were drying racks, and many halibut were spread out to dry in the sun. Anin told the others that he needed to be alone in order to give thanks to the Creator for protecting the clan and its new chief during his long voyage. He took a caribou blanket and walked to the far end of the small island. The other clan members decided to rest, having nothing else to do but feed the young ones and themselves. They would sleep soundly until sunrise. Robb and Gwenid drifted off "to explore the area," they said, in the opposite direction from the one Anin had taken. Gudruide sat down with her child in her lap, gazing peacefully at the mainland opposite.

Inside the mamateek, Woasut had finished nursing Buh-Bosha-Yesh and the child was already sound asleep on his wooden board. He would eat some mashed fish later. Della had been watching Woasut closely the whole time. When Woasut lowered the board so that the child would sleep more comfortably, Della asked her if she could lie down in her arms. Woasut smiled, and the Scotswoman slid over to join her. She removed her upper garment and nestled against Woasut, who was also naked from the waist up. Body against body, the two women lay quietly in each other's arms for a long while. Then Della looked into Woasut's eyes.

"I want you," she said.

Woasut, though taken aback by this abrupt approach, did not respond negatively. The young slave raised her face towards Woasut's and touched Woasut's lips with her own. Softly, she kissed her chin, her cheeks, her forehead, and the dark skin of her neck and shoulders. Woasut felt a tingling spread through her body. Taking the initiative, she kissed the young Scotswoman fully on the lips and rubbed herself against her chest. Then, clasped in a fiery embrace, the two women rolled together on the soft floor of the mamateek. For the first time in Beothuk and Addaboutik memory, two women loved each other passionately and yet tenderly. Let it be recorded that on the last night of Anin the Initiate's voyage around the world, two women of the Bear Clan expressed their feelings for one another without reserve, convinced that they were but strengthening the bonds of the clan. When Gudruide entered the mamateek she found them sleeping on the sealskin blankets, still clasped in each other's arms. She smiled, certain now that the clan was united, and that its members had learned to live together without the smallest cloud of jealousy to darken its future.

21

THE CLAN WAS awake by sunrise the next morning. Anin had already performed his duties as chief by preparing all the members for their meeting with the villagers of Baétha. He advised the four pale-skinned members to speak as little as possible for the first few days, and not to show impatience with the villagers who would certainly want to touch them.

"It may be irritating to you," he told them, "but that is what happens to people who are different."

He also suggested that they not remove their clothes when bathing, since the hair around their sexual organs would be sure to cause much laughter and derision, which would be even more difficult to tolerate. Robb, in particular, whose chest was completely covered with red hair, should keep his upper garment on at all times, at least until he was better known to the village. "When our stories have been told and accepted," said Anin, "the time for ridicule and joking will pass. Then my people will show nothing more than genuine curiosity towards you, a healthy desire simply to get to know you better." He counselled Gwenid to exercise a certain amount of restraint when among the villagers, especially the men. She could smile at them in a friendly manner, but she must keep her true nature hidden, because the young men of the village were not prepared for someone of her impetuous temperament. Gwenid must be careful not to provoke them. In a village, he said, the first impression the villagers form of someone quickly becomes the truth about that person. A bad reputation could cost a life. The Addaboutik do not tolerate dishonour. One of Anin's uncles had taken his own life when he had been caught telling a lie. Gudruide, he added, must tell the truth about her past. That was the only way that her fatherless child would be accepted. If the father was dead, the daughter would be received even though she was different from the others. Then he turned to Della.

"You will have no trouble being accepted," he told her, "since you are good at daily tasks and you adapt easily to new situations. You need only remain who you are."

To Woasut he suggested covering her skin with red ochre for her arrival, and washing it off later. It would be well, he told her, if at first she was thought to be an Addaboutik. He also recommended placing an ochre mark on Buh-Bosha-Yesh's forehead, to show the villagers that he was a chief's son. They would then show him the respect that was his due.

Anin also covered himself with red ochre, his whole body except for his face. He made an ochre mark on his own forehead to designate that the child was of his lineage. When the grooming was complete and everyone looked fresh and clean, Anin declared them ready to meet the people of Baétha. The tapatooks were placed in the water, but this time Woasut and Buh-Bosha-Yesh took their places in the large tapatook, with Gudruide in the bow and Anin in the stern. Della and Gwenid climbed into the second, with Robb paddling in the stern. Then they pushed off from the island. They were still within sight of it when they were met by a dozen tapatooks coming their way, filled with young men and women who had come from the village to greet them and escort them back. The young villagers called out to them, sang songs of welcome, laughed and paddled in circles around the returning voyagers. They looked in astonishment at the foreigners, but no sarcastic remarks or hurtful taunts came from their lips. There was politeness and respect from the start, and Anin was proud of them. Gwenid allowed herself several discreet smiles to those who took an interest in her, showing her white teeth.

Robb and Della contented themselves with smiling, but kept their eyes on where they were going. Gudruide seemed overwhelmed by all the attention. Woasut looked nervous. Her stomach was tight with anxiety. She felt like a small girl who had been caught doing something wrong and was waiting to be scolded by the clan elder. Her throat was dry and she found it hard to swallow. She wanted to cry, without really knowing why. She was afraid of how Anin's parents would receive her.

A large bay opened between two high hills, and the small armada turned into it. When they were between the hills, Gudruide was joyful. "Oh, how this reminds me of my homeland," she exclaimed. "We call this a fjord. You have a magnificent country, Anin!"

The passage between the high cliffs narrowed briefly, and then widened out again to form a kind of lake fed at the far end by a river that dropped down to a deep, rich beach. The beaches on either side of this river were crowded with people, and Anin signalled to Robb to leave off paddling before they beached the tapatooks.

"I am Anin, formerly of the clan of Edruh the Otter," he called, addressing the people on the shore. "I left here three season-cycles ago to journey around the land, and I have fulfilled my promise not to return until I had done so. On my journey, I met several people from other lands, and I am bringing them back with me to prove that what I have to tell you is the truth. I have returned here to Baétha, my home, to be welcomed by two clans, each on its own side of the river. I am an Addaboutik, and I have formed a third clan: the Clan of the Bear. If I were still of the Edruh Clan, I would land on the right bank of the river. If my mother were on the left bank and were claiming that for her own clan, that of Appawet the Seal, I would honour her clan and land on the left bank. But I am Anin, chief of the Clan of Gashu-Uwith, and I have no connection with any other clan. I therefore do not know where to land so that I may not offend one clan or the other. I and the other members of my clan will stay in our tap-atooks until the village has resolved this dilemma."

Anin waited. A whispering arose among the people who had come to welcome him. He had posed the question formerly asked only by the Innu, who came down from the region of cold. On what side of the river should they land so as not to offend the other side? The village of Baétha was formed of two distinct clans, and so it did not have a single chief. The question of diplomacy was raised and had to be debated each time a visitor arrived. If the visitor disembarked on one side of the river and brought difficulties with him, then the other side would withdraw, saying, "He's your visitor, not ours." Now the question was posed again, and the visitor this time was a member of the village whose father and mother, each belonging to a different clan, refused to settle the debate.

While they discussed the issue, several of the escort tapatooks landed on either side of the river. However, three remained in the water with the new arrivals, awaiting the village's decision before accompanying the members of the Bear Clan to shore. The Addaboutik were well known for their formality, and everyone understood the situation. But never before had one of their own members forced them to resolve this difficulty once and for all. Suddenly a murmur arose from those on the right bank, and a man well advanced in years walked out into the water until it reached his knees.

"We have found a solution," he said. "We of the Appawet Clan will cross the river to join those of the Edruh Clan. But it will take some time. The young are good swimmers, but the older ones must cross by tapatook, or else climb up the cliff and ford the river before it descends to the shore. Since it is only a question of time, the solution is therefore a simple matter of patience."

When the elder had finished speaking, those of the Appawet Clan who had tapatooks began ferrying the elders and the women with young children across the river, while the younger members and older children dove from the bank and quickly swam to the other side. The members of the Bear Clan watched patiently from their tapatooks until the last Addaboutik had crossed. Then they brought their tapatooks up onto the left bank, to be greeted by the united clans. There was much laughter and back-slapping and shouts of welcome. Although Anin was without doubt the hero of the day, all were embraced and made welcome in the village.

The whole day was given over to feasting and celebrating. In fact the celebrations lasted several days, with songs and dancing going on until the entire village was so exhausted that the people lay down where they were and went to sleep.

A mamateek had been set up in the village for the members of the Bear Clan, and was provisioned with food as a welcoming gift. Clothing for the women, necklaces for the men, and small packets of red ochre for each person were set out around the central firepit. Swaddling clothes for the babies were arranged on two small beds, and two ornately carved carrying planks were hung near the door. The villagers had thought of everything in advance, with but one exception: on which side of the river the newcomers should disembark.

22

THE TWO VILLAGES were comprised of a hundred and twenty people each, with forty to fifty mamateeks on either side of the river. The river descended through a kind of canyon, and so the villages had been built up the sides almost to the top of the cliffs. Small streams ran through the centre of each village, providing the inhabitants with drinking water, and cascaded into the canyon to join the main river a short way upstream from the point at which the voyagers had landed their tapatooks. People on either side of the river climbed the cliffs by means of steep, zigzagging paths. During the warm season the elders set up their mamateeks at the beach level, so as not to have to climb these paths too often, but when the falling-leaf season came with its high tides, they would dismantle their mamateeks and move them higher up the cliffs, to avoid being flooded out. That is why a mamateek had had to be set up at the beach level in order to welcome the members of the new Bear Clan.

When he saw that clothes had been set out in the mamateek for them, Anin realized that his fellow clan members were going to be examined carefully by the members of the village. In other words, he knew that the two pale-skinned women were meant to take off the long robes that covered their legs all the way to the ground, and expose as much of their skin as possible to the curious eyes of the villagers. He would not have a chance to tell about his adventures and explain who these newcomers were before they were subjected to the village's scrutiny. Della's legs were already exposed, but Robb wore a vest and leggings that hid his sand-coloured body hair, and the two other women were also very light-skinned. The young villagers would ask Anin questions that he was not ready to answer directly.

After bathing in the stream and cleaning himself with sap from an oily plant that frothed when rubbed against the body, Anin put on a pair of new moccasins decorated with red ochre with little tufts of caribou hair arranged to look like wildflowers. His dingiam was made of sealskin with the hair turned outside. He also wore a sleeveless vest whitened with a powder that was found on the sides of rocks at the farthest limit of the Addaboutik territory in the direction of warmth. Around his neck he placed a necklace of otter teeth that he had been given as a child, and on his head a covering made of eagle feathers and the head of an otter. He painted his face with red ochre, leaving a bare spot in the centre of his forehead, which he painted with the same powder that had whitened his vest. Then he instructed Woasut to make the same white circle on Buh-Bosha-Yesh's forehead.

Woasut wore a dress of caribou hide dyed blue and red at the openings. The dress was loosely tied at the side to allow her to nurse her child when he was hungry. Similar dresses had been laid out for the three other women, who were more than happy to change from their old clothes. Della executed a small dance, asking the others if she looked more feminine in a dress. Everyone began to laugh. Anin had explained that not wearing the dresses would be seen as a rejection of the friendship they represented. Robb also wore new footwear: red-coloured moccasins without the wildflowers. He also wore a new dingiam and vest, but put them on over his leggings and sleeves. The sleeves were joined together by leather thongs that crossed the opening in his vest. The women decided to paint his face red, like Woasut's, but Anin would not let them give his forehead a white dot. Then the three pale women decided to cover their skin with red ochre, and promptly painted their legs, arms, breasts, and sides, wherever their white skin was exposed to view by the loose-fitting garments.

Thus prepared, the members of the Bear Clan joined the festivities. It was dark, but many fires had been lit around the village. A caribou was cooking over a large, central fire, and two seals were roasting on a smaller fire nearby. Farther off, a beaver was also being cooked, its fat dripping noisily into the coals. Many kinds of shellfish were also cooking in a large, earthenware vessel, and water was boiling in a second vessel, set on a large stone in the middle of a fire. There were several other fires, and on each of them something else was being prepared: squids, lobsters, halibut, snails, rabbits, puffins, and ducks. It was to be a feast-for-everyone, and no one could leave a feast-for-everyone for fear of offending the two host clans. The first animal consumed was always the emblem animal of the host clan, and when it was eaten its bones were thrown into the fire and the ashes from that fire were spread in the animal's natural territory. This feast-for-everyone was presented by the Seal Clan, and so the clans ate seal meat first.

All the members of the new Bear Clan were seated together. One by one, the others came up to speak to them. Anin had visited his parents before the feast, to pay them his respects. His mother was still in good health, but his father was suffering from a strange malady and could walk only with much difficulty. His feet were so swollen they were almost completely round, his fingers and toes crossed over themselves, and his arms and legs ached constantly. It was said that he had caught this sickness when he had been lost at sea for many days several season-cycles before. He had disappeared during a heavy fog, and seven suns passed before he was found on a small island, half frozen and nearly dead. He had been in pain since that time, and each season-cycle brought him more suffering, and each sun seemed to take away more of his strength. His wife took good care of him, and never left his side. Even so, it was with some surprise that the villagers saw the old couple seated at the large central fire, beside their son Anin, chief of the new Bear Clan.

Anin was urged to tell his first story as soon as the seal meat was completely eaten. One of the elders asked him why he had changed clans, and why he had chosen the bear as his emblem. Gashu-Uwith, said the elder, was a scavenger who would eat anything that came to hand; what was there about the bear that deserved such honour? Anin told them about the many times Gashu-Uwith had come to his aid by warning him of some imminent danger, how each time the animal had saved him from peril. When he recounted the story of the two Ashwans who had been ripped open by the bear, members of both clans cried out and beat their drums with appreciation. The Ashwans were the sworn enemies of the Addaboutik, and Gashu-Uwith had just made two hundred and forty new friends. The elder who asked Anin the question stood up and apologized for having insulted Gashu-Uwith, and begged Anin to remove the mean-spirited words of an old, ignorant man from his memory. Gashu-Uwith was obviously a spirit protector to the Addaboutik. Anin declared that the elder's words were easily forgotten, and no one would henceforth recall them to mind.

"Anin and the other members of the Bear Clan have already forgotten your words," he said, "except for those that were pleasing to their ears."

Another villager stood up and asked Anin how he had met the pale-skinned ones. It seemed to him, the villager said, that even red ochre looked less red on their skin than it did on his own. Anin patiently told the story of his first meeting with a Bouguishamesh, and showed them the scar on his thigh that proved he had been struck by the stranger's cutting stick, which he promised he would show them on the second day of the feast-for-everyone.

"Anin has two cutting sticks to show that he killed two more strangers to protect Woasut and Gudruide."

"You say that these strangers were taller than you, taller than us?"

Anin told Gudruide and Gwenid to stand up, and he stood up beside them. Gwenid was a full head taller than he was, and Gudruide half a head.

"You can see for yourself how tall they are, and these are females. The males are even taller."

The others murmured with wonder. Anin went on to explain that their language was also different. Everyone wanted to hear this language, and Anin asked Gwenid to sing one of her songs. Gwenid needed no further prompting, and sang a rousing song in praise of the war god Thor. She was avidly applauded by several young men, who asked Anin if these strange women were made the same way as Addaboutik women. Anin thought it best to move on to more serious topics, and explained that there were many different lands in the world, and that the people in one land were different from those in every other. The two tall women with hair the colour of dried grass and skin as white as caribou milk, for example, came from a land that was far north of Baétha. But Robb and Della came from a different land that was an island much like their own, and Robb had hair like red ochre whereas Della's hair was also the colour of ochre but somewhat darker. The villagers pressed closer to Della and looked at her for a long time. Then Anin asked Robb to remove his sleeves and leggings as well as his vest.

"These people have hair on their bodies, just as we do from time to time. But Robb also has hair on his face, and if he did not cut it, it would grow until his entire head was covered."

This proved to be the high point of the evening. Once again the villagers lined up to touch the man with the animal fur. Some tried to taste it, some of the women wondered aloud how such soft fur would feel against their own smooth skin. Robb was not embarrassed at all by the attention, in fact found such frank feminine curiosity enjoyable. To bring the evening to a close, Anin announced that the women were also furred over, especially in their pubic area, where there was a tuft of hair the same colour as the hair on their heads. One young man cried out that the village would love to see such a sight, and Gwenid advanced, took off her dress, and displayed her naked body, even her pubic hair. She lifted her arms to show that hair grew under them as well. The entire village came close to see, and several young men reached out to touch her, which displeased the young Viking woman not at all.

But it was late, and even though the feast was far from over, Anin asked permission to retire with his clan members. Permission was granted, and someone took his place at the fire so that his absence would not put an end to the feast-for-everyone.

23

THAT NIGHT THE whole clan slept soundly. Their sleep was filled with dreams, but they were good dreams. In the morning, Anin decided to bathe as he had during his youth, and he told the women that now that the curiosity about their bodies had been satisfied, they too could undress and bathe without causing a disturbance in the village. The clan members accordingly left their mamateek and bathed in the stream that passed through the village. All the village children crowded the stream banks to see the sun's rays glancing off these strange creatures with light skin and hairy bodies.

Gudruide was still shy, but Gwenid evidently took much pleasure in being watched, constantly turning this way and that to show her body to the youth of Baétha. When they were dry, they put their clothes on and returned to the feast-for-everyone. The food that was left was common to the entire village, and everyone helped themselves to large portions. Questions were flung at the new clan members from all sides at once. Had they been afraid? How cold had it been? Had they met with any other dangers? Were there monsters? How did Anin meet Woasut? Where was her people's village? How many lived in it? How big were the Bouguishamesh boats? How many Ashwans did Anin kill? What did he eat when he was travelling? How long had he been unable to travel because of his wound? Why did the Bouguishamesh come to this land? Were they camped far from this place? What kind of animals did they keep?

Anin spent the whole day answering these questions. In the evening, the elders asked him to recount the story of his entire voyage, from the day he first left the village until his return. They wanted to know what to expect if they left this place and paddled directly into the warm wind, as Anin had done. Anin was obliged to begin at the beginning. He had always known that his story would take several days to tell. It was the final night of the first feast, but when it was ended the elders immediately declared the beginning of a new one, Anin's initiation feast, to celebrate the official establishment of the Bear Clan. And so the feasting continued, in the course of which the Addaboutik were better able to make the acquaintance of the new strangers, the pale northerners and the red-haired Scots. Robb was renamed Drona the Hairy One. A few of the young women asked permission to touch his hairy chest. Others stroked his arms. Some wanted to run their hands along his legs. One came up to him and said: "I would like to touch all the hair on your body. I invite you to my mamateek."

Robb did not know how to respond in the presence of so many others. To recover from his embarrassment, he told the woman she could touch him wherever she wanted right there in front of everyone, except in the places where he was hidden by clothing. Gwenid knew that performing the sex act before the other members of her clan was natural and strengthened the bonds of kinship among them, but not with an entire community watching. She had felt a distinct rush of excitement when she took off her clothes and allowed the villagers to touch her, but she realized that to let it go further would not be acceptable to these people. She could already imagine the remarks of the elders, who seemed to believe she could not understand their language. She knew it was going to be difficult to keep her own name; the young people were already calling her Boagadoret-Botchmouth, which meant Buttocks-and-Breasts. Della, too, had been given a new name: Red Ochre.

While Anin was recounting his adventures, Woasut and Gudruide often returned to the mamateek to nurse and change their babies, and to rest. Like good friends they talked openly about everything and nothing, without restraint or embarrassment. Gudruide told Woasut that she had seen her and Della sleeping in each other's embrace on their last night on the island of the fishermen, and that she had found it beautiful and very touching.

"It is good to know that there is no jealousy among us," she said.

Woasut admitted that if such an incident happened spontaneously, and if no one was hurt or offended by it, then she saw no reason why she should be prevented from doing it just by tradition.

"So far as I know, there is nothing in our customs that speaks of such relations between women," she said. "It is said that when a man has several wives, the women must understand and agree with one another, and live together in peace so that the man will be easy in his mind when he goes to hunt and fish. But there is nothing to say that the women may not express their friendship for one another in a physical way."

Gudruide said she thought that since Anin's wives were not related by blood, it was normal that they would be physically attracted to each other, especially when they were neglected by Anin or when they felt lonely. In her land, she added, it often happened: "The men would go to sea to win new lands. If a man had his own boat he would take his wife with him, but if he merely worked on a boat or was unmarried, he would be alone. They would often turn to each other, or to slaves like Robb, when there were no women. At the same time, the women who were left behind would become lonely and desperate for companionship. If they were rich enough to have slaves, they would use them to take their husbands' place in their bed. Those who could not afford slaves would turn to one another to satisfy their desires. But since the missionaries have come to our land, this pleasant custom has been forbidden. The god Thor, it seemed, did not approve of satisfying one's natural needs, such as the mutual satisfaction of physical desires, unless it was between a man and a woman."

Woasut listened carefully to Gudruide's words. If such things had occurred in other lands and in other times, why should they not occur now and here? Why had no one spoken of these things until now? Why was there so much talk about the duties of wives towards their husband, and none about the duties wives had towards each other? When she had taken Della in her arms it was out of sympathy for her, because no man seemed interested in her. But then it had been out of desire for her that she had responded to the Scotswoman's ardour with her own. She did not regret it — on the contrary, she had found the experience immensely satisfying, even more than satisfying, especially when she recalled the

soft attentions that Della had paid to her, how she had anticipated her needs and not stopped until Woasut had achieved her
ecstasy. It was a degree of deference she had never experienced
before. Except for that last time, she had always had to tell Anin
to keep going until she, too, was satisfied. Usually, he withdrew
from her as soon as he had had his own pleasure.

"Woasut is not sorry about what happened. Woasut wants it to
happen again and again. But she is confused. She does not know
why she has never heard anyone speak of these duties of a wife
before. Such talk would have made it much easier for her to
understand the meaning of such words as love, tenderness, friendship, companionship, and understanding."

24

THE CELEBRATION OF Anin's initiation that followed the feast-
for-everyone went on for half a moon. It was the longest feast
held by the Addaboutik known to the elders. According to the
Living Memory, who was the repository of the oral traditions of
the Addaboutik, descendants of the first Beothuk, no celebration had ever been held for a hero like Anin. Anin had travelled
completely around the known land in three season-cycles. He
had faced the sea and its dangers, fought the Bouguishamesh
and taken two of their cutting sticks. He had met the Ashwans
in single combat, saved the life of the last surviving Beothuk,
taken her for his wife and had a child with her. He had also
faced a bear for many suns without knowing that he was
meeting his spirit protector. He had been saved by this animal,
which killed two Ashwans. He had spent three cold seasons in
unfamiliar lands, in forests he did not know, with animals and
plants he had never seen before. He had saved the life of a
Bouguishamesh woman when her own people wanted to kill her.

He had slain three giants with his own hands, and saved three other strangers by adopting them. Finally, he had founded the Bear Clan, so named out of respect for an animal that was more benevolent to him than malevolent.

What other village could boast so great a hero? Anin deserved all the honours accorded him. Most of all, he deserved to be named the first Chief of the Addaboutik of the great Beothuk nation. Anin, founder of the Bear Clan, was the son of the two Addaboutik clans, the clan of Edruh the Otter and the clan of Appawet the Seal, and so the proper leader of this great people. Until now, the two older clans had not wanted to place a single chief at their head for fear of causing quarrels between them. Anin had settled the matter by refusing to land his tapatook without the unanimous consent of both clans. He had created harmony between the Addaboutik peoples. His good sense and impartiality had made him the greatest man in the nation. Because there were many young people, it was necessary that the community have a model at its head, in order to give the nation the spirit it needed to survive.

So spoke the elder of the Seal Clan, with the agreement of the elder of the Otter Clan. Anin was no longer just the chief of the Bear Clan, he was the first Chief of the entire nation. In honour of Woasut's people, and because the Addaboutik had once belonged to that family, the new nation would be called Beothuk. The elder also told the young people and the new Beothuk that they must follow the counsel of this man who had just proven beyond all doubt that he was the greatest of the great. He explained to the young people of the new Beothuk Nation that courage, boldness, and valour in combat were not enough to make a great people. If those qualities were not united with wisdom and respect for the rights of the community, they were not worth speaking of. He invited anyone who was not in agreement with him to explain their reasons at this time. If they had not done so by the rising of the next sun, it would be too late and Anin would be the new chief for the rest of his life. The elder also said that the first Chief, in council with the elders, must choose his successor when the time came. He stipulated that if the nation had not produced another hero of Anin's stature at the time of Anin's death, then Anin's oldest male child would automatically be named the first Chief of the Beothuk Nation.

No one dared to stand in opposition to this decision, since no one felt powerful enough to take on the task of directing this nation of individuals who lived only for the good of their community. Anin was proud, but he understood that this honour was like a weapon that cut on both sides. He knew that from now on he could no longer live solely for his own family and for his own clan, that he must keep the good of the entire community in view. He knew that one of his dreams during his voyage, that of ensuring the expansion and spreading of his people, began with assuming the responsibilities of the chief. His time was now the time of the Beothuk, and his alliances were now as important as the wars he would have to conduct in the case of invasion. This island was his country. He had claimed his right to it by being the first to encircle it during his journey of initiation, in the name of his people. He also knew that exploring and settling the interior of the island was equally important, and that the occupation of the sun-rising coast, the central areas, and the region of cold was of the first importance in establishing the Beothuk territory.

In view of all that, he must now rest for several suns. Later he would take counsel with his elders and the bravest of the young people. This night, in the midst of the celebrations honouring the nomination of the first Chief of the Beothuk, he had become a thoughtful man, conscious of the enormity of his responsibilities. Although honoured and proud of having attained the ultimate goal of his life, he was none the less troubled. More and more strangers were coming into his territory, and he did not know how to keep everyone on the alert. How could he stop those huge tapatooks that moved by the force of the wind, filled with so many warriors, from taking possession of his own people? Had not Gudruide told him that a single invasion of the Viking drakkars could bring more people than all the Addaboutik that now lived? That was the first problem he had to face. The council would meet tomorrow to form a plan of expansion, and that plan must include ways to increase the number of individuals. Consultations would be held. Everyone must be made aware of the importance of settling the land within the territory.

That night, around the fire, he spoke at great length with the other members of his clan. He required much information from the Viking women and from the two Scots members who knew a great deal about the lands Anin had never seen. The questions he posed to them were answered clearly, but the chances of limiting or countering that which he feared would happen seemed small. He learned that his dreams could very well remain dreams, and that to realize them would take longer than the lifetime of one man. But his people had already lived for many generations, and he hoped they would continue to live for many generations to come. He could make plans that could be carried out over several lifetimes. Perhaps he would return for another lifetime after this one, in order to complete his work? That night he had no heart to ask one of his wives to couple with him. Gwenid had not returned to the mamateek. Robb had been invited to stay with the parents of a new friend he had made, and Gudruide was already asleep, her child in her arms. Della was lying in the arms of Woasut, who was holding her with tenderness . . . and with love.

25

THAT WARM SEASON there was an exceptional amount of activity in the Beothuk village of Baétha, situated where the river of gulls joined the sea of winds. Everyone able to walk was employed in amassing great stores of provisions for the coming season of cold and snow. Contrary to custom, children carried the catch of the fishermen from the tapatooks to the drying racks and smoke huts that had been built along the shore. All the fishing vessels were constantly plying the open sea, casting for halibut, cod, salmon, lobsters, and herring. The women and younger children gathered snails, clams, and other shellfish, as well as wild fruit. Herbs were also collected to be used in preserving first the snails and then the other food that came from the sea.

Just before the season of falling leaves, all the men of hunting age were divided into two groups. The first group began the cold-season hunt, while the second broke up into three smaller groups, each of which went off to explore separate areas in the island's interior. The group led by Anin headed off to the sun-rising coast; another, led by Whooch the Crow, went north toward the region of cold; and the third group went to the bare mountains, the source of cold winds, led by Berroïk the Cloud. The three groups were told to be back in Baétha before the season of cold and snow set in. Only the elders, the women and children were left in the village. They were given the task of gathering small game and preparing for the cold season. That season of falling leaves was a long one for the women of Baétha.

For the first time in memory, no guardians were left behind to protect the village from attack by the Ashwans, the people the Viking women called Skraelings. There was, however, a plan of defence: the older children were placed on sentry duty up and down the coast, constantly scanning the horizon as well as the shore at the base of the cliffs. At the first alarm the entire village would be abandoned, the people retreating into the interior while the sentries ran to alert the hunting groups. The seal hunters, being closest, would form the first line of attack, acting as shock troops until the others arrived from farther away. The women were trained in the use of spears and arrows, so that they could also take part in the fighting. Woasut, who had seen what had happened to her own people, was not entirely content with these preparations. She knew how crafty were these Ashwans, who moved with such stealth down from the cold and attacked when they were least expected. She knew that prisoners taken by the

Ashwans lived short but horrible lives, submitted to unimaginable tortures. She also knew that these barbarians never took male prisoners, and killed without mercy. She remained anxious and lived in constant fear. She described the massacre of her clan the previous warm season to Gudruide, Della, and Gwenid. She also told of an earlier attack on her village when she had been a young girl. She sketched scenes of horror with such vividness and emotion that when she was finished the four women huddled together in sympathy, shivering and afraid. This reminded them that they would have to endure an entire season with no male warmth to comfort them. They began speaking of their physical needs and the effect this isolation would have on their moods. Gwenid said she knew what it was like to be neglected. She said that at first she was so afraid of becoming dried up that she had made up her mind to seduce Anin when they were alone together in the forest. She told them about the anger that dwelt in her heart when the clan chief coupled with Della in front of the other women, after the birth of Gudruide's child. She explained how she had hated the young Scottish slave at that moment.

"I do not think that our condition has changed very much since then," she said. "Now the nation is everything, and we are more and more neglected for the greater good of the people. My need for physical satisfaction grows stronger and yet is not appeased. I have a great need to please, and a strong desire to be pleased. I am always ready, I think about coupling constantly. I would even gladly couple with you, Della and Woasut."

The three women burst into laughter at these words. The laughter was a sign of the frank honesty and friendship that existed among the wives of one man. It rose from the understanding that must exist among such women, whose lot is for each to await her turn, believing that her turn will come, that their husband will be fair and not choose the same woman twice in a row. Encouraged by this understanding, Gwenid continued her confidences.

"During the home-coming feast, my desire was so strong and my frustration so great that I coupled with three young men, each of whom came to me one after the other, and none of them satisfied me. That is what we have to look forward to during the moons that lie ahead."

Gudruide regarded the three other women sadly, and lowered her head. No man had desired her since the birth of her child.

"I have not even had the comfort and caresses of other women," she said. "I am not as fortunate as Woasut and Della, who miss no opportunity to show their affection for each other. I do not say this in reproach. I speak only out of sorrow for myself."

Woasut looked at Gudruide with sympathy. "But know that I love you as well as I love Della," she said. "I do not give my caresses to Ashwameet, little Red Ochre, because I prefer her to you, but because I sense that her need is greater than yours. She needs sympathy and understanding, and I have enough for both of us. You seem so strong to me by comparison, so removed from such needs. It never occurred to me that you would feel neglected."

Woasut turned to Della. "The affection we feel for each other does not come from any desire to possess each other to the exclusion of others, does it, Della?"

Della smiled, but did not know what to reply to Woasut's appeal. She looked at her Viking sisters. "When I felt such longing for tenderness," she said, "it could have been satisfied by anyone whom I loved. I had no intention of playing favourites, because I knew that we all had to learn to live together in peace if we were to survive. I love you both equally, Gudruide and Gwenid, and I would never discourage your offers of tenderness and friendship."

26

BY THE END of the falling-leaf season, there were enough provisions for the entire season of cold and snow, since the hunters had been bringing in game steadily for several moons. The cold season was approaching rapidly. Each morning the ground was covered with a soft blanket of frost that drained the green from the plants. The weather turned cold and windy, and gusts of snow swirled and melted in the pale light of the sun. The hunters began to wait for the snow that remained on the ground so they could hunt fresh, red meat. The caribou would soon be leaving their warm-season grounds to seek shelter in the forests or food on the high plateaux, where the snow was less deep and lichen grew on exposed rocks. In the meantime, there were beaver pelts and rabbit furs and sealskins to provide, and clothing to be made for the cold season. The previous cold season had been mild, and there was general consent that nature's balance would be restored this time around.

With the explorer groups still gone, the hunters felt themselves obliged to show that they were responsible men. Each night, one of them, named Kabik, laid out the strategy for the next sun's hunt, explaining how each animal was to be hunted and advising each hunter to hunt only the animal he was assigned. Thus each morning the hunters left the village with a definite plan and a destination in mind. There was no duplication of effort, and therefore no wasted time. Occasionally a chance encounter with unexpected game would cause a hunter to change his plan.

Besides Kabik, another hunter, a young woman barely old enough to take a husband, was in the process of making a reputation for herself among the people of the new Beothuk Nation. She had developed great skill with the bow and arrow. The elder who made the clan's weapons had made her a gift of three bows. The least taut she used to hunt small game from short distances; the bow of medium tautness was good for larger game; and the tautest bow was for killing caribou and marine mammals. Her name was Boubishat, which meant fire, because of her spirited character and boundless energy. She had been raised by a woman who had never taken a husband. No one knew who her father was, and she did not wish to find out. It was her mother who taught her how to hunt small game, and she had gone out with the young men to learn how to shoot larger animals. She had practised her skills for many suns until they were perfected, until

she could shoot a bird from the air as easily as one that was standing motionless on the ground. There was no one in the village to
equal her in contests of skill that did not require great physical
strength. And even in contests in which skill was not the sole
requirement, she acquitted herself well. She backed away from no
one and nothing, and the other young people knew better than
to provoke her. Her forceful character made her a formidable rival
in everything she undertook. If she did not place first, she went
away and trained until she was able to issue a return challenge.
But despite her popularity, she had no male suitors. The young
men of the village respected her abilities so much they forgot to
consider her as a woman. Also, she and Della had become great
friends. Boubishat taught Della the use of the bow and arrow, and
Della showed Boubishat how to wield the Viking axe. The two
women would often hunt together. A firm friendship was established between them, and the young huntress spent many nights
with the Bear Clan women, listening as Anin's wives recounted
the adventures they had undergone during their husband's
voyage of initiation. Woasut would often invite Boubishat's
mother to eat with them, and she, too, became a frequent visitor
to the mamateek of the leader of the Bear Clan and first Chief of
the Beothuk Nation.

Thus the circle of neglected women grew with each passing
sun. While performing such communal tasks as drying and
smoking meat, they would often discuss the customs and traditions of the Beothuk people. Whenever they disagreed on a
point, they would consult the elder. If the elder was unable to
decide because he had never been asked that question before, the
women decided the correct way to proceed among themselves.
Then they would go back to the elder and tell him that from then
on such and such would be integrated into the clan's customs,
because they, the women, had determined it to be the best way.

And since the women had been left alone in the village while
the men were exploring, they demanded the right to sit on the
national council. They explained to the elder that he must convince the other council members of the legitimacy and desirability

of this decision. Once the principle was accepted, they held a meeting among themselves to elect a representative. The old man, who was the true Living Memory of the traditions and customs of the ancient Addaboutik people, descended from the even more ancient Beothuk, realized he had much to learn from these women. He was proud of them, since to his knowledge no women before these had displayed such interest in the affairs of the nation. He was a wise man, and not at all disturbed by these new ideas. He understood their legitimacy right away: if women were being called upon to play such an important role in the growth of the new nation, they obviously must have a say in the nation's destiny. If they agreed to have children to increase the population, which would allow the nation to spread into new territories, they must also take part in the nation's decisions. Any other arrangement would not be fair.

The voice of Gwenid, who was now known to everyone as either Boagadoret or Botchmouth, that is Buttocks or Breasts, was the loudest and strongest in demanding this new right for the nation's women. Woasut supported her demands and said she was willing to try to convince Anin of their justness, if he needed to be convinced. Thus the four wives of the Beothuk chief concluded a pact among themselves: they would be united in their appeal to their husband.

When the first group of explorers returned to the village, disappointment showed clearly on their faces. In the direction of the warm wind, they said, the mountains were completely bare. No game, no good sites for establishing a village, no trees to provide wood for the construction of mamateeks, and only the sea to provide enough food to enable them to survive. On the other hand, the high plateaux were easy to defend from any eventual invaders. There were a few beaches that curved into points that stuck out into the sea, where the wind had deposited much sand and formed steep dunes. But that was all. Berroïk, who had led the expedition, reported to the council that no one but the best hunters of sea mammals could survive in this region, and even then they would also have to be good at fishing. He described rock-strewn shorelines dotted with small beaches of fine sand. He thought that perhaps settlers there could gather shellfish along these beaches, but added that the lack of vegetation would allow no variation in their diet and that would lead to much illness during the long seasons of cold and snow. He suggested they await the findings of the other explorer groups, but in his mind the lesson to be drawn thus far was that the first Addaboutik people had chosen well when they established their village at the mouth of the river of gulls. Berroïk also said that they had seen several islands a short distance offshore on which there appeared to be large colonies of nesting birds, which might provide another source of food for anyone attempting to settle in the region.

27

THE FIRST SNOW that remained on the ground had fallen. The central fires in each mamateek were lit, and the women rose often during the night to tend them. The caribou hunters had prepared their snowshoes and were ready to set out. One night after dark the exploring group led by Whooch the Crow returned to the village. The men were exhausted and asked to be allowed to sleep before they recounted the tale of their discoveries.

As soon as the sun rose, the entire village gathered in a small clearing in a sheltered part of the forest to hear the explorers' story. But no sooner had Whooch begun to speak than the group led by Anin also returned to the village, and it was decided to let these travellers rest and to resume the assembly when the sun was at its highest point in the sky. When Anin entered his mamateek, the four women greeted him with shouts of happiness. Anin was surprised, but pleasantly so, and smiled while Woasut helped him remove his outer garment.

Then Gudruide made him sit while she removed his caribou-skin leggings. At the same time, Gwenid lifted his long-sleeved shirt over his head and Della removed his dingiam, which left him completely naked. Somewhat disconcerted by this unaccustomed welcome, Anin asked the women what they thought they were doing.

"The four wives of the first Chief of the Beothuk Nation," said Woasut, "have missed their husband. They have been physically neglected since the beginning of the season of falling leaves, and now demand immediate compensation for their loss of the first Chief's body."

So saying, Woasut threw herself upon Anin, with Gwenid and Gudruide following, and all three women began covering Anin's body with rough caresses and gentle biting. They laughed heartily as they did so, and Della, who did not join in, nonetheless smiled as she watched them. Anin was smiling also, aware that the women were playing a sort of game with him. But he was also astonished at their behaviour, since until then they had seemed to him more reserved.

"Do you not wish to join us?" Anin said to Della.

Della looked at him and said she was content to see if there was anything left to eat when the three starving women had finished their meal. Then, also uncharacteristically, she laughed loudly. The three other women went on with their merrymaking, allowing one to take off her clothing while the other two occupied themselves with Anin. When all three were naked, they stood up and spoke simultaneously:

"You will take all of us, one after the other, and you will not leave this mamateek until we are all satisfied."

Then Gudruide threw herself upon him, declaring herself first, while the others said they would wait their turns. Gwenid invited Della to disrobe, which she did. Anin realized that although the women were laughing, they were still quite serious. He told them he was not sure he was able to accommodate them, taken as he was by surprise and tired from his long journey; perhaps he lacked the strength or the desire to perform the act. The four women faced him and Woasut spoke for them all:

"We have not had a man with us for more than three moons. We have worked hard to prepare for the season of cold and snow, and now that you are back you are telling us you might be too tired to think about our needs? You have four wives who want to couple with you, and we believe that you owe it to us to make the effort. We wish you to pay your respects to all four of us before the sun has gone from the sky."

The three other women emitted cries of agreement. Seeing that he had little choice in the matter, Anin gave in.

"But help me a little, Woasut."

The young Beothuk leaned down and embraced Anin, caressing her husband as tenderly as she herself wished to be caressed. The other women retreated to another part of the mamateek and, covering themselves with caribou skins, awaited their turns. As they watched, Gwenid and Gudruide caressed young Ashwameet, much to her enjoyment. Although they had expressed their needs pleasantly, the four women were serious about the point they were making: they wanted the chief to realize that it was impossible for one man to keep four women completely satisfied, especially when he was away for such long periods of time. They had discussed this among themselves during Anin's absence, and had determined to play the scene out to the end. It was vital to their plan to have their own opinions taken seriously. Woasut therefore took her time, keeping Anin inside her until she was completely satisfied, which was long after he had achieved his own pleasure. No sooner had he withdrawn from her than Gudruide threw herself upon him, kissing him and cajoling him, embracing his body until he was ready once more. She, too, took her time, and when she was finished with him Anin was limp with fatigue. He begged the others to give him time to recover; perhaps after the assembly. But Gwenid and Della both began caressing him together, coaxing his resolve to stiffen again, and soon the young Viking was satisfied. Then Della turned in appeal to Woasut and Gudruide: "Since there does not seem to be even a crumb left for me to eat, I suppose I must rely on you to help me out of my bad humour." The women laughed and began to stroke Della tenderly.

The assembly did not begin at the moment the sun reached its highest point in the sky. It could not begin without its chief, and at that moment the chief was busy. In fact, he remained busy until the following morning. During that time, a serious conversation took place in the mamateek of the first Chief of the Beothuk Nation. The women expressed their grievances, explaining that they wanted their own voices to be heard on the national council. They pointed out that although their tradition described the duties that a wife bore to her husband, it neglected to mention the duties of husbands towards their wives. They discussed the many agreements that must be made between spouses, and the absence of any directives by which those agreements could be reached. They also raised the question of the attraction that grows between women when they are neglected by their husbands, telling him of their own experiences during his absence. They explained to him how united the four of them were, and that they felt absolutely no remorse for their behaviour; they did not find anything reprehensible about it so long as they continued to respect their duties towards their husband.

Anin was taken aback by this long conversation, which lasted well into the night. But he promised to think about the matters they raised, and to speak to them again when he had done so. When the two mothers had fed their babies, the four women and their chief finally went to sleep.

28

THE ASSEMBLY BEGAN as soon as the sun was at the highest point in its journey across the sky. The elder asked Whooch the Crow to start. Whooch told how his expedition had explored the regions of the high mountains and plateau country in the direction of cold. There were many trees, rich lands, small ponds, high waterfalls that tumbled into the sea, long arms of the sea that reached deep into the land between cliffs so high they had made him dizzy to look down from them. There were many advantageous places that gave a wide view of the sea, so that anyone approaching would be seen well in advance, but there were not many good hunting places except at this time of the season-cycle when the caribou migrated to the uplands to eat moss. It was a country well suited to anyone who loved nature, he said, but not for the establishment of new villages.

Then it was Anin's turn. He told about the expedition that crossed the forested parts of the island. He recounted how the two coasts of the island were joined by running water:

"Between the rising and setting coasts," he said, "there are large rivers and long lakes that would permit us to travel great distances in our tapatooks. We could cross from one coast to another in less than one moon, if we did not have to stop to hunt. Along the length of this crossing, there are caribou that dwell in the forest and do not migrate to the high country, as do the herds that live in the cold region. There are, of course, wolves that hunt in packs or families, but if our hunters are skilled the wolves will not rob us of meat. There are numerous places that would make excellent camps during the season of cold and snow. The forest is thick everywhere and provides perfect shelter from cold winds. There is much small game as well: rabbits, hares, beavers, otters, and martens. Some of the rivers that run toward the rising-sun coast fall into deep bays when they reach the sea. And when we were passing a large lake at the very centre of the island, we came upon a Beothuk village, so there are other people living on this island. We did not come into contact with these people, because we did not want to be mistaken for Ashwans. But we saw many areas where wild fruit grew in great abundance in the forests and along the shores of the rivers and lakes. It would also be possible to gather shellfish and other sea creatures. In fact, the best plan would be to establish villages at the ends of the deep bays, where we would be able to keep an eye on the inland territories without being visible from the sea, so that we would not attract the attention of Ashwans or the Bouguishamesh. We could do this at the beginning of the season of new growth. With our present population, and our knowledge of how quickly our numbers have increased over the past generations, we could spread out over the whole island in fewer than five generations. That way we will be assured of keeping our island to ourselves, by preventing our enemies from coming and murdering us all in one attack. We must also ensure that the region we inhabit now remains inhabited. This is an ideal spot for guarding the sun-setting coast. How many of you are ready to establish villages on the sun-rising side?"

Three-quarters of the men in the assembly raised their arms to signify their interest in Anin's plan. Not a single woman raised hers. Anin sensed that the women had come to the assembly with their own plan. Had not Woasut told him that they wanted their own voice on the national council?

"Are no women ready to establish their families on the sun-rising coast?" he asked.

Woasut stood up and approached the chief of the Beothuks.

"The women of the Beothuk Nation make up more than two-thirds of the population, if you include female children," she said. "And yet, until this sun, they have never had any say in making the decisions that affect their lives and those of their children. They wish to be represented on the council of the Beothuk Nation. The five men who now make the decisions have nothing to fear from us. One woman on the council would represent the wishes of all women. We swarm like bees, and we would be consulted."

Her words were followed by a long silence, which was broken by the Living Memory, who cleared his throat before speaking in favour of the demand of the women, as he had promised:

"If I may speak after Woasut," he began. "It is true that Beothuk women have not until now taken part in the decisions of the assembly, but that is because not until now have they expressed an interest in getting mixed up in the business that has always been the concern of the men. But it is clear now that the women wish to have a voice, and I do not see how we can prevent them from having one. There is, however, a condition for taking part in the council. When the council meets, it makes decisions for the entire nation and in the nation's name; it does not make decisions to please any one individual, or even one group within the nation. If the women accept that condition, I am prepared to accept a female to sit on the national council. I leave it to the other members of the council to express their own opinions."

The elder of the Otter Clan nodded his head. Whooch declared that he had no objection, and Berroïk said that he had been thinking about just such a move for a long time. Only Anin had not spoken. He stood up.

"In truth, I do not have a choice in the matter," he said. "I would be the only one to oppose the move. But I do fear that the women may be too emotional to make the kind of objective decisions that the council must make. However, as long as you accept the condition mentioned by the Living Memory, then I believe that you should be given a chance to prove that you can act objectively and practically. You will designate a representative to the council, and she will participate in the first assembly tomorrow morning. I have spoken."

The public assembly ended with Anin's words. It remained only to elaborate on the plans for the nation's migration towards the sun-rising coast. When they sat during the following sun, the six members of the national council of the Beothuks would establish these plans.

The women of the three Beothuk clans held an immediate meeting to nominate their representative to the national council.

The meeting continued into the night, since each person had the right to express her opinion as to what she expected from such a representative. To everyone's surprise, the spokeswoman selected turned out to be Gudruide, the Viking, the foreigner. The young huntress Boubishat was chosen as her replacement if Gudruide was unable to attend a council assembly. Gudruide was greatly honoured to have been chosen, but she protested all the same that she was a foreigner and unfamiliar with all the customs of the Beothuk. The other women replied that she did not need to know everything because all she would be doing was relaying to the council the decisions reached by the women themselves, and if she was ever in doubt she had only to ask the others. They then spoke of the important points that Gudruide must bring to the next meeting. Then the meeting ended.

Each woman returned to her mamateek. The young people sought out companions for the night. Robb, who had accompanied Anin on the expedition to the sun-rising coast, entered the Bear Clan mamateek and whispered a few words into Gwenid's ear. Anin called to him:

"Robb, it is time for you to find a companion in another clan. From now on, the four women in this mamateek are all my wives. Do you remember what you once told me? That when I have decided which woman is my favourite you would not consort with her? Well, I have decided that all four women are my favourites, even though Woasut will always be my first wife."

Robb moved away from Gwenid and lay down to sleep. Once again, thought Gwenid, she was to be frustrated in her desire for a man. The young huntress Boubishat was already asleep in the arms of Ashwameet, Red Ochre. When the sun rose, Robb gathered up his personal things and left the mamateek of the Bear Clan.

29

WHEN THE SEASON of new growth arrived, the members of the Otter Clan left for the sun-rising coast. They were led by Whooch, and Robb went with them. He was now known as Drona the Hairy, and he took with him two wives from the Otter Clan, two sisters. He wanted to establish a family and to be firmly identified as a member of the Beothuk Nation.

Anin appointed Berroïk to remain at the head of the Seal Clan and to maintain the village at the mouth of the river of gulls. Nonetheless, some members of the Seal Clan decided to join Anin and the Bear Clan to set up a village deep in the interior of the island.

This is the story of how the two founding Addaboutik clans expanded to fill an island. This is how the Addaboutik established the great Beothuk Nation! This also tells the value of Living Memory to the heart of the people: it is through our Living Memory that future generations of Beothuk learn that they are eternal, that they will live forever.

Anin and his four wives established a village on the large lake known from then on as Red Ochre Lake. Over a period of many season-cycles equal to twice the fingers on two hands, his wives produced a great number of offspring. Woasut met two of her cousins and five other Beothuk women who had escaped from the Ashwan massacre; these seven Beothuk became members of the Bear Clan.

At the end of a period of twenty season-cycles, every important region of the island was occupied and patrolled by the Beothuk. My father, Kabik the Careful, took two other wives after the death of my mother, who was the young huntress Boubishat, as well as his own mother, and installed himself and his family on the Bay of Exploits, so named in honour of Anin, who had first met Woasut on this bay.

Whenever a foreign ship anchored in a bay to provision itself with fresh water, the members of the Beothuk Nation demanded some form of compensation. The most coveted items were those made of metal: fish hooks, axe heads, knives, or sometimes just unformed pieces of iron that the Beothuk artisans, who had been taught by Drona the Hairy, would fashion into useful tools. The two swords and the axe that had belonged to the Vikings were carefully preserved and carried by Anin and Ashwameet, and were much in use. Anin's four wives gave birth regularly. The young Scots woman, despite her preference for her own sex, brought four infants into the world, three males and a female. Woasut also had four more children after Buh-Bosha-Yesh. Gudruide gave birth to six children altogether, four of whom were males. As for Gwenid, the fires of desire burned so brightly within her that she brought forth no fewer than eleven young ones into the world. In the entire memory of the Beothuk and the Addaboutik, that is, in the entire history of our people, Anin's family was the largest. All his children increased the Bear Clan in fewer than twenty season-cycles.

Many times Anin descended the river of two waterfalls to hunt and fish in the Bay of Exploits. One sun he went alone in his tapatook to the island of birds that was at the mouth of the bay, and he did not return. The entire nation went in search of him, but neither he nor his tapatook was ever found, neither were any of his hunting or fishing tools. There was no sign of what had happened to him. His four wives have kept his memory alive. There are also the stories of his voyage around the land, which have been kept by us. It has now been three times the number of fingers on my two hands since he disappeared. And still his family awaits his return.

His son Buh-Bosha-Yesh had been raised with the knowledge that eventually he would replace his father as head of the Beothuk Nation, and with Anin's departure it was he who became chief of the six clans that live on this island. There is no bay, no headland, no rivermouth that is not closely watched by the guardians of the island's nation. Powerful, yet peaceful, is the Beothuk Nation. Harmony reigns at all times.

The families grew large, and since the warriors had no wars to fight, the number of males came to match the number of females. It is now rare for a man to have four or five wives, and so the customs of the people have changed in some ways. The Ashwans returned to the island from time to time, but they were always repelled by the nation's guardians, thanks to their watchfulness.

This is how the peace and happiness of simple living have endured, so that the Living Memory of the people did not die.

Every night until their own death, the four wives of Anin stood on the shore and searched the horizon, hoping for his return.

II

THE INVADERS

The Red Men's island,
approximately five hundred season-cycles later

30

THE SUN HAD not yet risen over the northeast coast of the island of the Beothuk. At the horizon, a thin band of light announcing the appearance of Kuis the Sun was taking on a red hue, a sign that when he came he would bring hot and humid weather.

The old man sat on a flat rock overlooking the sea and contemplated the approaching light, giving thanks to Kobshuneesamut the Creator for adding another beautiful day to the season of abundance. He would make use of this fine weather to speak to the young people of the clan about pathways. He was the clan's Living Memory, charged with keeping the past alive; he had been instructed to do this by his ancestor Anin, the first Beothuk to travel around the whole land now occupied by the Beothuk Nation. The old man would tell the Addaboutik children how their courageous ancestor had overcome many unknown dangers in order to teach his people to preserve their land and be nourished by it, as they had been doing for longer than even he could remember. When he passed on to his eager young students the knowledge acquired by Anin during his voyage of initiation, he would also be reminding them that all knowledge begins with the experience of the elders, whose most important task is that of remembering. He thanked Kobshuneesamut once again, this time for putting into his head such thoughts that he might pass on to his people.

Today he would tell them about the hero Anin's second wife, the woman who came from the land of the Bouguishamesh-Vikings, where the cold also comes from. She was the first woman to sit on the national council. She had pale skin and hair the colour of dried grass, and she taught the people that the cold was called north, the wind was west, the rising sun was east, and warmth came from the south. He would explain to them the mixing of blood that gave the Beothuk their great strength, and of the gift of metal, which they received from their enemies. Then he would explain why it was necessary to protect the island of the Red Men from strangers if they wanted to continue living in peace. For longer than his memory, whenever a strange ship stopped to take on fresh water, the Beothuk had benefited from its arrival without allowing any of its passengers to stay on the island and compete with them for the land. He would have to explain why they must accept only those new people who wished to live among the Beothuk, and to become part of the Beothuk Nation, so that they might learn from them. And why, on this the longest sun of the season-cycle, they must give thanks to the Creator for having preserved them from invaders.

"The young people think we must tolerate all strangers, so that we will learn from them more quickly about the world we do not know. But every time strangers have come they have killed, tortured, and stolen from us, and they have shown no respect for the Beothuk people." That is what the Living Memory of the Appawet Clan would tell the young people at this feast, on the longest sun of the season-cycle.

He would also explain to them how he came to be called the Living Memory, how a long time ago when a young girl became lost in the forest and the villagers wished to know what it was that had made her go off by herself, away from her people, it was he who had remembered that when the girl was very little she had been fascinated by the dragonflies that flew in the marsh.

He reminded them how she had spent whole days watching the dragonflies without growing tired. She had especially liked to watch them coupling in the air as they flew, remaining together in their fashion for long periods of time. The searchers went to the marsh and found the girl sleeping at the foot of a huge birch tree. She had indeed gone there to see the dragonflies. It was then that the village had decided that one with such a long memory should be of service to the people, and since that day he had been the Living Memory. He had been given no choice in the matter; when the people decide who you are, you are obliged to be that person. A talent must be placed at the service of those who recognize it.

Slowly the village was awakening. The young people were splashing about in the sea, while the older clan members con-tented themselves with bathing more quietly in the river. The women were restoring the fires from last night and putting out food for those who were hungry. It was going to be a good feast, a feast-for-everyone, filled with happiness. Many visitors would come in from neighbouring clans to await the return of Anin, who disappeared into the sea more than five hundred season-cycles ago. Since that time, Anin's family had never accepted that their hero-ancestor was dead, and so they awaited his return from the sea as once they had awaited his return from his voyage of initiation around the Beothuk land. The old man knew that no mortal man could ever live so long. But perhaps Anin was not a mortal man? Perhaps he would return again, as he had returned the first time, on this the longest sun of the season-cycle?

The old man was still sitting on the rock when a young man called out that a sail had entered the bay. The elder told the young man to hurry to alert the guardians, and the youth ran at full speed towards the river, carrying the news with him. Before long a group of twenty men were on the shore, standing beside their tapatooks, ready to set out if the need arose. As they waited, armed with fishing spears and bows and arrows, they were joined by another twenty, as well as by many women and girls who formed a second line of defence behind the guardians.

This was the plan of defence that had been practised for hundreds of season-cycles. It had protected the nation many times before. The plan was to make the invaders understand that this was Beothuk land, and that if they wanted to take something from it they would have to negotiate for it first.

The chief of the Appawet Clan arrived on the shore, accompanied by his two wives. He was called A-Enamin the Bone because he was so tall and thin. He had lived for thirty season-cycles, and his wives had borne him five children, giving him five reasons to believe that he would continue to live after his death. He would speak on behalf of the clan of Appawet the Seal, after consulting with the clan elder, Asha-Bu-Ut the Blood.

There followed a long wait, because the boat was too large and too heavy to come close to the shore of the Beothuk. Nevertheless, its crew members dropped many sounding lines to see how close the ship could come. Finally, the strangers lowered a smaller boat into the water, with six men rowing and two others standing up in it, one in the bow and the other in the stern. This boat was much smaller than the first, but still it was five times bigger than the Beothuk's largest tapatooks.

When the English boat touched bottom, the six rowers jumped into the water and dragged the boat onto the shore. Then two of the rowers crossed their arms and joined their hands together, to form a sling in which the first standing man, the one in the bow of the boat, could sit. The sailors carried this man higher up on the shore, so that when they put him down he did not get his feet wet. The second standing man remained in the boat, surrounded by four rowers, who stood ready to push the boat back into the water if the need arose. The two standing men were obviously dressed for some ceremony, whereas the clothing of the other men, the rowers, was quite different.

A-Enamin raised his hand in salutation to the newcomers. The other man did the same. A-Enamin smiled at all the strange men and introduced his elder, Asha-Bu-Ut, by pronouncing his name. The stranger said something that no one understood, but which they supposed was his own name. Then he turned and, indicating

the man standing in the boat, said "Kapitan Jon Kabot." All the
children laughed at these strange words. Their laughter lightened
the atmosphere. By mimicking the act of filling barrels, Kapitan
Jon Kabot's representative indicated that his men wanted to take
on fresh water. The Beothuk understood what he wanted, since
he made the same gesture that all strangers made when they
wanted water. A-Enamin indicated that the Beothuk were
willing to exchange their water for tools.

One of the Beothuk guardians went up to the stranger and
showed him an axe with a large head. Another brought out a
handful of fish hooks. A third, a harpoon. A fourth took out
his metal knife. Then the man who was still in the boat had his
rowers carry him to shore and, smiling, he held out his hand
towards A-Enamin and to Asha-Bu-Ut. The two Beothuk men
smiled back, and held out their hands towards this Kapitan Jon
Kabot. The kapitan seized their hands and shook them up and
down vigorously, a thing that made the Addaboutik people roar
with laughter. It was the way these foreigners had of signalling
friendship with one another, but it never failed to make the
Beothuk onlookers laugh.

The Beothuk chief indicated to the strangers that they were
welcome, and made signs inviting the kapitan to join the feast-for-
everyone. The kapitan turned to his six rowers and gave them an
order, using their guttural language that the Red Men could not
understand. The sailors immediately pushed their boat back into
the water and rowed to the big boat, while the two stranger-chiefs
followed the Beothuk towards the mamateeks. The guardians
divided into two groups. The first group and all the women accompanied the visitors to the mamateeks, while the second remained
on the shore in case the newcomers proved treacherous.

For nearly half the day the visitors were entertained by the
Red-Ochre people. They were escorted to the feasting area,
where several young people were already singing and dancing.
And throughout the day members of neighbouring clans continued to arrive, and the feast-for-everyone on the longest sun of the
season-cycle was well underway.

All this time, sailors from the larger ship had been coming ashore in three small boats with many barrels, which they filled with fresh water from the river and rolled down the beach to be stacked in the boats. Three of these men now joined the kapitan and his lieutenant, carrying iron tools, as had been agreed. There were three axe heads, three harpoons, one hundred fish hooks, twelve knives, and one bolt of red cloth, which the women quickly unrolled and admired. The exchange permitted both peoples to obtain what they needed in friendship and understanding.

Everyone was enjoying the feast and their friendly feelings towards one another. The guardians relaxed their vigilance and joined in the festivities. When the sun fell behind the island, Kapitan Jon Kabot invited the Appawet Clan chief and one of his two wives, along with the elder, to board his larger ship. By signs, he indicated that he had more gifts for the chief. A-Enamin eagerly accepted the offer, not for the gifts but because he was curious to see what the larger ship looked like from the inside. Asha-Bu-Ut, however, absolutely refused to go, and attempted to dissuade the chief as well, but A-Enamin was convinced by Kapitan Jon Kabot's friendliness that there was nothing to fear. The elder tried to persuade the chief at least to take some guardians with him, but even this A-Enamin refused to do, saying that taking guardians would be an insult to these dignitaries, who had spent the whole day among the Beothuk people without guardians of their own. The chief did, however, ask one of the young Beothuk hunters to go with him in the elder's place. As soon as all three were seated in the small boat that took them to the ship, Asha-Bu-Ut spoke quietly to the Beothuk guardians, telling them that as soon as darkness came they must take their tapatooks out to keep a watch on the English ship as long as the chief and his party were on board.

The kapitan's three guests were welcomed on the larger ship and given salt pork to eat and rum and wine to drink. They did not eat the salt pork, and the rum made them feel sleepy, but the chief greatly enjoyed the wine, and asked for more. Suddenly a strong wind came up, and Kapitan Jon Kabot ordered that the ship's anchor be raised silently and the mainsail hoisted without the usual shouted commands.

When the guardians in the tapatooks that were hidden along the great ship's flanks saw the anchor being raised and the great sails hoisted, they raised the alarm. A-Enamin's wife heard them and began to cry out, demanding that she and the two others be put ashore. The chief and the hunter were in no condition to defend themselves, however, and they were easily overpowered, despite the fact that they were larger than any of the English sailors.

Hearing the shouts of the guardians and of A-Enamin's wife, the villagers hastily launched the rest of their tapatooks and attempted to stop the ship from leaving the bay. In no time they overtook the ship, and many tried to climb aboard, but the sailors had already put down large nets, like fishing nets, to prevent them. Not even when Kapitan Jon Kabot ordered cannons to be fired among the tapatooks did the Beothuk give up the chase. They followed the ship as far out to sea as they could, but it was no use. They had to admit that they had not been prepared for such a turn of events. Frustrated and desolate, they returned to the village, where the feast was terminated and the news that the Appawet Clan's chief and two others had been carried off by the English caused great sadness within the Beothuk Nation.

Sorrow and confusion continued to dwell with the Beothuk people. They had been deceived like children by the Bouguishamesh's show of friendship. Asha-Bu-Ut blamed himself for not doing everything in his power to prevent the chief from accepting the English offer. He was even more distraught when he saw how A-Enamin's second wife and their five children wept and pulled their hair in anguish at their loss. Three of the children had lost their mother. All of them had lost their father. The clan mourned the loss of their chief, and vowed never again to be deceived by the false smiles of foreigners. From that day to this, no Bouguishamesh has ever been welcome on the island of the Red Men. The Living Memory explained that in Beothuk legend, foreigners were always depicted as hypocrites and untrustworthy men. Strangers did not come to the island to establish true ties of friendship with the Beothuk. That was why he himself had refused the kapitan's invitation to board his ship.

Long were the lamentations following the disappearance of their beloved, if careless, chief, who had allowed himself to be so easily deceived by the foreigners. Messengers were sent to all the villages of the Beothuk Nation, carrying the unhappy news and warning all other clans to be on their guard against the traitorous people who came to the island on ships bearing the colours of the King of England.

The Appawet Clan elected a new chief, one of the guardians, one who would be more prudent than his predecessor had been. From that day to this, the shores of the bays and the rocky cliffs at the mouths of the deep inland rivers have been kept under strict surveillance by the guardians of the nation. Whenever a foreign vessel was sighted, Beothuk warriors lined the shores and the riverbanks, and no foreigners were allowed to come ashore to replenish their water supplies. Their ships were followed until they were well out at sea, out of sight, and their crews were showered with storms of arrows, so that never again would they consider casting their anchors near the island of the Red Men. The Beothuk had become the enemies of all foreigners. Never again would they be fooled by the hidden intentions of those who came from far away. The Red Men had lost their innocence.

The young people did not remember this lesson, and so the Living Memories of each clan were charged with reminding them of this sorrowful incident, as well as telling them of all the dangers experienced by their ancestor Anin during his voyage around the land of the Beothuk.

This longest sun of the season of abundance would remain in the minds and the memories of the bearers of the Beothuk tradition. Asha-Bu-Ut was sorry that he was not able to pass on what he knew in time to save the three Beothuk who were stolen from among his people. He was saddened, but took comfort from the knowledge that this lesson would be remembered for a long time:

"The entire nation must now be aware how dishonest and treacherous strangers are. All Beothuk must learn never to put their trust in strangers, especially not in those who smile too easily.

"Men with beards, men who wear fine clothing, men who are afraid to get their feet wet, these are not men like the Red Men. They do not keep their word as the Addaboutik people do. An Addaboutik who has given his word and does not keep it is punished, often by death, because his untrustworthiness threatens the lives of the other members of his clan. If the other members are judged by his example, then they, too, will not be trusted. No nation wants a clan in its midst whose word cannot be trusted. The entire nation suffers when a single member breaks his word."

31

IWISH STORMED OUT of the mamateek. She was furious, and the whole village knew it because they had heard her shouting at Gobidin the Eagle, chief of the Seal Clan, throughout almost the entire council meeting. Clan chief or not, Gobidin still had to listen to the words of his councillors, and stop thinking that he was perfectly capable of making important decisions all on his own.

Iwish was the second wife of A-Enamin, the Seal Clan chief who had been stolen by Kapitan Jon Kabot. She represented the Seal Clan women on the clan council. She thought that the village should be divided into smaller units so that it would not be totally destroyed if attacked by an enemy, or subjected to a surprise raid. With her feminine logic, Iwish was concerned with the survival of the nation, and was impatient with the proud males who believed they could handle any danger that came their way, without taking any precautions against it. She reminded them that this sort of thinking was exactly what had resulted in the theft of her husband and two other clan members by the English, right from under their noses and without anyone being able to prevent it. She also reminded them how once, when she was a young woman, an Ashwan raiding party had attacked her village at dawn and killed nearly all the adult males and taken most of the women as slaves. When she remembered these things, she told Gobidin, she could not bring herself to believe that the clan chiefs took adequate precautions or always made good decisions.

But Gobidin was a member of the guardians, and he firmly believed that the guardians were strong enough to repel an attack from any large ship that sailed into the bay. When Iwish reminded him that the English had taken her husband, his first wife, and one hunter without him and his guardians being able to stop them, he spoke about the treachery of the English, of how his guardians had been taken by surprise, and how their mistake had been in allowing the foreigners to come off their ship onto Beothuk land. He was of the opinion that the best way to prevent such a thing from happening again was to prevent any foreigner from stepping onto Beothuk land. That would solve the problem. Iwish protested that no amount of force would stop foreigners from leaving their boats if they decided to attack the village. But Gobidin remained firm: if the guardians prevented these foreigners from landing, they could not use their weapons of deceit and cunning against them, even under the guise of friendship.

Still Iwish persisted. It was not necessary, she said, for the foreigners to leave their ships in order to attack the village. The ships of the English-Bouguishamesh had cannons, their sailors had firesticks. Such an enemy could laugh at the Beothuk guardians. Gobidin assured the other councillors that all the bays were under constant surveillance, and no surprise attack was possible. Faced with such an attitude, Iwish became very angry; she demanded that Gobidin return her husband to her, then, since a surprise attack was so impossible that he must not have been stolen from her. Even when the elder spoke in favour of her proposal, saying that Iwish's suggestion was pregnant with wisdom, Gobidin refused to listen to her, saying that her arguments were groundless. At this, Iwish lost control of her anger, and called the chief of the Seal Clan a pebble-headed idiot. She shouted that the Eagle was a very large bird with a very small brain. Then she left the mamateek before the council meeting was ended. This was a grave insult, not only to the member who had called the meeting, but also to the other councillors who had troubled themselves to attend it. But worst of all was that by leaving the council meeting she had shown great disrespect towards her clan chief. She had questioned his competence and called him a self-important imbecile. This was clearly a transgression of Beothuk law. Rather than calmly discussing the important issues confronting the nation, she had allowed herself to be ruled by anger, and had insulted the chief before the other councillors. She had caused him to lose face, an unpardonable breach of etiquette, not only for a council member but also for a woman. Only two options lay before her. She either had to prove beyond a doubt that she was in the right, or else she had to make a public apology for her behaviour. The very fact that she had transgressed her duty as a woman to be respectful to men, who were the providers and protectors of the clan, made it impossible, in the people's eyes, for her to prove that she was in the right. It was therefore necessary to hold a public ceremony, during which Iwish would ask the forgiveness of the assembled villagers. Nothing else would remove the offence. The council agreed, however, to delay this special ceremony until such time as Iwish was calmer, since at the moment she was much too angry to be reasoned with.

Iwish, meanwhile, had snatched up a handful of spears and gone off into the forest to practise her skill at throwing this most favoured of Beothuk weapons. She was followed by a group of young women who, like her, were well trained in the use of arms and who took Iwish's advice. Since the theft of her husband, Iwish had not accepted the so-called superiority of men. Males, she said, had grown stupid and complacent. She formed a sort of sub-clan of women dissidents who were ready to raise the call for the defence of the Beothuk territory. Nearly all Beothuk women were aware of this movement, and discussions in the village mamateeks had been lively and long. The women believed Iwish was in the right. Iwish had become the official opposition within the clan council. She was also the women's representative on the national council. She had great influence among her people, and the male clan members were well aware of her power and did not like having their authority questioned by such an irascible woman as Iwish, who refused to recognize good, masculine common sense when she saw it. On the other hand, though they resented her belligerent attitude, there were men who recognized the selflessness of her intentions and the depth of her thinking. She thought about a great many matters, and was always willing to seek counsel, at least from other women.

Within this sub-clan, Iwish had formed an elite corps of women who were as proficient with weapons as any male hunters of the clan of Appawet the Seal. In a very short time, these women had become the pride of all the women of the clan, which created, in the minds of the men, an unhealthy form of heroine worship within the heart of the village. Every adolescent woman wanted to belong to this elite group, and they already behaved as though they were the equal of the male hunters. And indeed, as warriors and hunters, these young women were more skilful than many of the young men, and more alert. Their determination was unshakeable; nothing and no one could dislodge them from their path. The women had acquired such self-confidence that the men did not dare challenge them except in contests of brute strength.

The most effective argument that the men could raise against Iwish's proposal to divide the village was that since the disappearance of A-Enamin and his first wife, not a single foreign ship had been allowed to replenish its water supply on the island. The clan had successfully defended its territory even though many were the sails that had been seen crossing the entrance to their bay and the narrow strait leading to the land of their friends the Innu, whom the Beothuk people called the Sho-Undamung.

Iwish did not accept the submission of women and the superiority of men. She was descended from the Bear Clan; her people reached back to a daughter of the famous huntress Boubishat the

Fire and to a son of Anin himself, the national hero of the Beothuk. She believed that the two sexes were equal in most things, and that women were superior in others, since it was women who brought children into the world and were the first teachers of all Beothuk, without exception. Everyone was born of woman, and this gave women superiority over men. If women simply refused to bear and raise children, it would mean the end of the human race and of the Beothuk Nation. Women therefore had the right to be heard and to have their words respected by all. Now was the time to claim that right, to demand it with all their strength, to force the men to listen to their words.

Such was the pass to which the nation had come, a nation whose only common hero was a man. Anin the Voyager, the father of more children than any other man known to the Living Memories of the Beothuk people. The men said that for three season-cycles no foreign ship had come to take fresh water from the island of the Red Men, and that this was proof that Anin's original plan, which had been respected and enforced for count-less generations, was a good plan. Why divide the village when all its strength lay in its unity? The Iwish women thought only of defeat, were fearful for no reason. Like all women, they were weak and dependent on men.

On that sun, the women of Iwish's sub-clan dismantled their mamateeks and took the bark and poles to a place deep in the forest, to the south and west of the bay, to establish a second village. They did this in support of Iwish and her plan to divide the village in order to avoid the complete destruction of the pop-ulation in the event of a surprise attack by a foreign enemy. The women believed that what they did was necessary, that the wishes of the men had to be ignored in order to ensure the safety of their children. Thus the division that raged in the heart of the village was not between families, but between men and women, whose views were now diametrically opposed.

That same night, the young guardians watching at the coast signalled that two ships were passing the mouth of the bay, out beyond the islands. The ships showed no sign of entering in search of fresh water, as so many other ships had done, even though they would have been able to see, from the different colour of the water, that a large river flowed into the bay from inland. The two ships continued sailing past the bay and disappeared beyond the tongue of land that separated the Seal Clan bay from the next bay along the coast. The guardians shouted their belief that word had passed among the men on board such ships that it was useless to try to take on fresh water in the deep bay of the large river with two waterfalls. The Red Men of that bay were too powerful and would prevent them; it was better to continue farther south, to one of the places where no Beothuk lived. They said that the women were wrong to fear these foreigners and to move the village into the forest.

According to the Living Memory responsible for this period in Beothuk history, the captain aboard the first of these two ships was named Gaspar de Côrte Real. He had sailed from Portugal and had been warned by a Portuguese fishing boat that the bay he had just passed was well guarded by the Red Men, but that the next bay to the south, called Bonavista, was not protected and fresh water could be taken from a stream that emptied into it. Some fishermen had even crossed the tongue of land separating the two bays and seen the village of the Red Skins; it would be a small matter to attack this village from landward, they said. Such an attack would weaken and perhaps even eliminate the stranglehold maintained by the ferocious inhabitants of this New Found Land, as the fishermen called the island.

Côrte Real's ships took on fresh water in Bonavista, and when night fell the captain ordered seventy of his men to pass through the forest on the tongue of land to the Beothuk village. The men were guided by one of the fishermen who had been to the place before. Their orders were to capture as many of the Red Skins as possible so that they might be taken back to Portugal alive.

Even though seventy men could hardly move silently through the forest, with the aid of the fisherman they made their way to the Beothuk village undetected. A handful of them quietly entered the village and, at a signal, simultaneously set fire to a dozen birchbark mamateeks. When the members of the Seal Clan ran from their burning homes, they were captured and chained together by the Portuguese sailors. When the sun came up, the entire village of the Appawet Clan, fifty-seven men, women, and children, were herded like cattle into rowboats waiting at the shore of their own bay, and transported around the tongue of land to Côrte Real's ships. It was a catastrophe for the Red Men.

While Côrte Real's raiding party waited on shore for the boats to return for them, a band of warrior women descended upon them, and before they could mount a counterattack twenty of them had been killed by Beothuk spears. The attack was led by a wild woman who shouted and whirled in a frenzy, her short sword striking at anything that got in her way. She was a veritable demon, reported one of Côrte Real's men. The Portuguese had no choice but to flee back to Bonavista along the path they had taken the night before. Even so, they were pursued by the women led by Iwish, and ten more were slain before they could reach their ships. Thirty men in all had been killed by the Beothuk women.

Seven of the captured Red Men were placed on Côrte Real's flagship, and the other fifty were tied together and left on the open deck of the second vessel. Then both ships set sail for Portugal. The fifty-seven Beothuk were never seen again on the island of the Red Men. It is said that they were sold as slaves.

While returning on the path to the village of the clan of Appawet the Seal, the women came upon a Portuguese sailor who was wounded but still alive. They made him walk back to the village, in the hope that he could be made to tell them what had happened to their people. It was from him that they learned the name of the ships' commander was Gaspar de Côrte Real.

News travelled quickly on the island of the Red Men in those days, and Iwish was named chief of the clan of Appawet the Seal, and also leader of the guardians of the nation, for her foresight as well as for her ability to oversee the island's defence. She was the first woman to become a clan chief, and the first to sit on the national council as a full councillor, rather than as a representative of the nation's women, and the first to be the leader of the guardians. She knew, however, that she had been accorded these honours because she had acted like a man; if her words had been heeded by the others, she would have demonstrated her usefulness to her people as a woman, and not simply as a replacement for a man. She was determined, she was strong, and she was as capable as any man, but she considered herself a woman, and preferred to be seen as a woman. She obeyed the laws of the nation and observed her duties as a woman and as a wife.

She had no intention of neglecting those duties when she assumed the role of clan chief and leader of the guardians. She stoutly maintained that if a man were more competent she would relinquish her titles, go back to being a woman, and forget these man-tasks that had been thrust upon her. She was well aware that her most important role as chief was to find a male replacement for herself, and to restore the confidence and dignity of the stronger sex, which had been diminished by her own success and that of her female followers. There was nothing wrong with the models followed by young Beothuk males for hundreds of season-cycles; they must be put back in place as soon as possible so that virility would return and the women could once again enjoy life in confidence, as they had before.

For that to happen, it was absolutely necessary to rid the clan council of its prideful and complacent men who believed they were the only ones with knowledge and power. These men must now look to the women for counsel, and not simply as bearers of their children. Her work would begin immediately. She had to reorganize the defences, since there was no doubt in her mind that the next warm season would bring more foreign ships to their shores. Every season-cycle brought more and more ships to the island to take fish that belonged to the Beothuk, thereby preventing the Red Men from taking the nourishment from the sea that they needed for survival. The fish in the inland ponds would eventually disappear, and the clams and shellfish they gathered in the bays were already becoming fewer.

How were they to fish for cod and halibut? They dared not take their tapatooks beyond the bay for fear of being captured by the foreign ships. When such encounters occurred, the Beothuk were saved only by the swiftness of their paddlers. Somehow they had to put these fears aside and return to their traditional way of life. There must be peace, not war. That was the task that fell to the Great Iwish, the first female clan chief of the Beothuk Nation.

A new clan council was formed and a second woman was named to it, but Iwish also named three men, including the elder who had escaped from the Portuguese raid by joining the women in the forest the night before the attack. He had endeared himself to them by saying that he, too, had had a presentiment of disaster, perhaps a feminine one, but a true one nonetheless. They said he was wise. But he rather thought of himself as prudent, as opening his spirit to all good ideas, whether they came from a man or from a woman.

32

IWISH HAD BEEN chief of the Appawet Clan for a full season-cycle. She had doubled the guard along the coasts, and at her orders Beothuk tapatooks regularly crossed the bays and skirted the cliffs, keeping watch on the freshwater brooks that tumbled down from the highlands and splashed into the sea. The men had become trained warriors: they attacked and faded away almost simultaneously. Such a war of harassment was the only possible way of meeting an enemy as numerous and well-armed as the newcomers from the far-off continent. first the English, then the Portuguese. The invasion had to be stopped by some means, or it would no longer be possible to protect the abundant land that had once belonged solely to the Beothuk Nation.

The clan chief learned much from the Portuguese sailor who had been captured by the guardians. His wounds, staunched with his own hair, had healed quickly, and in less than one moon he had been put to work gathering clams and shellfish with the elders of the village. At night, Iwish questioned him at great length about Portugal. She learned that his people came to the island in search of a metal they called gold, and that possession of this metal was deemed wealth in Europe. She also learned that the prisoners taken by Captain Gaspar de Côrte Real had in all likelihood been sold in exchange for this metal, that they would then be forced to do the work of their new owners. The prisoner explained that they would be beaten and whipped, and that at the slightest sign of resistance they would be killed. She was told that in the eyes of these foreigners, anyone who did not adhere to the same religion as they did were regarded as inferior beings, lower than beasts, and that their religion then gave them the right to mistreat such beings without fear of punishment. Iwish refused, however, to treat her prisoner in the same way: it was one thing for him to be made to contribute to the well-being of the people of the island, but quite another for him to be mistreated. He would be killed if he could not be put to good use, but in the meantime there was much she could learn from this sailor.

She was surprised, for example, to discover how hated the Beothuk were by the crews of the ships that fished the waters surrounding their island. Her people were considered demons, creatures from hell, and it was necessary to kill them so that Europeans could move in and live freely on the land. All these things she was told by the sailor, whose name was Miguel Ferreira. From their conversations together, she also learned that the Beothuk were at least as intelligent and humane as the people who came from away, since they did not force other human beings to do the work for them that they did not wish to do themselves. "When we become too lazy to do our own daily tasks, there will no longer be a reason for our nation to survive," she told herself. "We will have become useless."

One night, the Portuguese sailor expressed his confidence that his people would return to the island, because the market for slaves in Europe was a lucrative one for those who could supply it. He gave her this information as a warning, and Iwish passed it along to all the members of her clan and then to all the other clans on the island of the Red Men.

Then the sun came when Iwish was informed by a paddler that the two Portuguese ships that had taken fifty-seven of her clan members prisoner the previous warm season had returned to the bay next to that of the Seal Clan, and that the guardians were preparing to attack the sailors as soon as they landed to fill their water barrels. Iwish ordered everyone in the village to prepare themselves, and sent a hundred extra guardians to increase the strength of the Beothuk defending the island against the invaders. As quietly and quickly as possible, the word was passed throughout the village, and everyone set to work, the men, women, and even the children. First, small sticks were sharpened until they were as sharp as knives, and then stuck into the ground or set into the trunks of trees so that they would tear at the flesh of anyone who brushed against them. If the village was attacked at night, as it had been the last time, these little sentries would alert the villagers to impending danger.

Meanwhile, the defence system was put into action under the direction of Camtac the Speaker. From their hiding places above the bay, guardians watched as four large rowboats were lowered from the ships, each one loaded with empty water barrels. They continued to watch as the rowboats made their way towards the brook at the head of the bay. Each rowboat contained six rowers and two sailors armed with muskets. If each rower was also armed, there would be thirty-two armed men to attack.

Camtac went to each of his archers and told him that he must take aim at a particular sailor and release his arrow, and then rush down to the shore with his spear in case the arrow failed to find its mark.

The archers picked their targets and each one placed himself in the best position from which to achieve his objective. When the rowboats landed, the sixteen barrels were rolled to the brook one at a time; two men remained at the boats, muskets at the ready, while the other sailors made their way to the creek, each with musket in hand.

When Camtac gave the signal, thirty-two arrows were released at the same time, and thirty of the Portuguese sailors fell, dead before they touched the earth. The two sailors waiting at the boat were immediately rushed. One of them had time to raise his weapon and fire at the attackers before he was hacked to pieces, along with his companion. The shot, however, alerted the sailors in the large ships, who could be seen shouting and gesticulating on the decks. The Beothuk warriors launched their tapatooks and began paddling furiously towards the Portuguese ships. In preparation, they had tied birchbark and dried moss to a quantity of arrows and placed these in the tapatooks; now they set fire to these arrows with burning sticks, and sent a volley of flaming torches into the ships' rigging and onto those areas on the decks where they could see piles of flammable materials. Soon both Portuguese ships were in flames, and sailors were jumping into the water or desperately lowering the ships' boats in order to escape. Both captains began shouting orders in Portuguese, and to some effect, since their crews could be seen to be grouping for a rush towards solid ground. The guardians waited for them in their tapatooks, which were light and much more manoeuvrable than the rowboats. There was some musket fire from the ships, and several of the Beothuk, those who had not heeded the plan to strike and retreat swiftly, were killed, making their fearlessness also the cause of their deaths, and making themselves dangerous to their companions.

As soon as the sailors stepped onto dry land they were attacked by the guardians sent by Iwish. There followed a veritable massacre: the Portuguese were slaughtered mercilessly down to the last man. The enraged Beothuk sought revenge for the fifty-seven clan members who had been taken prisoner during the previous season of new growth. They took many heads, including that of Captain Côrte Real, and these were distributed among the Beothuk villages throughout the island. The bearers of the heads were careful to avoid the sharpened sticks that had been placed around each village. They knew how and where such weapons were placed, and everyone was mindful of where not to step. That night there was a great feast, and the dancing in celebration of the Beothuk victory over the Portuguese invaders lasted until the rising of the sun. But there were many families that did not share in the rejoicing, because they were mourning the loss of those who had been killed defending the island of the Red Men.

Iwish was angry that nothing had been saved from the two ships. There had certainly been tools on board that would have been valuable to the Beothuk: axes, sailcloth, metal implements of various kinds. The Beothuk had no use for Portuguese heads. What a waste! But her anger merely told the guardians that she was a woman, and therefore never satisfied, and that all the victories in the world would count as nothing in her eyes. Only Camtac was content with his reception after the great battle. Iwish led him to her mamateek and, after making him a gift of her short sword, gave herself to him to show her gratitude for his victory over the foreign invaders. In this, however, he had to obey her wishes, even in the matter of performing his duty as a man. The clan chief knew exactly what she wanted and how she wanted it. She it was who took the initiative, who climbed on top of Camtac rather than letting him mount her. She perched upon him, her back turned to his face, so that he felt he was simply being used by her for her own satisfaction, that he was nothing to her but an implement of pleasure, not a mate participating in an act of mutual enjoyment. He was humiliated by this, but at the same time realized that he must speak to no one of his humiliation, for fear of being publicly ridiculed. If others found out how he was being used by Iwish, he would lose the status of being her favourite, and therefore would lose his influence in Beothuk society. He must keep absolutely silent about his amorous adventure.

Was he the only man benefiting from the clan chief's favours, or was he simply one among many others? If the latter, then he was not the only one to know that men, to her, were nothing but accessories in her bed, not there to dominate her but simply to serve her physical needs! He would try to find out, so that he could learn more about her ways and also so that he would not make a false step within the Appawet Clan. Since her husband had been taken by the Portuguese, this woman had lived solely for the five children the three wives had had together. Rather than take a new husband, she satisfied her sexual needs with the young and vigorous guardians under her command. It was very difficult for a guardian to refuse her, since she was such a determined woman with a strong personality. Camtac was lost in thought, and Iwish looked at him from the corner of her eye.

"Did I not give you pleasure?" she asked him.

"Yes, but I do not feel that I have conquered you."

"Conquered me?" Iwish turned and looked Camtac straight in the eye. "For longer than anyone can remember," she said, "men have taken their own satisfaction without ever asking their women whether the act had given them pleasure or not. Do you not think that it is time for such things to be reversed?"

Camtac held her eyes and spoke his mind.

"For myself, I do not see why I should be blamed for the faults of men who have lived before me. I was under the impression that you wanted to thank me for saving the island from the invaders, not punish me for something that is not of my doing. I am not responsible for the conduct of my ancestors. I am the victor over the Portuguese, not their victim. I would have been able to give you as much pleasure as you have given yourself, perhaps even more, if you had given me the chance instead of thinking only of yourself. You have shown much disrespect for me, and a lack of confidence in my abilities and character. I am not proud of my accomplishments now, and not happy about our relationship."

Iwish replaced her dingiam and made to leave the mamateek.

"There is not now and there has never been a relationship between you and me," she said angrily. "I have been pleased by you and that is all that matters to me. The next time I wish to be pleased, I will look elsewhere. You are free to find another woman who will be more impressed by your masculine pride, and more attentive to your masculine happiness."

Camtac was thoughtful for the rest of that night. According to tradition . . . But what use was it to think about tradition? Were not the events of today the traditions of tomorrow? Perhaps things are never the same for long? What good were past experiences? Could they be used to determine the actions of tomorrow? Would that make them part of a tradition? Perhaps that was the use to which his experience with Iwish could be put: to teach him that that was the path things would always take, and to help him warn the next generation so that they would not suffer from illusions, or be as wounded by their experiences as they might otherwise be. At the very least, he must not allow himself to believe that all relationships were like this one, otherwise there would be no point in continuing to live. Surely there were other ways for men and women to live; all women could not be as domineering as Iwish.

Such were the thoughts that occupied Camtac's spirit as he sat on Iwish's bed, in the mamateek of the chief of the Seal Clan. In all Beothuk memory, this was the first time that a woman had acted like a man without incurring the respect of the others of her clan. Was she perhaps a man of the female sex? Then why did she not choose females for her sexual partners? Since she did not, did that mean that men were more able than women to give her satisfaction? With these thoughts plaguing him, Camtac left the mamateek of Iwish for the last time.

But he remained thoughtful for several suns afterwards. Iwish was a very beautiful woman. She was also much more experienced than he was, and that was not always a bad thing. She was tall and strongly built, with large breasts, soft skin, and a pleasantly proportioned body despite having given birth to two children. She wore her dingiam at all times, and a short skirt open at both sides that revealed her thighs. Her moccasins had leggings, made from the legs of caribou, that protected her from branches and sharp rocks, of which there were many in the forest and along the coastline of their land. Her skin was dark, like that of the ancient Addaboutik from which she was descended, and the hair on her head was dark red, almost black. She was taller than Camtac, and he was at least a head taller than the Portuguese sailor.

Iwish had lived more than thirty season-cycles, but she was still beautiful enough to fill the dreams of the young warriors of the

Beothuk Nation. There was not a male member of the Appawet clan, young or old, who had not at one time or another imagined himself sharing a mamateek with her. It was the women who began whispering about her faults. Since she had become chief, the prestige of the female guardians had decreased steadily, while that of her private, elite corps of males had risen to eclipse them. The women no longer felt they were vital to the defence of the nation. At the same time, Iwish declared that the male population had sufficiently increased that it was now of paramount importance to protect the females, who were the reproducers of the Beothuk people. Discontent at this turn of events continued to rise. The women felt they were held in less esteem, and many of the men continued to chafe at the idea of being ruled by a woman. Consciously or not, many clan members began to look for reasons to discredit Iwish in the eyes of the men who were still loyal to her, for a way to overcome the obvious physical attraction she held for them.

33

BUT THE SUNS that passed under the rule of Iwish, the Seal Clan chief, were happy and peaceful. A sense of security replaced the uncertainty that had preceded and immediately followed her election as the leader of the guardians. Every day she was told the number of foreign ships that prowled about the island; she knew that there were more than a hundred of them, from several foreign lands, some to catch fish and others to hunt seals. There were Basques who came for the whales in the northern passage, towards the land of the Sho-Undamung, also known as Innu or Montagnais, who were friends of the French, or Malouins. There were also Portuguese, Spanish, and English vessels everywhere. By now the guardians of the nation could recognize the country of origin of these ships by the flags that flew from their sterns. The Portuguese sailor had taught them the colours and insignia of each nation. They also knew that they need only keep watch on the rising-sun coastline to assure themselves that they were not about to be invaded. The Malouins fished well to the northwest, but took on fresh water only on the north coast of the passage to the land of the Sho-Undamung, their allies. These observations were confirmed by the Portuguese sailor.

After nearly two season-cycles had passed, Iwish was informed that two more Portuguese ships had arrived off the coast, and that they seemed to be searching for the ships of Gaspar de Côrte Real. Their sailors watched the shoreline constantly from the decks. Iwish doubled the guard and assigned extra guardians to watch the village during the night, in case of a surprise attack. Around the village, workers sharpened more sticks and placed them along the creek beds, for added protection. The bays were constantly patrolled by tapatooks, so that no movement from the foreign ships would go unnoticed. One night, they saw two Portuguese ships drop anchor at the mouth of a small brook near the island where the Beothuk cut their hardwood.

Iwish ordered the guardians to attack the ships, but to return to the brook immediately after the initial raid. Camtac was still in charge of the largest group of guardians, and he knew exactly what to do and how to go about it. As soon as night fell, the tapatooks left the creek and, entering the bay, circled around the two Portuguese ships in the darkness. Before long they saw a large rowboat filled with sailors make its way from the ships towards the hardwood island. Five tapatooks silently followed, and when they came within range the guardians let loose a hail of arrows into the Portuguese rowboat. They were so close that they could hear the sailors cursing; many of them were hit before the rowboat even reached the shore. When the sailors tumbled out onto dry land, they turned and fired their muskets into the darkness, but the Beothuk warriors were shielded by the night, and none was hit. More rowboats were lowered from the main ships, but by the time these reached the island the Beothuk had disappeared, vanished into thin air, as Iwish had instructed. When the sun rose the next morning, twelve sailors lay stretched out on the beach, killed by the arrows and hunting spears of the invisible Beothuk raiding party. The surviving sailors gathered driftwood and began to prepare their food, but as soon as they lit the fire a fresh volley of arrows killed a dozen more. Once again they fired their muskets blindly, this time into the thick woods, in the hope of hitting the ghostly Savages. Once again, no one was hit. When the sun had mounted high in the sky, the sailors on the island watched as fifty or more Beothuk tapatooks left the creek opposite and headed towards the two Portuguese ships, firing flaming arrows into the sails and rigging as soon as they were close. They saw hundreds of Beothuk warriors climb up the ropes hanging over the sides of the ships. There followed a horrific battle; terrible screams could be heard coming from the burning vessels. The sailors launched their boats and rowed furiously to the aid of their countrymen, but by the time they reached the ships the Beothuk once again were gone. The Red Men lost twenty guardians, but the Portuguese losses were at least three times that many.

The Portuguese captain was Miguel de Côrte Real, the brother of Gaspar. He ordered all his men to arm themselves and attack the Savages in force. But no sooner had his men reached shore than half of them were levelled by a single flight of arrows, and the other half immediately turned and rowed back to the Portuguese ships, which were still burning. Côrte Real could do nothing but raise the anchors and let the ships drift towards land. They soon beached on the sandy shore, and the sailors worked to put out the flames lit by the Beothuk torch-arrows. But they suffered more losses in doing so, since the Beothuk guardians took advantage of the diversion to launch their tapatooks and shoot at the sailors lined up along the shore like so many ducks as they passed buckets of water to fight the fire. Côrte Real fired cannons at the Savages, but managed to overturn only one tapatook, and all five guardians from it were rescued by their fellows. Then, as at a signal, all the Beothuk disappeared. The Portuguese thought they had been frightened off by the cannons. But that night, the Red Men descended again upon the beached Portuguese vessels. This time they climbed aboard and quickly killed all the remaining Portuguese. The head of Miguel de Côrte Real, like that of his brother before him, was severed from its body and exhibited in all the Beothuk villages for almost an entire moon, until worms began to wriggle from its eye sockets. This time the tools from both ships were salvaged and distributed among the Beothuk villages. The unburned sails were cut up and used to make new mamateeks and to wrap up provisions for the coming cold season. Iwish was satisfied with the result of the battle. The Portuguese would now know what to expect, even though not one member of their expedition had survived to tell the tale of the massacre. When the guardians had set fire to the two ships, they released the Portuguese sailor who had been their prisoner for almost three season-cycles. He was given a tapatook and a paddle and told to carry the news of the great battle to the foreign fishing boats that were waiting at the periphery of the Red Men's island, and to tell the foreigners that the Red Men would defend themselves without mercy from any future Portuguese invasion.

For five season-cycles after this battle there was peace on the island. No foreigners dared to land for fresh water. The Red Men were savages, they said, barbarians who would no longer trade for their water with any foreign nation. They guarded their coasts so fiercely one would think the very rocks contained some precious metal, perhaps the very metal that all European explorers were looking for. The rumour began to circulate on the fishing grounds that the island of the Red Men did indeed contain vast quantities of this precious metal; if not, how to explain the jealousy with which these people protected their land from foreign invaders?

After each victory, Iwish continued her habit of rewarding one of the guardians by inviting him into her mamateek. And each time, the young warrior would leave her bed feeling frustrated and angry. He may have enjoyed a new experience, but he knew he had simply been an instrument of pleasure, at the service of a woman. Because he himself was unsatisfied by the experience, he would let it be known that the clan chief was herself insatiable. She became known as "the devourer of guardians," and she did nothing to prevent the rumours from spreading. She gave birth to two more children, neither of whose fathers were known. If their mother knew their identities, she kept the secret to herself. She would allow no competition for her role.

Iwish, the hard one. Iwish, the devourer of guardians. Iwish, the protector of the Beothuk nation. Iwish, the uncontested chief of the Appawet Clan, the Clan of the Seal. That is how she would live in the memories of all the Beothuk on the island of the Addaboutik, the island of the Red Men. The nation's Living Memories would be sure to relate the story of her life for a long time to come. But Iwish was still at the head of the clan and leader of the guardians when six of her own clan members were taken prisoners by a French ship while they were crossing the northern passage to the land of the Sho-Undamung. That was the beginning of the end for the clan chief. She was reproached for allowing the six brave warriors to cross the channel without a proper escort to protect them from attacks by the foreigners. They held her responsible for not foreseeing the danger: Must not a chief be something of a sorcerer? Must she not be able to see into the future if she is to have the honour of leading her clan through it?

Not one man who had been frustrated and humiliated by her in her bed would come forward now to defend her. Any man who did would have been ridiculed throughout the Beothuk Nation. He would have been called her love slave, and would not have been able to bear such an insult. It was therefore true that Iwish had not understood her own weakness or foreseen her downfall. She, the devourer of guardians, was devoured by her own failure to guard. This was an unpardonable crime. Her closest friends abandoned her, and the other clan chiefs, the members of the national council, did nothing to save her. Iwish's mistake was to have been right so often and for so long. She was guilty of doing nothing to prevent the deaths of six clan members, even though she had saved hundreds from being captured and sold as slaves.

She had neglected to boast of her accomplishments, to broadcast each victory and describe her own role in them. She had been totally unaware that the six warriors were planning to cross the northern channel to the land of the Innu, but she now had to expiate her guilt by removing herself from the position of clan chief, even though she would long be remembered.

She passed into the Living Memory of the Beothuk. A leader, even a leader in bed, cannot make mistakes. As soon as she was shown to have made one, she died by her own hand. That is how Iwish died many season-cycles before her actual death. The Living Memory would remember her in the future; why, then, would people try to glorify her in their memories of the past?

She had no choice: she was told she could no longer direct her clan because she had lost the trust of her people. She moved to a remote part of the village with her seven children, and lived in a mamateek she made herself. She was avoided by the other villagers. Her children had no friends. When one has lost one's usefulness to the nation, one cannot hope that one's children will be successful. Iwish could no longer find anyone to share her bed, and no one came to ask her advice, despite her great knowledge and past experience. She was not even allowed to become an elder: she had made too many enemies and her judgement was no longer valued.

Iwish, the first woman of the Beothuk Nation to become a chief, no longer existed. Many chiefs before her had made mistakes, some of them more serious than hers, but they had been male chiefs. Iwish's fault was that she had been an authoritarian female, determined and sure of herself. She spent the rest of her days eking out a small existence. Her children took care of her. She never lacked for food, her daily rations were always sufficient. She suffered only from loneliness, from having no friends to talk to. She suffered from the knowledge that none of her children, no matter how competent or talented, would ever be called upon to fulfill a public function in the Beothuk Nation. She suffered even more from being forgotten by those she had once favoured over others. And she suffered these things without complaint, with as much pride as any male would feel. Forgotten by her contemporaries, she was remembered by the nation's Living Memories only as a woman who had been right too often. Even in these former times, women, important though they were, could expect justice only from those whose sole duty was to remember.

34

FOR HIS MILITARY successes, Camtac was named the new chief of the Appawet Clan and leader of the guardians of the Beothuk Nation. He, too, was a direct descendant of Anin, the ancient hero of the Beothuk Nation and the first of the great explorers. But Camtac had not been the only candidate. The council had thought of placing Woodamashi in the position. Woodamashi was the Messenger, the one who carried the news from village to village. He was always jovial, well liked by all and ever ready to be of service. But in the end Camtac was chosen for his exemplary courage and his cunning. A man's value was still measured by his deeds. Twice had Camtac defeated the Portuguese, the slave-trading invaders who had come to the bay south of that patrolled by the Seal Clan village. Twice had he and his guardians exterminated the vermin that came from Europe, the continent where every nation was at war with every other nation.

Together, Camtac and Woodamashi planned the repeopling of the island. For several season-cycles the nation had suffered severe losses. Men had been killed in battle or taken by slavers. Women once again outnumbered men in the villages. Because of its location, the Seal Clan village had suffered more losses than the others, and many men had been killed. Polygamy was once more practised in the village. Woodamashi carried this news across the island.

As an example to his people, Camtac took three wives. For twenty-three season-cycles he reigned as chief of the Appawet Clan and leader of the guardians without once having to go into battle. He led his people in total and complete peace. A wise man has said that it is often necessary to live through war in order to understand peace, and perhaps it is for that reason that warriors are often chosen to become leaders of nations. Certainly it is true that the Beothuk's lives had been greatly disturbed by the foreigners' invasions of their land. They had seen the invaders take their fellows to become slaves. They had even had to establish a second corps of elite female warriors to replace the men who had been taken prisoner by the Portuguese. A female warrior did not always produce children for the nation. And a mother does not raise her children to watch them die in battle. Or, worse, to see them become slaves to foreigners.

Camtac was a tall man and very thin. His long, gaunt face and sharp eyes gave him the appearance of a marten. His arms were long and well muscled. His legs were long, too, but powerful. His body had been hardened by his training as a guardian: for example, he could run for many suns and never tire. Throughout his life as a warrior he wore only a dingiam to cover his sex. During the cold seasons he wore a vest and sleeves made from caribou skins. His leggings were also made from caribou skins, turned fur-side in. His face and body were painted with red ochre powder, and his clothing was decorated with alternating yellow ochre and black stripes. To denote his authority he always wore a leather belt with the short sword that Iwish had given him when she was still young and beautiful and he had shared her bed. He was a decisive leader, very slow to change his mind once he had reached a decision that he thought was right. He listened to his councillors, however, and followed the traditions of the nation rigorously. His courage was unquestioned; gladly would he have sacrificed his life to save the nation or any other Beothuk. He lived first for the good of the people, second for his family. His own wishes and desires came last, after all his other responsibilities had been met.

He had a daughter, Ooish, so called because of her full, red lips and her independence of spirit. She was always talking, and was one of the elite female guardians of the Beothuk Nation. But there was nothing mannish about her. She was tall and thin, agile as her father, good-natured and playful, everything a man could want a woman to be. She refused, however, to settle for second or third wife, or to let a man provide for her. She preferred being a huntress and a warrior, to be free and not, as the saying was among the women of the village, married off. In age she was twenty season-cycles, and had been raised during the time when monogamy was the custom among the Beothuk. As the daughter of the clan chief, there were many youths who would marry her, but none of them would guarantee that she would be his only wife. She discouraged all suitors, and prided herself only on her skill at the hunt, her facility with weapons, and her prowess at wrestling. Her favourite weapon was a large hatchet, which she could wield more effectively than a spear in everything except fishing. She could hit a moving target with this hatchet at fifty paces.

It was not long before she had risen in rank within the corps of elite guardians. She had fine leadership qualities. But her father, Camtac, warned her constantly of the danger of taking on the role of leader without the unanimous approval of the community. Without it, at the first sign of weakness support would be withdrawn from her, by the very people whose lives she was protecting. He pointed to old Iwish, to whom no one in the village would speak a word and who lived alone in her mamateek, an outcast. Iwish was always being cited as a bad example to young women who were strong-headed and rebellious. Do not fall into the same trap as Iwish, they were told. As a result, these young women were careful not to excite the jealousy of men. With the exceptions of Woasut and Gudruide, the first two women to change the customs of the Beothuk people, women were still considered inferior to men. Such thinking was still firm in Beothuk traditions. It was better that way. Women were represented on national council, as they had been for five hundred season-cycles, and they should be satisfied with that. They were not to irritate the men for fear of stirring up the kind of competitiveness and frustration that defeated Iwish, the devourer of guardians.

Ooish was aware of these taboos, and observed them rigorously in all her endeavours. Although she was clearly qualified to serve as a leader of the guardians, she refused to act as their chief. She believed that an older woman would have more authority and be better able to maintain discipline and direct training. She loved to train, but she preferred to do so by herself rather than as part of a group. She wore her hair pulled up tight on her head and tied with a single cord, in the traditional Beothuk manner, so that it appeared to fall over her forehead like water bubbling up from a spring. During the warm season, her hair was the colour of dried grass, although it darkened as the seasons grew colder. Like her father, she wore only a dingiam and short leggings tied just below the knee; the rest of her body she covered with red ochre. Her leggings were the same colour as her skin, and were decorated with the outline of a seal, the emblem of her clan.

Once, when the members of the female corps of guardians were bathing in a lake of clear, calm water, two young men from the clan passed by and were invited in by several of the bolder women to help them wash. The two men removed their dingiams and jumped in without the slightest hesitation, to cries of delight from the women. It was not long before the men were showered with offers, and one of the women even dared the men to prove their virility by servicing as many of the women as they could manage. The contest was on. One after the other, the women knelt before the men to be serviced. This was not an occasion for romance, but for competition, and when the two men left the guardians' camp at sunset they were utterly exhausted. Ooish had observed the festivities, but had not joined in. As long as women behaved in such a manner, she told herself, men would always consider themselves to be their superiors. News of the orgy spread quickly throughout the nation, and the two men who had serviced fifteen women were acclaimed as men of great strength and fortitude, worthy to engender many new Beothuk. They were practically hailed as heroes. Ooish was disappointed in her fellow clan members, who apparently valued quantity over quality. She longed for tenderness, softness, mutual respect. Not serial servitude. She swore she would never give herself to anyone who took such pride in physical performance alone. She had often spoken of this aspect of love with her mother, one of her father's three wives. She had learned that Camtac was gentle and thoughtful, and never boasted of his prowess at being able to satisfy many women in a single night. Her mother told her that her father was discretion itself, and each of his wives enjoyed his complete attention when he was with her. That is what Ooish wanted: a man who was content to be with no one but her.

It was Camtac's twenty-sixth season-cycle as chief of the Seal Clan, and also the twenty-sixth season-cycle of Ooish's life, when three ships dropped their anchors in the cove south of their village. Ooish was at the head of a unit of fifty elite female guardians that watched as a large detachment of sailors rowed ashore to fill their barrels with fresh water. The ships were flying the flag of France, and the men were small. But there were too many; there could be no question of attacking them. The women continued to watch. One of the sailors attracted Ooish's attention. He was at the centre of the detachment, and stood at least a head taller. His hair was the colour of dried grass.

The sailor who seemed to be in charge of the detachment led several of his men, including the tall man, towards a wooden structure in which the Beothuk kept their cold-season stores. This was a sort of compound made of stakes driven into the ground and covered with an old sail from one of Côrte Real's ships, taken thirty-six season-cycles ago. It was filled with seal-skins. Ooish saw that the men took nothing from this structure, which made them different from all the other foreigners, who freely took what they wanted from such places. The tall man was standing at the edge of the shoreline, close to the trees from which Ooish was watching the sailors. He was carrying a weapon the Red Men of the island called a firestick. Ooish stood up and called softly: "Bouguishamesh."

The man turned and looked into the woods, showing no sign of being startled. He moved towards Ooish and left the beach just where she was hiding. Soon they were trying to communicate, but neither could make sense of the other's tongue. The man was dressed in a curious fashion, a black, sleeveless vest over a red shirt. His trousers were tight to his legs and ended just below the knees, and his lower legs were covered with thin stockings, as red as his shirt. On his feet were the same sort of shoes the captured Portuguese sailor had worn: Ooish's father had kept them to help him remember the man. The back parts of this unusual footwear were held off the ground by small blocks of wood, attached under the heels, which forced the wearer to walk either leaning forward on the balls of his feet or set back flat on his heels. Ooish thought that either way they were not meant for walking through a forest, and even less for chasing game. The wooden blocks also had the effect of making the man seem taller than he was; when he took his shoes off, Ooish saw that in reality he was no taller than she. He was, however, still taller than the rest of the ship's company.

When the others returned to their ship, they were short one man. His name was Jean le Guellec, a Malouin, and he stayed with Ooish, the daughter of Camtac. He kept with him nothing but a sort of firestick he called a blunderbuss, and a small pouch filled with black powder and metal pellets, which he called shot. Ooish took him to the camp of the female guardians and invited him into her mamateek, where she gave herself to him as she had never given herself to a Beothuk man. She found the French sailor handsome and very much to her liking. Although she could not converse with him, they were in perfect harmony together.

Jean le Guellec was kind and attentive to Ooish, everything she had dreamed of in a man, and she made every attempt to be the same to him in return. She felt herself filled with such deep joy that she could hardly wait until the morning to tell the other women about it. Her story of this night of love made more than one woman envious, and soon many tongues were passing the news throughout the island of the Red Men. For his part, Jean le Guellec had no desire to return to serve under his captain,

Jacques Cartier. He did, however, go back to the Bay of Catalina and convey to a comrade that he intended to remain on the island, and that Captain Cartier need not send a shore party to search for him. Deserters were severely punished on French ships, but le Guellec returned his pay to Cartier and hoped that this would incline the captain to overlook his departure. All captains, he knew, were fond of money and other forms of wealth. After making these arrangements, le Guellec returned to the guardians' camp and spent many happy suns with his wild woman of the New Found Land. When, ten suns later, Cartier ordered his men to weigh anchor, he had had no encounters with the Beothuk himself, but had lost to them a sailor who had decided that life among wild, Red Savages on the island was more agreeable to him than one on board a Malouin ship of exploration in the service of France.

Le Guellec had led his captain to believe that the Savages of the island were ferocious and uncivilized, that they bound their hair at the tops of their heads and that it was not wise to get in their way. In fact, le Guellec had at that time never seen more than one or two male Beothuk, and knew nothing about them except what he had learned from the women of the elite corps of female guardians, and from Ooish, whom he had known for only ten suns. The Addaboutik had assimilated another foreigner into their clan, and the guardians undertook to teach him their language. He was given the name Wobee, which meant white: Cartier left the island without trying to recover his lost crew member.

Ooish hesitated for many suns before returning to the village to introduce her father to the man with whom she wanted to live. She feared the chief's reaction, since Wobee had not made an official representation to Camtac for his daughter, as was the Beothuk custom.

She was afraid of her father, who was a kind and sympathetic man when it came to the needs of his neighbours. The people held him in great esteem as a brave warrior who had fought many battles. And yet, despite his fine character, people were reluctant to ask favours of him. This Ooish must do, and soon, since she was certain that her father would already have heard that she had taken up with a man. News travelled quickly on the island of the Beothuk, especially when the women of the elite corps of guardians got wind of it.

On the path to the village, the Malouin realized that his fine shoes had not been made for walking in the forest or on the rocky footpaths of the Red Men's island. He gladly took them off and accepted a pair of moccasins from Ooish. The moccasins were finely sewn from caribou hide, and were the colour of a woman's skin before she covered herself with red ochre. They covered the ankle as well as the foot, and were secured by two flaps below the knee.

This former sailor from the ship of Jacques Cartier also quickly learned that no cloth as thin and fine as the cotton from which his hose were made would last long in the rough environment of the New Found Land. They were soon reduced to rags by the pointed branches that protruded from the trees along the path, by sharp rocks and evergreen shrubs. The skin under this meagre material was also soon covered in scratches, scrapes, and bruises. The abrasions on his legs were so painful, in fact, that he began to miss the smooth decks of the French ships, and the cobblestones of his native village in France. But Ooish was very beautiful, and so passionate that he decided to suffer patiently and continue on his way to the Seal Clan village.

35

WOBEE WAS PRESENTED to Camtac, chief of the Seal Clan, leader of the nation's guardians, and father of Ooish. Camtac welcomed Wobee with a smile, saying that he must now learn to live like a Beothuk. Then Camtac turned to his daughter and asked her: "Are you his wife already?"

The young woman nodded Yes, and looked at le Guellec. The Malouin seemed taken aback by the direct question, not knowing if Ooish's father would accept their relationship. Using the few words he knew of the Beothuk language, he asked Ooish if he would now enjoy the same benefits as one who had been born a Beothuk.

Ooish said that he would, but added that this did not mean he was permitted to have more than one wife. She would not tolerate that. Camtac asked le Guellec if he accepted those terms.

"I do," said the Malouin, explaining that that was the custom in his own country, where a man never took more than one wife. Christianity forbade it, and he had been born a Christian.

"I declare you committed the one to the other and to the perpetuation of the Addaboutik race," said Camtac. "You must cover yourself with red ochre so that you will appear as the other members of the Beothuk Nation. Ooish will show you how. I am now old enough to withdraw from the affairs of the nation. You and the other clan members must choose my replacement from among the people of the clan."

That night, the clan council met and considered three candidates: Whitig the Arm and two women, Wedumite Who Embraces and Ooish the Lips. When the council was ready to discuss Ooish's candidacy, Camtac rose to leave, explaining that it would not do for his presence to influence the other councillors. He knew his daughter too well.

"In which case," the clan elder said to him, "you would be abdicating your responsibility as chief, which is to designate your own successor."

Hearing these words, Camtac answered that he would see his duty to the end, and remained seated in the council. He was opposed to those who would have a woman as chief, saying that he had lived during the time of Iwish the Devourer of Guardians, and had in fact been one of her victims. He believed that a male chief would do a better job. However, the other council members, including the clan elder, believed that choosing a female chief was no less appropriate than choosing a male.

"Your daughter is as knowledgeable in the bearing of arms as she is in the duties owed by a woman to a man. I do not understand your objection to her nomination! Furthermore, she is a direct descendant of Anin and Woasut, the first couple of the Bear Clan. Our tradition maintains that any descendant of our first couple is qualified to assume the leadership of the nation, and therefore is qualified to become a clan chief within the nation. My choice is therefore Ooish, leader of the guardians."

The other council members spoke in agreement, and Camtac had to accept their decision so that the deliberations of the council would be unanimous, as was the custom. That night there was a great feast-for-everyone on the shore of the bay at the mouth of the Exploits River. A new chief had been elected according to ancient tradition, and she was a descendant of Anin the Voyager, the hero of the Beothuk Nation. That she had chosen a Bouguishamesh for a husband was also according to the tradition started by Anin, who had had four wives, three of whom had come from other lands. Such mixing of blood strengthened the nation and improved the viability of future generations.

The new chief of the Appawet Clan accepted her election by giving her word that she would do everything in her power to conserve the unity of the Beothuk land. She proposed that Whitig become leader of the guardians, and that Wedumite take charge of the elite corps of female guardians. She promised to raise these candidates at the next grand council meeting, scheduled to take place during the moon of the longest sun of the season-cycle, which was to be the next moon, to be held at Red Ochre Lake.

After the feast, Ooish coupled with her new husband, Jean le Guellec, named Wobee. He was attentive during their coupling, eager to satisfy the desires of his wife. He thought it amusing to be both her husband and her subject, and teased her as she lay on their marriage bed.

"When we are here in our mamateek," she replied seriously, "I am your wife and simply a Beothuk woman. But when I am sitting in council, I am the chief. There is no need to confuse the two responsibilities. If I do, then it will be impossible for me to govern all members of the clan equally. You must remember that, and you must also remind me of it if I appear to forget. It is very important to me."

And they slept in peace, each in the arms of the other.

The nation's affairs proceeded as might have been expected. As a descendant of Anin and Woasut, Ooish was responsible for ensuring the repopulation of the island, and this required her to re-establish the rule of polygamy among clans in which there were more women than men. But she would not allow that rule to apply to herself. This caused her to be criticized by the other women of her own clan, as well as by the nation. When she learned of this she confided in Wobee:

"I do not know what to do," she told him. "It seems I have failed in my responsibility as a wife and a clan member. The need for polygamy is obvious, and yet I have made myself an exception to my own rule. This has put me in an embarrassing position with the other women. What do you think?"

"I would not object to having a second wife," said the Malouin, smiling, "or even a third. When you give birth to the child you are carrying, I will be required to take a replacement in any case. Otherwise we would not be contributing to the repopulation of the island, as you have ordered us all to do. If you are jealous, you could be the one to choose my other wives from among your friends. That way, you would be able to choose women you could control. In any case, you would always be my first wife."

Ooish thought for a long time before falling asleep in the arms of her Malouin husband who had become a Beothuk.

When Wobee woke up, Ooish was already gone. He stepped out of the mamateek and looked about for her. A young boy stopped and said to him:

"Ooish has gone to the female guardians' camp. She said she would return before nightfall."

There was nothing for Wobee to do but wait for Ooish to return. That, he reflected, was the chief occupation of the husband of the chief of the Seal Clan: to wait. When the sun was setting, Ooish came into their mamateek accompanied by two other women. The first was short and plump, the second tall and thin, like a rougher version of Ooish, without her attractiveness.

"These are the women I have chosen for you," Ooish told Wobee. "The name of the first is Obosheen, She Who Warms. The second is Badisut the Dancer. They have agreed to be your wives. Remember that you must honour them within the mama-teek. If you do not, I will consider you to be unfaithful, and I will kill you with my own hands. They have been informed of these rules. I want to know what you do with them. They have accepted this condition. Do you?"

Jean le Guellec, a Malouin formerly of the ship of Jacques Cartier, now Wobee the Beothuk, gladly accepted this condition, eager as he was to ensure the continued happiness of the household and of the clan. That night Obosheen, the fat one, asked to be served first. Their coupling had little tenderness and few caresses, but Obosheen seemed satisfied and soon went to sleep – in the arms of Badisut. The Frenchman, although he had been embarrassed to couple before two other women, also went to sleep without complaint.

The following morning Ooish took the two women to each mamateek in the village and introduced them as Wobee's new wives, thus putting an end to the murmurings and criticisms of the other women. She had now done her duty as a wife and a woman, like all Beothuk. At nightfall, there was singing and dancing in the clan chief's mamateek, by Ooish and Badisut. This was followed by two sessions of coupling, one with Badisut and the other with Ooish, after which the Malouin sailor slept soundly. The first session he had performed in a half-hearted manner, but the second, with Ooish, was a revelation to the new wives, who learned for the first time why Wobee referred to coupling as "making love." They followed the lesson closely, realizing that the act was more complex than the simple back-and-forth thrusting they had experienced before. They saw that the same kind of tenderness that existed between women could also exist between Ooish and Wobee. They had never suspected that it could be so . . .

It was still dark when a young hunter came to the mamateek of the clan chief. Everyone awoke.

"A pod of white whales has entered the bay," he told them. "It passed close to the islands and has not taken the deep channel back out to the open sea. Now is the time to hunt them. Everyone in the village who is available must come, quickly. An opportunity like this comes only once in the life of a hunter. Quickly. Get up. We must get some long cutters. Everyone, down to the beach!"

And he was gone as quickly as he had arrived. He could be heard rousing the other mamateeks: "White whales! White whales!" The whole village was awakened. The hunter had given Ooish a more detailed report so that she would be aware of the situation, but also as a way of telling Wobee that he too was expected to take part in the hunt. Nonetheless, it was with an ill grace that he searched in the darkness for his moccasins and dingiam. Ooish told him they were unnecessary, since he was going to get thoroughly wet in any case.

"Whether you are in a tapatook or on the beach, you will be soaked."

"I don't know anything about this hunt."

"Just do what the others tell you to do."

She left, naked except for her dingiam, ready to go to work. His two other wives, both experienced hunters and guardians, led Wobee to the beach, where fifty tapatooks were already lined up. Old Camtac explained to the paddlers that their job was to turn the whales back towards shore by forming a cordon across the mouth of the bay and beating the water with their paddles. Two paddlers per tapatook, no more. The others must stay on shore to assist in cutting up the whales and boiling the fat.

While the paddlers sprang into their tapatooks and set off, staying close to the shore so as not to chase the whales out of the bay, the older women lit fires on the beach. Around each fire they arranged birchbark containers that could be sealed shut with pine resin. On one fire they placed a large metal cauldron, obtained by trading with the last ship that had been allowed to take on drinking water.

The beaters had surrounded the pod of beluga whales, which had just discovered the deep channel to the north of the Island of Exploits. The tapatooks lined up across this channel, completely blocking it, then the paddlers at the bow of each tapatook began hitting the water with their paddles while the stern paddlers slowly moved the tapatooks towards the beach. The confused whales raced towards shore. The first to arrive near the beach were the juveniles.

As soon as a whale surfaced in the shallow water, two or three hunters closed in with their spears and harpooned the animal at its main artery, on the right side just below the vent. The whale lost all its blood very rapidly, and died. Then the women and the older men waded in and began cutting up the whale with semicircular cutters attached to the end of long poles. The cut pieces were as long as a man's thigh and the thickness of a hand. The youngsters carried the pieces to shore, where the older women attached them to tripods close to the fires, and placed birchbark containers beneath them to catch the dripping oil as the flesh baked. When the strips were partially cooked, the women removed them from the poles and placed them in the cauldron, into which they had already put equal parts of fresh water and saltwater. The whale meat was thoroughly boiled, to be eaten as soon as the hunt was over.

In such manner, twenty-two white whales were killed and rendered. The entire bay was red with their blood. The youngsters, despite being tired from the hard work, laughed and teased one another.

The meat from such a hunt would last the village several moons. Such an opportunity to hunt sea animals from the beach came only once every ten or fifteen season-cycles, and it was important to take advantage of it. Hunting white whales the usual way, from a tapatook, was dangerous: one tapatook in three did not return from such a hunt. The unfortunate hunters, usually the younger and least experienced ones, made the mistake of placing their tapatook behind the whale, where the animal could upset it with a single swipe of its tail. Or else, having harpooned the beluga, an inoffensive but powerful creature, they allowed it to drag them along until it decided to dive before the men could untie the cable. Many families mourned the result of such carelessness and inexperience.

Only one death occurred during this shore hunt: a young man had been too close to a whale's tail end when the animal tried to escape, and he had been thrown onto a rock that stuck out of the water. His skull had been fractured, he had lost consciousness and never awakened. His loss was regretted, but compared to the losses of a traditional whale hunt, the village counted itself lucky.

Wobee was impressed by the Beothuk's hunting methods. Nowhere in Europe had he seen whales caught in such a manner. There the animals were chased by oarsmen in swift whaling vessels. The harpooner threw his weapon and the oarsmen braced themselves against the whale's flight and sounding. Beothuk tapatooks could never withstand such force. The Malouin had learned much. He admired the ingenuity of these people, whom his countrymen termed "primitive and barbaric Savages."

"We Europeans are an ignorant lot," Jacques Cartier's former crew member told himself: "We talk about wanting to kill these people. I will do my best to prevent that from happening."

He helped carry slabs of whale meat and blubber to the cauldron until the setting of the sun. The villagers had been working since before sunrise, without a single break, adults and children alike. Only the three wives of the Malouin had slept, and they, too, had worked hard.

36

OOISH'S CHILD WAS a male. He had hair the colour of red ochre, his skin was light, and his eyes were very big. He had, however, a blue spot on his abdomen, like all the Addaboutik, indicating that he was a true member of the race of Red Men even though his father was a Malouin. He was a healthy child and the delivery was easy, and he was a strong child because he had been delivered in the traditional way. Ooish did not lie down during the birth, and she had no need of another woman to clean the child and cut the cord. For three whole moons Ooish had drunk an infusion of white birch leaves, an oily beverage that facilitated childbirth in women having their first baby. It also worked for later children; it was a beneficial drink that prevented all complications.

Wobee was very proud of his first-born son; he cuddled him and took him up in his arms, and talked to him as though the infant could understand every word. Sometimes he spoke to him in French, sometimes in the Breton tongue, the language of his ancestors who had been conquered by the French. The child would grow up speaking three languages, like his father. But he would be an Addaboutik, a member of the Beothuk Nation, an inhabitant of the island of Anin, the ancestor who first travelled around it, more than five hundred season-cycles before, during the time of the Vikings and the first women with pubic hair. It was now common to see women with pubic hair and with hair under their arms, but in Anin's time, the time of the ancestor, women did not have such coverings. It was the Viking women and the Scots woman Della who introduced this feature into the Beothuk lineage. And body hair in men came from Drona, the former Scots slave whose entire body had been covered with hair, like the body of Gashu-Uwith the Bear. But Drona's hair was red.

Wobee's apprenticeship was long and difficult. He was learning that it was no easy thing to become a Beothuk. First he had to learn to light a fire using two small sticks of dry wood. Before coming to the island he had known how to make fire using a small stick with a ball of sulphur at its tip – a device the French called an "allumette" – or by striking a fire-stone against metal, or even by igniting a small amount of gunpowder. But never before had he seen anyone make a fire by rubbing two sticks together using a small bow, as the Beothuk did. The men in his family had all been mariners, fathers and sons, and they knew that oak was the best

wood for building ships. But they knew nothing of the many qualities of the birch tree, the Beothuk tree of life, which even provided
them with nourishment. There were birches in France, to be sure,
but the French were ignorant of the tree's virtues. Birchwood was
sometimes used for trim in shipbuilding, but no one had thought to
make canoes from birchbark. Snowshoes were unknown in Europe,
as were sleds for pulling heavy loads through snow. Ropes had been
made from hemp for many years, but European women did not
weave dried grasses into cords fine enough to be used as rabbit
snares. Such work even among the Beothuk was a rare skill, and
those who had mastered it sold their wares.

Jean le Guellec travelled in the interior of the island, visiting
all the Beothuk villages and clans. He was guided by Camtac,
who also taught him much about the Beothuk way of life. First he
taught the Malouin about survival. Le Guellec swiftly learned
that if he were abandoned on this island he would soon perish
from starvation or cold. He compared the extent of the knowledge of the Red-Ochre people with that of his own people, and
discovered that Beothuk knowledge was put to use every single
sun, not just on special occasions. He learned that true knowledge
came from studying one's surroundings, not from a school. The
French had adopted an alphabet so that they could read and
write. By so doing, it seemed, they had lost the kind of knowledge
that came from their environment. They could no longer read
the wisdom of nature and the elements. Only sailors could still
read the sea and the weather. Mariners were the only ones left
who were close to nature. There were many new inventions, such
as gunpowder and firearms, but these were instruments of death,
not aids to survival.

Slowly but surely the Malouin learned the Red Men's way of
life. He learned which forest plants were needed to heal wounds,
how to survive in the season of cold and snow, never to refuse aid
to another, since life often hung by a thread when one was alone
in the bush. The only way for people of nature to survive was to
help one another. Together, anything was possible; alone, life itself
was difficult. Wobee learned to respect the other creatures of the

forest, the animals and the plants. He learned that plants and trees were living beings. He learned that the trees, the plants, and the animals were possessed of souls, and that they suffered just as human beings suffered. He learned many things of which he had been ignorant before coming to the island. He learned that here there were no privileged classes, no masters and no servants. All beings were equal, and women, although less important, were nonetheless equal to men. He learned that women had been taking part in the political life of the nation since time out of mind, and that the Living Memories encompassed all eternity. He struggled at times, but he learned. Camtac told him that his apprenticeship would last his entire life, and that his most important legacy would be what he could teach his children while he was alive. Total knowledge came only with death and reincarnation as a new being. That is how men accumulate knowledge. In one life, one learns enough for that life. After reincarnation, one teaches what one has learned to others, passing on to future generations the memory of those that have gone before. That is how a people, a nation, survives. All the knowledge one man has is worth nothing if it is not passed on. And knowledge that is passed on is worth nothing if it is not understood. That is why it is necessary to keep one's ears open to listen, and one's eyes open to see and to understand. That is the secret of Beothuk existence. That is why the Beothuk will live forever, according to Camtac, even after the last Beothuk has died. The Beothuk will continue to live through others. In the memories of others. In the teaching of others. Camtac said that the Beothuk were without end. The Beothuk were life itself. There will always be Beothuk in the world. As long as there was knowledge to teach and to learn. The Beothuk were the true men. There will always be something for true men to learn. Their need to learn, to know, and to give, is without end.

The Malouin listened to the father of his first wife without once interrupting him, which was one of the first Beothuk rules.

"If you want to learn, you must watch and listen. Do not ask needless questions. You might force a person to lie. Remember the words of Anin the elder about lying, which he spoke during his long voyage. Lying is bad and the liar deserves to die. Lying is death. Only the truth exists. Only the truth deserves to live. Lying kills, it kills from the inside by eating the guts of the liar. The ugliest truth is worth more than the most beautiful lie."

As they travelled to the many villages on the island of the Addaboutik, the Red Men, the Malouin, the former member of the crew of Jacques Cartier, thought that if lying killed the liar, then all Frenchmen would have been dead a long time ago.

The journey was a long and exhausting one. The two men stopped at a food cache, where the Beothuk laid away provisions for the season of cold and snow. The caches were placed a half-sun apart between each village, so that travellers could eat without having to carry heavy loads. They served as the stages in a journey from one village to another. It was necessary to know the correct path in order to find them, because they were not always placed in plain view of any casual passerby. One had to know the ways of the Red Men to find them. Camtac knew these ways well. He was a cultured man. Even if he forgot all that he had learned in his life, his culture would remain with him, because culture is what is left when all learning has been forgotten. Culture is life. Culture is group instinct. The right way to prepare food. The right food to prepare. Culture is being. Without culture, without daily life, there would be no dancing and no singing. Songs teach. Dances teach. Culture lives. That was the teaching of Camtac, elder of the Appawet, of the Beothuk Nation, of the Addaboutik, of the New Found Land.

The two men took caribou meat from the storehouse and cooked it over a fire using branches from the Beothuk tree of life. They were careful to close the entrance to the cache to prevent animals from stealing the meat that belonged to the humans of the great nation of Red Men.

The two men, from different worlds, returned to the path leading to their home village on the Bay of Exploits, the scene of Anin's triumph over the Ashwans who were pursuing Woasut. When they arrived, they were welcomed by their people as heroes who had come a great distance. The two men had been travelling for three whole moons, and were very glad to be back among their people, and their own families. When Wobee entered his mama-teek, his three wives gathered eagerly around him. He thought he was going to be embraced, but as soon as she was close to him Ooish backed away.

"You stink," she said to him. "Have you not bathed for three months?"

The Malouin admitted that it had never occurred to him. "It has not been warm enough since we left," he said.

To which Ooish replied that if all Beothuk refrained from bathing except during the warm season, then the foreigners would smell them from across the sea, and have no desire to land on their island.

"And you would be the first man I would refuse to make love with. Go and wash yourself. I want a man who smells like a man, not one who smells like sweat. Go wash in the river and come back to honour the three of us. We have been waiting for three months."

Wobee made his way to the river moaning and groaning that this Beothuk habit of washing was going to be the death of him. He could catch a cold and die from an infection of the lungs. No one should take their clothes off during the winter, when it was cold.

When he was clean, he returned to the mamateek where his wives were waiting for him. He told them about his journey with Camtac and everything the elder had taught him. The three women were astonished at how much he had not known. A nation of warriors like the French, able to construct huge ships that could withstand the worst storms at sea, a nation that knew how to make fire by striking small sticks against a rough surface, that could make guns that killed from a great distance, and yet did not know the beneficial properties of a birch tree? Unbelievable! The Beothuk women were shocked at the apprenticeship this Malouin sailor had had to undergo in order to enter the Red Men's world.

When the conversation died down, the women said that it was time for Wobee to honour them. The Breton-turned-Beothuk was able to satisfy two, but to perform the act a third time was too much for him, and his third wife complained loudly that she had been neglected by a husband who had been away for three months, so loudly that the people in the neighbouring mama-teeks could hear her complaints, although they did not interfere in any way. When their husband, exhausted, fell asleep, the two wives who had been satisfied consoled the wife who had not, so that peace would return to the family of four.

In the morning, Wobee awoke with the intention of satisfying his third wife, but he found himself alone in the mamateek. All three women had already left to assume their daily tasks.

"Too bad for her," he told himself. "All she had to do was stay behind. She scolds me for not honouring her, and then when I am ready to honour her, she is no longer here."

He put on his dingiam and his moccasins and also left the birchbark mamateek. The sun was very warm and bright, even though it was the season of falling leaves. It was the time for hunting. Wobee had to learn the methods the Beothuk used to prepare for the season of cold and snow. The young people of the village told him that they were leaving to hunt caribou. Realizing that he must prepare for the hunt by making arrows and hunting spears, he went into the forest to look for straight trees that would serve for spear shafts. As for arrows, he had seen the elders cut wood and dry it so that the ashwogins would be light and yet strong. He had also watched them make the strong bows needed to hunt the larger animals.

He had already become proficient in the use of such weapons, since his blunderbuss was no longer useful, having run out of powder and shot. He had practised pulling the bow for many suns before he was able to rely on such primitive but essential tools for survival on the Red Men's island. After much practice, he had become skilful enough that he no longer invoked the laughter of the children, who were always eager to make fun of the smallest mistakes. He had not yet acquired the skill of his first wife, Ooish, who could hit a moving target with her hatchet from fifty paces.

When he had cut a dozen good trees for making spear shafts, he tied them together, lifted them to his shoulder, and returned to the mamateek. Using a very ancient tool consisting of a metal blade with two wooden handles, which the village had received in trade from a ship that had come for fresh water, le Guellec began to shave and smooth the round shafts of the spears until they were small enough to fit comfortably in his hand. This operation took him almost two complete suns. When the shafts were ready, he took them to young Bashubut the Scraper, who was the most skilled in the village at splitting flintstone to make spearheads. From Bashubut he received ten points, whose wide ends were grooved in such a way that they could be attached to the spear shafts with thin cords cut from sealskin. When he had tied the points to his ten shafts, he secured a length of thin cord to each point. When the point entered the animal, it became detached from the spear shaft. If the animal died right away, or very soon, the point could be retrieved from the carcass by pulling on the cord. If the animal did not die immediately, by pulling on the cord and removing the point from its body, the hunter caused the animal to bleed excessively, so that it would die rapidly rather than suffer for many suns.

Satisfied with his new weapons, Wobee entered his mamateek to attend to his three wives and his son.

37

WHEN THE MOON of the falling-leaf season was half dark, thirty hunters left the village of the Seal Clan for the interior, travelling towards the mountains that ran the length of the island, from south to north. It was time for the herd of woodland caribou on the island of the Red Men to migrate to the highlands, as it did every autumn, to return to the moss pastures in preparation for the season of cold and snow. Some of the women, children, and elders would follow the hunters later, to skin the animals they killed, seal the meat in birchbark containers, and build caches in which the provisions would be stored for the winter. The hunters' first task was to locate the herd and to make a barrier across its migration route, in order to direct the animals into an enclosure where the hunters would be waiting for them.

The hunters split into five groups and went off in five different directions to look for the caribou. As they were travelling lightly, carrying few provisions, they had to hunt small game along the way for their food. Rabbit snares set the night before provided their morning meat. Fine-meshed nets were set to catch the willow ptarmigan. And beaver from the inland lakes provided the hunters with excellent meals. Sun after sun, the hunters watched the animal trails, waiting for signs that the caribou herd was on the move.

Early on the seventh morning, a hunter ran into one of the camps to tell his companions that he had seen the herd heading straight for the great clearing, which was only a sun's march from Red Ochre Lake, where the Bear Clan had its village. The messenger and the others of his group had to tell the four other groups to meet at the clearing. The Bear Clan hunters would surely be the first on the scene, and it was important that all the meat be evenly divided between the two clans. Two men left to go towards the cold, now called the north, and two others went south, to find the rest of the Seal Clan hunting party. Wobee was left behind to make his way directly to the great clearing, to arrive there before the caribou, and to begin constructing the enclosure. When he caught up with the herd, he made a wide detour around it, so as not to frighten the animals, who were moving in a leisurely way and grazing on tree moss. It took Wobee two suns to reach the clearing. Many hunters from his own clan were already there and had started to build the pole enclosure. The next morning, hunters from the Bear Clan arrived to help the Seal Clan. The enclosure was completed in two suns. There was an opening on one side. When the caribou entered the enclosure, the hunters had only to place more poles across this opening, and the slaughter could commence.

Then the beaters left and formed a huge circle around the caribou herd. On the morning of the third sun, they began to walk simultaneously towards the herd, making as much noise as they possibly could in order to drive the animals into the enclosure. Hunters with their bows and lances waited for two more suns before the first caribou trotted into the clearing. Wobee had been placed in a group of beaters, so that he could learn from the more experienced men on either side of him. The job of his group was to prevent the caribou from leaving the clearing once they saw the enclosure. Several times, at great risk to their lives, they ran in front of the animals, especially the females, to prevent them from breaking through the line of beaters. When the first caribou, a female, arrived at the end of the fence, it hesitated before entering the enclosure. Three hunters were posted at each end of the enclosure, a hundred arrows piled beside each of them. Four lance-throwers stood behind the section of the enclosure called the cap. Their job was to finish off the wounded animals that were slow to die. At the edge of the forest, twenty young, strong men were ready to carry the dead animals from the enclosure to the skinners and preservers, where the animals would be dried and smoked, ready for the birchbark containers. One container for one caribou, complete with its tongue, brain, heart, kidneys, and liver.

Some of the women had laid fires, and near each fire was a drying rack. Others had made smokehouses covered with birchbark, and had lit small fires inside that would produce great amounts of smoke. They had also readied piles of wood shavings, which had been soaking in birchbark containers of water. When the fires were lit, they would throw the wet shavings on the flames, and the resulting smoke would do a better job of preserving the fresh meat when it was placed in the storehouses.

At first, everything went well. Then the main body of the herd, frightened by the beaters, charged as one to the end of the enclosure, running right over the animals that were already dead, so that the young carriers could not remove the carcasses. Two of them were trampled by the panicking animals' sharp hooves, and were seriously wounded. Panic spread to the hunters surrounding the herd. Caribou carcasses piled one on top of another, live caribou were charging back and forth, and finally the wall of the cap collapsed. The four lance-throwers behind the cap were crushed by the wall, and two were killed, their faces pounded by the hooves. Many animals escaped into the forest.

Unaware of the catastrophe that was taking place at the end of the enclosure, the beaters continued to drive more caribou through the opening, making as much noise as they could and thereby making the situation worse. The wounded carriers and bowmen were taken out as quickly as possible, and other hunters took their places, but by then the entire caribou herd was in a panic. Animals ran about in all directions, charging the walls of the enclosure until one whole side collapsed. The herd then rushed towards the opening, forcing the carriers and skinners to flee. The smokers also ran to get out of the way of the stampeding animals. Only the driers remained at their fires, and they were kept busy because they were attending to the wounded, whose number was constantly increasing. When a runner finally reached the line of beaters to tell them to stop, there were thirty gravely wounded men lying on the ground. A hundred caribou were dead, but four hunters had paid for them with their lives.

Work went on around the wounded, for the animals had to be cut up and the meat carried to the fires to be smoked and dried. The survival of the Beothuk people depended on it. No matter how many setbacks hit them, they could never lose sight of the fact that the nation's survival depended on the annual caribou hunt. Some of the wounded hunters had been trampled by the caribou's sharp hooves and had open wounds in their chests and abdomens, and on their legs, arms, and faces. Others had suffered broken legs and arms. One of the younger hunters was so disfigured that he was almost unrecognizable. Two of the dead had had their skulls crushed, and the two others had smothered to death under the collapsed wall when the caribou stampeded over them. Never in Beothuk history had a caribou hunt turned out so badly. A fatal error had been committed: the enclosure walls had not been reinforced by poles angled outwards to hold them up. Also, the walls had not been built high enough; the caribou had been able to see over them.

Several elders began to sew the wounds of the hunters, using long hairs taken from the heads of the fallen. The women searched for pitcher plants to make a paste to apply to the wounds that were too large to be sewn closed. Others fashioned splints with which to bind broken limbs. The disfigured young man moaned that he would rather die than live without a face. He was blind, but he still tried to find a weapon with which to take his own life. It took four people to hold him still.

When the beaters arrived they beheld a scene of indescribable horror and confusion. The blood of a hundred animals mingled with that of the dead hunters. No words could adequately describe the nightmare that greeted them on that field of death. The work of cutting and smoking the caribou meat, and mending and cleaning the many wounded, lasted three whole suns.

Wobee was in a state of shock for several hours. An elder told him that the next hunt had to be better planned and certainly better executed. The former Frenchman who had sailed under Jacques Cartier felt partly responsible for the human slaughter: he told himself that the beaters should have gone more slowly so as not to panic the caribou. Although the elders told him that it was the hunters' inexperience that had caused their deaths, Wobee did not believe them. He kept himself busy comforting the wounded, devoting himself to their care, and he made many new friends in both clans, the clan of Appawet and that of Gashu-Uwith. His dedication was noticed by all, and he acted like a true Red Man in their eyes. No longer was he looked upon as a stranger.

The young man whose face had been destroyed, whose name was Dogermaït the Long Arrow, was relieved by a dressing of healing herbs and no longer spoke of killing himself. His instinct for survival was returning. He even joked about his wounds, saying that from now on he would be known as Ashmudyim the

Evil One, the devil with the face that frightened children. Slowly, calm returned to the Beothuk people. It was decided to build a storehouse for the meat on the very spot where the acci-dent had taken place, as a way of reminding future hunters to take more care. The members of the Bear Clan suggested that all the wounded be carried to Red Ochre Lake, which was close by, until they had regained their strength. Then they could return to their proper villages. Half the wounded were Bear Clan members anyway. From then on, Dogermaït was called Ashmudyim the Evil One, but always with a smile, so that he would not be offended by his own joke.

Of the original thirty hunters belonging to the Appawet Clan, only fifteen took the trail back to the sea. Almost all the women and elders returned within a few suns. The hunting during this season of falling leaves would be remembered for a long time. Dogermaït chose to return with the hunters rather than stay behind with the Bear Clan. He wanted to be among his own clan members, despite his new ugliness. Most of all, he wanted to rejoin his companion Addizabad-Zéa the White Woman, to see if she would accept his disfigurement or be repelled by it. Would he be able to remain with his clan, or would he always frighten others? Since he still had two good legs and two good arms, he made the return journey without too much help. He had the use of only one eye, however, and often stumbled over objects on the ground. When he had to descend a steep slope and cross a stream by stepping on rocks, he said that since he could see only half of what he once could, he had to be twice as careful. The first time he fell a comrade reached out to help him; he erupted in anger. "I do not need anyone to help me correct my own errors," he said firmly. "If I have to learn how to do everything again, then I must do it on my own."

His companions complied with his request. When he tripped a second time, then a third, no one in the file tried to help him. They pretended not to notice, and several of them actually made a detour around him to avoid being tempted to help him when he blocked the path. Weakened, but with tremendous courage, he picked himself up each time. Even though the wounds on his face and his punctured eye caused him terrible suffering, he did not complain once. He managed to keep up with the other hunters. He would not become an object of pity to the other clan members. He would learn again how to be a fully participating member, completely capable of fulfilling his role for the well-being of the community.

Despite the young man's pride and determination, Wobee could not help keeping an eye on him. What courage he was showing, and what a will to live! The Malouin spoke to him from time to time, trying to understand certain attitudes and habits of the Beothuk. Amiably, without showing the slightest impatience, the wounded man answered the Malouin's questions, perhaps glad that he was still able to be useful despite his condition. Perhaps also Ashmudyim treated Wobee kindly because Wobee had tended him so devotedly after his injury. During the seven suns it took the hunters to reach their village by the sea, the two men became closely bound in friendship. They would remain so until one or the other left on his final great voyage.

When the village was but half a sun's walk away, the hunters sent a runner ahead to announce their arrival and to say that one of the men was wounded, so that the shock of seeing him would be lessened for his family.

38

WHEN THE HUNTING party left the forest edge and walked into the clearing where the Appawet Clan had their village, they were greeted by a large group of fifty children. Among them stood a beautiful young woman. She did not move, but her eyes searched among the hunters for her husband, and as soon as she saw him she ran towards him and threw herself into his arms.

"Dogermaït," she cried. "How happy I am to see you again, safe and healthy."

Gently, the wounded man pushed her away from him. "I am not Long Arrow any more," he said to her. "Now I am Ashmudyim the Evil One, he who frightens children."

"No, you are not!" cried the woman. "To me, you are still Dogermaït, the best archer on the island of the Red Men."

"Even with a face that looks like trampled grazing ground?"

"Even if you had come home in pieces," replied his wife, whose name was Addizabad-Zéa.

The young man embraced her and held her close, though he was careful to keep his bleeding face from touching hers.

Wobee was astonished by this scene. The young woman had not shown the slightest hint of disgust at her husband's face, even though it had been cut to ribbons by the flint-sharp hooves of a dozen caribou. How would the children react, he wondered? Their response could be decisive for the mutilated young man. But they made no allusion to the man's terrible wounds. They were not repelled by the sight of his disfiguration. On the contrary, they flocked around him.

"Dogermaït, when are you going to tell us the story of the hunt?"

The young hunter was so moved by this welcome that he began to cry like a child who has been taken from his mother. Still the children fired questions at him.

"How many caribou did you kill?"

"Did you miss many?"

"Where did the chief of the hunt place you?"

"Tell us the whole story."

"When are you going to tell us?"

When the young man was finally able to speak, he said: "As you can see, there was an accident during this hunt. The caribou used my face for their escape route and turned me into Ashmudyim the Frightful. I am surprised that you even recognized me!"

To which one of the children replied: "Your body and your heart are still the same. You didn't fool us!"

This caused the young man to burst into tears again, and even the other hunters had to keep tight control of their emotions. The brave man had almost died trying to procure their winter provisions, and everyone was aware of that fact.

"How can we call you Ashmudyim?" the children asked. "You are our hero. You are Dogermaït, he who shoots the longest arrows and is the best archer of the Beothuk Nation."

Once again regaining his voice, Dogermaït announced that at the clan's feast-for-everyone, which was to take place in two suns' time, he would tell them the story of the hunt from the beginning to the time he was wounded. Those who saw the accident would have to take the story from there. He explained that he first wanted to spend some time with his wife, his father and mother, before beginning the story. He thanked the young people for not making fun of his disfigurement. The youngsters had acted instinctively in accordance with Beothuk tradition: No one has the right to laugh at the misfortunes of another. Dogermaït asked them to leave him in peace for the time being.

"I desperately need to rest," he told them.

The youngsters were hardly gone when the parents of all the hunters arrived on the scene. Some of them shed many tears when they learned of the death of the four young men. Others were relieved to hear that their absent sons were resting at the village of the Bear Clan until they were strong enough to return to their own village. Dogermaït's father and mother took their son into their arms to show him how joyful they were that he had returned. Wobee watched their displays of affection and learned much about the great solidarity shared by these people, who were called blood-thirsty Savages by the Europeans who wanted to take the fish from their very waters. How could anyone have any idea of the degree of civilization attained by a people until they had lived among them? Le Guellec thought that though he no longer lived among his own people, and sometimes missed them, he would never regret having left the ship of Monsieur Jacques Cartier.

39

WHEN HE ENTERED his mamateek, Wobee found his three wives lying in one another's arms, hugging and kissing one another and obviously giving themselves a great deal of pleasure. He was scandalized by the sight. He started shouting and waving his arms, saying that in his country such behaviour was condemned by the Church and abhorred by all decent people. Ooish replied that in France a man had only one wife to satisfy, and even then, as had been told by Anin's Viking wives, no sooner was he away to sea than his wife found a replacement for him in her bed!

Jean le Guellec declared that what they were doing was an offence to nature and to God Himself. Badisut laughed at that, asking him when was the last time he had seen this God of his, and what had they talked about, since he seemed to know so much about the Creator's thoughts.

"You have a great deal of nerve, talking to us about God as though He were your best friend. We know nothing of your God, but we do know that Kobshuneesamut the Creator has never spoken against what we are doing. We would surely know if he had. Our God allows us the freedom to be ourselves. Why does yours want to come into our mamateeks and tell us what to do and what not to do? What does he gain from becoming involved in our private relations?"

Then Obosheen tried to explain that in a household of three wives, jealousy is the worst enemy. Without it, she said, there is friendship and agreement, which can grow into mutual tenderness.

"When a man goes away and leaves his wives unsatisfied," broke in Ooish, "what do you think they should do? Dry up? Rub themselves against trees? Only birch trees are smooth enough for that. The others have rough bark that scratches our soft skin. Beothuk women have satisfied each other since the beginning of multiple marriages. It isn't our fault that there are more women than men. As long as we don't neglect our duties as wives, we have been able to take our pleasures where we find them without being made to feel guilty about it. We have not deceived you with other men, nor even with other women. We have remained faithful to ourselves."

Badisut told him about the discussions that had taken place in the Grand Council during the time of Anin and his four wives. Only one of them had been Beothuk, but the others became friends of the Beothuk.

"As far as I know, there has always been peace in our households. Is that not what it means to respect our traditions? There are no specific rules about friendship between women in the Beothuk tradition. But what you tell us about your country says nothing to us about ours. We are Beothuk, not French. Our obedience is to Beothuk customs, not to French laws. Our friendship may anger you, but I think your anger is a form of jealousy. If you took care of us in the customary way, our little caressing sessions would be much less frequent. But do not come in here and accuse us of doing wrong. We have caused no problems among our people. We have preserved an atmosphere of understanding within our household by respecting Beothuk customs. And we have done our duty to the Beothuk Nation by increasing it with your babies. Ooish is going to have her second child during the coming season of cold and snow, and the others of us will give birth when the season-cycle begins again after that. Were you even aware of that? Have you shown any interest in us at all? You have nothing with which to reproach us. You also benefit from the peace that is in this household, so you must leave us to our friendship if you want it to continue. Never again reproach us for showing our tenderness and love."

Presented with these arguments, Wobee was silent and thoughtful. What would happen if the men outnumbered the women, he wondered? That thought had no doubt occurred to others before him. "Perhaps I should speak to Camtac," he thought. "He has an answer for every question. Maybe he will enlighten me."

Wobee left the mamateek and walked to Camtac's dwelling. When he arrived, he asked his father-in-law to accompany him to the seashore, so that he might seek the old man's counsel.

Camtac took up his walking stick and followed. He did, indeed, have answers to the questions posed by the Malouin.

"We often discussed these practices you speak of at the national council fire," said Camtac. "We came to the conclusion that as long as the women did not neglect their duties as wives we could hardly prevent them from giving pleasure to themselves, since it was we who had asked them to share a single husband. The council has no authority to dictate conduct within families. Its only concern in that area is to make sure that the birthrate is maintained. If there are sufficient births, what more can we ask? It is true that our tradition does not speak of this practice, but why should a person's pleasures be controlled by tradition so long as his or her duties are being fulfilled? If women began to prefer such pleasures to repopulating the island, then the council would be justified in stepping in to remind them of their responsibilities. But I do not believe that is the case here, and so I would not be concerned about it. I have often seen our young men seek such pleasure among themselves when they are deprived of women, as when they are on long hunting and fishing journeys. I do not think the nation has been made weaker by such things. Or that we have become less attentive to our duties. I think it must be the same for all peoples who live as we do, the men being away from their women for many moons at a time. One thing I can tell you, such practices are never found among wives chosen from the same family. Sisters never show such tenderness and affection for one another. Sometimes it exists between cousins, or between an aunt and her niece. On the other hand, if a man marries sisters and shows too much favour to one of them, there are often disgraceful scenes between them, acts of mutilation and sometimes murder. You must therefore pay heed to this more than to excessive affection between wives."

Wobee listened, and the old man continued.

"Do not compare the customs of your old country with ours. You are living as a Beothuk now. Always remember that, and you will commit no more errors that threaten the peace of your household."

While the two men continued their walk along the beach, children played freely about them and couples walked hand in hand. It was one of the last beautiful evenings of the season of falling leaves. Saying he was very tired, Camtac left Wobee and returned to his mamateek. In reality, the conversation had stirred his sexual appetite, and he was eager to hasten back to satisfy his desire with his new wife, who was twenty season-cycles younger than himself, and who had recently replaced Camtac's first wife, the mother of Ooish, who had died the previous season of new growth. She had died of a fever that was new to the Beothuk, and against which their herbal medicines had proven ineffective. Wobee recognized one of the couples on the beach; it was Ashmudyim and Addizabad-Zéa, walking with their arms around each other.

That night, Wobee the Malouin watched Ooish and Obosheen making love-between-women while he was honouring the tall dancer, Badisut. Everyone went to sleep feeling happy.

In the morning, he asked his wives if they had ever seen two men satisfying each other. All three women laughed, and Badisut asked him if he was looking for a male partner. He also laughed, then, realizing the naivety of his question. Never again in his household was the friendship between wives called into question; from then on, their mamateek was a place of complete freedom. During the season of cold and snow, Ooish gave birth to a second son, and in the season of new growth Badisut had a girl child and Obosheen had twin boys.

Wobee continued his apprenticeship into the life of the Beothuk people on the island of the Red Men. He also occupied himself with his growing family, as all Beothuk fathers were required to do to assure the continuity of the race, the nation, and, above all, of the family.

Ooish remained clan chief until she reached the age of sixty-eight season-cycles. She had four children, Badisut had five, and Obosheen four. In all, there were seven male and six female descendants of Jean le Guellec, the sailor from Saint Malo in Brittany and the former crew member of the French explorer Jacques Cartier. Though a foreigner, he was welcomed into the heart of the Beothuk Nation on the island of the Red Men. He grew old and wise, and no one noticed any differences between him and any other Red Man on the island. His conduct had, quite simply, made a man of him. Because of his generosity and devotion, he was a friend to all. Since the time of the four foreigners who had come with the ancestor Anin the Voyager, no other adopted member had been so completely integrated into the nation. Wobee did not attempt to change the Beothuk people into copies of the French. He knew too well that he would never be able to weaken the power of the traditions that had been established by Anin more than five hundred season-cycles before, and kept alive by the Living Memories of the nation. Since they had a history that had lasted so long, how could he, a simple sailor, hope to change their way of seeing the world?

When Ooish became sick, she did not suffer long. The fever took her in only a few suns. Such medicine as was known on the island was not strong enough to save her. No one understood how a person who had been so strong could, in so few suns, become too weak to fight off this mysterious sickness that was attacking the men and women of the island.

Jean le Guellec, who as a Beothuk was called Wobee, did not take a new wife when Ooish died. He continued living with the two wives she had chosen for him, and educating the children she had borne him. Badisut the Dancer was taken as quickly as Ooish, and the Malouin found himself alone with his small, fat wife Obosheen, She Who Warms.

40

THE OLD, WHITE-HAIRED man, who was the Living Memory of the Beothuk people on the island of the Red Men, sat on his rock beside the beach fire and continued speaking to the young people who had been chosen to replace him as holders of the history of their people. The group who listened to him was composed of a dozen adolescents of both sexes, each of them eager to learn the traditional values and knowledge of the past that would help them in times to come. They let the old man recount his tale of the Beothuk without interruption, so that nothing would cause him to become confused in his telling of the stories of their ancestors.

"When I tell you of all these hardships," he said, "it must seem to you that they will go on without stopping, forever. But our people have also experienced hundreds of season-cycles of peace and contentment as well as extraordinary events. When Ooish died, her place was taken on the council by her oldest son, Ahune. He was reasonably well experienced and spoke his mother's language, also that of his Breton father, as well as the language of the French.

"Under his governing, a new policy was born. The island was opened to strangers. Eager to know more about the way of life of those from other lands, he decided that we must be more welcoming to the newcomers. The next time a ship entered the bay, Ahune did not prevent the foreigners from landing. He had never known war and the sadness of losing his parents and friends to kidnappers, and so he welcomed the Englishman Martin Frobisher with open hospitality, and traded with him for much iron. Then he accepted Frobisher's invitation to go on board the English ship, although he took with him an armed escort of twenty guardians, whereupon the same thing happened to him as had happened on the ships of Cabot and Côrte Real: his guardians were overcome and sent ashore on boats, and Ahune alone was taken prisoner by the Englishman. Although we managed to kill five of the foreigners, we lost another of our chiefs.

"He was replaced by a member of the Otter Clan from the River of Gulls, a man named Gigarimanet the Fish Net. Despite his mistrust of foreigners, he agreed to take in two English couples and three Basque sailors who had been abandoned on our shore by the captain of a ship that was sailing along the coast. It was also during Gigarimanet's time that a man representing the King of England landed at St. John's Cove and declared that from then on our island belonged to his king. This was the worst thing that had happened to us. From that time on, our island no longer belonged to us and we had to compete with newcomers for our food. This was the beginning of the war. Whenever our guardians saw a ship entering a bay, they alerted all the island and we chased the ship back to the open sea. Between each attempted invasion, we would have ten, fifteen, sometimes twenty season-cycles of peace. Whenever the peace lasted too long, our young people would begin to criticize our council members. They would reproach Gigarimanet for always making decisions on his own, without consulting the people. 'When I make a decision,' he would say, 'it is because I have given much thought to the matter. If I make a wrong decision, you will have only me to blame. None of you will have to bear the guilt.' Then he would say, 'The worst danger is believing that many empty heads are more valuable than one full one.' When he was criticized for being too lenient in his stand against the English, he would reply: 'Have we been at peace too long, perhaps? Do we need more battles to remind us how sweet it is to be at peace?'

"He would also say something that you must remember in the future: 'Being defeated is bad for a nation. But being victorious is not always good, either. How many lives must we sacrifice to gain a victory before our cries of joy are drowned out by our lamentations for the dead?'

"These are words that you would do well to remember before you criticize those who prefer peace to war.

"For a long time our Beothuk people of English origin would go to the peninsula near St. John's Cove to learn what the English who landed there were doing. One day they told us that the English were planning to place a permanent settlement there, and that the leader of this movement was a certain John Guy. At the end of an unusually warm season, a ship entered Conception Bay and sailors from it built a fortress of pine logs. The logs were placed lying down, not standing up as is our custom. To show our good faith, we left provisions for them for the season of cold and snow, but when the snow melted they left. Two season-cycles later, in Trinity Bay near Eagle Rock, eight fishermen from the Seal Clan met with this John Guy and traded with him, giving him food in exchange for metal tools. One of our English clan members agreed to meet with John Guy at Trinity Bay the following warm season, telling him that all the Beothuk people would be present at this meeting. When the next growing season arrived, eight hundred members of our nation gathered on the shores of the bay to meet with John Guy. When an English ship entered the bay, our people paddled out to meet him in their tapatooks, to accompany his boats to the shore.

"Then suddenly the eight fishermen who had met John Guy the previous time shouted in alarm that this was not the same ship. The tapatooks tried to return to shore, but they were too late. The ship's cannons thundered, and despite the attempts by the paddlers to avoid the cannon balls, many of our tapatooks were hit, and many women, children, and elders were killed and drowned. One hundred people in all. Wobee the Malouin, the elder of the Seal Clan, escaped the massacre. He was more than one hundred season-cycles old, but he was still very strong and was able to swim to shore.

"That was the end of Gigarimanet's time as chief. He was replaced by his harshest critic, Shéashit the Grumbler. I have been told this part of the tale by Wobee himself. This was the end of the line of chiefs that were descended from Anin, the hero of the island. This Shéashit formed a new clan, which he called the Rabbit Clan, to show how little respect he had for the tradition of the spirit protector. He established this clan on the large Bay of Odusweet, where Anin spent his third season of cold and snow with Woasut, and where his son Buh-Bosha-Yesh was born. It was in this part of the island that Shéashit made his name when he defeated a company of French soldiers that had come to kill all the Beothuk on the island.

"These soldiers, armed with muskets with long knives attached to their ends, were all dressed exactly alike. They wore leggings the colour of snow and vests the colour of the sky just before nightfall. At first light, when the soldiers were occupied with mosquitoes and blackflies, Shéashit's men killed seven of them and cut off their heads so that they would not be recognized by their families in the Afterlife. On the second sun, when the soldiers were marching in closer formation, the guardians killed nine more of them, and cut their heads off also. Then on the third sun, twenty-one more soldiers lost their lives and their heads. Not a single surviving soldier had seen a Red Man, and since the blackflies had all but blinded them, they turned and raced back to their ship. Our people had enjoyed a great victory without losing a single warrior. That is the story of the glory and adventures undertaken by our people.

"Knowing what was to follow, it seems to have been a small victory.

"The English were becoming more and more numerous in the large bays along our coast, and the strange sickness continued to afflict our people, a sickness for which our herbal medicines and the skill of our medicine men could do nothing. Wobee told us that even in his former country, the medicine men were powerless against this sickness. When a person, usually a female, came down with this strange fever, she began to vomit and was unable to keep food in her body. After several suns, red marks would appear on her arms, face, and other parts of her body. Then she became very sick and died almost right away. It was at this time that Wobee, who was born Jean le Guellec, was found dead in his mamateek.

"It was also at this time that the Shanung, also called the Mi'kmaq, pretended friendship with us but were actually in the pay of the Malouins. They cut the heads off four of our guardians who were protecting the southern coast of our island. The Shanung who lived at Bay d'Espoir were our friends, but those from St. George's Bay we killed. During a feast given by Shéashit and others of the clan that lived on River of Gulls, some children came and told Shéashit that the heads of four of our beloved guardians had drifted in in their tapatooks. Shéashit's men therefore went out and cut off the heads of fifty-four Shanung, after warning their friends, the Sho-Undamung from the north coast, that this was none of their affair. When the account was settled, the feast was resumed.

"These same Sho-Undamung invited the Beothuk to come and live among them before they all died at the hands of the English, or the Malouins, or the Shanung. That was when Shéashit conceived his plan, the last chance for the Beothuk. It was becoming quite clear that living close to the sea on the island was too perilous, and so Shéashit convinced the other clan chiefs that their only hope for survival was to attack the English and chase them off the island.

"Keep these stories in your memories, my young friends, so that the Red Men will live forever. You are the nation's future. Remember Anin, the ancestor of us all, and you will live forever in the memory of he who was the bravest among us."

41

ONE MORNING FIFTY paddlers in ten tapatooks set out to cross the Strait of Belle Isle, an expedition led by Shéashit to the land of the Sho-Undamung. Each tapatook carried five paddlers carefully chosen by Shéashit: they were the fifty strongest warriors of the Beothuk Nation. Strong, fearless, and so brave that Shéashit himself could hardly hold them back. These were the warriors who had collected the fifty-four Shanung heads during the feast at St. George's Bay. They were the most devoted of men and the most worthy of confidence.

The crossing took only as long as it took the sun to reach its highest point in the sky, even though they paddled against a strong wind. If the weather were favourable, the return journey would take still less time, since the wind would be at their backs. For those who do not know the tricks of the wind and the treacherousness of the waters that pass through the strait, this crossing can be a true adventure. But these men had made the crossing before, and to them it was unexciting. It had become easy to travel to the country of the Sho-Undamung, also known as the North Shore Innu. In fact, the crossing was called "the passage to friendship." The strait was also familiar to the young people, because it was the perfect place to hunt belugas and other whales. During some crossings, the white whales would escort the fleet of tapatooks to the north shore. The Beothuk would then know that the weather would remain favourable for the rest of that sun. It was almost as though the whales brought the good weather to the Red Men of the island. When the mammals remained hidden, it was a more difficult crossing. Whales do not like bad weather and storms, and stay longer under the water.

On this day, the Beothuk were escorted by two humpbacked whales and two narwhals throughout the whole of the crossing. They were so curious and kept so close to the paddlers that twice the tapatooks almost capsized. However, these incidents brought only shouts of laughter from the warrior paddlers. To them it was nothing but a moment's diversion. They teased one of the younger guardians, saying he had fallen in love with one of the whales. "Don't get so excited," they said to him, "or we'll all take a bath. If you can't control yourself, jump in and go for a swim with her, so we can complete the crossing safely."

Even though crossing the strait had become child's play, the warriors had not neglected to arm themselves well. Living Memories still told of the six warriors – in some accounts there were seven – who, a long time ago, had been captured by a French ship. Furthermore, each had prepared for the crossing by undergoing a period of sexual abstinence that lasted half a moon. Then, when they arrived at the large bay at the start of the crossing, the men had gathered before a fire and devoted themselves to Kobshuneesamut the Creator, and asked for his protection for the well-being of the nation. No warrior worthy of the name ever asked the Creator for something for himself. This period of preparation and gathering had been so intense that some of the participants entered into a trance and remained prostrate on the ground for two and sometimes three suns; the others waited patiently for them to come back to themselves, with much respect and without talking. Silence was the rule so long as one person remained in the gathering. During this ritual, no food was eaten and water was drunk only when thirst became overpowering.

On the night before the crossing, a small ceremony took place during which each warrior received an amulet from each of his companions of the crossing. The amulets were tokens of mutual devotion that united them in case of danger. Each giver of an amulet was promising to come to the aid of all others during the crossing.

When the paddlers reached the coastline of the north shore, nearly two hundred Innu were waiting for them, chanting and singing. The arrival of visitors was always an excuse for a large feast. They held a macoushan, a sort of feast-for-everyone, after which some of the hardier young people danced until they collapsed from exhaustion. The Beothuk were welcomed with open arms. The Red Men presented a striking contrast to these Sho-Undamung. They were much taller than the Innu, who were small and stocky. The Beothuk's legs were strong, while those of the Innu or Montagnais seemed weak and short. The Beothuk's arms were long and muscled; those of the Innu were shorter, but also well muscled. The Beothuk laughed a lot, but were no match in this area for the Sho-Undamung, who laughed constantly, at anything. Nothing seemed to bother them; they were always playing tricks, some of which were outrageous to us but seemed necessary to them to maintain their courage.

The feasting lasted so long that the Beothuk were unable to return on the same day, as they had planned. The Innu women were very interested in these tall, strong men from the island. Conjugal fidelity was not one of the Innu's virtues, and many were the moans and amorous groans coming from nearly every habitation that night. The Beothuk were very well treated during their stay among the Sho-Undamung.

The Sho-Undamung chief's name was Wapistan the Marten. When he saw so many tapatooks approaching from the island, he thought the entire Beothuk Nation was emigrating to his shores. He had invited Shéashit and his people to come and live among them, and when he realized that this was not why they were coming, he was disappointed. Shéashit explained to him that he wanted the Innu's help in putting his war plan against the English into action. Wapistan listened to the request without interrupting the son-in-law of Wobee the Malouin.

The plan was to attack the English colonists from two directions at the same time. The Sho-Undamung would attack from the sea, and the Beothuk from the land. They would cause as much damage as possible to the colonists who were spread out along the coast and on the islands. These colonists had firesticks and knew how to use them. When the firesticks were aimed at someone, that person almost always died.

"Their weapons are more powerful than ours. They do not even need to come close to us in order to kill us."

Wapistan smiled and let Shéashit speak on for a while. Then he said he knew about these weapons; he and his men already had ten of them.

"The problem with these weapons," he told Shéashit, "is that we must depend on the French to supply us with powder and shot. And the French make us pay dearly with skins in exchange. One rifle costs fifty beaver skins. A pound of shot is ten marten. A pound of powder, two beavers."

The situation was clear: the wise old Wapistan was waiting for the Beothuk chief to make him an offer. Shéashit thought it over for a moment.

"We will give you enough skins to pay for the powder and shot you use during the battle," he said. "We will place these skins at the mouth of the large bay at the beginning of the crossing. How many do you want?"

Now it was Wapistan's turn to think.

"We have ten French rifles and will need enough ammunition for twenty shots from each rifle. We will bring the arrows and spears for hand-to-hand fighting. My men are not as large as yours, but as you know they are all valiant warriors. That makes one hundred beaver skins and twenty seals."

"How many men will you send to help us?" asked Shéashit.

"About a hundred. In twenty-five canoes."

"In that case, everything will be ready for the attack."

Their conversation continued late into the night. The two men drew up a plan that allowed them to attack simultaneously on all fronts. They decided that the first attack would take place in Notre Dame Bay and on the nearby islands. The time was quickly chosen for the attack, and for the retreat and the many other preparations. There would be a smaller engagement prior to the main attack, in Gander Bay, two days before Notre-Dame, which was exactly one moon away.

As soon as it was light, the fifty Beothuk paddlers were ready to return to the island. The weather was promising, and all the Innu gathered on the shore to bid safe voyage to the Red Men. The tapatooks were launched, and the westerly wind pushed the men swiftly towards the New Found Land. The crossing was uneventful. One of the tapatooks took on some water, but three of the paddlers chewed resin from the white pine and in a few moments the leak was sealed. Then the water that had entered was scooped out with a bowl carved from a tree knot. No one was worried and the incident was soon forgotten. The same four whales accompanied the paddlers on the return journey. It was suggested to the young warrior who had been teased earlier that his whale was jealous of the Innu women. "You had better calm her down before she tries to get revenge for that little morsel you were with last night," they told him. "We don't want to take a bath on your account."

The portage from the large bay at the beginning of the crossing home to Hare Bay took less than two suns. The men arrived fresh and alert, not at all tired from their long voyage. Their wives welcomed them with open arms and raised dingiams. Most of the men fulfilled their husbandly duties, despite the celebrations that had taken place on the north shore.

Shéashit immediately sent runners to each of the Beothuk villages to inform them that the attack against the colonists at Notre Dame Bay was scheduled. The date was fixed for the moon of falling leaves. It was to be a strong attack; the future of the nation depended on it.

For the next several days there was much coming and going between the villages. The village on Hare Bay was abandoned and the women and children were sent to visit their families and friends in other villages. The three other large, permanent villages thus received many visitors. But since all the men of combat age from these same villages had left to gather at the Bay of Exploits, no village had more people than it could feed and shelter. The village of the Gashu-Uwith clan on Red Ochre Lake contained many women and children, but there were few men left to protect them.

The village of the Otter Clan on the River of Gulls on the west coast was also deserted by the men, and there was an air of reunion among the women and children gathered there. In the village of Appawet the Seal, there were many meetings among the chiefs, the warriors, the young recruits who were about to engage an enemy for the first time, and the elders who already had much experience in fending off the invaders. The experienced men explained how things would happen during a battle. The young men listened, eager to learn and to take part in their first war.

Shéashit said clearly that it was not necessary to kill many people during this battle. The important thing was to attack from many places at the same time, so that the English would see that the island did not belong to them, that it was inhabited and defended by the Beothuk, and that permission to remain on the island must be sought from the Beothuk. They had to frighten the English and thereby gain their respect. It was especially important not to kill randomly. Since the English never used women in their battles, the Beothuk women would not be asked to participate in this one. As for children, they were not responsible for the actions of their parents. As long as they were unarmed, children would not be killed. During the battle it was permitted to take all the metal tools they could find. They could also steal fishing nets and ships' sails, and cut the ropes of the boats. One of the young warriors asked Shéashit a question:

"If we cut the ropes of their boats, how will they be able to leave our island? We'll have to put up with them for a long time."

Everyone laughed at this, but Shéashit was not perturbed. "You are right," he said. "We must not cut the ropes if we want them to leave the island."

The assembly broke into laughter again. And thus the war against the English began in joy.

42

THE SHO-UNDAMUNG WARRIORS were at Gander Bay at the time of the new moon of the season of falling leaves. There were one hundred and four of them, and they arrived in twenty-five canoes. They brought with them ten firesticks, with powder and shot. They were also well supplied with spears and bows and arrows. Their bodies were painted many bright colours for this special occasion.

The Beothuk of the Rabbit Clan were already there, and were soon joined by those of the Seal Clan. The men from the Otter and Bear clans arrived the next day. In all, there were two hundred and twenty Beothuk ready to go into battle. There were no women among the warriors, which was unusual among the Beothuk.

It was decided that the Sho-Undamung would attack the islands while the Beothuk occupied themselves with the dwellings on the mainland of the New Found Land itself. They would rendezvous the next morning at sunrise, and the Beothuk would set out on foot for Notre Dame Bay. The Sho-Undamung would wait until evening, and then paddle out to the islands in the bay.

The Beothuk warriors left the moment the sun cleared the horizon. They were divided into small groups. Since the dwellings of the colonists were distant from one another, the groups of warriors set off in many different directions. The bay was very large, and most of the islands were occupied by the English colonists. Many of the groups had left during the night, so as to be ready when the sun arrived.

The warriors were still travelling when they heard the first shots coming from the islands. The Sho-Undamung were attacking too early. Shéashit and five warriors hurried towards Fortune, while twenty others paddled in tapatooks to Twillingate. The first dwelling in Fortune was made of squared timber, the home of a fisherman. There were three fishing boats pulled up on the beach. Shéashit advanced upon the dwelling slowly, convinced that all the inhabitants inside were asleep. Suddenly, he gave a loud war cry to frighten those inside the dwelling, and at the same time a puff of smoke rose from the house and Shéashit received a shot in his chest that cut his war cry off short. His five companions charged the house, but more shots rang out and all five fell back, mortally wounded. After a moment's silence, a man, a woman, and three boys came out of the house, each carrying an English musket.

No one knows how or by whom, but the English colonists had been warned of the massive attack being prepared for them by the Beothuk, and they were ready for it. Men, women, and all children old enough to fire a musket had been on the alert and waiting for the Red Men, or Red Indians, as they were called from then on.

At Fortune, at Twillingate, and on the Island of Exploits, the same scene repeated itself. The Sho-Undamung and the Beothuk received many shots. The Red Men had intended to sow fear, but what they reaped was death. More than a hundred and sixty-eight Beothuk warriors were killed that sun, which from then on was called the Morning of Death. The Innu fared slightly better, losing only thirty warriors and eight wounded. They had been able to retreat to Gander Bay when the shooting started.

The question the Beothuk had asked themselves was clear: Could they continue to live as they had before? And now they knew what the answer was: No, they could not.

The retreat was painful, since they had to travel deep inland, as far as Red Ochre Lake. There were not even enough members of the Rabbit Clan left to return to their bay. The death of so many men in a single battle once again gave the women a huge majority within the Beothuk Nation. Winter was approaching, and there seemed to be nothing but misery ahead. And once again, the Beothuk had to choose a new chief.

During this time, Wapistan and his warriors were portaging to the large bay at the crossing to the north shore, on the northwest coast of the island's northern peninsula. They collected the bundles of furs left by Shéashit's men, put them and their wounded in the canoes of the Innu who had been killed in battle, and returned to their land without complaint. Their Beothuk friends had not wanted to disappear without a fight, and they had tried to help them, but they had been defeated by a superior force. And by a people who had been well prepared to defend themselves, obviously warned of the imminent attack.

The people of the Seal Clan on the east coast had to take down their mamateeks and transport the poles and coverings inland to Red Ochre Lake. The people of the Rabbit Clan helped them, while the people of the Bear Clan returned to their homeland. The few men left in the Otter Clan helped the Bear Clan complete their return as far as the lake, since it was on the way to their own village on the west coast.

The retreat was like a long funeral procession. It lasted eleven suns. The people were beaten, and those who had lost a loved one in the battle cried. The Beothuk men, who ordinarily did not cry, were inconsolable. They saw their entire lives, their culture, their way of living, die along with their loved ones, never to return. Everything was lost, family, friends, companions in arms, hunting and fishing partners.

The path that followed the river of two falls was worn more than usual during the eleven days of the long migration to the island's interior. The Beothuk were people of the sea, but they were now forced to become people of the land. No more enjoying the sea's abundance, no more collecting shellfish and sea cucumbers. No more simple life. Only misery, and the forest's innumerable blackflies. The Red Men could not maintain their territory, which was apparently coveted by others. They had lost their paradise, their garden, as they called it. From now on, they would have to share the fruits of the earth with strangers, with the Bouguishamesh. And such sharing would never be carried out in a spirit of equality. This sharing would have to be won dearly.

The English had become masters of the island. The English king now owned it. How would he treat its original inhabitants? Kobshuneesamut alone knew, or the god of the Englishmen, if not their king. The area surrounding Red Ochre Lake could not sustain so large a population. The children quickly learned to fend for themselves. The women once again were obliged to share their husbands. And the range of choices was much smaller than it had been before.

The national council met for five suns without arriving at a unanimous choice for the new chief. No one seemed to have the courage it would take to renew the nation. Never in the nation's memory had the Beothuk been so beaten as following the defeat on the Morning of Death.

However, among the survivors, one young man, almost still a child, named Dosomite the Pine, began speaking to the people. He found it inconceivable that the Beothuk had succumbed so easily to despair.

"How can you even dare to call yourselves Beothuk," he harangued them, "if you walk around looking like the living dead? You have no right to give in so easily. You must either go on beating yourselves slowly to death, or else have the courage to kill yourselves, all of you, without exception, right now. When you no longer have the strength to live, you must at least have the courage to die. It's the only dignity that we have left. As for me, I've decided to go on living. If there are those among you who no longer desire to see the sky, the rivers, and the trees, let them withdraw from my sight. I only want to be near people who want to live. The others can go and throw themselves before the English muskets. That's all they're good for . . ."

This is another speech related by the Living Memories. The youngest chief of the nation had suddenly appeared among the Red Men. There had been no need to give him a name. He had been raised by himself, by the strength of his word. This did not proceed according to the tradition; he had just created his own precedent. A chief raised by himself, say the Living Memories, having lost his father in the final battle of the Beothuk. It was a rare beginning in those former times. It is still rare in modern times. Dosomite, the son of Shéashit, had a great deal of spirit. He was a great-grandson of Ooish and Wobee, and he would never spend his life moaning about the past. We must begin again, he said, and he had the courage to do it. But he refused to take on the necessary courage for others who did not have it. He made sure of that by rejecting all those who wallowed in despair. It was cruel, but he also knew it was essential.

The young man made friends in a few suns. All those who wished to live came to speak with him. The others did not dare. One day he said to a group of young people:

"As long as I can see how beautiful are the flowers of this tree, as long as I can see them change colour before falling, I will want to live. When this tree seems ugly to me, I will know I am ready to die."

Slowly, day by day, life began to return to the nation. There was no more talk of clans. Everyone belonged to the new nation of the Beothuk. The Otter Clan joined with the clans of the seal and the bear, and the most recent clan, the Rabbit, disappeared altogether. There were no more clans, there were only Beothuk. All the clans had been established before the need for survival. Only rarely was the name Addaboutik mentioned; the Beothuk most often referred to themselves as the Red Men or the Red-Ochre people.

The people adopted a way of thinking: the Beothuk were eternal, they would never die because there were too many things to learn, too many beauties to contemplate, too much love to share. The English put their events on paper. They would need a lot of paper if they tried to write down all the things the Beothuk were unable to make them understand.

Dosomite the Pine continued to lead the nation without officially becoming a chief. The national council gradually ceased to exist. The elders, the Living Memories, the medicine men, were often consulted. They were the Living Memories of the people, the seers, the wise ones who had experienced life.

But the Beothuk, despite the example and courage of Dosomite, continued to live in desolation.

III

GENOCIDE

The eighteenth and nineteenth centuries

43

ALMOST ALL THE bays along the rising-sun coast of the Red Men's island were now occupied by English colonists and fishermen who had come to settle the New Found Land. The Beothuk had left the coasts to seek refuge in the interior, in order to avoid attacks by the colonists and fur trappers. The failed attack against the inhabitants of Notre Dame Bay had made the English bold. They spoke of the great adventure that had ended with the deaths of nearly two hundred Savages, some of whom had come by canoe, others by foot. The word was spread around: "They are easily killed. They do not know the power of our weapons. They expose themselves to musket fire like children, and *Bang!* Like shooting ducks on a pond. What's more, they shout a warning before they attack. They are incredibly stupid."

I am Wonaoktaé, the Living Memory of the Beothuk people on the island of the Red Men, of the Addaboutik descended from the hero Anin. I was designated the bearer of historical tradition, the first female to have been conferred this honour. I am the younger sister of Tom June, who was said to have been Anin reincarnated. He lived in the eighteenth century, according to the English reckoning. I will tell you his story a little later. First, let me recount, in order of occurrence, what happened after the death of the last storyteller, the one who has already told you our history as it unfolded. As I said, I am Wonaoktaé of the Beothuk, but my true name is Demasduit, which means the flower that grows by the lakes. Here is the rest of our story.

What I said before introducing myself is true. The English considered us to be animals, inferior to them in every way. News of their victory over our people spread quickly to England. More colonists signed up, drawn by the possibility of earning large sums of money in the fur trade, the natives were so naive. The English who were already here wrote to them saying they could get furs from us for nothing and sell them for high prices on the British market, and they believed this. The island became more and more populated.

But the Beothuk never really left Notre Dame Bay. They continued to haunt the fringes of the settled areas. Fishermen would find their nets and lines stolen, settlers would lose their metal tools, and axes and knives would disappear as if by magic whenever they were left unattended, even on the doorsteps of their houses. Among the Beothuk who still lived near the coast, the word was passed around. Our elder often warned them that the English left their tools lying about specifically to lure the Beothuk into taking them: "Whenever one of us lets himself be tempted by a tool, the English have an excuse to come after us. We must always be on our guard. Remember Ebenezer Triton," said the elder. "In one summer he killed eight of us himself. Scalped them all. He was an evil brute who killed for the sheer pleasure of killing. Our young men were foolhardy. As far as the English were concerned, we were stupid because we never fought back. This Ebenezer Triton thought of us as rabbits. All we were good for was running away, zigzagging to avoid his musket fire. Our young men made fine moving targets for anyone who cared to fire at them. They could run fast, but not faster than lead balls, or the buckshot with which the English loaded their muskets. Our young men are condemned to die if they do not learn this."

One day the Ashwans attacked Twillingate and three settlers were killed. The Beothuk were blamed because no one in Twillingate could tell the difference between a large Beothuk and a small Ashwan. To the English, all Savages looked the same and had the same physical stature. It was impossible to tell one from another, especially if they were all the same sex.

During this time, at Red Ochre Lake, which the English call Red Indian Lake, the sickness was sweeping through the people. The winter after our retreat to the interior, more than two hundred died of the fever that changed the colour of our faces. More than half of those were children under ten years of age. It was a devastating blow to our families. The whole life of the Beothuk is based on the family, the continuation of our spirit through our children. The death of a child is a terrible punishment. Every adult is affected by the loss. Mothers were reluctant to have more children for fear of being forced to watch them die of hunger or disease. Food became more and more scarce. A diet based exclusively on game from the interior was all that was available to us. Before, our people ate mostly fish and other foods from the sea, shellfish and crustaceans, not so much meat. Now we had to develop new ways to hunt, we had to kill as many caribou as possible. The English call these animals reindeer, although there are no deer on the island you call Newfoundland.

The winter following the failed attack at Notre Dame Bay was deadly for the Beothuk. Almost every adult was sick and unable to hunt. There was much famine, and worse. Mothers were too badly nourished to make milk for their babies, the babies became sick with the fever and were too weak to resist it. If the Beothuk believed in mass suicide, they would have given themselves willingly to death.

It was a catastrophe. Of the two thousand Beothuk who sought the interior, we were reduced to fewer than five hundred. And most of those were females.

A once proud and happy people had been reduced by famine, disease, and persecution by the English to the blackest of misery, and in only a few moons. Once a people busily expanding their territory, they had become a people on the edge of extinction. Instead of helping us, the colonists, fishermen, and trappers preyed on us. To kill a Red Indian was seen almost as a sport: they bragged about it as they would about shooting a caribou.

The elder said that it was difficult to blame the new inhabitants of Newfoundland for this attitude. The Living Memories of the Beothuk Nation reminded us of many instances of treachery practised against the newcomers, and they told us that the colonists and fishermen came to this island ignorant of the customs and desires of the native people, and believed they were encountering true Savages. "Both sides are to blame," said the old man. "The Living Memories stir up hatred of the English by recounting tales of treachery and deceit. And it is true that the English did not try to understand our ways, or to get to know us at all. By taking us prisoners they thought they were learning something from us. Perhaps they mistook us for animals that they could tame and put to their use."

People who live in freedom are always misunderstood. The single greatest fault of the English, in my view, is their belief that they are the sole possessors of the truth. And yet they do not know that we live by truth and die by falsehood.

One fine morning a ship dropped anchor in the Bay of Exploits. It was observed by Hadalaet the Ice and several of his young companions, to whom he was teaching the names of the plants of our island. When the sailors saw that there were natives on the shore, they lowered a boat. One of the men in the boat was dressed differently from the others. The elder, Hadalaet, heard one of the sailors address him as "Sir," and call him Scott. The name was familiar to Hadalaet; when he was a younger man he had gone with his mother to gather clams, and he had heard an Englishman call another Scott. Several seconds later his mother lay dead, shot through the forehead by an English musket ball. The name Scott remained in Hadalaet's memory like a horrible stain, and it made him sick to hear it. He had lost his mother and had lived a life of terror; whenever he ran, he zigzagged in order to avoid the musket balls of the men who killed his mother.

Hadalaet and the other Beothuk watched the English sailors. The English watched the Beothuk. Neither group dared to approach the other. After a while, however, Hadalaet left his companions and walked toward the English. Scott left the sailors and walked to meet him. This man Scott was young and strong. He was not afraid of an old man. When he came up close to Hadalaet he raised his hand in greeting. Hadalaet opened his long coat, which covered his body down to his knees, and taking his knife from his belt, stabbed Scott three times in the chest. The Englishman fell to the ground, killed outright. The sailors ran towards Hadalaet, at which point the other Beothuk took their bows and arrows from under their long coats and killed four more Englishmen. Then they turned and fled into the forest, taking the old man with them.

Instead of chasing the Beothuk, the sailors who were not killed ran towards their boat, leaving their dead companions stretched out on the shore of the bay. This was another story for the Living Memories to tell to a nation that had been decimated for many years. Later, Hadalaet himself told this story to several young people, as though he were a hero.

The same sailors landed another time on the north shore of the Bay of Exploits and discovered a storehouse of food that had been placed there by the Redskins but not well hidden. In it they found hundreds of furs of every kind of animal that lives on the island: bear, marten, beaver, wolf, fox, and many others. They took these furs to pay the costs of their expedition. They also took all the dried and smoked meat that was there, forcing the Beothuk to make another hunt to supply themselves with food for the winter. A voyage to the land of the Beothuk was never without profit, even if it cost the lives of a few sailors: an expedition was always rewarded.

The old man and his six warriors were bitterly accused by the rest of the Beothuk of attracting more hatred to our people, and of continuing the war between the Beothuk and the English. They were punished for their act of vengeance. They were told that the nation could not endure another attack by the foreigners. Our position was too precarious. There were simply not enough Beothuk left on the island to continue to defy the powerful invaders.

It was decided that such an error must never be repeated. Our only hope was to become invisible to the English, to make the colonists and fishermen forget that we existed. We could no longer live near the coast, or hunt there, or fish or gather shellfish from the sea. The chief at that time was named Bawoodisik the Thunderbird. He was a descendant of the ancestor Anin, but he was chief not because of his lineage but because he was elected by the people.

Bawoodisik was a serious man, taciturn and solitary, and had become wise at a young age because of all he had lived through. He had been raised in the most absolute misery, and learned to content himself with little and to share whatever came his way from fishing and hunting. The great-grandson of Dosomite the Pine, he had learned from his grandfather never to be discouraged or to give in to despair. As a young man he had learned to love what he saw and not to look upon what he could not love. His environment did not allow the slightest error, and so he had had to know it intimately. Every sun brought him another opportunity to learn something to his advantage, and because of this he found life interesting and worthy of cherishing. Bawoodisik received his name because, on the morning of his birth, his mother had seen a large bald eagle flying very high in the sky. Several moments later, a thunderstorm began that lasted half a sun. Bawoodisik was born during the storm, and so she could give him no other name but Thunderbird.

The young Bawoodisik learned to hunt almost before he could walk. His great-grandfather, the Pine, was still alive at that time, and taught him many things. The Pine would never speak to anyone who was easily discouraged, and counted among his friends only those who desired to live and to learn. He spoke to Bawoodisik about Kobshuneesamut the Very High, the Creator of all things, and told him how Kobshuneesamut left the Beothuk free to do either good or evil, but to accept the consequences of their actions whatever they may be. He taught the young boy that lying, evil-doing, the killing of one of his own people, jealousy and envy were weaknesses, and degrading for a real man.

He also learned to recognize the qualities that pleased Kobshuneesamut. These were truth, sharing, love of younger people, independence, and caring for the elders. He learned that truth and falsehood belonged to the same family, as did good and evil, as did beauty and ugliness. He learned that everything had its opposite, and that knowing that was the only way a young man could decide what to do. He learned that night was the opposite of day, and that neither was evil in itself. Each has its usefulnesses, just as men and women have their different usefulnesses. Just as the child and the adult, or the tree and its fruit. He learned all these things as a boy, and as a man he was as beloved by the people as his great-grandfather had been. He did not become the man he had dreamed of becoming: he became the man he had learned how to become, and was neither better nor worse than what he had been taught to be.

Bawoodisik was very tall, and his great strength was well known among our people. He was muscular and could endure great physical hardship. He could carry heavy loads for great distances, like the Sho-Undamung. In short, his abilities were those of all the Beothuk who survived this period of misery. The less able and the less talented died before they became adults. That was how difficult it was to survive in the interior of the island of Newfoundland during this period of suffering.

44

SIX SEASON-CYCLES PASSED after the story of old Hadalaet and the man named Scott. Nothing changed in the life of the Beothuk. They still had to steal tools from the colonists, for they needed tools more than ever in order to survive. And the colonists continued to shoot them on sight.

Many Sho-Undamung would come from the north shore to hunt on the island. But because they knew of the great misery that dwelt in the heart of the Beothuk Nation, the northerners did not impose themselves on the Beothuk as guests. Knowing how difficult it was for the Red Men to survive, they frequented instead the Shanung, at the Bay d'Espoir, the people the English called Micmacs. These people lived along the river that emptied into the Bay d'Espoir, and were also no strangers to misery. Twenty-eight of their most valiant hunters had been surprised by a violent storm during a whale hunt, and were lost at sea. The women were therefore more numerous than the men, and many young Montagnais or Innu huntsmen who came to the island to hunt decided to remain here among the Shanung. The community thus became one of mixed blood, and their contact with the English was much more frequent than it had been. The Micmac already spoke the European language. The Innu soon learned to speak it as well. As the Red Men had for thousands of season-cycles, this community of Mixed-Bloods grew and prospered. It often happened that one of their hunters shared the success of his hunt with the Beothuk at Red Ochre Lake. Relations with these people became normal again after many seasons of cold and snow following the deaths at St. George's Bay, on the southwest coast.

One day Bawoodisik and five companions saw an English expedition in the Bay of Exploits. The Englishmen were examining the forest plants and conifers, and were led by a Mixed-Blood guide from the Bay d'Espoir whose name was Paul. This guide was well known to the Beothuk. The chief knew that he would not take the English near Red Ochre Lake even though he had been a faithful friend for many years and knew exactly where to find the Beothuk. Bawoodisik and his companions watched the English for two suns with none of the English party being aware of it except the guide. When the man called Paul came and stood close to Bawoodisik, the chief learned that the Englishman who was so interested in the forest plants was named Sir Joseph Banks, and that he was a learned man who had come to study the flora and fauna of the island. The Mixed-Blood assured the Beothuk of the scientist's good intentions, and said that he was not an enemy of the Red Men. The chief and his companions were therefore content with simply spying on the party and watching their curious movements. When he returned to the Englishmen, the Mixed-Blood told Sir Joseph that if the Beothuk were as savage as the English said they were, then he and his expedition would have been dead long ago, without their even having been aware of the Beothuk's presence.

"They are actually all around us," Paul said, "and you don't even smell them."

Sir Joseph replied that while examining the soil he had seen tracks that gave him to believe that the Beothuk still numbered about five hundred, and that they lived close to this spot.

"But I am not here to chase Beothuk," he said. "My mission is entirely scientific. I am not a soldier. If the authorities want to establish contact with the Red Men, that is their affair, not mine. As long as they leave us in peace . . ."

And he continued his investigations without the slightest concern for the presence of the Red-Ochre people. Bawoodisik and his companions, convinced that these particular Englishmen were no threat to the Beothuk community, returned to their families. Since the epidemic killed mostly women, and each man was capable of seeing to the needs of only a small number, the households had once again become monogamous. Abundance was a thing of the past, and each of us had to look after his or her own necessities as well as those of the community. Children also had to do their part or else risk dying of hunger along with the adults.

Each spring the whole community dispersed up and down the coast between the English settlements. Each family found its own place to set up camp and to fish, staying in the forest but always close to the sea, and so they were exposed to reprisals from the newcomers to the island. But that was the chance they had to take if they were to survive at all, if they had any hope of repopulating the land of the Beothuk with new Red-Ochre people.

The word nation was hardly heard among us any more, and the idea of expansion was completely abandoned. We spoke only of the family. We had even forgotten the notion of clans, symbolized by an animal whose spirit protected humans. There was no more question of occupying the bays to defend our ancestral territories. We lived in the bays only during the summer, and for the sole purpose of finding enough food to survive for another season-cycle. The children were taught to avoid and even fear the bearded strangers whose faces were as pale as death. They were instructed in the art of concealment, of camouflage, of disappearing suddenly into the forest, which had become the last refuge of the people. The Bouguishamesh were afraid of the forest.

During the warm season, Bawoodisik chose a small cove in the northeast for his summer camp. Two complete season-cycles had passed since the Englishmen had been seen with the naturalist Sir Joseph Banks. To give the time as it is reckoned by the English, the number of years past the middle of the century was twice the number of fingers on two hands. That season-cycle was a very important one for the Beothuk, because during it many unhappy events came to pass that determined the fate of the Red Men, the descendants of the ancestor Anin the Voyager.

In early spring, when the families had already moved to their summer residences, another expedition was seen to disembark in the Bay of Exploits. This time the expedition members landed and travelled inland towards Red Ochre Lake. Since no Beothuk lived there during the summer, the expedition was allowed to go in peace. We did not even hurry to collect the furs and provisions we had left there. Usually we took our furs and often our food with us. But we would not kill over these items, and there were no Beothuk left in the village at the lake. The expedition leader was a soldier, but most of the men in his command were colonists from Notre Dame Bay, and were very familiar to all the Beothuk who were then alive.

Bawoodisik was one of the last of the Beothuk to have more than one wife. He had Adenishit the Star, mother of a male child of about six season-cycles, and he had Basdic, her sister, who was pregnant with her first baby and was expected to give birth shortly after the first snow. These four had built their mamateek on the shore of Seal Cove, not far from Catalina. It was almost a moon before the longest day of the growing season. The sun was rising over the beach when Bawoodisik awoke, along with Adenishit and her still unnamed child. Basdic was already awake and was collecting clams on the beach. The three watched her from their mamateek. She was naked from the waist up, and wore her dingiam under her big, round belly. Suddenly they saw an Englishman run up behind Basdic. When Basdic saw him she threw herself on her knees and showed him that she was pregnant, but the man grabbed her by her hair with one hand and with the other took out his knife and slit open her belly. Then he lifted Basdic by her hair and plunged his free hand into her bleeding belly and took out her baby. She was still alive and struggling. The man stuck the baby on the sharp end of the stick that Basdic had been using to dig clams, and lifted the child above his head and held it like a torch. Several other men ran onto the beach then and congratulated the Englishman for his bravery, for his warrior-like conduct: eviscerating a pregnant woman and proudly displaying the skewered body of a Beothuk fetus.

All this happened so quickly that neither Bawoodisik nor Adenishit had time to react. Their child watched the whole barbarous scene. Bawoodisik's second wife had just been cut open before their eyes, and there was nothing they could do to protect her. The Beothuk chief collapsed onto the ground and cried for a long time, which he considered to be further evidence of his weakness.

It was no use for Adenishit to tell him that it had happened too quickly, that even if there had been a hundred warriors they would not have had time to stop the Englishman from murdering Basdic, for Bawoodisik was inconsolable. Gradually his pain gave way to anger. That night he took his bow and arrows and travelled north, to the place where the fur traders had anchored their boat. There he found two Englishmen sitting on the beach around a fire. The others were still on the boat.

Bawoodisik crept up on the fire slowly. It was a moonless night, and he was protected by the darkness. He took three arrows from his quiver and shot them in rapid succession. One pierced the throat of one of the men, and the other two lodged in the thigh and right shoulder of his companion. The Beothuk chief leapt upon this second Englishman and finished him with his own English knife. Then Bawoodisik took his English hatchet and cut off the heads of the two men, and ran back to his second wife's body.

He and Adenishit dug a shallow grave near the seashore and laid Basdic's body in it. They carried rocks all night to cover her body so that animals would not profane it. Then, on the pile of rocks, he placed the two English heads as symbols of his revenge. In every English community on the island, the savagery of the Beothuk was condemned, and praises were sung for the brave fur traders who had succeeded in killing a Red Indian. "There's another one who will not grow up to trouble the peaceful colonists in this New Found Land," they said. I am Wonaoktaé, the Living Memory of the people of Red Ochre Lake, and I tell you I am sickened every time I tell this tale of horror.

Bawoodisik prayed on Basdic's grave every day. He brought her the last flowers that bloomed in the evening, so that the beauty of her native land might comfort her in her eternal sleep. Adenishit and her son continued to live from day to day, digging clams and collecting the eggs of shorebirds, and the chief continued to hunt seals and catch the many kinds of fish in the bay. Two moons passed. One day, while Bawoodisik was fishing, Adenishit and her son were digging clams at the edge of the forest when a group of fur trappers emerged from the woods. Adenishit tried to run, but one of the trappers raised his musket and shot her. The child threw himself on his mother when he saw the blood flowing from the wound in her chest. The trappers took him prisoner and carried him away. They gave him the name John August, because of the month in which he was captured. He was not asked if he already had a name. In any case, the name they gave him was not valid, because he was not English.

The child was frightened and trembled all the time, and cried whenever anyone tried to touch him. He would not let any stranger come near him. He was tied up with a cord that cut into his wrists and ankles so badly that he would bear the scars for the rest of his life. Since it was impossible to tame him, he was sold to a fur trader who brought him to England, to live with the trader's brother in Liverpool.

A terrible anguish engulfed him when he saw the ship was pulling away from the coast where he had once played with his mother, happy and smiling. He felt his insides being torn apart when he realized he would never see her again, nor ever again have anyone who would love him. If only his father would come back, he thought, he would stop these strangers from taking him away. He had seen the face of the man who had killed his mother, and never would it leave his memory. Nor the face of the man who had eviscerated his aunt Basdic, at the beginning of the warm season. That is what he said later to Tom June, and what Tom June told me.

All during the long voyage to St. John's and later, during the crossing to England, the child heard the name with which he had been encumbered: John, John, John, August, August, August. The two words pounded in his head like the drum that is beaten when a Beothuk is buried who has had the fever for which there is no cure. John August had terrible nightmares. Someone would cut his stomach open and take out all the Beothuk people he knew, one after another, and stick them on lances and let them dry in the sun. When he was able to calm himself and go back to sleep, he would rest peacefully, dreaming that he had found the two murderers, the men who had killed his aunt and his mother, and had cut their skin up into long strips and made snowshoes out of them, and put them on his feet. He smiled, thinking that at last he had found a use for the English.

Suns passed, nights passed. He found himself in England, in a large village, bigger than any he had ever seen before. He was placed with a family by the name of Gardener. The Gardeners already had three sons of their own, the oldest of whom was fourteen. The Beothuk boy was put in his charge. As he soon discovered, the English boy was cruel and violent, and greatly enjoyed every chance he had to kick and punch the newcomer. John August, however, did not take this treatment without fighting back. He would pick up anything he could find in the house and throw it at his tormentor. When Gardener senior had had enough of this, he whipped the boy, and told his oldest son that he could whip him as well, as long as he did not mark him too badly. The little Savage would have to be sold, and they wanted him to fetch a good price.

The next year, in 1769, the English king, George III, became uneasy about the turn of events in Newfoundland, and issued a proclamation "forbidding the colonists of Newfoundland to molest the Beothuk." But Newfoundland was out of sight and far from the control of royal sanctions. Life went on, and the massacres continued. We heard rumours of this royal proclamation, but we knew that there was no cure for those who came to exploit our island's natural resources. They were just words, nothing but words, words written on English paper.

45

JOHN AUGUST TOLD Tom June that he was kept in a cage and exhibited to the public, who paid money to see him. The newspapers described him as a Red Savage from Newfoundland, and his owners painted his skin with watercolours so that the people who paid tuppence to see a young Savage would not feel cheated when they saw a boy who looked like any other boy. They tied his hair up on the top of his head like a sheaf of oats, in the manner of Beothuk women. They made a loincloth for him of cowhide, one side left rough, with the hair on, and the other side lined with suede, in the European fashion. The loincloth was also painted red with watercolours rather than red ochre; it gave him a grotesque but artificial appearance. He looked nothing like a true Beothuk from the island of the Red Men, and he knew it, despite his young age, because he spoke to Tom June about it when he was no longer a child.

He remembered that they gave him a stuffed animal for company. It was a tiger; he did not know what it was until one day he saw a picture of one on an advertisement for a circus. He would amuse himself by throwing the toy at the bars of his cage to frighten visitors who came too close. When he tired of this, he curled up in a corner, his thumb in his mouth like an infant who has been taken from his mother too early, and refused to move until Mr. Gardener took a stick and poked him sharply in the ribs with it. This was to show visitors how ferocious he could be.

He told Tom June that he learned to speak English by listening to the visitors. His adoptive parents rarely spoke to him. Whenever he did something that displeased them he would be harshly, but wordlessly, beaten for it. Mr. Gardener kept a leather razor strop for that purpose. John grew quickly, and always nurtured his plan to return to Newfoundland and avenge the death of his mother. He also hoped to see his father, Bawoodisik, again. But he was closely watched, and the elder Gardener boy, Peter, reminded him constantly that he was in their power. The young John August saw how true were the stories told by the Living Memories, that the English are a cruel people. He grew up with a single idea in his head: to escape and return to his homeland.

He managed to escape three times, but each time he was caught. He did not speak English well enough to get by on the street. Although they did not become rich, the Gardeners lived well off the revenues of exhibiting John to the public. They took him on tour throughout England, and finally in London one of the visitors was Sir Joseph Banks, who successfully petitioned the King for his release. John was then fourteen years old. He had been in a cage for eight years. He had all but forgotten the language of his people. Sir Joseph paid for his passage back to Newfoundland and even gave him some pocket money so that he would not be destitute when he arrived in St. John's. He told John that he was sorry he had to leave for the Indies and could not accompany John on his journey back to his people. John later said that Sir Joseph was the only Englishman he had ever met who showed the slightest sympathy for him; he was sorry that he never saw Sir Joseph again.

That is how young John August returned to the island of the Red Men. All he remembered of it was the name of the place where he had been taken on the first night of his captivity: Catalina. He also remembered the face of the man who had murdered his mother. Sometimes, in his dreams, he also saw the man who had killed his aunt two moons before he was captured, and when he awoke he would be uncertain which of the two men he most wanted to kill. But it did not matter, for both were in mortal danger as long as John August was alive. He had sworn to find each man and identify himself to him before killing him, after having made him suffer as much as possible.

In St. John's he learned that a boat was leaving for Catalina. He was able to secure a position on board as the captain's cabin boy. This captain made the journey to and from Catalina once a month, and it was arranged that for the five days that the ship was in port there, John would be at liberty to roam the town. Although only fourteen, he was able to frequent the taverns in Newfoundland. He was looking for two faces. He did not know the names of the men he was seeking, or their size, or their ages. Would he still recognize them after eight years? He did not know, but he lived for nothing else. He spent so much time in the taverns that he soon became dependent on alcohol. He drank beer, also rum and sweet wine. Within a few years he became an alcoholic. He suffered from terrible nightmares. One night when he was drunk he got into a fight with four men from one of the ships in the harbour, and was beaten up quite badly. The next morning he decided to leave Catalina to look for his father.

He left on foot. He walked along the coast, heading first west and then southwest, looking for the area where he had been raised. He went as far as Trinity Bay, in Smith Fjord, but recognized nothing. He returned to Catalina and then crossed the peninsula to continue his search in Bonavista Bay. At King's Cove he met an old man who had worked on the cod boats who remembered hearing of "a Beothuk savage who lived on Fogo Island." This Beothuk had been captured in 1770 and raised on Fogo, and eventually he became master of a fishing boat that sailed from the island. John decided to go there to meet this man, who was Tom June, my brother. He left Catalina again, once more on foot. Fogo Island was situated off the southeast point of Notre Dame Bay, in the mouth of the Bay of Exploits. It took him thirty days to walk to Dildo Run, from where he was able to make the crossing to Fogo Island. On the way he begged meals from colonists and fishermen. He never told anyone that he was Beothuk, and he was taken for a young Englishman. He therefore did not know whether the people who helped him were kind people, or whether they were only kind to other Englishmen. It was autumn, and the weather was turning cold.

We were now nearing the end of the century, and young John had been searching for his mother's murderer, or for someone who knew his family, for two full season-cycles. He had no difficulty locating Tom June. Tom June was very tall, with dark skin and black hair with hints of red in it. One side of his head was shaved, "my initiation to the life of a sailor," he said, laughing.

Over a pint of beer, John August told him how he had been taken prisoner when he was six years old. He told him about the death of his mother and the murder of his aunt. Tom June was saddened by the tale.

"The colonists are very powerful," he said. "They are also very ignorant. They honestly believe that we are monsters, and that we are only waiting for an opportunity to kill them. The men you are looking for are Albert Fenton and Guy Jersey. I don't remember if it was Fenton or Jersey who killed your mother, but one of them still brags about how he shot her from a great distance."

Young John instantly became so furious that he had to be held down by the patrons of the tavern. He wanted to kill all Englishmen. Tom June, who was well known in the place, was embarrassed and excused himself to the other patrons. Then he literally dragged John to his cabin on the beach near the Fogo wharf, laid him out on his own bed, and wrapping himself in a woollen blanket, slept on the floor beside him.

When he woke up, John was still incensed that his Beothuk brother had apologized to the English for his behaviour. Tom June made him listen to reason: in the first place, a tavern filled with English drinkers was not the best place to announce that they were Red Men, Beothuk. Suddenly recalling the name of his father, Bawoodisik, John asked Tom to take him to the land of their people. To calm him down, Tom promised to take him to the interior of the island on his next shore leave.

Tom June had been taken prisoner at the age of ten season-cycles, when he still spoke the language of the Red Men fluently. For the first few years of his captivity, he escaped several times and returned to live among the Red-Ochre people on the coast, but after a few suns he always returned to Fogo. He did not feel that he belonged in either world. He was a visitor among his own people, and also a visitor among the people who had taken him prisoner. He was not happy in either place. He himself said he was nothing, not Beothuk, not English. No English father would let him call on one of his daughters. And when he was among his own people, he was not allowed to speak to a Beothuk girl for fear that he would try to persuade her to leave the community to live among the invaders, the very people who amused themselves by killing Red Men.

And so when the English asked him to teach them the Beothuk language, he told them it was too difficult for civilized people to speak. And when his own people asked him to give them English lessons, he told them he could not find the time. The elders remarked on how much he had come to resemble the English: not enough time, not enough time . . . as though time was something you could make and use to cause pleasure or joy. Time was an insubstantial thing, an invisible thing, no one could hold it in his hands. It was like the cycle of the seasons, uncontrollable. But the whites cherished it as they cherished their own children. That is what becomes of a young Beothuk when he is taken to live among the Bouguishamesh: he learns to worship time instead of Kobshuneesamut. Both are insubstantial, and both have their uses, but they are different. Time was all that the Beothuk had left, they did not need to work to find it.

Tom June had been raised by an Anglican pastor who had come to Fogo Island to Christianize the savage Redskins. He had not had the courage to travel deep into the forest to meet these Savages, and so he had contented himself with raising this captured child. He was helped by his wife, Elizabeth, who taught Tom to speak English and to read and write, and in four years she transformed the young Savage into a little English gentleman. But he still lived in Newfoundland, and there was nothing of the gentleman in the other children on Fogo Island. He adopted the manners of a young lout, much to the dismay of the good Elizabeth. The children on Fogo ran completely wild, and the dual personality of her young charge discouraged the frustrated teacher. Saving the young Beothuk's soul was her only mission in life.

He remembered his true name, which was Deed-Rashow the Red and had been given to him by his father, Doothun the Forehead. However, Doothun was not his real father, because he had been orphaned by the fever for which there is no cure. The elderly Doothun, whose young wife would bear him a daughter the same year that the young man was drowned, raised Tom until his capture by the colonists when he was digging clams on the beach. As a young man, Tom would visit his adoptive father whenever he had the chance. I did not know Deed-Rashow personally, but I have heard him spoken of so often that I feel as though I know him very well. It was my father who first told me the stories of Tom June and John August. When Tom June took John August back to his people and introduced him to his uncle, the old man told the boy that his father had died about ten season-cycles after

John had been captured. He had been unable to live with the shame and the sense of guilt that haunted him.

John August had no family and did not speak the Beothuk language. He had no way of communicating with his people, and could not hope to be able to resume his life among them. With a sad heart, he returned to Catalina and continued to drown his sorrow and despair in the taverns. Before he died, a certain Albert Fenton was found floating in the Catalina harbour. As for Guy Jersey, he was found hanging from a tree not far from a tavern, also near the Catalina wharf.

It is said that one night, after a bout of drinking, John August became very sick and choked on his own vomit. It is also said by malicious tongues that he suffered such a violent fit of delirium tremens that the crew members aboard the ship he was working on had to knock him hard on the head to calm him down, and he died from the blow. However he died, his reputation as a trouble-maker was well-known and it was not difficult to convince everyone that death came to him as a result of his drinking. He was the first Beothuk child to be exhibited in England like an animal in a zoo. At the age of seventeen, he had had six years of freedom, eight years of captivity, and three years of hell. A hell worse than death, a hell of not knowing who he was, of never seeing his own family, of losing even his language, of having no friends in whom to confide.

Thus died the last descendant of the hero of the island of Newfoundland, Anin the Voyager. John August was the final chapter in a sad family saga, a family that had influenced the whole culture of the island for nearly eight hundred season-cycles.

What I find the strangest thing of all, however, as the Living Memory of my people, is that the colonists of the island of Newfoundland did not try to use these two young men as go-betweens, or even as interpreters, when they sent their military expeditions into the interior of the island to establish contact with our people.

Tom June lived another five years on Fogo, always in the same job. One autumn morning they found his body floating in the water of the harbour, beside his overturned tapatook. There had been no storm or strong wind for several days. He was a little over thirty years old and was an excellent swimmer. His death remains a complete mystery. As he had neither close friends nor mortal enemies, it was put down to an accident. No one seemed to mourn his disappearance, and no Beothuk came out of the forest to claim his body. Two days after his death, his tapatook also disappeared. It had been recovered by the owner of the boat on which Tom was working, but no one knows who came to take it away.

I, Wonaoktaé, his younger sister, grew up and became the Living Memory of my people. I am the first woman to whom the memories of so many others have been given. I am the daughter of Doothun. I was taught at a very early age how to use my memory to learn about the past and to recall the present, so that future generations will know where they came from. The world is a series of worlds. Life is a series of lives. I will never forget the lives of Tom June and John August.

46

BAWOODISIK WAS NOT dreaming. He had heard a musket shot. The sound worried him: a musket firing had been a bad omen ever since the English first came to the island of the Red-Ochre people.

Still troubled, he decided to give up his seal hunt and return to the land, to Adenishit and the boy. The child was the first-born of Bawoodisik and Adenishit, and was the last of the line descended from Anin the Voyager, the hero of the island and the first to travel completely around the Addaboutik land. It took him three season-cycles, and his voyage united the clans and created the Beothuk Nation through his marriage to four women: one Beothuk, two Vikings from Ice-land, and one Scotswoman. His progeny had been great: he had fathered more children than any Beothuk that followed him. He was a wise man, who saw his people expand their territory until they occupied the whole island, so that they could protect their land and keep it intact. He withstood great hardships and much danger, which until that time had been unknown to the Red-Ochre people. Protected by Gashu-Uwith the Bear, he had established his own clan and the Beothuk Nation.

Bawoodisik thought it was time to give a name to his son, so that he would perpetuate the unending tradition of the Beothuk people in the vast reaches of the universe. He must take good care of this child to assure his own continuity, make him into a man strong of body and of spirit. It meant instilling in him a sense of his great responsibility.

Bawoodisik rounded Owl Island and looked towards his mamateek. There was no smoke rising into the sky. Adenishit never let the fire go out. Even when she was digging clams, she would return often to the mamateek to make sure the coals were still alive. Bawoodisik paddled faster. As soon as he set foot on the beach he felt a deep anguish. He knew that something serious had happened. He saw the prints of English boots in the sand, leading into the forest. He also saw the tracks of Beothuk moccasins, those of his wife and his son. Then he saw his wife, stretched out on her back on the beach. She had been scalped. Her hairless skull was a hideous thing, encrusted with coagulated blood. The marks of small moccasins about her body told him that his son was still alive. He threw himself on Adenishit's lifeless body. He had loved her deeply. He held her in his arms and wept for a long time, unable to imagine life without her.

He spoke to her softly, gently rebuking her for exposing herself to the enemy. He reminded her of the many methods of concealment taught by the Living Memories of the nation. He reproached her for letting the fire go out. He tried to wake her up. He called his son's name over and over: "Buh-Bosha-Yesh," the name he had decided to give him, the name of Anin's first son, but he knew that there would be no answering call. He felt worse than he had ever felt before. He was angry with himself for blindly following tradition. . . . He should have stayed to dig clams instead of going to hunt for seals. . . . He should have . . . forgotten that men must hunt and women must dig clams. . . . He should have . . . but he had not done what he should have done, and he was angry with himself.

When his body was emptied of all its tears, when his throat was so dry that he could no longer swallow his saliva, when his very saliva hurt his throat as though he was swallowing sand, he knew that he would never cry again. He raised himself from the ground, and lifting the body of his wife in his arms, carried her to the grave of his other wife, Basdic. He laid Adenishit beside her sister and covered her body with freshly picked flowers before piling stones on her grave. It took him a long time to find enough stones to protect his wives from being dug up by scavengers. Then, like a man walking in his sleep, he began the long march to his winter camp in the interior of the island, at Red Ochre Lake.

The rest of the community did not try to draw him out of his silence. They respected his grief, and did not wish him to relive his horror by recounting it to them. Other members who had passed by Bawoodisik's summer camp and read the signs were able to reconstruct most of what had taken place there. And they could imagine the rest.

Such scenes were frequent enough that the Living Memories could easily fill in the details of the story, and they repeated them often to the children, so that the children would be cautious and even defiant when they came into contact with the English.

When Bawoodisik spoke again, he said that now Anin the ancestor had no more descendants, it was time to name a new chief, one who was not in his direct line. He then went many moons without uttering another word. He had no advice to give the council concerning the affairs of the nation. The people could go to the elders and the Living Memories if there were important decisions to be made. Bawoodisik died long before his body ceased to live. He died with Adenishit, and with the disappearance of his son, Buh-Bosha-Yesh. Life for him was no longer worth living. To him the trees had become ugly, the sea was a monster that swallowed without chewing. The spirits of the forest

no longer protected the Beothuk. He thought that the spirit protector of humans no longer influenced the understanding of men
and women. He told himself that it would be good to sleep and to
not awaken, so that he could join Adenishit and Basdic in the
land of eternal voyage.

One morning they found Bawoodisik sleeping in his mamateek. He had eaten dozens of the marvellous mushrooms that
grew in the forest, brightly coloured on top with many white dots.
The father of the last descendant of Anin the ancestor had lost
the will to live when he had lost his love for the island. He had
lost his three reasons for living. He had left for his eternal voyage
on the same day that another child of the Beothuk nation was
captured: a young boy of ten season-cycles who was also taken to
Fogo Island, like Tom June.

No one felt strong enough to go to get him back. They had
gone to Bawoodisik's mamateek to ask his advice when they
found him poisoned. No Beothuk had committed suicide in the
hundreds of season-cycles known to the Living Memories of
the community of the Red Men, because our instinct for survival
was too strong. Bawoodisik's death brought darkness to the heart
of the survivors of the Beothuk Nation.

The new council was made up entirely of women. The members
made several important decisions. They decided it was time to
come out of hiding. As soon as the weather permitted, they would
go to the bay, all the community together, to dig clams until the
season of abundance returned. Hant's Harbour was the ideal place
for digging clams in the spring, and so all the men, women, and
children would go there together. No one would be armed. There
were three moons in which to spread the word.

"We must force the English to respect us and to accept our
presence on the island," said the women. "They must understand
once and for all that we are not evil monsters, but men and
women of a different colour. We must do this for the sake of those
who remain, and in memory of those who are no more. We must
do this for our future children."

This female movement had grown from the despair of the nation's males. Broken and demoralized, the men had let themselves become soft, and were afraid to make the smallest decision. The women saw this and got together to form a new council. They did not elect a chief, saying that the people had fallen into the habit of relying too much on one person, and of therefore neglecting their own personal responsibilities to the community. They decided unanimously to govern by consensus, as all the councils of the nation had done since the creation of the Beothuk people.

The women decided they had to take the situation in hand. The elders worried, but the women were young and had an unshakeable faith in the human spirit. They reminded the others that young Deed-Rashow the Red was being raised by the English in Fogo. If he was still alive, then perhaps he would help his people make peaceful contact with the English.

"We must meet with them and learn how we can live together in peace. Otherwise they will kill us all. It is not good for us to hide and run from this new civilization that has come from away. There must be a way to learn how to live side by side without killing each other."

The council adopted the following strategy: the women would show themselves first, with their children, then the elders. The men would come out last. Everyone would begin to dig clams and collect shellfish. If the English arrived, they would continue what they were doing as though they were alone.

If they had to acknowledge the English presence, they would keep smiling so that the colonists would understand that the Beothuk were also human beings and intended no harm against anyone. If verbal contact was possible, they would of course try to make them understand, but as a group: no one should try to make contact individually.

"We will go out together, and it is as a community that we wish to be accepted."

The women were very proud of their plan. Once again, they had contributed to the preservation of the Beothuk Nation. Perhaps even to its expansion. They were energetic, proud, almost arrogant. The men were not asked to express their opinion at all. They had had enough opportunity to improve the life of the Beothuk Nation and they had failed to do so for a hundred season-cycles. It was now time for the women to make the decisions.

What would they do, then, if the English were frightened by the sight of so many Beothuk in one place, and fired at them without trying to make contact? They would raise their arms above their heads to show that they were not carrying weapons. Would the English refrain from firing upon an unarmed enemy? They would not kill the entire community! Such a thing was inconceivable. The important thing was not to panic.

Before going to Hant's Harbour, they had to make baskets for collecting the clams and shellfish. Everyone had to set about this task so that they would be ready to leave at the start of the warm season. Throughout the winter, mussels and other shellfish buried themselves in the sand on the beaches; the harvest would be plentiful.

"If the English leave us alone, we could hold a feast-for-everyone again."

The women made the rounds of the mamateeks to collect all the dried grass that had been picked during the previous falling-leaf season. Then they gathered in the large central mamateek to share the work of making baskets and other containers. The people spent much of the season of cold and snow preparing for the public demonstration, the first in the history of the Beothuk. During this time of feverish activity, Mixed-Bloods from the Bay d'Espoir came with sacks of dried and smoked meat to help the Beothuk through the season of deprivation. The Mixed-Bloods seemed to be prosperous. When the Beothuk asked them how they got along with the English, they replied that the foreigners seemed to have accepted their presence well. They even spoke of regular meetings to exchange furs for things like cookstoves, iron cauldrons and pots for carrying water, as well as knives and axes. They told the Beothuk about precautions they took to avoid conflict with the newcomers. They warned them never to accept alcohol from the English, because the English would then cheat them by taking things they wanted and leaving nothing in exchange.

"What is worse," said one of the Mixed-Bloods, "is that that drink makes us crazy and causes us to fight among ourselves, which is never good for us. So no matter what bargain you are offered for it, do not accept it. You will lose everything."

When the Bay d'Espoir people left, one Beothuk couple expressed their desire to go with them and to live among them. The Mixed-Bloods agreed to take them and even invited all the Beothuk to join them. But the council of women politely refused this offer. They had determined to try to make their own peace first. If that attempt failed, then they would think about joining with the Mixed-Bloods.

The council warmly thanked the Mixed-Bloods for so generously sharing their food with the starving Beothuk, a people who were once the uncontested masters of the island now called Newfoundland.

47

JOHN AUGUST AND Tom June were not the first children to be stolen from the Beothuk. Our people still talk about young Ou-Bee, whom the fur trappers took while they were looking for beaver. They broke into a family's mamateek at the head of a bay on the south shore, at the edge of the evergreen forest. The family was sleeping soundly after having worked hard to set up their summer camp. Ou-Bee awoke at the sound of a musket being fired at close range. The first thing she saw was her father covered with blood, still lying where he had been asleep. She then saw her mother being shot full in the face. Then one of the trappers slit her younger brother's throat with a long knife. There was blood everywhere.

Ou-Bee was naked under her caribou blanket, and when she leapt to her feet and tried to escape she was stopped at the door by one of the men, who slapped her face so hard that she fell backwards. Another man held her down by the shoulders while the man who had struck her pulled down his cloth trousers and raped her. She screamed and tried to fight him off, but he was like a starving animal and did not stop until his appetite was appeased. Then a third man held her on the ground, squirming in her own family's blood, while the second man took his turn with her. Then it was the third man's turn. Ou-Bee was completely exhausted from screaming and fighting, and she was in terrible pain, not only in her body but also in her spirit. She was in pain from having been soiled by the English pigs. Pain from rolling in her family's blood. Pain from having seen her loved ones being murdered, and of being alone. And pain from being helpless, unable to do anything to punish their murderers. If she could only get her hands on a weapon she would kill them all, as they had killed her family. But she could not move, she could only vomit on them, and even then she was beaten even harder by the men, who felt no pity for a young girl of only twelve season-cycles, a girl whose life had just been lost to her forever. Because they had taken a live Beothuk captive, each of the men received a reward of ten pounds.

Ou-Bee was sent to England, where she was adopted by a family named Stone. They tried to give her an English name, but she steadfastly refused to respond to it. She responded only when they called her Ou-Bee. Whenever Mr. Stone was alone with Ou-Bee he tried to kiss her, but then she would scream like a terrified animal. Her screams would anger Mrs. Stone, who would come into the room and beat Ou-Bee to shut her up. But her terror of Mr. Stone was so great that she would start to scream as soon as she was alone with him. This apparently causeless screaming exasperated Mrs. Stone even more. Ou-Bee began to have nightmares in which she relived the scene of her rape, and she would wake up screaming, which of course brought Mrs. Stone into her room, to beat her until she was quiet. Somehow, the young girl survived. She was even able to laugh at the blows she received.

Mrs. Stone struck her so hard and so often that eventually her heart began to give out. After that, Ou-Bee paid no attention to the treatment she received at the hand of Mrs. Stone.

It was men she feared. For the rest of her life she detested the presence of men. Mrs. Stone complained that the girl had a mean streak in her, that she never smiled, replied only listlessly when spoken to, and refused to play with children her own age.

It was a friend of the Stone family, a certain Reverend Clinch, who taught Ou-Bee to read and write English. He described her as "happy, playful, fond of teasing, and good with children, with whom she enjoys playing constantly." He said she learned faster than any English child her age, and that after only two years of instruction the English language held no secrets from her. In fact, Reverend Clinch even began to learn the Beothuk language from Ou-Bee, and compiled the first collection of Beothuk words. Ou-Bee lived until the year 1788, when she died of tuberculosis, a disease to which native people have no resistance. Her story was later told to the Paul family in Bay d'Espoir by a soldier who had met the Stones, and I heard it directly from Mary Paul herself.

Meanwhile, in keeping with the decision taken by the women of Red Ochre Lake, as soon as the growing season commenced, when the clams and mussels were most plentiful in the sand on the shores of the bays, more than four hundred women, children, elders, and young men old enough to dig them up, travelled to Hant's Harbour, in Trinity Bay, and showed themselves openly on the beach. As agreed, no one was armed: their aim was to convince the English settlers that the Beothuk people were tired of hiding in the bush like wild animals.

Suddenly a group of fur trappers appeared on the beach, heavily armed with rifles and muskets. There were perhaps twenty-five of them. Instinctively, and in a manner that had not been foreseen by the council, all the Beothuk ran out onto a rocky point that protruded out into Trinity Bay. As though that was a signal, the English began to fire on the unarmed people at the tip of the point. Some of the younger Beothuk jumped into the water and tried to swim away, whereupon the English marksmen made a game of shooting them. The terrified people cried for mercy, imploring the trappers to show them some measure of pity. But the shooting did not cease until all the Beothuk on the point, without a single exception, were dead. Those who witnessed the scene said that the sea and the rocks ran red with our blood.

Such carnage had never been seen before. Four hundred dead. The Living Memories of the Beothuk Nation were all killed at a single stroke. All but one, the one who is telling you this story, Wonaoktaé, also called Demasduit. Of course, the perpetrators of this heinous act were not punished for their barbarity. As usual, official history turned its back on us.

This took place at the end of the eighteenth century. It was also at this time that Tom June was spending much time with the man who had raised him, Doothun, my father. Each time he visited, he coughed more often and seemed sicker than the last time. He had the English sickness, tuberculosis, and he probably contaminated all those with whom he came into contact. But after the massacre at Hant's Harbour, the English sickness spread more slowly throughout the island.

The community at Red Ochre Lake was now reduced to a pitiful few, those who had already been too weak to go to Hant's Harbour. They were now too feeble to hunt or fish for themselves. Many of them died of starvation at this time. There were perhaps a hundred left in the community. Most of them were determined to do whatever they could to survive. They learned to set fire to clearings in the bush and to collect and eat the insects from the burnt grass. They gathered edible plants without caring about how they tasted. The combined wisdom of all the ancestors was called upon and put to use. The inside bark of the birch tree was dried and pounded into a kind of flour, which they used to make bread. This was to be the Beothuk's food until the people reached the end of their history.

Storehouses for dried meat were now well hidden, so that they would not be discovered by the English expeditions that were becoming more and more frequent in the interior of the island.

Whenever a Red Man was sighted he was shot at. There were very few members of the community who had not been wounded in this way. Buckshot from an English musket spread in all directions, and pellets would often lodge in a person's skin without killing him. These wounds would become infected, and would have to be treated. The skin would have to be cut open, and the cuts would then have to be healed with plants gathered from the bush. The healing process took a long time, because the people were already weak, sometimes too weak even to gather the healing plants.

At the start of the season of falling leaves, a trapper named William Cull saw a Beothuk woman on the beach in Gander Bay. She appeared to be alone. There was no one else in sight. It would be easy to catch her. The reward for the capture of a live Beothuk was now fifty pounds, almost a whole year's income for this coarse and greedy man. With the aid of three sailors, William Cull began to chase the woman. She ran from them in the zigzag pattern that had become customary with us, until her four pursuers were completely winded. When they finally captured her, she too, was exhausted, but because of her swiftness William Cull thought that she was a young woman. That, at any rate, is what she told everyone.

During the season before the coming of cold and snow, the English of the island always held a ball. That year the main attraction was the close examination of this Beothuk woman, who was dressed up like a Savage. All of the local high society were there. But the Beothuk woman was uncooperative, and spat on anyone who tried to touch her. Some white-haired gentlemen declared that she was already of a certain age and that her character had been formed by her existence. If she would spit in the faces of English women, she would certainly scratch the faces of English men who simply wanted to see if her skin resembled the skin of humans or was more like that of animals. What was more, she coughed, and was suspected of having "the consumption," as the English called their own disease. It was decided to remove her from the ball and return her to the family that was keeping her. She lived with that family surrounded by children, whom she loved as though they were her own. She had clear, auburn hair and she was slightly taller than English women. After a year it was noted that she seemed to be very sick. Since they did not want to have her death on their consciences, the family contacted William Cull and asked him to take her back to her own people. This he agreed to do. When she was back among her people, however, she spread the contamination, which had not been prevalent since the slaughter at Trinity Bay, and so the English were soon to be rid of the troublesome Savages, as we had become in their eyes.

William Cull was not a man to go to unnecessary trouble on behalf of a Beothuk. He saw no reason to make the twelve-suns' journey through the forest to Red Indian Lake just to return a sick old woman to her people. He abandoned her on the shore of the Bay of Exploits to wait for her people to come and get her, without leaving her so much as a blanket to keep herself warm. It was the end of the month of falling leaves, and it was already turning cold on the island. Later William Cull was suspected of having killed her, but no proof of this was ever found. All that was known for certain was that the Beothuk never saw the old woman again.

One day during the season of abundance, another royal edict was issued forbidding the people of Newfoundland to molest Beothuk. This time it must have been taken seriously, because that year, although there were several recorded encounters between red men and white, no deaths were registered officially. However, the reward for the capture of a live Beothuk was raised to one hundred pounds.

That year a certain Lieutenant Spratt undertook to make contact with us. This officer brought many objects that we might find useful, and had them placed on the beach at the Bay of Exploits, as bait. Our people went down to look at what was there, but they touched nothing. Spratt never saw so much as a hair on the head of a single surviving member of our people. Throughout the entire operation the Beothuk kept watch on the beach around the bay, aware that the English had set a trap for them. They were not about to let themselves be taken by surprise again. There were not enough of us left to risk such a thing. Ever since Hant's Harbour, the English disease had continued its ravages, and the number of living Beothuk was sinking rapidly. Births were rare, since the women were too unhealthy to keep their babies.

It is said that at the end of the eighteenth century there was one man who came to the defence of the Beothuk. His name was G. C. Pulling, a lieutenant in the English navy. He apparently wrote a report in which he strongly denounced the atrocities and acts of barbarism that had been committed by the colonists, fishermen, and fur trappers in the northeast quadrant of our island. According to Lieutenant Pulling, there was more violence against the Beothuk Nation than the Living Memories were able to recount.

48

AFTER RECEIVING A large reward for capturing the old Beothuk woman in Gander Bay, William Cull realized that there was much more money to be earned by trapping Beothuk than by trapping beaver, and so he organized a larger expedition with the aim of bringing in, by force if necessary, more Savages. Cull decided to take his men to the centre of the island to surprise the Redskins, as we were now known, in our winter homes. If, all things being equal, the reward remained as high as the one he had just received, then capturing twenty Redskins would make his fortune. He persuaded his brother John to join him, and the two men enlisted the aid of John Waddy, Thomas Lewis, James Foster, and a fourth man named Joseph. All these men were well known to us, as we had kept a wary eye on them during the warm seasons.

The expedition left from the Bay of Exploits at the beginning of the season of cold and snow. It was also the first year of the nineteenth century. The English travelled during the winter so that they could walk on the frozen river. That way they were sure to find Red Ochre Lake. In other seasons they would have to walk through the woods and try to keep track of the many bends in the river, and would run the risk of not finding the lake. Surrounded by bush, they would also be more vulnerable to attack by our warriors. Also, there was not much else for the English to do during the winter to earn money. Since they still had to live, why not hunt Redskins? Just before they left, they learned that in the last proclamation of the governor of the island, Vice-Admiral John T. Duckworth, the reward for capturing a Beothuk alive was still one hundred pounds. The men were encouraged by the thought of how much money they could earn.

But as soon as they entered the woods they became nervous. The Cull brothers and their men were afraid: at the least snap of a twig they would spin around, their weapons ready to fire. The two Mixed-Blood guides they had hired were more afraid of the expedition members than they were of the Beothuk, with whom they were on good terms. As far as they were concerned, they were not leading the English on a raiding party into Beothuk territory; their job was simply to guide them upriver on the ice, showing them how to avoid the dangerous places where the ice was likely to break through. The two guides were very familiar with the river's treacherous currents and eddies.

On the fourth day of the march, the men discovered one of our food caches. The storehouse contained one hundred caribou, well dried and sealed in their birchbark containers. Each container also held the heart, kidneys, tongue, and liver of the animal. They also found more than a hundred prime furs and animal skins in the storehouse, which they took. To ease their consciences, in place of the furs they left us some broken tools, which they thought that we, simple Beothuk Savages that we are, would find useful.

The next morning two of our men showed themselves to the expedition, and so the English knew that we were aware that they were a raiding party, that they had come into our territory to capture us. The two men vanished into the bush on snowshoes as rapidly as they had appeared. It was now clear to the expedition that they had been under surveillance from the start. The guides laughed and talked to each other in their own language, which the English did not understand.

Weighted down with their stolen goods, the English did not continue their expedition to make contact with the Red Men, the last Beothuk to inhabit the island of the Addaboutik. Instead, they returned to the Bay of Exploits. Still, the expedition had been a profitable one for the men, since they sold the stolen furs at a high price, and it had cost them nothing to obtain them.

Later that same year, in August, Lieutenant Buchan arrived in the Bay of Exploits on the ship *Adonis*. Since it was late in the season, Buchan decided to spend part of the winter in Ship Cove, to wait for an opportune moment.

During the cold season, Lieutenant Buchan undertook to travel up the Exploits River, led by William Cull and his friends. Matthew Hughster, Thomas Taylor, and twenty-three men from the *Adonis* crew formed this new expedition. Although the leader was different, most of the members were the same men, and were well known to us. They were Redskin hunters, and the Beothuk were wary of them whenever they came near. However, the expedition brought provisions and many useful things which they intended to give us, nearly two tons of useful merchandise. All the items had been loaded onto twelve sledges and pulled by sailors from the *Adonis*, who were armed with pistols and swords. The fur trappers insisted on carrying their long hunting muskets, and Buchan gave them permission to do so.

The expedition experienced great difficulty in travelling up the Exploits River. The members were clearly unskilled at using snowshoes. They did not lift their feet high enough to clear the front of the snowshoe. When there was even a light crust on the surface, the snowshoes would catch under it and the men would trip and injure their legs or twist their ankles. Novices tend to tie their whole feet to their snowshoes, but only the toe is supposed to be attached, leaving the heel free. That way, the tail of the snowshoe never leaves the snow, and there is always some contact with solid ground. When the foot is raised, it must be placed down ahead of the other foot. If you set it down beside the other foot, you will become tired very quickly. You must also take turns breaking trail. After a snowshoer has broken trail for a while, he must fall back and let another man take the lead, otherwise he will soon become exhausted. That is the secret of walking on snowshoes.

One morning the expedition came upon the remains of a mamateek on an island in the middle of the river. After ten more suns of marching, they found one of our storehouses. It was circular in form, which was how our ancestors built their storehouses. It was made from small trees cut and stuck straight up in the ground, and covered with caribou skins sewn together.

A Beothuk could make the trek from the Bay of Exploits up the river to Red Ochre Lake in less than six suns. Often we could do it in five. The English had been travelling for twelve suns and were still one sun away from our lake. They made camp at the base of a rapids, and the next day Lieutenant Buchan decided to leave the provisions behind with a guard of fifteen sailors, and to continue upriver with eight of his best snowshoers. That day they felt they were being spied upon by shadows in the woods. They became very nervous. They knew that their presence had been noticed.

The next day they entered a clearing near Red Ochre Lake, where they found three mamateeks: two of them close together, and the third about two hundred paces distant. It was early morning, and the Beothuk were still sleeping. The intruders could hear them snoring. Since there were nine English, all well armed, they decided to break into all three mamateeks at the same time, to profit from the element of surprise. At a signal, the three doors of the mamateeks were thrown open and we were startled from our sleep.

That winter my whole family had decided to camp on the south shore of the northern arm of the lake. When Lieutenant Buchan crept into our clearing like a thief, our family was divided into three mamateeks. In the first, the one separated from the others, was my brother Mamjaesdoo and his family, including my niece Shanawdithit. I was in the middle mamateek with my father, my mother, and my brothers and sisters. Shanawdithit's uncle, her mother's brother, was in the third mamateek. His name was Nonosabasut, the handsome one, who was as strong as a bear. With him was his brother L'Oignon, so named by the French of our nation. In all, we were twenty men, twenty-two women, and thirty children. Seventy-two people in three huge mamateeks. I was twenty-one season-cycles old. I had been born the year they found Tom June drowned in the harbour on Fogo Island.

Farther away, on the south shore of the lake, was a camp consisting of two mamateeks containing five men, seven women, and five children. Closer to our camp were two more mamateeks, with only four men, three women, and six children. In the three camps there were one hundred and two people, all that was left of the two thousand or more who had made up the Beothuk Nation only a few hundred season-cycles before.

When Lieutenant Buchan arrived in our camp, we were sleeping comfortably in our mamateek. The coals in the firepit were still warm, and since it was not very cold outside life seemed good to us. When the sound of voices reached us, my father woke up and tried to understand what it was we were hearing. Then the other adults sat up, each of them alert. I sat up, too. From where I was, I could clearly see the others' faces in the soft light from the embers. Suddenly the door-covering of the mamateek flew open and men wearing blue and red clothing surged into our home. We were completely stunned by this sudden intrusion. The men in blue with bright buttons down the front were not known to us, but the other men, the men wearing caribou skins and carrying long muskets, we knew all too well. By their presence we knew that some of us would die that day. One of the men in blue, a small man, smiled broadly and began seizing the hands of our adults and shaking them vigorously up and down, as the English do so often among themselves. When he came to a child, he stroked its head in a friendly manner, as we ourselves do with our children. Slowly, our fear subsided, and the adults became curious, admiring the shining buttons of the men in blue. My father got up, stirred the fire to life, and invited the men in blue to sit down beside it.

The adult women, including my mother, took some caribou meat and began to cook it on the fire on the ends of small sticks. Then she offered it to the Englishmen, who took it without showing any of the distaste that non-natives usually show when we offer them food. All this time one of the men, a fur trapper, was looking at me. I could see his eyes travelling up and down my body. My chest was bare, as were those of the other women in the mamateek. I know that English women do not bare their breasts. Even when they are nursing, they just loosen their dresses and reveal only the tip of their nipples to their babies. But this man stared so long at my breasts that I began to be afraid, and pulled the blanket up over my body. This uncovered my legs and my sex. At that, the man's face went completely slack, and I quickly grabbed my brother's blanket and covered myself. His expression troubled me deeply. His chief saw that something was wrong, and said something to the man that I could not understand, and the man turned his face and stared into the fire. By their gestures, we understood that these men did not mean to harm us. They indicated that they had gifts for us, but that these gifts were at the end of the first rapids below the lake. We put on our outer clothing and everyone left the mamateek. All the other Beothuk were outside already, talking with the rest of the Englishmen, but no one seemed to understand what anyone else was saying.

With more gestures, the English chief gave our men to understand that he had gifts for us, but that we must come to their camp below the rapids to get them. He asked if any Beothuk would accompany him to his camp. Still suspicious, our men consulted with each other. In the end, four men, including Nonosabasut and his brother L'Oignon and Ge-oun the Jaw, decided to go with the English. Nonosabasut said to his family:

"We will go with them to get them away from here. When we're gone, you must all get away. We'll lose them on the path, since they cannot chase us very well on snowshoes."

But this plan was ruined when the lieutenant left two sailors with us, "as a sign of good faith," he seemed to be saying. The two men were James Butler and Thomas Bouthland.

Buchan left with six of his men and four of ours. The four Beothuk told us later that the English were visibly ill at ease as they returned to their camp. Nonosabasut thought that the men believed they were being followed. In fact they were right, because two Mixed-Bloods had been following them since they left the Bay of Exploits. These had been William Cull's guides on the previous expedition. When they had gone only one-quarter of the way back to the English camp, Ge-oun explained by gestures to the lieutenant that he was going back to his people, to see his small baby. Nonosabasut decided to go with him. That left only L'Oignon and the other warrior, whose name I do not remember, even though I am the Living Memory of the nation.

As soon as the nine men reached the top of the hill overlooking our camp, the Beothuk who was with L'Oignon, seeing much smoke and many men in the English camp, decided to go back to his family. He ran away, calling for L'Oignon to run, too. But L'Oignon replied that he was not afraid of the English, and continued with Lieutenant Buchan. When Ge-oun and Nonosabasut reached our camp, the two sailors left to wait with us became afraid, and raised their pistols and pointed them at the men.

When my mother and older sister saw this, they grabbed two bows that were hanging on our mamateek and quickly shot two arrows at the sailors, hitting them in the back. Almost at the same time, two young men also fired arrows at the sailors, also hitting them in the back. The sailors sank to the ground. Nonosabasut and Ge-oun were angered by this survival instinct that had caused four of our people to defend themselves from the threat of the pistols. But three of the four had been wounded by English muskets. My mother had been shot three times, twice so badly that she had almost died from the wounds. Nonosabasut decided that the bodies of the English sailors could not be left in camp, and he lifted one on his shoulders to carry it somewhere else. He ordered the rest of us to hurry to the next camp as quickly as possible.

Faster than it is taking me to tell it, we gathered up our things and ran to the next camp. Nonosabasut cut the heads off the two corpses. This was a symbolic gesture meant to say there was no glory in their deaths, that death for them was anonymous and they should not be recognized by their relatives in the Afterlife.

The next morning Buchan and his men returned to our camp and found no one there. We had all disappeared, including his two sailors. Buchan distributed his gifts to the three mamateeks. And since it was late and the sun went down early in the cold season, he decided to spend the night in our homes. The English were very nervous. One of them, John Grimes, heard a sound outside the mamateek and, without looking to see what it was, shot his musket through the bark covering. There was a loud shout of anger, followed by much cursing in English: Thomas Taylor had had his sleeve burned by Grimes's ball. Taylor was extremely angry, and it was all Buchan could do to prevent him from attacking the sailor who had been so nervous that he had fired his musket without looking. L'Oignon wondered what would have happened if the man outside had been a Beothuk.

The expedition left for the coast the next morning, leaving the two sailors behind to fend for themselves. L'Oignon, the only Beothuk still with them, broke trail for the English on his snow-shoes. After a while he stopped, told the others he had seen something, went up to the spot where he said it was, and vanished into the bush. When Buchan reached the spot himself he found the decapitated corpses of his two sailors. When the expedition arrived at their food cache, Buchan saw that all the bread had been taken but the pork meat was still there, although it had been thrown about on the ground. The Beothuk do not eat salt pork, not even when they are starving.

For the next two suns no one in the expedition closed their eyes. It was supposed to have been an expedition of peace, but now they were so afraid of the Red Men that they practically ran back to the bay where their ship was anchored. They were followed and watched the whole time. L'Oignon the warrior had quickly rejoined his people, including Gausep the Breath, whose name I had forgotten earlier in my story. Ge-oun was with him also.

"You took your time getting away," Ge-oun said to L'Oignon. "If you had stayed with them much longer, we would not have been able to save you."

"Why were the two sailors killed?" asked L'Oignon.

"We had no choice. When Nonosabasut and I returned to camp, they became frightened and pointed their pistols at us. Before they could kill us, our women shot them with arrows. Their two arrows would have been enough, but then two young men also fired at them. We had no cause to kill them before that. All we wanted was for everyone to get out of camp and return to the lake. You never know what to expect from these people. They are completely unpredictable. They shoot at anything."

"I know. One of them shot through the wall of the mamateek during the night and almost killed a white chief. They are afraid of us. And when those people become afraid, the Beothuk suffer. What are we going to do now?"

"Keep out of their way, if that's possible," said Ge-oun the Jaw.

49

HOPING TO SPEND the rest of the season of cold and snow in peace, we moved our camp to the opposite side of Red Ochre Lake, and at the far end of it. It took us four suns, travelling through the cold and the deep snow, to reach this place, where we were certain no Bouguishamesh had ever set foot.

It was very difficult for us to build new, comfortable mama-teeks. Those who had already been sick became worse and died. I was in good health, and was strong, and so even being who I was, Wonaoktaé, known by my people as Demasduit, the Living Memory of the few Beothuk people left on the island now called Newfoundland, I worked like everyone else to care for the sick and share what I had with them. It was during this season of cold and snow that Nonosabasut noticed me for the first time. In the former days, when a woman reached twenty-one season-cycles she would have had to have been very ugly if she was still untaken. But now, with so much sickness and so many of us killed by the invaders, everyone was too busy keeping alive to think about such things. It was not possible to enjoy life, to live in peace as our ancestors had been able to do. Those who lived before us also had problems with the foreigners, but they also knew long periods of quiet, many dozens of season-cycles when there were few worries. The foreigners came to this island and our people saw them come. Now they lived here, in our bays, on our shores, they prevented us from digging clams or gathering food from the sea, they did not allow us to fish in the abundant waters that surround our island. They even chased us into the deepest parts of our forest. It had become intolerable for us. We hardly dared to close our eyes at night for fear of being attacked in our sleep.

Our people were not entirely without fault. We often attacked the colonists and the fishermen and the fur trappers. But we only attacked them after they had shown themselves to be hostile to us. If the fishermen had been content just to fish, we would have been able to continue gathering our own food from the sea. But the fishermen hired fur trappers who, instead of trying to trade with us, killed us and stole our furs. The Shanung and the Sho-Undamung traded with the French and the English for three hundred season-cycles, but the fur trappers took our furs and offered us nothing in return. They signed treaties with the Mixed-Bloods from the Bay d'Espoir. Why did they never sign a treaty with us?

When Lieutenant Buchan took us by surprise, there were still a hundred Beothuk living. When Nonosabasut came to ask if he could share my mamateek, three season-cycles later, there were only sixty of us left. The others had either died of the English disease or had been killed by the English fur trappers.

In the twenty-four season-cycles of my life, I had often travelled with small groups of attackers. We would hide in the bush and steal tools and fish hooks, just so we could take salmon from our own rivers, which the English had claimed for themselves. They blocked the mouths of the rivers with weirs and nets to stop the fish from migrating into the interior of the island, where we lived. We had to travel down the rivers to spear our own salmon in the ponds of the palefaces. If we were careless enough to let ourselves be seen, the English would shoot at us. When we offered to share with them the fish we had taken from the ponds, they fired at us anyway, to punish us for taking them. It took us a long time to understand this way of thinking. To obtain the things that we needed to stay alive, we had to risk being killed. At first it seemed like a game, but we soon learned that the muskets were fired at us in earnest. We had no choice. We could not confront people armed with muskets and pistols. Even if we could obtain muskets and pistols of our own, who would give us powder and shot? Certainly not the same people who were firing at us.

In the early days of our union, Nonosabasut and I were happy despite our fear of the English. We had lived with that fear since the day we were born, and had become used to it. People were dying all around us, the fur trappers stole our furs, shot at us as though we were rabbits, and prevented us from procuring the food of our forefathers. But we were happy. The joyful laughter of our children took our minds off our troubles, as children had always done among our unfortunate people. And I, as the Living Memory, continued to frighten them with stories of the Bouguishamesh, who killed Beothuk children for sport.

Our men persisted in provoking the settlers along the coasts by stealing the things from them we needed to survive. Whenever I could, I would accompany these raiding parties: we would often spend several suns watching the foreigners without their knowing, waiting for the right moment to steal their tools.

After a while, by listening closely, I was able to understand some of the words that came from the tongues of the English. Slowly I was learning their language. The first Europeans to settle in Notre Dame Bay were the French. Their villages were called Toulinguet, Fougue, Fortune, and Change, and the region they inhabited was called *la côte des Français*. When the English came, they changed the names to Twillingate, Fogo, Change Island, and so on. Nonosabasut's brother had been called L'Oignon by the French because of his strong breath. It seems that the English took over this region without the permission of the French, and there was much ill feeling between them, although not as much as there was against us.

Nonosabasut and I were always together, and it seemed to me that we were becoming one and the same person. There was no need for us to speak because I always knew what he was going to say. When he made a gesture, I knew immediately what it meant. I had watched him for such a long time, in fact since my earliest childhood, that I knew him as well as I knew myself.

The feelings I had for this man were stronger than a simple wish to couple with him, or to make love, to use the phrase taught to us by Wobee the Malouin, who married Ooish and two other Beothuk women in the time of Jacques Cartier, the explorer. The feelings I had were deeper than that; I would give my life to save his. When I told him of these feelings, he laughed.

"If you ever see anyone point a musket at me," he said, "don't be foolish enough to get yourself shot with me. Save yourself, run as fast as you can, in a zigzag. Never trust those people. You are the Living Memory of the nation, you know better than anyone that we have always suffered when the English come near us."

My feelings for this strong and powerful man were such that I can find no words to express them in your language. I was filled up with them, and I wanted nothing more than to be with him. I made his clothes for the cold season by sewing beaver skins from the interior. We both wore the same coats in the cold season. We wore leggings of caribou hide with the hair turned in, and moccasins that went up to our knees. Beneath our coats we were naked. Since the English seemed unable to tell the difference between a man and a woman, we told every Beothuk woman: "Whenever you are in danger, open your coat to show that you are a female. It may save your life." But this did not always work. In my history of the Beothuk people I have already told you the story of Basdic, the pregnant wife of Bawoodisik, who showed herself to a fur trapper and was eviscerated alive anyway.

In the course of my short life, I have had to learn the entire history of our people. It took me a long time to learn it. When I had it all in my memory I taught it to my niece, Shanawdithit, who is now fourteen season-cycles old, and therefore old enough to find a husband. But there are no more free men in our community, and the women now refuse to share their husbands, as they did before. So Shanawdithit is dry, and the nation does not expand.

The year before my union with Nonosabasut, the governor of this island, who lived in the cove called St. John's Cove, issued another edict aimed at helping us. But he also continued to offer a reward for our capture, and since the English loved rewards they continued to hunt us in order to get them. Money in exchange for a Beothuk seemed to be a good bargain. As for us, we would have given away all the English on the island in exchange for a bit of peace and freedom. But they did not know that.

One day we were walking along the Exploits River when we came upon a winter camp that someone had built at the bottom of a high falls. It was late in the falling-leaf season. We examined the camp and found metal traps, enough food for the whole winter, and a small pond filled with a hundred salmon. We took the traps and speared twenty of the fish. The men went through the provisions and took some tea, but they destroyed the pork, that disgusting, salty meat that the English love so much. Suddenly a man named Morris appeared. He was a trapper, and well known to us. We quickly ran off into the woods, but Shanawdithit tripped and fell down. When she stood up again, she was hit in her right breast by a musket ball.

Nonosabasut shouted so loudly and fiercely that the trapper took fright and ran off as fast as he could. My husband picked my niece up in his arms and carried her to our camp at the top of the great falls, where we cared for her for twelve suns, applying to her breast plants that heal wounds and prevent infections. Poor Shanawdithit suffered terribly, and with only one breast she felt herself to be less of a woman. Men were already scarce; how would she find someone who would take her now? A woman with one breast would not be able to provide enough milk to feed a child. This was the second time my niece had been wounded by an English ball. The first time she had lost part of her calf. This time it was a breast. The poor girl. And despite her trouble she also had to learn all the events of the past, so that she could become the Living Memory when I was gone.

Some of the members of our small community thought that we should make peace with the English, but I was able to give them a hundred reasons why that was impossible. Throughout the whole of our history we have been constantly tricked by those people. Even Lieutenant Buchan, who expressed so much sympathy for our families and our children, formed an expedition made up of the most ferocious and outspoken enemies of the Beothuk.

And what of the four hundred Beothuk killed at Hant's Harbour? How could we trust a people that would do that to us? And the four men who had gone with Lieutenant Buchan, if they had not seen smoke at the bottom of the rapids and returned to our camp, would they not have been killed also? It was true that they did not attack L'Oignon, but that was because he was alone: the English knew that if they killed Nonosabasut's brother they would never make it back to the Bay of Exploits alive. They let L'Oignon go out of fear, not from any generosity of spirit.

When Shanawdithit regained her health and her strength and was able to make the journey back to Red Ochre Lake, we set out on the trail. Snow began to fall, and since we had not taken our snowshoes we had to walk quickly. During the season of cold and snow, a Mixed-Blood from Bay d'Espoir named Paul Paul came to bring us the latest news. He told us that Morris was working for the young John Peyton, the son of a famous hunter of Beothuk. This Peyton had been given the right to trap salmon on the Exploits River, our river, which now no longer belonged to us. It belonged to Peyton. And we received nothing in return. I was careful to memorize this news so that I could tell everyone about it.

When we began to think about everything that had happened to us, we realized that we were all going to die. But we determined that we would not give up without a fight. There were still ways we could harm our persecutors. L'Oignon, Nonosabasut, Gausep, and Ge-oun decided to undertake a series of raids against the English colonists. Shanawdithit, who cared nothing for danger, decided she would accompany them. I went also, since I did not want Nonosabasut to go into battle without me.

We left at the end of the season of cold and snow. As soon as the ice melted, we searched along all the rivers that ran down to the rising-sun coast, which was now called the east coast. The first thing we did was destroy all the salmon nets we found in the rivers. We took them out of the water and cut them up into small pieces. We then went to Exploit-Burnt Island and stole all the sails. Even though there were ten or twelve of us, carrying those ships' sails was not easy. They were very heavy, even when they were folded. We also cut the ships' hawsers at high tide and pulled them in close to shore, so that when the tide went out they were beached. Then we took the rest of the sails and all the tools we found in them. We took a sail belonging to John Peyton Jr. and another belonging to George Tuff.

That is how we took our revenge on you heartless and pitiless people. Our pride was wounded, but it would die only when we died. Not before.

50

THE TWO BROTHERS who fished for salmon in the West and South West brooks running into New Bay were of quite different characters. George Roswell was kind and generous: whenever we came near his fishing grounds he let us take a few salmon, knowing that we needed them to survive. He also turned a blind eye when some of his hooks and other tools disappeared. He understood that those items were a small price to pay for his peace of mind. He was able to fish in our waters for more than thirty years without once being bothered by a Beothuk. George lived on the West Brook. He had come across Beothuk at leat twenty times during his life, and since he himself was never armed he never needed to defend himself against us. The Beothuk trusted him, and not once did he betray our trust.

But his brother, Thomas, who fished the South West Brook, always carried his large hunting musket when he went out. He bragged that he had never missed a Beothuk. But he had wounded many of us. In 1789, I think it was, he wounded an old woman who was unable to run fast enough. She was shot in the shoulder, and ended up losing the use of her arm. The wound itself took a long time to heal because the tendons of her muscles were completely severed by the lead ball. The woman was in her fortieth season-cycle. She suffered terribly. After that, the families that spent the warm season in New Bay avoided the South West Brook area and Thomas Roswell, but they continued to hold a grudge against him. Two young men of about sixteen or seventeen season-cycles went there to watch the salmon ponds. They watched for three suns, but every time Thomas went out to check on the ponds he was accompanied by several other men who were well armed. The two young men did not risk an attack.

But one day Thomas went out alone. He leaned his long musket against a tree and bent over the pond to pull out an enormous salmon using a net with a long handle. That was the signal. The two young men came out of their hiding place and called to him. When the fisherman turned to grab his musket, two arrows with metal tips entered his chest, and one of them pierced his heart.

The two men walked up to him and began naming all the people who had been shot by Thomas Roswell, either wounded or killed. When they had finished their litany, they cut off the man's head to show to the other Beothuk that their families had been avenged. This story has come down to me. I am telling it so that everyone will know that the Red Men will not die without a fight.

Little by little, the young members of our community were getting to know the ways of the English. The Mixed-Bloods from the Bay d'Espoir, who had many contacts with these people, told us much about them. They said that all the chiefs of the English nation on the island lived at St. John's Cove, which they now called simply St. John's, which was on the Avalon Peninsula, a place where nothing grows, and where the wind is always in the trees. The trees bend over to let the wind go by, because they are too weak to resist its passing.

Nonosabasut told us of his final plan. He said that if a fire broke out in that town during the season of cold and snow, when the wind was strongest, the flames would quickly spread to every building. Without their houses, the English chiefs would have to return to England, and perhaps the colonists and fishermen would go with them. Without their chiefs, the others would feel lost.

It was decided to make an expedition to St. John's the next winter, that is, during the third season-cycle of my union with Nonosabasut. It was a dangerous expedition, because there were many rivers and brooks to cross, and a narrow strip of land on which there were no trees to hide in. This was the thin passage that joined the peninsula to the rest of the island. We would have to make many camps in the open, and wait for the wind to go down before we could make a fire. But we were a courageous group. Nonosabasut would be our leader. There was also L'Oignon, his brother, and Gausep the Breath, Shanawdithit my niece, and myself, the Living Memory of the Beothuk Nation. It would be easier for a small group of five people to travel quickly, and harder for the non-native people of the island to see us.

When the ground was frozen solid we set out for St. John's, first crossing the mountains south of Red Ochre Lake. Nonosabasut had already made the journey to St. John's once, and told us that it would take as many suns as three times the fingers on both hands to get there, and the same to get back. We left the main group at the southeast end of the big lake, at a place where a natural harbour came in through the trees, and made our way towards Snowshoe Lake, so called by our people because even in the warm season we had to wear snowshoes to walk across the marshes that surrounded the lake, because the small bushes the Shanung call sagakomi grow so thickly. In winter the springs make the ice so treacherous that we have to wear snowshoes to spread our weight over a wider surface. Even though the snow had not yet fallen, we strapped our snowshoes to our backs before setting out.

This first part of the journey was very difficult. The land had been part of Beothuk territory for thousands of season-cycles, but we seldom hunted on it, and allowed several Mixed-Blood families to use it. The Paul family had made it their hunting and fishing territory. They were the largest family in Bay d'Espoir. At the end of two suns of rapid, steady travelling we reached the large lake that the Mixed-Bloods called Maelpaeg. We had climbed up and down many promontories, cliffs, rises, hills, and mountains. We had crossed dozens of brooks, including the one that bordered the Paul hunting grounds. When we arrived at the head of the lake, we looked about and found a canoe made of birchbark in the manner of the first Shanung to live on the island, and quite unlike our tapatooks, but strong enough to allow us to do some fishing. There were freshwater salmon in the lake, as well as Atlantic salmon and sea trout. At the outlet, the water flowed into the river of white water, which in turn emptied into an arm of the sea known as the Northeast Arm. L'Oignon took the canoe and went fishing while we built a temporary shelter for the night. The weather warmed as evening fell, and it rained during the night, a heavy, persistent rain such as arrives at the end of the falling-leaf season. Our bark shelter kept the rain off well, but we were still cold and we slept curled up close to one another, to conserve our bodies' heat. L'Oignon had caught twelve medium-sized trout and we had eaten well before going to bed. But in the morning we had to catch more fish before continuing our journey. We wanted to have dried and smoked fish for the days when fishing or hunting would not be possible. We left our camp late that day, but we quickened our pace and did not stop until we had reached a beautiful lake that was the source of a river filled with salmon. There were so many salmon at the head of this river, where it left the lake, that it was child's play for Shanawdithit to catch two with her fishing spear. Then she made a good fire of dry birch branches and cooked the fish on a large, flat rock with their skins on, so that they kept their flavour.

The next morning we set out again, this time to reach the Bay d'Espoir, the home of the Mixed-Bloods. These people used to be called Shanung, but that was before the Sho-Undamung came to live with them, making the Mi'kmaq a mixed-blood people. We were welcomed with much festivity, and fed with many kinds of game that had become unfamiliar to us. The Mixed-Bloods were a truly generous and sympathetic people. We had never believed the stories circulated by the English, that these people had come to the island to kill us. The English said such things only to appease their own conscience, and to distance themselves from our troubles. First the Shanung, then the Mixed-Bloods, had often brought us fresh meat to help us through the cold season. The English never once gave us anything. We had never been attacked by the Mi'kmaq, nor by the Innu, but the English never missed a chance to shoot at us. The Mixed-Bloods lent us their canoes. The English beat us back whenever we came close to them. The English never welcomed us into their villages, as the Mixed-Bloods did. To get even close to their villages we had to hide and use forest paths unknown to them. The rumours they spread about the Shanung were meant only to cause trouble between us, so that the English could kill us more easily. It is true that we had had our differences with the Shanung more than a hundred season-cycles earlier, but that was long over.

We stayed with them for two whole suns, sleeping in warm beds and not having to use up our own food. We were served like chiefs of the old days, when our nation was still strong and we held feasts-for-everyone. Now we had become poor and could barely feed ourselves, let alone others. There were no more feasts-for-everyone. But our friends remembered the past. I met the Living Memory of their people and learned many things from him about our common histories that I did not know.

For example, he told me that his people had been living here long before the French and the English came. His ancestors had seen Anin pass through on his voyage of initiation. But they did not speak to him because they were afraid he might be an enemy. He told me that his ancestors had also seen the men with hair the colour of dried grass, and who sailed in huge boats, at the same time as Anin. I asked him if this meant that the island belonged to them as well as to us. Why hadn't our two peoples made contact, if that were the case? He replied that there were too few of his people in those times.

The soft living in the Mixed-Blood community could easily have seduced us for a long time. We were among people who had once belonged to our nation and who had freely chosen to be in this place, to live here in peace. We could not blame them. They still called themselves Shanung, but we knew they were Mixed-Bloods.

The next stage of our journey was the pond at the Blue Coast, a section of sea-cliff that was so high that when you stood on it looking straight out all you could see was blue sky. The cliff was peculiar in that the trees that grew on it did not point up to the sky, but followed the slope of the incline. Here the word "sky" did not seem such an inadequate word to designate what we used to call "the immensity of the spirit."

I remembered being told by the Living Memory of the Mixed-Bloods that, unlike us, they each had two names, because they had been baptized in the Christian manner. These Christians had chased the Vikings out of their country many . . . a very long time ago. Their religion allowed them to kill anyone who did not follow their teaching. They were like the English, who are also Christians. And the French, and the Spanish, and the Portuguese. They all have permission to kill anyone who is not a Christian. That was why the people at Bay d'Espoir were allowed to live in peace: *because they were Christians*. The English could not kill them. If we became Christians, perhaps we would not be killed by the English. I spoke about this with Nonosabasut, who laughed at the idea.

"Perhaps," he said. "But then, wouldn't we have to stop killing them, too? Would we not be able to avenge our dead? The English would still rob us: only then they would be robbing us of the pleasure of watching the bastards die for having shot at us for the past how many hundreds of season-cycles! No. I could not accept that."

And he laughed again.

"Besides," he said. "Have you never heard of the wars that those Christian people have fought between themselves? If they can wage war on each other, why could they not still wage war on us? If they refrain from killing the Mixed-Bloods, it's because the Mixed-Bloods are useful to them, as guides and hunters, to provide them with food and furs. Not because they are Christians."

His reply made me thoughtful and sad. I believed that I had found a solution to our troubles. But now I wondered if the Beothuk even wanted to survive physically. I was no longer sure. Perhaps it was better to go on being the Living Memory of my people than to try to find simple solutions.

The next stage took us deep into the heart of dangerous country, the region where the English lived. We would also be close to the passage that would take us onto the Avalon Peninsula, between the two large bays called Placenta and Trinity. It would be a critical stage in our journey. We would have to sleep surrounded by Bouguishameshes. The very thought of it made my skin contract like that of a plucked ptarmigan. The evening of the next day we slept near Arnold's Cove. We could see the houses of the colonists and smell their domestic animals, which were still rare on the rising-sun coast but more numerous down here on this part of the island. There were horses, a grey one and a brown one. They were pulling a huge wagon filled with fish. The English found many ways to avoid doing physical labour themselves. It would have taken twenty Beothuk a whole sun to carry that many fish as far as these two horses were moving it. But there was no room for horses at Red Ochre Lake. They need plenty of space to be useful. I prefer our ways.

L'Oignon told us that these animals were very inconvenient. You have to give them so much food, and since they can't find it themselves you have to dig up the ground and grow it for them.

"Digging up the ground to feed horses," added Nonosabasut, "and then to use horses to pull food for humans, is a form of slavery. Once you begin you can never stop. The way I see it, you end up eating to work, instead of the other way around, as it is with us."

He gave his loud, sonorous laugh, even though we were supposed to be as quiet as possible. We signalled to him to stop and he did, but he continued to let out snorts of laughter from time to time. It was difficult for him to keep his good humour in check. He laughed much more than the rest of us. He was big, tall, and strong as a bear, but he was as gentle and tender as a mother with her child. That's how he was, my husband, the most beautiful man in the entire Beothuk Nation.

L'Oignon was always trying to make out that he was more handsome than Nonosabasut, which made us laugh. Gausep, too, would strike poses and twist his face to make himself look fine, but he was very ugly to begin with, and his contortions only made him look uglier, and that would make us laugh even harder. The laughter helped us to forget our troubles for a short while. Shanawdithit took advantage of this quiet time to stick close to me and learn about our history, and her apprenticeship progressed more swiftly than usual.

Although there were many English houses about, there were also many clumps of stunted trees, and we had no difficulty finding places to hide. We had more trouble with dogs on the farms; they would smell us from far away and bark and bark, and sometimes keep us awake all night.

Our real problems began when we reached Conception Bay. Here the houses were closer together, and there were many more people out and about. Nonosabasut decided that we could no longer travel during the day. We would hide and rest and continue our journey to St. John's by night.

It had now been two full moons since we left Red Ochre Lake, nearly twice the time we had anticipated. But we had learned much about the world about us, and about the English ways of life.

At last we arrived at the edge of a small forest on the east side of a high hill that overlooked the village of St. John's. From here we could watch the activities of the whole community. Snow had been falling steadily for two suns, and the cold was beginning to bother us. But we did not dare to light a fire for fear of being discovered.

The wind changed just as the sun was going down. It came from the east, and blew hard all night. That was our signal to begin our final preparations. Nonosabasut and L'Oignon were to start their fire at the eastern end of the village. Gausep would go to the south and Shanawdithit and I would go north. When we had set our fires, we would flee back along the same route by which we had come, and go all the way to Conception Bay before stopping. There we would rest and wait for the others in a small hiding place we had built for that purpose.

When we had all heard the plan, Nonosabasut said it was time to make a fire to warm ourselves. He said we should wait to start our fires until all the lights were out in the English houses.

But since we could not be sure that all the English would go to bed at the same time, Shanawdithit and I decided to start our fires in a barn in which there was a great deal of dried grass for the horses. Shanawdithit had to call the farm dog inside and cut its throat with her long knife to shut it up. Otherwise we would have been discovered by the dog's owner, who was constantly looking out his window to see why the dog was barking. There was a good stand of conifer trees near the barn, and the next house was close to the buildings of this one, and so the fire spread very rapidly. In fact, it spread so quickly we were almost caught in our own trap. We had to run like the wind to escape, and we kept on running until we reached Conception Bay, where we finally stopped just as the sun was beginning to rise. We waited there for a whole sun, but no one seemed to have come after us. During the night we were awakened by footsteps: it was Gausep. He had run all the previous night, but during the day he had had to hide until night-fall again before he could join us. He assured us that we had no need to worry about Nonosabasut and L'Oignon, because the corner of the village where they had gone to start their fire had taken well, and they were able to get away quickly.

But the wait was terribly long for me. My man, my husband, my companion, my whole life, was absent from me. I did not once close my eyes. I had never found time annoying and I used to laugh to hear Tom June say he never had enough of it. But that night I realized what time is. It is a martyrdom that never ends. An eternity.

Shortly before daybreak my head was filled with the sound of footsteps. It was Nonosabasut. But he was crying like a baby. We could see that everything had not gone according to plan, but we did not question Nonosabasut. We did not say a word. When my husband was ready to tell his story, he would tell it. There was no use asking questions. When he had calmed down, he told us that his brother L'Oignon had been burned alive when he had tried to run through a wall of fire that had cut the village in half. It was his clothing, his cotton clothing that Lieutenant Buchan had given him during the expedition five season-cycles before. L'Oignon had worn these clothes especially for this occasion. If he had been wearing clothing made from caribou hides, he would not have died. Our clothing does not catch fire so easily.

When I learned that the wall of fire had been near the place where Shanawdithit and I had set our fire, I felt guilty for having started our fire too early, and cutting off L'Oignon's escape route.

I am the Living Memory of the Beothuk people, and I must remember the story of this expedition, and the tragedy that marked it, for the rest of my life.

51

IN SOME PLACES the river is calm, in others it rushes through narrow rapids. When it is calm it seems to be resting up for a tumultuous, growling cascade, and then it is calm again when it widens to become the long lake known to us as Red Ochre. It begins in the mountains that rise to protect the rising sun, and it flows towards the north-northeast. And although it appears calm for its journey through Red Ochre Lake, after two suns it picks up speed again as it drops into a series of small ponds, each lower than the other, and gains more water from the many brooks that feed into the ponds. It finally loses itself in the Bay of Exploits, where it forms the south arm of huge Notre Dame Bay. Six or seven suns to travel seawards from the mountains to Red Ochre Lake, two suns through the lake, and from the top of the cascading ponds to its mouth in Notre Dame Bay another eight to ten suns, altogether making a river the length of two moons. No other river in Newfoundland carried so many salmon. But the Exploits River, the Beothuk's source of life, can no longer feed its people. It has been robbed of its life-giving power by the holding ponds built by the English colonists. The fish no longer come to the high inland ponds at the heart of the island.

That heart has also been pillaged by the English trappers, who compete with the Beothuk for furs. From the beginning they have done all they could to procure the furs that are so eagerly bought by the European markets. The Beothuk simply needed the furs to make clothing for the long seasons of cold and snow.

When a fur trapper broke into our storehouses and took our furs, we had to start all over again.

Every time the English tried to establish contact with the people of the island, they hired guides who were well known to us as Beothuk killers. How could such contacts be peaceful? If peace was their intention, then why did they come armed to the teeth, and why did they track us down with these hunters of Redskins? If George Cartwright and Buchan and Glascock had been honest soldiers, and if John Peyton Jr. was a humanitarian, why did they come to us in the company of people who could never be trusted by the Beothuk? William and John Cull, Thomas Taylor, Matthew Hughster, John Peyton Sr.?

That is how the last survivors of the proud race of Red Men saw things. They had lived on this island since the beginning of time, longer than memory. The elders said that non-native people have always been afraid of wolves, and tell many stories about those animals in Europe. Their wolves seem much different from the wolves we know on our island. Here the wolves feed on caribou and other animals. They do not eat Beothuk. Non-natives have always been afraid of Beothuk, and they have killed almost all of us.

"When there are no more of us left, the non-natives will have to start killing wolves," the elders said. "That is what happens when you are afraid. Rather than try to conquer your fear through reason, you destroy its source."

So said the last elders of the small community at Red Ochre Lake, during the winter of the great fire at St. John's. When we returned to the lake after setting the fire, we had to take a different route. We decided to travel by day, and whenever anyone saw us they grabbed their muskets and fired at us. We were not hit because we knew how to run, by fanning out and running in a zigzag pattern. But our journey was long and dangerous. We would travel days on end on snowshoes. And I was pregnant. During the season of dead leaves, I gave Nonosabasut a son.

That summer, the few Beothuk still surviving had to steal salmon from the English holding ponds so that our elderly, our sick, and our pregnant women would have enough to eat during the season of cold and snow.

Our lake now had only pike, and our river yielded only the occasional sea trout. Our season of abundance was now a season of famine, a time when our men had to work as hard for food as they did during the season of cold and snow. The caribou were also hunted by the swelling masses of European immigrants to the island. There were many Irish living here now, in Notre Dame Bay. These people penetrated farther into the bush in search of game. Knowing little or nothing about us, they thought nothing of shooting at us as though we were wild animals. Our land, once so vast, shrank a little each day, rain or shine.

All the leaves had fallen when I gave birth to a male child. He was not big, but he was healthy. I was in my twenty-seventh season-cycle, but this was my first child and my milk was not abundant. We had to start him on solid food very early so that he would grow and survive. But I was very happy, and Nonosabasut was watchful and attentive. Shanawdithit helped me with my daily tasks. She was now seventeen season-cycles, but there was no one to take her for a wife. This is sad for a people who for hundreds of season-cycles have lived only for the family, the clan, and the nation, whose strongest urge is to populate the island and defend the integrity of their territory. If we were more numerous, we would have declared war on the invaders who used any means within their power, including violence and trickery, to kill us.

There were not enough resources on the island to feed a larger nation. The only way for us to survive was to drive the palefaces out of our country. That was our dream. But it remained nothing but a dream.

During the winter after the birth of my child, Shanawdithit was wounded again by a fur trapper who surprised her at one of his marten traps. This time she was hit in her right side, up high where her coat was attached. She walked for half a sun to where Gausep and his wife were hunting, and they cared for her well. Despite her third wound, Shanawdithit was always smiling. She said that if she was shot three or four more times there would not be enough left of her for a husband. She also calculated that at the rate she was going, she would have enough flesh for a hundred season-cycles.

Time passed and the number of Beothuk decreased. The fever that followed a dry cough and a general tiredness continued to take us. Three men and two women and four babies died during this last season of cold and snow.

Then the warm season returned, and with it the heat, the sun, the berries, the blackflies and mosquitoes. It amused me to think that these tiny insects would bite us and then fly off to bite the English. I wondered if our blood tasted the same. I also wondered why the English did not cover their skin with red ochre to protect themselves from fly bites. I thought that blackflies must be able to find many nice, comfortable places to go about their business under those dark, heavy clothes the English wore. The thought of it made me laugh. It wasn't much, but it was some compensation for all that we had lost.

Throughout the warm season we talked about the things we would need for the winter that would come after the season of falling leaves. We would have to steal a few more sails in order to cover our mamateeks. Birchbark was becoming scarce. The trees were being cut before they could grow to their full height. At Notre Dame Bay, where we traditionally went for the largest trees, the English had cut them all down for firewood, the biggest trees first. We had to make our tapatooks smaller and smaller. We had to take their sails because they had taken our trees. The same may be said of other things. We would have dug clams, but when we went down to the beaches at night we would find that there were no clams left in the sand, the English had gathered them all during the day and left none for us. They blocked our rivers and prevented the salmon from swimming up to us. They hunted our game and prevented us from making winter clothing. It took Nonosabasut a whole winter to trap ten beavers to make me a coat for the season of cold and snow. Fortunately the meat from that animal is the best of all those that live on our island, and is very nourishing to those who know how to prepare it.

It was decided that as soon as the season of falling leaves came, a small group would go down to Notre Dame Bay to steal some sails. At the beginning of the falling-leaf moon, five persons left for the bay: they were Shanawdithit, Nonosabasut, Gausep, his wife Mamatrabet the Song, and Shanawdithit's father, Mamjaesdoo. When they arrived, they observed the activities of the English from the top of a small hill we call the tapatook, situated just behind the house and wharf belonging to John Peyton Jr. From there they saw that Peyton's men were loading a ship with salmon taken from our Exploits River. When the ship was loaded and ready to leave, Peyton had to wait for high tide so the ship would not be grounded on the many reefs that fill the bay. He appeared to be nervous. He walked back and forth between his ship and his house. He walked up and down the wharf. He sensed that he was being watched, but he could see nothing. He was a sensitive man, was John Peyton. This story was told to me in detail by Shanawdithit and Mamatrabet. In telling it, the women shuddered again with their fear of being caught before the mission was completed. In order to get the sails, they had to cut the ship's ropes, get to the tiller, direct the ship towards the beach, ground it, take down the sails, and then carry them back to Red Ochre Lake.

It was a moonless night. The mission had to be carried out silently. Gausep carried the tapatook down to the beach, accompanied by Nonosabasut and Shanawdithit. The three of them paddled without taking the blades from the water, sculling in the Beothuk manner, towards the wharf. Suddenly they saw Peyton come out of his house and walk out onto the wharf to the ship. They barely had time to glide under the wharf, which was mounted on pylons, and to wait there without moving, without even breathing, until the nervous Englishman went away. The wait seemed so long the two women thought it would never end. Finally Peyton returned to his house. As soon as he

was out of sight, Gausep climbed onto the ship and helped
the others up. They tied a rope to the tapatook, and lifted it to the
deck of the ship. Then the two women cut the hawsers. Slowly
the ship drifted away from the wharf, pushed gently by a north
wind, and headed towards the beach. Gausep was at the tiller
while the two women cut the ropes attaching the folded sails to
the mast, and laid them out on the deck, near the tapatook.
Then they lowered the tapatook into the water. There
Nonosabasut and Mamjaesdoo, along with four other men who
had just come in from fishing halibut, were waiting in water up
to their waists for the others to lower the sails. They placed the
sails in the tapatook, pulled the tapatook to the shore, and lifted
it out to carry it to Red Ochre Lake. Gausep found two muskets
in the captain's cabin. He broke them up into pieces, in recog-
nition of all the wounds that had been inflicted on us, and for
the dead of the Beothuk Nation. Then he gathered up all the fish
hooks and hatchets he could find and plunged into the water to
join his companions.

It was not easy to transport those sails to our camp. The men
cut two long poles and strung ropes between them to form a kind
of netting, then they placed the sails on the netting so that two
men could carry them. By changing places from time to time,
they were able to make the return journey, which otherwise
would have taken ten suns, in only seven.

No lives were lost to the community during this expedition. As
soon as they returned to camp, it was time to dig the pits for the
winter mamateeks and to put the poles in place around them, and
then cover the poles with the sails from John Peyton Jr.'s ship.
Then the women made a second wall inside the first, to the level
of their heads, and stuffed dried moss between the two walls.
They also laid pine boughs on the ground around the central
firepit. Finally, the pine boughs were covered with caribou hides
to make the mamateek comfortable and warm.

It took many suns to make a mamateek for the season of cold
and snow, for there were many important precautions to take.

The positioning of the mamateek had to be right, at the top of a small rise so that water would not run into it. Also, the ground around had to have good natural drainage, so that the mamateek would not become an island in the spring.

It was in this mamateek that I spent the season of cold and snow with my husband Nonosabasut and our male child.

52

IT IS WITH great sadness that I take up the telling of this history of my people. I am Shanawdithit, of the Beothuk Nation, the niece of Demasduit. I am now the Living Memory of the Red-Ochre people. My aunt passed on to me the duty of relating the events that followed her telling.

With the aim of getting back what had been stolen from him, John Peyton Jr. obtained permission from the governor, Sir Charles Hamilton, to recover his goods. He also received permission to capture one or two Beothuk in order to establish contact with them. It may be, as the historians of that period say it is, that the governor was concerned with the well-being of our people, and that John Peyton was truly a philanthropist and humanitarian, but it would be hard to prove it by those who were primarily concerned in this matter.

When the Mixed-Blood hunter Paul Paul saw the expedition set off from Upper Sandy Point on the morning of March 1, 1819, he recognized the two John Peytons, senior and junior, Dick Richmond, John Day, Jacky Jones, Matthew Hughster, William Cull, Thomas Taylor, and a man named Butler. From this list he knew that something unpleasant was about to happen to the Beothuk people. Although advanced in years, and taken with the dry cough, the half-Shanung, half-Sho-Undamung hunter hurried on snowshoes as fast as he could to warn us of the coming danger. He hurried so as not to lose time, and soon became exhausted with the effort. It was reckless of him, because the people of the forest know better than to venture into such an immensity of cold and snow alone.

Despite the advanced age of John Peyton Sr., the expedition made good time, covering much ground each sun. They knew exactly where they were going. They slept little and walked with a determined rhythm, like soldiers who have received precise instructions.

During this time, poor Paul Paul was having more and more difficulty catching his breath, and had to stop more and more often. Finally, completely exhausted, he sat down to rest, and did not get up again. Far from his own people, far even from the Beothuk camp, he went into his final sleep beside Badger Brook on March 3, 1819, without being able to warn us that the enemy was approaching. His body was eaten by wolves and other predators, and was found in the spring by one of his sons, who had gone out to look for it.

We thought that we were about to spend a peaceful season of cold and snow. We forgot that we had enemies. When the leaves had fallen, we had the two sails taken from Peyton Jr. and we did not expect him to come after them until the spring. However, we had taken great care not to take any of his fish. No barrel on his ship destined for England had been touched. We took only two sails, ten fish hooks, and three boarding axes. It is true that Gausep broke the muskets, those weapons that had caused so many deaths and had wounded so many of our people, including myself three times.

The month of winds came, and we thought we had escaped the vengeance of the English for another season-cycle. We were wrong. Many of us were gathered in the mamateek of Nonosabasut and Demasduit, known as Wonaoktaé, the Living Memory of the Beothuk Nation. The sun was going down rapidly, and it was almost twilight. There was a shout – "Bouguishamesh!" – and we all ran immediately outside and fled into the woods.

Demasduit, carrying her infant son, was the last to leave. One of the Englishmen ran after her. Seeing that she was going to be caught, she literally threw her two-season-cycle-old son to Gausep, who caught him and threw him in turn to me. I muffled him up in my fur coat to keep him warm, and hid myself behind a stand of white pine, along with several others. The man caught up with Demasduit and, as we had been taught to do since we were children, she opened her coat to show him that she was a woman. Then she touched her breasts, which were swollen with milk, to show him that she was nursing a child.

We all recognized the men as Beothuk killers. The one who caught Demasduit was the son of the old assassin, Peyton Sr. Although he had not yet done anything to us, the loss of his sails certainly meant he was not well disposed towards us. Gausep and his young son took out their bows, ready to attack the butchers from the Bay of Exploits. But Nonosabasut stopped them by saying that he was going to try to talk to them first. He advanced towards the group of men and, looking the old Peyton straight in the eye, told him to tell his son to let Demasduit go. When John Peyton tried to take out his pistol, Nonosabasut, swift as lightning, grabbed the weapon from his hand and threw it far away. It landed in a mound of snow covered with a crystal crust. Then Nonosabasut, the husband of Wonaoktaé, seized the old murderer by the throat with his left hand and, threatening to hit him with his right, said to him: "Tell your son to let my wife go, or I will kill you."

Then Peyton Jr. ordered Nonosabasut to be killed. One of the men raised his musket, which had a bayonet fixed to the end of it, and plunged it into Nonosabasut's back. Our friend fell to his knees.

Nonosabasut picked up a small, forked stick, raised it into the air as a sign of peace and friendship, then touched his forehead with it, and trying to stand up, offered it to Peyton Sr. The old man became afraid, thinking that Nonosabasut was attacking him again. "Are you going to let him kill me?" he shouted. We all knew what his words meant. When he had shouted them, Dick Richmond raised his musket and shot Demasduit's husband in the back. Nonosabasut fell face down on the snow, but still he was not dead. He got to his feet again and grabbed old Peyton by the throat. Then a number of muskets all fired at once, Nonosabasut fell, and this time did not get up.

I know that now everyone says that it was Nonosabasut who, unarmed, first attacked those poor, helpless murderers who were armed to the teeth, but I, Shanawdithit, tell you that although Nonosabasut was courageous and loved Demasduit very much, he was also not stupid, and would never have faced ten well-armed men, with their muskets and pistols, alone and weaponless as he was. He was only trying to save his wife. One day I heard someone say that the English thought that Nonosabasut was an enraged monster. Nonosabasut was well built, strong, and impressive of stature. But he was not a monster, and he was not enormous. He was an ordinary Beothuk, and because he was not motivated by fear, but by love, his enemies were afraid of him and saw him as bigger than he was. He was a good husband, a gentle and caring father. He loved Demasduit deeply, and she loved him in return. Such men gain in stature when they are dead, and those who kill them are the ones who should be reproached.

When Lieutenant David Buchan came to make contact with us when I was still a young girl, he spoke to Nonosabasut for a long time and did not report being overly impressed by his size. We are always astonished by lies when our tradition has taught us that only truth exists. If lies killed, then all the non-natives on this island would be dead. I no longer believe that truth alone is the means to life. Our tradition definitely does not apply to the English.

Nonosabasut was not our chief. Our community had been reduced to only a few individuals. We were families, not clans. Nonosabasut was the most energetic of us all, and the most experienced, but it is wrong to say that we were all under Nonosabasut's authority, or that we were still a "tribe." That at any rate is a non-native expression, unknown in our language. We were once a nation, divided into separate clans, and each clan was symbolized by an animal spirit-protector in whom the reincarnated spirits of our ancestors resided. Is that clear to you all? I, Shanawdithit, the Living Memory of the Beothuk Nation, do not wish to repeat it.

The expedition had taken only five suns to follow the river up to the lake, but it took many more to return with Demasduit as a prisoner. Her hands and feet were tied tightly, and she was drawn on a sled so that she could not escape. She was cold and hungry. Whenever they gave her that horrible salt pork to eat, she would spit it out and vomit, unable even in starvation to overcome the revulsion she felt for that meat. But she played with her captors, ordering them to lace her moccasins for her, and to wrap her more tightly in her blanket. That is why the English thought they had captured a Beothuk princess, the wife of a Grand Chief.

One night, while her captors slept, Demasduit succeeded in loosening the ropes that tied her to the sled, and slipped quietly out of their camp. She tried to cover her tracks in the snow with her coat, but without snowshoes she quickly became exhausted and was recaptured. For the rest of the journey to the Bay of Exploits she remained calm and quiet, staying as close to John Peyton Jr. as she could. She had picked him out as the leader of the expedition. She would not let Dick Richmond come near her. He had been the first to shoot at Nonosabasut. Whenever Richmond tried to touch her she flew into a terrible rage and struck at him like an evil spirit, and spat in his face.

For the first few days she was kept in the home of the younger Peyton. Then she was transferred to the house of the Episcopal missionary at Twillingate, a Reverend Leigh, who turned her over to Mrs. Cockburn, his housekeeper. From then on, Demasduit was never called anything but Mary March.

When the ice melted, Reverend Leigh brought her to St. John's. When he learned that Demasduit had a young child of only two or three years, he decided that she should be returned to her people. No one had thought of that before: it had never occurred to her captors that that was why she had shown them her swollen breasts. It was only when she tried to express the milk out of her breasts that the reverend understood that she was a nursing mother. She gave him her word that she would return to the English settlement of her own accord if they let her go back to nurse her son. She would return as soon as her son was weaned. And since a Beothuk's word is the witness of the truth, she really did intend to return. John Peyton Jr. went with Reverend Leigh to St. John's to see Governor Hamilton.

The governor ordered Captain W. N. Glascock to take command of Her Majesty's Ship *Sir Francis Drake*, and to go to Notre Dame Bay to return Mary March to her people. She could nurse her child and, perhaps later, help to establish peaceful relations with the Beothuk. He also ordered John Peyton Jr. and Reverend Leigh to accompany the woman until she was once again among her people.

Meanwhile, an inquest was held into the death of Nonosabasut. All the members of the expedition were questioned, and the conclusion they came to was this: "The grand jury is of the opinion that no malice was demonstrated during the events and that it was not their intention to spill blood while detaining one person. It seems that the victim died as a result of his own attempted attack against John Peyton Sr. and his men. The men acted legitimately in their own defence."

However, I, as the Living Memory of the Beothuk people, must note that Demasduit was never interrogated, neither at the inquest nor by the grand jury nor by Governor Hamilton. Perhaps they did not think she was intelligent enough to tell the story of what happened. But she was, at that time, the Living Memory of the Beothuk people. Non-natives are always minimizing our ability to understand what is happening to us. If I have since learned that Christianity is the road to truth, I also know that justice is without colour. It is completely pale.

One of the things that surprises me as I grow older and my responsibilities change is to see how our views of events that once seemed harmless to us also change. There was a time when I felt under attack. Since available men were so few among our people, I behaved like a man. I fought alongside men without even thinking of myself as a woman. Only now that my aunt

Demasduit is no longer among the living do I fully understand that I will never have a Beothuk husband, and that makes me very sad. I will never experience the joy of being a woman, of giving my life to another, of sharing the feeling of being a part of Kobshuneesamut the Creator. I remember the words of Nonosabasut, who said that Kobshuneesamut lost his power as the Creator when two Beothuk died for every one that was born. Despite his sadness, he never lost his ability to laugh out loud whenever the opportunity arose. What was the sense of crying when there was nothing to be done anyway, he would say. We had become the laughing-stock of the island when we had once been its masters.

Our family had become very small. There were only my mother, Doodeebewshet, my father, Mamjaesdoo, my sister, Dabseek, the fourth-born of our family, who was a little younger than me. There was Gausep, his wife, and their young son of twelve season-cycles. There was an elder who, at the time of the events surrounding Demasduit's life that I am recounting now, had gone to Gull River to see if he could find any surviving members of the Otter Clan living there. But we knew that that was only an excuse. All the Otters had come to live with us many season-cycles before, back when the last descendant of Anin the Ancestor was still among us, and was our chief. The elder left so as not to be a burden to the other survivors. He went nowhere, and would not return. He left us telling a lie, because he knew that lies kill.

53

BEFORE LEAVING FOR the Bay of Exploits, John Peyton and his men looked inside the mamateek in which Demasduit had lived with Nonosabasut and their son. They were astonished at how clean and orderly it was. For them, a camp in the forest was a place where chaos reigned, where cleanliness left much to be desired. Paul Paul, the Mixed-Blood who used to visit us often, told us that he had never seen the English wash themselves or take a steam bath when on an expedition. They let their bodies become dirtier and dirtier and give off an increasingly unpleasant odour of sweat. We would bathe ourselves even in the winter, and clean ourselves in sweat lodges, an ancient custom of our people reintroduced after our defeat at Notre Dame Bay, when we realized we could smell the English coming a mile away. The trappers smelled particularly strong, but the fishermen smelled worse, especially the deep-sea fishermen, who came back to port with their cargo holds full of cod and halibut. Even when we were very busy cleaning and drying fish, we would wash ourselves many times so that we would not bring the smell into our mamateeks.

During this visit to their mamateek, Peyton picked up a mask that had been carved by Nonosabasut shortly before his death. "A pagan idol," Peyton called it. Demasduit flew into such a rage that the men became frightened of her: that mask had been made by her husband and was sacred to her, and no one had the right to touch it. She reached up and tore off a small cross that Peyton wore around his neck, and threw it to the ground. Her mask, she said, was no more a pagan idol than his white-man's cross was. She ground the cross into the earth with her heel, much to the displeasure of Peyton, who had received it from his father. He knelt down and recovered the small cult object to which he seemed to have attached as much value as Demasduit did to her mask. It was a disgraceful scene, and it proved that it was impossible for any understanding to exist between our two ways of seeing life.

No Beothuk had ever before attacked a cult object belonging to another person, since belief is a personal choice that must always be respected. Is the worship of crucifixes, or of images of people floating in a circle around someone's head, any more sacred than an object created by a loved one who has just been killed? As the Living Memory of the Beothuk, my duty is to remember, and here I am trying to understand things that the killers of the Beothuk have never even considered.

If Demasduit's hands had not been tied she would have inflicted a severe punishment on the man who had profaned the object that she cared so much about, especially after the death of Nonosabasut. Before setting out for the coast, Peyton reproached the trapper who had stabbed Demasduit's husband with his bayonet. The trapper was not contrite. "It was only a Redskin," he said to Peyton. "I've killed a hundred like him."

That was when Peyton decided to keep Demasduit as a prisoner. But since she had insulted Peyton by tearing the cross from his neck, he refused to take her son with them. It was Peyton's decision alone. "After she has been civilized," he said, "she will perhaps lose her primitive ways and we can use her in our negotiations with her own people. We shall see."

Peyton's men celebrated his decision by drinking that horrible navy rum that makes people mad and burns their throats and turns their bowels to water. They became crazy. They thought they were alone in the world, but we were watching them closely, hidden in the shadows. If they had not been so drunk they would have sensed us breathing down their necks.

Demasduit, tied up tightly and watched by two men who were not drinking rum, cried the whole night. We were very close to her, but there was nothing we could do to free her. The balls from the English muskets would have killed us. But we were able to frighten them during the night. When the men were all asleep, we crept up to the mamateek and suddenly cried out as loud as we could. The guard shouted, "The Indians! The Indians!" and when everyone ran out of the mamateek they saw our footprints everywhere. That made them very nervous, and they began firing their muskets in every direction, hoping to scare us off.

I am trying to imagine how Demasduit must have felt, lying in her own mamateek with the men who had just killed her husband and the father of her child. Was her pain greater than her rage? I cannot say. If it were me, I would have had only one desire: to kill as many of the English bastards as I could. But for my poor aunt, perhaps the pain and the humiliation were almost unbearable.

The rest of us did not know what to do. We were as powerless as Demasduit. We seemed to be free of the constraints that held her, but we were just as much prisoners of our destiny as she was. We knew now that our survival was only a temporary thing, and that eventually the Beothuk Nation would disappear. We knew that our spirits would not be passed on to others. We knew that fate had reserved that for us.

There was no more hope, but we would not allow ourselves to die without acting. We had to go on fighting until the end. But the end of what? Of our lives? Of our race? The end of our nation? Or the end of our world? We had no more dreams. We had no more fear. We had only the instinct to eat and not die, to await death only when there was nothing more to eat. Who could do more than that?

With Demasduit gone and Nonosabasut dead, their child refused to eat solid food. None of our women were with milk, so no one could help the infant survive. Four suns after the departure of his mother, despite all the care we could give him, the continuation of Nonosabasut's male line died. The next days were devoted to ceremonies for our dead. The ground was frozen, so we built a scaffold of wood. We dismantled an old mamateek and used the birchbark from it to wrap the corpses of father and son. We laid the corpses on the scaffold and made a huge fire, around which we all prayed, and cried, and sang, and cried again, for two whole days without eating. When the whites left us, they took with them our winter stores and all our furs. Later I was told that this had been a peaceful expedition; it made me shudder to think what a war party would have been like.

That winter in our camp, total desolation reigned. Gausep the Breath, his wife, and his child decided that as soon as the ice thawed they would travel north to live among the Sho-Undamung. Ge-oun the Jaw went to join the Mixed-Bloods at Bay d'Espoir, where he knew of a young girl who was descended from the first Beothuk family to move there.

We were the only Beothuk left at Red Ochre Lake: my mother, my father, my sister, and me, the last Living Memory of the once great nation of the Beothuk of the island of Newfoundland, the country of Anin.

For the first few suns when we were alone, my family and I experienced feelings that I cannot describe. When we were a community, we encouraged one another all the time, we told each other our dreams and shared our hopes and desires. It never occurred to us that our way of life would change with the sudden departure of three of us. If sickness had taken away the last of our friends and relatives, we would have spoken of fate and the will of the Creator. But what had happened to us was not sickness. One had been brutally murdered while his wife and child were watching, and the mother had been taken away by the invading savages, and the son had died of starvation.

Even when I go to the most profound depth of my memory I cannot come up with a situation similar to this, one that would so change our way of confronting life. There was nothing in our history to guide me. I could say: "This is the first time this has happened in the Living Memory of the Beothuk." And with equal truth I could also say: "In the Living Memory of the Beothuk, this will never happen again." I am the Living Memory, and I know very well that I am the last of the great nation of Red Men. In my memory, which is still living, I can find the words that I have been taught and that have come to me from the ancestors:

"The Beothuk people will never die."

"The Beothuk people are eternal."

"There will always be Beothuk, because there will always be real men."

"The Beothuk are the real men. Real men always feel the need to know, to learn, to understand. These things are eternal."

All these words resonate in my head, but they no longer mean anything. They do not describe our present situation. I know now that they are symbols only, and that their meaning at any one time is not the same as it was in their original context.

In actuality, we were literally dying of starvation, cold, and soli-
tude. We had been a gregarious people who moved forward into
tomorrow. We had become a family living in hell who had
nothing but our memories to live on. When life is reduced to
memories, the end is near. The world had once been a series of
connected worlds, life was a chain of connected lives, the
Living Memory was one in a line of related Living Memories.
Now, for our people, there were no more tomorrows.

We will therefore end our lives by the telling of it. We were
the last family of native people on this island, the last to have the
same kind and amount of pride as the first family. That was certainly true. There truly had been a first family on this island.
What if we pretended that we were that first family?

At the time that the first family was established, there were
no Bouguishamesh here. There were certainly no English. The
two daughters of the original family somehow found husbands
to continue their line. Were we not, my sister and I, two daughters without Beothuk husbands, and with no men around us
from whom we could fashion one? Not even a block of wood
into which the creator Kobshuneesamut could breathe life? Yes,
but. . . . Where is Kobshuneesamut? Did anyone know?
Nonosabasut was right: the creator was finished with his creat-
ing. He had forgotten us.

54

AT REVEREND LEIGH'S residence in Twillingate, Demasduit was
described as being quite different from the Eskimo. She had small,
delicate bones. Her hands and feet, although very small, were
magnificently formed. Her skin tone was pale, lightly coppered,
but soon came to resemble that of Europeans. Her hair was black
and fine. Her eyes were larger, more expressive and more intelligent

than those of the Eskimo. Her teeth were small and straight and she kept them very clean. Her cheekbones were high, but her general bearing was pleasant and she expressed herself well.

Demasduit felt lost in this unfamiliar environment. On her first night at the Leighs' home she tried to escape twice, but was caught each time and brought back. After that, she was kept under close surveillance. She became calm only when she realized the hopelessness of her situation.

Reverend Leigh reported that she seemed to appreciate the comforts of civilization. In order for her to consider herself a human being, it was absolutely necessary for her to have a Christian name. They christened her Mary, and because she had been captured in the month of March, her family name became March. That was the tradition: Tom June had been captured in June, John August had been taken in August. The word went around that Mary March never rose before nine o'clock in the morning. She ate very little: a few crumbs of bread, some dried raisins, hardtack dipped in tea. She refused anything that contained alcohol. When she was given European clothing she immediately took off her beaver coat, folded it carefully, and placed it in her chest. Reverend Leigh added that she was extremely selfish, and never allowed anyone to touch that coat. It was the only thing she had that reminded her of Nonosabasut, who had worked all one winter to obtain enough beaver skins to make his wife a coat.

Still according to the reverend, Demasduit was shy and very reserved, did not allow anyone to touch her, either affectionately or otherwise. From her, Reverend Leigh learned that the Beothuk were not naturally polygamous but lived in families, even extended families: cousins, uncles, and aunts were all part of the Beothuk clan community. Mary March carried the family of Demasduit in her thoughts at all times; she spoke of them as though they were alive and well. "When will I be allowed to return to my family?" she was constantly asking.

She said that there were sixteen members of her family. Everything she received she divided into sixteen portions and laid them out separately. Some of her clothing disappeared, and it was found that she had taken them apart to make other articles from them. In her locker they found sixteen pairs of moccasins and two small pairs of children's leggings. The leggings had been made from two cotton nightcaps.

Whenever the reverend's housekeeper entered her room, she found Demasduit curled up on the bed in a fetal position, pretending to sleep. The housekeeper never succeeded in catching her making these articles for her family. Naturally, since Mary March was an object of Christian charity, the housekeeper accused her of having stolen the two cotton nightcaps, but Demasduit replied angrily that they had been given to her by John Peyton Jr., who later confirmed this.

Reverend Leigh also made note of the fact that Mary March had a well-developed sense of humour. She could imitate the housekeeper, the blacksmith, the cobbler, and the tailor, who wore spectacles, to great effect. She imitated their manner of speaking English.

During the summer that followed her capture by Peyton and her return to St. John's, Demasduit was impatient to be returned to her people, as the governor had ordered. But Captain Glascock was busy charting the Bay of Exploits with John Peyton Jr. Her child had no doubt learned to feed himself, assuming he was still alive, as Mary most assuredly did. Her own health, however, began to decline. She began coughing frequently.

On the seventeenth of June of that year, Captain Glascock, in the company of Reverend Leigh, John Peyton Jr., and Demasduit, set sail for New Bay, where many Beothuk had been spotted over the previous few years. Two days later, they returned to the *Drake* without having seen a single one.

On the twenty-second, Captain Glascock sailed with John Peyton Jr. and Demasduit to the Bay of Exploits, and followed the Exploits River as far inland as the first rapids. They made as little noise as possible so as not to frighten off the Savages. Glascock and his men went ashore to explore the surroundings. They found mamateeks that had been abandoned the previous winter. They returned to the *Drake* on the twenty-fifth of June.

These sea voyages did not help to improve Mary's health. Her cough worsened. She also began to have fainting spells and frequently had to lie down in the ship to rest.

Glascock sent out many shore parties to explore the small bays along the coast, in search of Beothuk. None was ever seen. If there were any Beothuk in the area, it was very unlikely that they would show themselves. The search along the Exploits River continued from the twenty-eighth to the thirtieth of June, when Captain Glascock and three of his crew members became ill. They had been almost eaten alive by blackflies and mosquitoes. The men's faces became so swollen they were temporarily blinded, and they all came down with fever.

During this time a ship's officer, John Travick, spotted three Beothuk in a tapatook crossing Badger Bay. In order to alert them to the fact that he wished to speak to them, he fired his musket in their direction. The three Beothuk were me, Shanawdithit, my father, Mamjaesdoo, and my sister. We were hunting for shorebirds on one of the islands when the English rounded a point in a rowboat upon which a small sail had been fixed. First they shouted at us. Then, seeing that we did not wait to listen to them, they fired at us. We paddled as swiftly as we could to escape from them. We had too many memories of bad experiences with the English.

Five suns later, well hidden in the thick conifer forest that surrounds Badger Bay, we watched another rowboat enter the bay with Demasduit on board. Even from a distance I could see that she was sick. When the English officer and his men landed, she did not have enough strength to get out of the boat on her own. She remained on board. I now think that she could sense our presence, that we were quite close. But what could we do for her? There were only four of us, and we had no medicines to make her healthy again. We did not know how to cure her of the English disease.

We continued to watch the small boats in the bay for several more suns. From time to time a boat would land and the men would come ashore. Only once did Demasduit make her way up a path to the old mamateeks, where some of her people had once wintered. The English left some things in it for us: tea, a few needles, some fish hooks, and a quantity of red cloth, which no doubt would enable us to be more easily seen. We sensed a trap, and did not reveal ourselves.

The men wanted to leave Demasduit behind, but she refused. She must have known she was incapable of looking after herself, sick as she was. The disease made her extremely weak, and she had seen men much stronger than her unable to raise themselves from their beds once the fever had taken hold. Without weapons, without even red ochre to cover her skin, she would quickly die. She shouted something in English and finally the men gave in and allowed her back in the rowboat. They returned with her to Twillingate.

Governor Hamilton was still determined to return Demasduit to her people. This time he instructed Captain David Buchan, a naval officer, to sail in the *Grasshopper* as far up the Exploits River as the section known as Peter's Arm. He and his men prepared to spend the winter. Meanwhile, John Peyton took Demasduit from Reverend Leigh's house in Twillingate to Captain Buchan's ship. They arrived on the twenty-fifth of November, 1819. A woman was brought along to take care of Demasduit, who by this time was so sick that Captain Buchan soon realized he had very little time to get her to Red Ochre Lake. She could no longer stand without the aid of at least one person, and sometimes two.

She had begun to complain of being separated from her son. Even in her sleep she called him by the name she had intended to give him: Buh-Bosha-Yesh, the name Anin and Woasut had given to their first child more than eight hundred season-cycles before, during the life of the glorious hero of the island of the Red Men.

The season of cold and snow had been upon them for a while. Demasduit called to John Peyton and David Buchan: "I know I am going to die," she told them. "I can see the colour of death all about me . . . it is white everywhere I look. I want you to take me to Red Ochre Lake, where my son is. I want to see him one more time."

The two men gave her their word that they would take her to Red Indian Lake. On the morning of January the eighth, 1820,

John Peyton made a circuit on his snowshoes, as he had been doing every morning, in order to keep himself in good physical shape. While he was away, Demasduit was seized by a violent fit of coughing, after which she had much difficulty breathing. She recovered slightly, but several minutes later her coughing fit returned, this time even stronger than the first. She was suffocating. David Buchan was called back, but there was nothing he could do for her except to watch her take her last breath. She died saying the name John Peyton.

Buchan declared that her death did not mean that they should change their plan. "We promised to bring her with us to Red Indian Lake," he told his men, "and we will bring her to Red Indian Lake."

The ice on the river was not solid enough to travel on until January the twenty-first. The men took every precaution necessary, but it was a march of more than one hundred and twenty kilometres undertaken by a group of sailors who had never worn snowshoes before. They had somehow to avoid frostbite and cope with damp clothing, heavy packs, and so on. A team of ten men broke trail for the others at least as far as the second set of rapids. They were followed by fifty men carrying packs and pulling sledges. On one of the sledges was the body of Demasduit, also known as Mary March.

That winter the ice was badly formed. As well, the portages and forest paths, usually well maintained by the Beothuk, who used them often, were grown over and difficult to negotiate. Many sledges broke and had to be repaired. Much time was lost. On the eighth day, a huge ice dam formed on the river, swamping the banks and forcing the men to walk through water. Their provisions were lost and the men's feet froze.

On the eleventh day, the ice dam broke and the men's lives were saved only by the swiftness of their reflexes. Even at that, thirteen men had to return to the ship on the thirteenth day. One had split his foot with an axe, and eleven were suffering from frostbite. The thirteenth was an officer who was ordered to accompany them to safety.

The expedition arrived at Red Indian Lake on the twentieth day. They saw many mamateeks, all of them empty. Only one showed signs of having been recently used; it was ours, which we had quickly abandoned when we had heard the army of men approaching our lake.

The men placed Demasduit's red coffin, with its copper ornamentation, on the scaffold that we had built the preceding spring for the body of Nonosabasut and the child Demasduit had named Buh-Bosha-Yesh. She had returned to her son and her husband, the man who was her life and her death. Buchan remained in the camp with his men, and we continued to watch them. He knew that we were nearby, but like all whites he could not see us unless we showed ourselves openly to him. When we were not taken by surprise, we were invisible to these people.

After resting for several suns, the expedition left. We know that later on the party split up, and some of the men went to Badger Bay to attempt to meet our people. Of course they did not find any of us. We learned of this from some of our people who had gone to live with the Mixed-Bloods at Bay d'Espoir. For three suns after their departure, we prayed for the remains of my mother's brother, my father's sister, and for Buh-Bosha-Yesh, their son. We were happy that they were together again for their long voyage.

We were certain that Nonosabasut would have waited for Demasduit before setting out on that long journey. He never went anywhere without her. And she, Demasduit, known as Mary March, Wonaoktaé of the nation of Beothuk before me, had returned to the place of her birth, and was once again among her people.

Welcome home, Demasduit. Welcome to the well-springs of your life.

55

NOW WE WERE truly lost. There was only my family left. No one else in the world but the four of us. The sky was always grey, and the sun did not shine as it once did. The moon made only brief appearances, and there were no more stars. The nights were cold. And my mother's tears flowed more frequently! My father never smiled any more, and my sister did not speak. We were torn open, our insides ripped apart, all our bones ached, and the bones of our ancestors ached as well.

When the naval expedition left the lake and we were alone again, Ge-oun the Jaw visited us before returning to the Mixed-Bloods. He had married a woman from the community who was neither Innu nor Shanung, but a bit of both, although she wasn't sure how much. She didn't know what she was. In that community, no one really knew who they were, and they did not wish to know. Everyone lived from day to day, asking only that they had enough to get them through to the next morning. They were an unbelievably generous people, but uninterested in their identity as a nation. Iwish said that a people with no memory is a people with no future. Iwish the Devourer of Guardians. . . . A people with nothing left but a Living Memory, Iwish, what kind of people are they? Tell me. Explain it to me, renew my hope in life so that I can give hope back to my family. Tell me, Iwish, when all there is is memory, what good is it? And for whom?

My father hardly had enough energy to hunt for food. My mother coughed all the time. My sister felt herself weakening also. It seemed I was the only one left capable of smiling, or speaking, or thinking, of wanting to go on. To live. Is it living when all you do is subsist for the day without knowing what will be left for tomorrow? Is it living to know that when you die there will be no one to continue being what you have been? Is it living to think that there is no hope of finding a companion to share the way with? I no longer knew whether I wanted to go on living or not. If a Bouguishamesh aimed his musket at me, I did not know if I would have the strength to run. I would open my coat so that he would at least know that he was shooting a woman. "Go on," I would say, "do me a favour. Kill me."

I do not think I would be afraid. There was no place within me for fear to reside. There was no place within me for joy. There was no place within me for hope.

Sometimes we had to walk for days to find rabbit tracks. The ptarmigan no longer came to mock us, as they once did. For as long as I could remember the caribou always came from the end of the lake to winter in the mossy valley near the natural harbour at our end of the lake, but this winter they did not come. Red Ochre Lake had been abandoned not only by the Red-Ochre people, but also by the very animals that once lived there.

One morning, Mamjaesdoo, my father, slipped on an icy rock and hurt his leg. After that he could not walk without leaning on a stick. I was the only one who could find us something to eat for the next few suns. The next day I would leave with my sledge for the bare mountain, where I might find some caribou. That night I slept to make up for all the nights I had stayed up to watch the English sailors.

My mother coughed all the time. I was very worried about her. "It would be better if you did not go, Shanawdithit," she said to me. "I won't need you much longer."

During the night I had terrible nightmares followed by dreams of hope. In the nightmares, I was captured by white men who changed into sea monsters and chopped me up into little pieces, although I was still alive, and they ate me as they gazed out over a furious sea. In my dreams of hope I was lying in the arms of a handsome young Beothuk man who had just come down from the north, where he had been secretly raised. He loved me, and gave me four beautiful children at once. We started a new nation. We covered the whole island with our children and their children, and drove out all the foreigners. We lived happily, surrounded by our own people. Everywhere we went the game was plentiful.

In the morning, cursing my dreams as well as my nightmares, I left for the bare mountain. Nothing in life could have been as frightening as those dreams had been. But neither could life ever be so beautiful. I became angry with my dream spirit for bringing me such visions of life that vanished when the morning came. As I walked, I began to dream again. My stomach woke me up to tell me that if I did not eat something soon I would die. I had some smoked fish in my pack. I ate a piece of it before starting again for the mountain. At the end of the day I did not have to make a shelter for the night because I found two mamateeks that had been built during the previous season of cold and snow. I chose the least damaged one and made a good fire in it with dried wood that I found neatly stacked inside, and ate the rest of my smoked fish. Before going to sleep I looked outside the mamateek and saw rabbit tracks, so I set several snares in the hope of having fresh game in the morning. Then I lay down and very quickly went to sleep, exhausted by the long distance I had come during the day.

At daybreak I heard a sound outside the mamateek. I took my bow and an arrow, opened the door covering and saw three beautiful caribou. I made sure I had a second arrow ready, and quickly went outside, setting the first arrow to my bowstring. The closest caribou was barely twenty paces from me, and I shot it in the heart. I let my second arrow go too quickly and it went wide of its mark. In my defence, I should say that as soon as I left the mamateek two of the caribou began to scurry away; only the male remained still, and that was the one I hit.

I made certain that it was dead before I went close to it, then I took out my long English knife and made an incision in its chest just below the sternum, and opened its chest cavity right down to the penis. I went around the penis to the rectum, went around the rectum also, and, with a single heave, pulled out the lower intestine. I knotted the end of this so that the animal's excrement would not spill out into the body cavity. The warm blood that ran out over my hands kept them from freezing, but it was still cold work. When this first operation was completed, I carefully skinned the animal, being sure not to let the knife slip and cut through the hide. I scraped it well to remove every last trace of flesh, then folded it hair-side to hair-side, and tied it into as tight a bundle as I could manage. Then with my axe I quartered the meat by cutting through the sternum and then along the vertebral column, separating the two hind quarters and cutting the thorax in half. I tied everything to my birch sledge. I took the caribou's head and cut out its throat up to the lower jaw, and removed the tongue, which I placed on the coals inside the mamateek to cook. I placed the heart, the liver, and the kidneys in my pack to give to my mother and sister when I was back in camp, since they were sorely in need of fresh organ meat. Only then did I eat the tongue, the outside membrane of which I could easily cut through with my teeth. When I was well warmed and fed, I began to walk back to our camp, pulling the sledge behind me. My bow and arrows were tied to the pile of meat on the sledge.

As night fell, I began to sense a presence around me. I looked carefully in all directions, but could see nothing. It was probably an animal that had picked up the scent of caribou blood. I could not walk as quickly as I had the day before, because of the heavy load on the sledge, but I knew I had almost reached the north end of Red Ochre Lake. I was too tired to continue, however, so using my snowshoes I dug a hole in the snow and made a fire in the bottom of it. I pulled the sledge over beside the hole so that the fire would keep predators away from the meat, and covered myself with the two caribou hides I had brought with me. No sooner had I laid myself down when I heard a loud howl. It was a wolf that had been following me. Another wolf replied from some distance away towards the south. Then another from the north! After a few moments there came another howl from very close, and then the others howled again, this time from not so far away. The pack was closing in for the feast, and I would be part of the meal if I did not move quickly. I jumped up and laid four more fires, completely surrounding my shelter. Then when I heard the wolves howling again I lit the fires. Now all I had to do was make sure I had enough wood to keep five fires going all night. I took a torch to go into the bush to gather firewood, but when I stood up I found myself nose to nose with a wolf, all its teeth bared: I jumped back, and so did the wolf. It ran off into the darkness, and I ran back to my shelter in the snow.

My heart was pounding like a drum made tight by the heat of the fire. I spread one of the caribou skins on the ground and sat on it, then I began to laugh: the wolf had been as frightened as I was. Its heart must be pounding, too. I could not stop laughing. I laughed until I was so exhausted I fell asleep. I did not hear another howl all night, and I slept without feeling any more fear.

I had had an experience that I would not have missed for all the stories in the world. Even though my father had always told me that a wolf never attacks a person who is standing, I felt I had had a very close call.

During the night I dreamed about the wolf nation. It, too, had been attacked by the English fur traders. Every trapper on the island wore a long coat made from wolf skins. It was necessary to kill wolf after wolf. Then all the wolves changed into Beothuk, and the fur coats on the traders were made from the skins of Beothuk, without hair. The island was completely cleaned of natural predators. As the Living Memory of a people on the verge of extinction, I was convinced, in my dream, that the wolves were suffering the same fate as we were. When I slept, I thought of myself as another person, someone else who was telling my story! Was I becoming crazy? Hadn't I always been a bit simple-minded? That would make me someone special! That must be why Demasduit chose me to tell the story of our past. That was why I was the past. If I am the past, I cannot at the same time be the future. That would explain why I had never found a husband. That was why I would die alone! I knew then that I am the past. I knew then that I would die alone.

In the morning I woke up with the sun. It was going to be a beautiful day. As I checked each of my fires to make sure that they were completely cold, I saw dozens of wolf tracks and I studied them carefully. There were three distinct sets of prints; three animals had spent the night circling my shelter. I had seen only one. If I had seen all three, perhaps I would not have slept so soundly. Wolves are not as vicious as people make them out to be. They are like Beothuk! The Shanung who guided the Englishman Banks more than two hundred season-cycles ago was right. He said to the scientist that if the Beothuk were as vicious as the English said they were, they would have killed all the new-comers to the island and would never even have let themselves be seen. It was the same with the wolves.

The sun had still not reached its highest point in the sky when I arrived at our mamateek. Mamjaesdoo, my father, was outside, waiting for me.

"I was worried," he said. "I heard wolves howling last night, and I was worried about you."

I looked at him in surprise. "Was it not you who always told me that wolves do not attack a man when he is standing up?"

"Yes, but you are not a man!"

And he laughed for the first time in many moons. It was good to see and hear my father laugh. It warmed my heart. But when I was untying the caribou meat I remembered that I had not removed the snares I had set for the rabbits. I was mortified. That was something we Beothuk had always been taught: never set snares unless you know you are going to be able to check them. An animal that is killed and abandoned has died for nothing. Everything must be used. Especially during a time of famine, as we were now in. My father's smile faded. When I saw him I told him I would go back to check the snares. He asked me how far it was, and when I told him that it had taken me almost an entire sun to get there, he said it was too dangerous to travel so far for so little.

"You must not risk your life for a few rabbits," he said.

However, my father had often risked his life for less than that. He had run for ten suns after stealing a few fish hooks, chased by two fur trappers carrying muskets. I tried to persuade him, but he refused to let me leave that day. "Later," he said.

"Later, the rabbits will have been eaten by the wolves," I said.

"Wolves must eat, too," he replied.

Although his leg was still badly swollen, he helped me carry the meat and called my sister out to lend a hand as well. He told me that I had done enough for the time being, and said I should rest. He was a brave man, my father. Brave and kind. May Kobshuneesamut preserve his life for a long time.

I went into the mamateek and lay down. Pulling the loaded sledge had exhausted me. My father cut up the caribou meat and hung the pieces from a tree, then came inside so I could tell him of my dreams. When I had finished he remained quiet for a long time. When evening came he looked me in the eyes and said: "Shanawdithit, we must not abandon hope. As long as one of us is still alive, we can hope to see the good days return. Kobshuneesamut cannot abandon us after so many season-cycles. One day he will remember that we are here. One day he will think about all the glorious days of our past. The foreigners cannot always be in the right. Give me your word that you will continue to fight until the end. I could not continue to live knowing that you had abandoned all hope."

"I give you my word, Mamjaesdoo. I will not give up. Even when I am dead, I will not give up."

56

TWO SEASON-CYCLES HAD passed since Demasduit was reunited with Nonosabasut and Buh-Bosha-Yesh. The snow had melted quickly and the warm season had begun earlier than usual. With the return of good weather, my mother's health improved and my sister also seemed to get better. They coughed less, seemed to have more strength, and took part in the daily routines with my father and me. Mamjaesdoo was getting old, but he was still a strong woodsman who was used to working hard to assert his right to live. That summer he decided that we would hunt in the terri-tory belonging to the Mixed-Bloods, south of Red Ochre Lake.

"The Shanung are not starving because all the game has trav-elled onto their land," he said. "We will let them share their good fortune with us for the summer."

Three suns later we took our tapatooks and paddled south across the lake. At the end there was an outlet where small trout entered a large brook. When we arrived there, Mamjaesdoo and Doodeebewshet took out a long net made of fine, light string, and walked some way down the brook. They stretched the net all the way across the brook and walked back with it against the current toward the lake. Meanwhile, my sister and I waded into the brook where it left the lake and began beating the water with spruce boughs. The trout became frightened and swam downstream right into the net held by our mother and father. And so we ate fresh trout every day for several days, and had enough left over to smoke and store for later in the growing season.

We repeated this fishing method every morning, and each time we caught many fish. The rest of the day was spent hunting and gathering other kinds of food. There was a time when we had considered this region poor hunting grounds, but now it was the best place on the island. My father was expert at throwing a net to catch birds, and he soon had a large number of ptarmi-gan who thought they were well hidden against the ground, because their feathers had turned from white to reddish-brown. Although it was mating season, the ptarmigan remained together in flocks, so that it was not unusual to catch ten or twelve of them with a single cast of the net. We roasted one or two and dried the rest near the fire that we always kept going when we camped.

Mamjaesdoo was lucky enough to come upon a female caribou that was still feeding a calf that had been born during the winter. He killed it with a definite purpose in mind: he wanted us to eat the fermented contents of her stomach, a delicacy he had learned about from the Sho-Undamung on the north side of the strait.

After skinning the animal and cutting the flesh into thin strips for drying, he explained to us what he had done. He had taken the closed part of the stomach and added the female's own milk to it, and mixed in some of the fresh blood from the same animal, and hung the sac between two small trees, having made a support for it by weaving rawhide strips together as when making snowshoes. He then covered the sac with another piece of caribou skin to keep the flies from eating it before we could, then he let the mixture ferment for five or six suns.

Then, one night, he announced that dinner was ready, and came into the mamateek carrying his fermented caribou stomach. Our mother found the smell revolting and made retching noises. My sister said she did not even want to look at it, saying the sight of blood made her sick. But I had always been close to my father and was willing to try anything as long as he had made it. But I have to admit even I found the texture a bit repulsive.

By closing my eyes and trying not to inhale, I tasted this food that no Beothuk who had not left the island had ever tasted before. I was surprised by the delicate flavour, a taste I will never forget. When Doodeebewshet heard my exclamation, she decided to try it too. She liked the taste, and then my sister joined in. In the end we were eagerly eating this new food, at least new to us: the Innu had been eating it for hundreds of season-cycles. Father said that it was one of their secrets for surviving the extreme cold and the long migrations they undertook each season-cycle.

The next morning my father left the mamateek and returned a short time later. He seemed pensive. When my mother asked him what was troubling him, he admitted to us that he had detected the presence of whites.

"When I left the mamateek I smelled something," he said. "I had stopped to determine which direction the wind was coming from, and I smelled that odour of cocoa that every sailor and every cod fisherman trails behind him. That told me there were English in this area. The French do not drink cocoa. I will follow the scent to see what they are up to. Do not make a fire, and

remain here quietly until I return. If I do not come back by nightfall, Shanawdithit, you are in charge of the family. You are best
able to assume that role."

And he was gone.

Mamjaesdoo had always been known as an excellent hunter.
He knew how to stalk game without being detected. It was an easy
matter for him to get close to something he had scented from a
distance, without being seen or heard. Even on the flat plateaux,
where there were no trees, he knew how to follow the contours of
the land, to take advantage of small stands of bushes, to skirt the
edges of the hills and make long detours, without anyone
knowing he was there. Moving in this way, he saw two men
sitting on the ground eating bread and drinking cocoa.
Mamjaesdoo knew one of them very well. His name was Jos
Silvester, a Shanung. He used to live at St. George's Bay, but now
he had moved to Bay d'Espoir to live with the Mixed-Bloods. He
was a real Shanung, a Mi'kmaq. He was wearing Beothuk leggings
made from caribou skins turned hair-side in, despite the mildness
of the weather. Even in the warm spring air he would rather be
hot than have his legs torn by the small evergreens that grew
everywhere on the south part of the island. Silvester also wore an
English shirt of red flannel, a small sleeveless vest made of caribou
skin, and a wide-brimmed hat that was especially prized by
blackflies, which flew to it as bees flew to honey.

His companion was tall and thin, and wore clothing made from
skins, except for his cloth trousers, which fit him tightly from his
knees to his heels. Both men wore moccasins. The palefaced one
also wore a wide-brimmed hat. They both stank of bear fat, with
which they had probably smeared themselves for protection against
fly bites. If the flies were leaving them alone, however, it probably
had more to do with the smell than with the repellent powers of
bear fat. Our father said that when a blackfly became stuck in bear
grease it had only one thought: to get out as fast as it could.

The two men finished their meal. Then the paleface began
taking down the small shelter made of sailcloth that they had slept
in the night before. Silvester, however, stood up and walked

straight toward my father. Mamjaesdoo knew that it was a waste of time to try to hide: the Shanung had sensed his presence. While still walking in my father's direction, Silvester said quietly: "Surely you didn't think I wouldn't notice the smell of a Beothuk."

"I thought the stink of bear grease would drown out all other smells," my father replied.

When they were standing face to face, each man reached out his right hand and touched the other's shoulder. That was how two men greeted each other when they were not enemies, but not exactly close friends either.

"Who's the Bouguishamesh?" my father asked.

"His name is William Cormack, an English scientist who wants to meet the Beothuk to see why they are dying."

"Well, he came just in time," said my father. "We're almost all dead. He can study us as much as he likes. There's no one to stop him."

"He would like to meet with you to talk about it."

"We would rather discuss our way of life. We will talk of death when we are closer to it. We don't want to attract it by talking about it."

Jos Silvester looked my father in the eye. "If you do not want to talk to him, he will never see a Beothuk. I give you my word."

With that he turned on his heel and went back to Mr. Cormack. Mamjaesdoo returned to our camp and asked us not to make a fire that day. "By tonight they'll be far enough away that we can go back to our normal lives," he said.

When morning came we went back to our fishing and drying, to prepare for the season of cold and snow. But our catches were becoming smaller and smaller, because it was already the season of falling leaves. Mamjaesdoo looked at the amount of provisions we had put away, and said to us: "There is not enough here to last us until the next growing season. We will have to go to the coast as soon as spring comes to dig clams until the hunting season begins."

We settled down to pass the season of cold and snow in the Mixed-Bloods' hunting grounds. In the middle of that winter,

Jos Silvester came to visit us and spent several days in our winter camp. He told us how his people were able to get along with the English: "We are different from you," he explained. "We never show any animosity towards them. We do not necessarily like them, but we have no choice, there are many more of them than there are of us. So we smile at them and make them believe that we think as they do. They hire us from time to time as guides. They buy our furs. We were friends with the French before these came. The English beat the French, so we either play their game or else the same thing happens to us as is happening to you: we die."

There were some angry words exchanged between Silvester and Mamjaesdoo. Father did not like the hypocrisy of Silvester's attitude towards the English after all that we had suffered at their hands. Jos had an answer for everything.

"They have done nothing to us. And look at us: we are still alive!"

This made father very angry. "When my family is dead, there will be no one for you to sell to the English but the other Beothuk who have gone to live among you."

"If we wanted to sell Beothuk," Silvester retorted, "you would have been sold long ago, you and your family. But we too take pride in protecting the people who are like us. You are different from us, but we are alike in the way we live and where we come from. Only our languages are different."

This conversation went on late into the night. Their positions were very different, and very emotional, but Silvester had not lost all his people, as we had. He could not begin to understand my father's bitterness.

The season of cold and snow gave way to the melting season, and then to the season of new growth. It was time for us to travel to the coast. Father wanted us to go to the south coast, but we preferred the east, where we knew we would find sea food. However, if we had known what was waiting for us in that direction, we would have followed the wishes of the only man left in our family.

We loaded our remaining provisions on our backs and set out on snowshoes to the north part of the lake before turning east to follow the Exploits River. It was a difficult journey, because the snow was melting more each day. In the morning it was not so bad because it was colder and more granular, but when the sun came up and warmed it the snow became soft, and our snowshoes broke through it often and we would sink, finding ourselves with our noses in the heavy blanket of spring snow.

Although their coughs had returned, my mother and my silent sister never complained. They hoisted their loads in the morning and did not set them down again until my father or I called for a rest. It was as though they were trying to be as little hindrance as possible. They insisted on doing their share of the work. But the sickness was gaining ground.

I was becoming more and more worried. Mamjaesdoo was also anxious, but he was more discreet than I was. He had seen more people die of this disease than he could count. But he prayed to Kobshuneesamut in private, not wanting the rest of us to worry any more than we already were. The moon of winds had still not completed its cycle when we arrived at New Bay, a small cove in the Bay of Exploits. When we arrived we took over a mamateek that had been used before by Demasduit and Nonosabasut. We repaired it and made ourselves as comfortable as we could. My mother and sister were getting sicker and sicker. They coughed very often and were frequently too weak to move quickly. They spent a great part of the day lying down.

All this time, Mamjaesdoo gathered the sea food that became available in early spring. I spent my time looking after my sister, who I sensed was becoming more and more distracted. Every now and then she would begin to babble about things I could not comprehend. Then she would regain her senses and beg me not to pay attention to her when she was like that. She said she was tired.

One morning when Mamjaesdoo was digging clams he stood up and saw two fur trappers coming from behind a pile of rocks. Taking no chances, he began to run in a zigzag, fleeing towards a small brook across the cove, which was still frozen over. The two trappers ran after him. He was not wearing snowshoes, but still he risked crossing the cove. The ice covering was very thin and gave way under his weight. He disappeared under the ice and did not come back to the surface. The two trappers were disappointed that they had missed one of their last chances to kill a Beothuk.

They began to walk around the bay, convinced that there must be other Redskins to massacre. They walked, they searched, they peered, and finally they saw . . . my mother, who had gone for a short walk to get some fresh air. When she saw them, she turned and ran back to the mamateek. My sister and I were still there, and so all of us fell into the hands of the most renowned Beothuk killer on the island: William Cull.

57

WHEN THE DOOR of the mamateek burst open and Doodeebewshet ran in, I was holding my sister Dabseek in my arms. She had just had a weak spell and was having trouble breathing. When we saw William Cull burst in behind my mother, neither Dabseek nor I had the strength to react. We were resigned to whatever was about to happen. We did not yet know that our father, Mamjaesdoo, was dead. Neither did our mother. Our first reaction was to let William Cull take us away from there as quickly as possible, so that our father would not be captured as well. When William Cull's companion asked him if it was necessary to retrieve the body of the drowned Indian in order to get the bounty, I realized what had happened. These men did not know that I understood their language. Cull replied that the governor did not pay for a dead Beothuk.

"He wants them alive," he told the other man.

From this I knew that I was now in charge of the family. I did not dare say anything to Doodeebewshet. She had troubles enough without my adding to them. And I was careful also not to breathe a word to Dabseek, the fourth and youngest member of the family. Picking her up, I carried her out of the mamateek, followed by my mother and the two men, who were holding their muskets at the ready. We walked for a certain distance until we came to a small boat with a sail, and we climbed into it. The men took us towards Exploit-Burnt Island, the home of John Peyton Jr. I knew this place well from having raided it with some companions five season-cycles before. This was where we had cut the hawsers of the ship carrying salmon, and stolen the sails.

Judge Peyton had an outside shelter built for us so that we would at least have the illusion of being free. Doodeebewshet was sicker than she had ever been, but she refused to sleep. She heated some rocks and placed them in water to make steam, the method for cleansing a mamateek that had become a religious ritual with us ever since our people had fallen into despair. My mother firmly believed that it was helping my sister. I thought that it at least could do no harm, and let my mother do what she thought was best. She never smiled any more. She was always sad. She asked me if I had enough strength to get away and find my father. I told her there was no question of my leaving her alone with Dabseek. I told her that in any case I was not well enough. She did not insist. Her will was already fading.

I cringed every time I heard one of Peyton's men refer to my mother as "the old sow," because they found her ugly and dirty. But I kept my feelings to myself so that they would not know that I understood their language. As soon as the ice left the harbour they loaded the ships, and we boarded one of them to be taken to St. John's, to the home of Governor Hamilton.

In St. John's we found that Governor Hamilton had gone to England and that Captain David Buchan was temporarily taking his place. It was two of Buchan's men we had killed when I was twelve season-cycles old, and it was Buchan who had returned

Demasduit's body to us three season-cycles before. Before he would even receive us he sent an English doctor to examine us. The doctor told us his name was Watt, which I found amusing because I thought he was asking us "My name is what?" Every time he turned his attention to my sister or my mother, I could not help laughing. This seemed to irritate him very much. When I explained to Dabseek and Doodeebewshet why I was laughing, they too broke into gales of laughter. The doctor's face darkened and he went off, apparently to complain about us to Buchan, but Buchan did not seem to be angry. At least he never spoke to us about our behaviour. Only one thing confused me: the doctor told Buchan that my sister and my mother were suffering from something called "consumption," and that they did not have long to live. I knew that they were very sick and would soon leave us, but I had not known that the English knew about this disease. Could it have come from them? Could they have given it to us deliberately? I did not know what to think. I understood English, but I did not know all the sounds. That angered me a little. What was even more frustrating was that I could not speak my mind to anyone. I did not want to worry my mother and sister, and I did not trust the English. The torment this created within me was very difficult to contain.

With an escort of a dozen people, we were paraded on the streets of St. John's. We were taken into stores, and by gestures we were told we could have anything we wanted, as much as we could carry. I told this to my mother and sister. My mother said: "They do not know how big a load a Beothuk can carry. They may be sorry they gave us permission." And for the first time in many suns I saw my mother smile and laugh. I did not know then that I was seeing it almost for the last time.

We looked at everything. Mother and Dabseek took whatever they thought would be useful or needed, such as kettles made from some light metal, tools and utensils, cloth, stockings, needles, some heavy thread for sewing, rolls of canvas. The only things they would not let us have were the things we most needed: knives and axes. I do not know why they refused us these things. . . .

Since those useful items were denied us, I amused myself by tying pieces of coloured cloth to myself, in my hair, over my arm, around my waist. This made the English laugh. Outside, children ran behind us calling us names: "Dirty Indians! Savages! Dirty women!" My mother and Dabseek did not understand their words and laughed. I frightened the children by making fierce faces at them and pretending to try to catch them. Beothuk children would never have been so rude as to insult visitors to their village. Beothuk children were well raised, better than these young English hooligans.

Captain Buchan ordered John Peyton Jr. to return us to our people as soon as possible. He did not want us to die in captivity. I pretended not to understand what he was saying, but I wanted to shout to him that "our people" were all dead. "You have killed them all!" I wanted to tell him. But I held back my words. They must never know that we were the last of our people! That would give them too much pleasure. I wanted them to remain afraid of us a while longer. I wanted them to tremble with fear every time they stepped into the forest on our island.

We had been taken to Exploits-Burnt Island aboard a ship called the *Anne*, belonging to John Peyton Jr., the same ship whose lines we had cut and whose sails we had stolen five season-cycles before. Now it took us back to the Bay of Exploits. Peyton let us off on the beach in Badger Bay, and left us there with enough food for several suns. We found an old mamateek and repaired it, and carried the food into it, then lay down to rest. Doodeebewshet kept saying that we had to find Mamjaesdoo, and I kept putting off telling her the truth about our father.

On the morning of the fourth sun after our return, we awoke to find that Dabseek had died during the night. My mother and I cried the whole day. She had been my little sister, I had taken care of her since she was a baby. I was miserable, and my mother was inconsolable. She cried and beat her chest, saying that Kobshuneesamut was unjust, that he did not have the right to take away young children who had not lived long enough to experience happiness. She said that the Creator should have come for her instead. But by nightfall she was calmer, and it was she who went out and found a small depression between two rocks. The next morning we placed Dabseek's body in it and covered her with rocks piled one on top of another, to discourage predators. She would wait there until she was ready to make her final journey. We worked all that day. In the evening, my mother was exhausted, and the next morning she, too, was dead.

I was responsible for the family. Me, Shanawdithit. But I was completely alone. What must I do? Should I just let myself die? I had no more food, no weapons with which to hunt, and no fish hooks to catch fish. I barely had enough strength to drag my mother's body out and lay it beside Dabseek's, and it took me the entire day to carry enough stones to pile on top of it. Then I decided it was time for me to die. I did not have a knife, or an axe, or an arrow. I had nothing sharp at all. I did not know which herbs were poisonous and I knew how to swim. How could I find death? I could wait. I had no food. I could simply sit and wait for death to find me.

Then I remembered that I had given my word to Mamjaesdoo that I would fight to the very end! That I would never give up. That I would never lose hope. Giving one's word is a sacred trust. Kobshuneesamut would never forgive me if I broke it. Mamjaesdoo would never forgive me, either.

Peyton had left a small, flat-bottomed boat at the end of the bay in case we needed it. I decided I had to return to Peyton's house on Exploit-Burnt Island. But it was such a long way. I began rowing and kept on without stopping until it was almost dark. Then I saw a small sailboat which I recognized as belonging to Peyton, and called to it. The men on board agreed to take me to Peyton. Everyone was sleeping at his house when we arrived, and as I did not want to disturb them I slept in the outside shelter the magistrate had had built for us on our previous visit to his house.

In the morning, Peyton's maid and cook found me sitting on the step outside his door.

58

I MISSED MY family very much.

My mother, my sister, and my father were so unhappy without
me that I often thought of joining them as soon as possible. But
my promise to Mamjaesdoo, given during that last season of cold
and snow, weighed heavily upon me. I could not go back on my
word. I could not betray my people. I was the last hope my people
had of being continued in others. I had to fight on to the finish.
Who knew? I could still marry a man from away who might agree
to live here with me on the island of the Red Men. Who could
say? We could have children, give birth to a new nation, perhaps
start a clan, or at least a family. I was dreaming with my eyes open:
I would never meet anyone who would be interested in me. I was
nothing but a servant in the Peyton household. Since coming
here I had done nothing but wash and dry dishes. Mrs. Jury taught
me how to do it, speaking harshly:

"You hold the plate like this, not like that. You take this
cloth and you dry the glasses first, then the plates. Why do you
not understand?"

I thought: It is you, Mrs. Jury, who do not understand. Soon I
will be twenty-eight season-cycles old. In the Beothuk world
I know how to do everything. I know how to hunt, how to fish,
how to kill white men. And you, what do you know? You are ignorant of every important thing, and yet you have the nerve to tell
me I do not understand. I understood your language before I even
met you. I knew exactly what time of day you took your meals,
what kind of bed you slept in, and what kind of awful, stinking
meat you put into your mouth. What do you know about us, Mrs.
Jury? What do you know about the Beothuk? What do you even
know about me, after five years of working in your damned silly
house, where people come and go without ever greeting the servants? The only kind people in this house are young Anne and the
boy, John III. They come to me, they seek me out, they run to me

and hug me. When they are sad it is me they come to. When Mrs. Eleanor spanks them, it is me who comforts them. Peyton Jr., your master, has spoken to me exactly four times in five years, and each time Mrs. Peyton, his wife, has thrown a jealous fit and has kept me away from the children for a month. She punishes me because her husband speaks to me. She punishes the children because she is angry with her husband. Is it my fault, or the children's fault, if her husband speaks to me? Will someone come down with "the consumption" if he speaks to me? I am a good little maid to work so silently in this house. If I left here I would miss only the children. They are so sweet. I love them more than anything in the world because they are all I have left. Peyton's employees are all brutes, and Beothuk killers. It must make them very unhappy not to be able to kill me. They are the same men who came into our forest and shot at our people. They do not know how much I hate them. They know that I hate them because I have told them so many times. But they do not know how much.

The other day a man came and spoke to me and questioned me for a long time. He seemed to be a kind man. He wanted to know about the Beothuk. He was the first person to show any interest in my people since I was in St. John's. When I was there, Captain Buchan gave me some paper and a pencil and asked me to draw my people. I enjoyed drawing very much. But in five years at the Peytons no one has ever given me paper. If I so much as pick up a pencil it is taken from me. They think I will write on the walls with it, as though I were a child. . . .

I miss my people very much. Here they call me Nancy April. I miss not being able to speak my own language with anyone. I was able to do so just once. I was told that a Shanung came here often, and the other day I saw him from close up. He was not a Shanung at all, he was Ge-oun the Jaw, who went to live with the Mixed-Bloods at Bay d'Espoir. I was very angry with him and hit him in the face with my fist, and told him never to come back here: if the people here found out that he was not Shanung but Beothuk they would kill him. Fortunately, no one understood our conversation. I told them he was a Mi'kmaq who had killed many Beothuk, and that I did not want to see him again. Then they treated him as a hero. They shook his hand and gave him rum. He sang Beothuk songs for them, and everyone thought he was singing in Mi'kmaq. But even if he escapes this time, they will kill him some other time. He must not come here again. It is too dangerous for him.

The kind gentleman who asked me questions the other day came back with a priest, and the priest scolded the Peytons for not having me converted to their religion. I have no use for their religion. Any god who allows his followers to kill anyone who does not think as he does surely does not deserve to be a god. Kobshuneesamut would never allow such a law. William Cormack, the gentleman who brought the priest, wanted to know about our way of life. I will tell him that I am the last one. I have told the others that there were still twenty-seven of us, but I lied. I must be careful, because lies can kill. Only the truth exists. If they find out that I have lied to them, perhaps they will kill me. That would be good, because then I could die without betraying my promise to my father. I must keep my word. I hope this Mr. Cormack comes back.

One morning when Mr. Peyton was away a man came with a paper. Mrs. Eleanor talked to him, then told me to pack a small bag but to leave here all the clothes she had given me. I could only take the things given to me by Captain Buchan, that is, one quilted dress, a pair of long stockings, and a pair of flat shoes. Then she told me to go with the man. She did not say goodbye or shake my hand, or do any of the things the English do when they part. I left, just like that, with no formalities. The man took me to a ship and informed me that I was going to live in St. John's with Mr. Cormack.

I was delirious with joy. I was going to live with the only person who had ever shown any interest in me in five years! Maybe he liked me a little? Maybe he didn't think I was ugly after all? If I was nice to him, maybe he would learn to like me? Mamjaesdoo was right, we have to go on hoping to the end.

When I arrived at Mr. Cormack's residence his attitude towards me seemed to have changed. He said it was necessary for us to keep our distance, because of "what people might say." I did not understand at first, but he explained to me that people would become suspicious of a bachelor sharing a house with a "wild woman." So he had to keep his distance from me. I asked him if he touched me would he leave a mark on my skin that people would see, and he said no, but in his conscience as a gentleman it would be exactly as though that were the case! I liked it when he took my hand to show me how to draw a circle with a pencil. I also liked the feel of his warm breath on my neck when he leaned over me to see what I was drawing. I wanted him to kiss my neck, to caress my shoulders. I wanted to be loved . . . but he never did any of those things. Alas. I was dreaming with open eyes again. The English said that he was not handsome, that he was too thin, too tall, too this, not enough that. All their remarks left me cold. To me he was a kind, gentle, sympathetic, and interesting man. He told me many things I did not know, and I told him many things he wanted to learn. Maybe more. I would have told him anything to keep him near me.

He explained to me that he had made a great study of native peoples. Once in a while I would ask him to tell me about these primitives, as he called them, just so that I could listen to his voice. Hearing him speak to me I was in ecstasy! He knew very well that I could understand virtually nothing of his dissertations, but he went along with it anyway . . . I think . . . I hope!

I was much happier staying with William Epp Cormack than I had been at the Peytons', but I missed the children. Still, Cormack charmed me. I would have loved him to take me in his arms and kiss me with passion, but he never did. Perhaps he sensed that I had contracted the sickness called consumption, like my mother and my sister. I was coughing more and more frequently, but I tried not to when I was with him.

Or perhaps he simply did not like me personally. Perhaps he was only interested in me as a Beothuk. He had started an institution that was named after my people. Towards the end of my stay with the Peytons we had moved into a new house, in Twillingate, a place to which I did not want to return.

I think I am getting weaker.

Cormack had other "primitives" who were staying with him, a Montagnais or Innu man and two Abenakis. They told Cormack that I was ill. I was furious with them, and told them so. A Beothuk never betrays another's secret, not even for the other person's benefit. Would Cormack now be afraid to come near me? Perhaps he would decide it was time to remove himself from me further . . . so he would not accidentally come to love me. He warned me that he would have to leave me for a while. He said that his life as a man of science, a man who sought to understand the ways of primitive peoples, was forcing him to go to England in order to sell some articles and earn enough money to be able to continue his research in the field. I tried to dissuade him from going. I told him that I still had many stories to give him, new ones that he did not know about the Beothuk, and the Addaboutik, about Anin and his four wives. . . .

He affected not to understand me. He became more distant, while I was burning up inside. I would have sliced my body and opened it up to show him what a Beothuk looked like on the inside if he had asked me to. I wanted to shout to him that I loved him. But I could never do that. I felt my life draining from me slowly. My final hopes were disappearing before my very eyes. I felt this man running through my fingers like a fistful of sand. I was desperate. I wanted to die. I was dying.

One morning when I came downstairs I was told that William Cormack was gone. It was the season of cold and snow. I was taken to the English governor's house. I was beginning to have frequent weak spells, and sometimes I would faint and not know what was happening around me. I spent whole days looking at my naked body in a mirror. I had only one breast. My other breast had been torn away by an English musket. The muscle on one of my legs was also missing, also torn away by an English musket. And there was a dark, dirty hole at the top of my ribcage, where part of my side had been blown away by an English musket. I suddenly understood why William Cormack would not touch me. I was not a complete person.

When the warm season returned I could hardly get out of bed. My legs, once young and strong, were too weak to hold me up long enough to go outside to breathe the fresh air of my island. I was dying to smell the flowers. I was dying to see the sun rise again over the sea. I was dying from never having known the heat of a man's love. But I could still be proud. I had kept my promise to the end. I had hoped that my people would go on living.

I knew that the Beothuk would live forever because there are still real men on the earth even if they do not have red skins. With what little energy I have I will fight against death until the last breath leaves my body. When that happens, the last Living Memory of the Beothuk people will vanish.

Shanawdithit died of tuberculosis on the sixth of June, 1829, in the hospital in St. John's, Newfoundland. She was buried in South Side Cemetery after a brief religious ceremony held in the St. John's Cathedral. No one attended the service. Some people still say she died for love, for the love of her people and for the love of William Epp Cormack.

CHRONOLOGY OF EVENTS

in the History of the Beothuk of Newfoundland

I – THE INTITIATE

About 1000 A.D.
Vikings winter on the northern peninsula of the island, an event confirmed in the Norse sagas.

II – THE INVADERS

1497, June 24, 5:00 a.m.
John Cabot (Jean Cabot, Giovanni Cabotto) sails into Bonavista Bay. When he returns to England, he takes three Beothuk with him and presents them to King Henry VII.

1500, October 18
Gaspar de Côrte Real returns to Lisbon with seven Beothuk, who are painted red. His second ship arrives two days later with fifty more Beothuk. All are sold as slaves.

1501, May 15
Côrte Real leaves Lisbon for Newfoundland to capture more slaves. He never returns from this voyage.

1503
Miguel de Côrte Real leaves in search of his brother Gaspar. He, too, is never seen again in Portugal.

1508
According to Father Charlevoix, the French ship *Bonaventure* brings six captive Beothuk to Rouen.

1523
Giovanni Verazzano sails the *Dauphin* to the waters off Newfoundland.

1534, May 10
Jacques Cartier sails into Catalina Bay, which he names Sainte-Catherine. He also visits Port de Rapont (Quirpont), where he finds Beothuk habitations covered with sailcloth, but does not make contact.

1583
Humphrey Gilbert arrives in St. John's Harbour and takes possession of the island. He leads two exploratory expeditions, one to the south, where no Beothuk are encountered, and one to the north, where he describes the Beothuk as "gentle, kind, and inoffensive." Gilbert writes that he counted sixty sailing vessels in Placentia Bay, all from St-Jean-de-Lutz. In Siburno and Biscay there are eight Spanish vessels. In Farillon (Ferryland), he sees twenty-eight English ships. In all, he records, ninety European vessels are frequenting the waters off the island of Newfoundland.

1609
James I establishes the first permanent settlement on the island. Under the auspices of the Newfoundland Plantation Company, John Guy publishes a pamphlet encouraging English settlers. He is named Governor of the colony and spends the winter of 1610–11 in Cupper's Cove (Cupids), Conception Bay. He encounters many Beothuk without experiencing any problems with them.

1612, June 7
John Guy returns to the colony after a stay in England. In October, he leads an expedition of twelve men to Mount Eagle

Bay (Spread Eagle) and Trinity Bay (Savage Harbour). On October 6, he meets eight Beothuk paddling a tapatook and holding up furs for him to inspect. George Whittington, one of the colonists, goes ashore, buys food and furs from them, and pays them with knives. There is dancing and singing, and a shared meal, and they arrange to meet again the following year, in August. The Beothuk present Guy with an eagle feather.

1613, August

Guy, still back in Bristor, does not keep his appointment. Instead, a fishing boat sails into the bay, where eight hundred Beothuk have gathered. They again hold up furs for the English to see, and dance for joy. When they launch their tapatooks and paddle out to meet the English, the ship's captain panics and fires his cannon at them. Many are killed. This is the last friendly encounter in the history of the Beothuk of Newfoundland.

1616

In Port-les-Oyes (St. Julien), eighty Beothuk attack a company of French soldiers that had come to rid the island of its inconvenient Savages. At Petty Master (Crock Harbour), the French, unaccustomed to the Beothuk way of guerrilla warfare, lose seven soldiers on the first day, nine on the second, and twenty-one on the third. Thirty-seven dead in three days, and they never see a single Savage. The company returns to France.

1610–1635

The Malouins (from the port of St. Malo, in Brittany) make repeated demands to the authorities in their home port that they be allowed to hunt the Beothuk, who are preventing the fishing fleet from landing to acquire fresh water and food. They say they have to pay the Mi'kmaq to perform these tasks.

III – Genocide

Eighteenth Century

In Notre Dame Bay, the Beothuk take to stealing fish hooks and axes from the colonists and fishermen. This is used as an excuse to hunt them down.

The Beothuk abandon the island's coastal areas and retreat inland, where they mix with the Mi'kmaq.

In St. George's Bay, the Mi'kmaq cut the heads off their Beothuk victims in order to collect bounties. When Beothuk children discover these severed heads, they inform their parents. The Mi'kmaq are invited to a Beothuk feast, and fifty-four of them are massacred during the meal.

At about this time the Innu (Sho-Undamung) cross over the Strait of Belle Isle to the island.

1758

One morning at sunrise, several trappers burst into a Beothuk mamateek and kill a man, a woman, and a child. A young girl is taken captive. Her name is Ou-bee. She is sent to England to live with a couple named Stone. Ou-bee's lexicon of the Beothuk language is the only one in existence, and is the basis of what is reproduced at the end of this book.

1760

A naval officer named Scott builds a fort in the Bay of Exploits, after arriving by ship from St. John's. He is approached by several Beothuk. An elderly Beothuk man leaves his companions and walks towards Scott. As they meet the old man takes a knife from under his cloak and kills Scott. The other Beothuk take out their bows and arrows and kill four more sailors.

1766

Sir Joseph Banks studies the flora and fauna of the island. According to him, there are still five hundred Beothuk living within five miles (eight kilometres) of Fogo. A Mi'kmaq guide tells him that the Beothuk are not dangerous; if they were, all the English on the island would be dead without ever having laid eyes on a Beothuk.

1768
Lieutenant George Cartwright, under orders from the governor, Sir Hugh Palliser, arrives on the *HMS Guernsey* and sails up the Exploits River, Cape John, and Cape Freels.

1768, June
A trapper surprises a Beothuk woman while she is gathering clams. She throws herself to her knees and implores the man not to harm the child she is carrying in her belly. The trapper eviscerates her, impales the fetus on the fork of a sharpened stick, and parades it before his companions.

1768, August
Some trappers encounter another Beothuk woman and her six-year-old child. She trips while trying to run away and is killed. Her son is taken prisoner and displayed in Liverpool that winter, for a fee of two cents. He is called John August, marking the month of his capture. Much later he returns to Catalina to seek the men who murdered his mother, and dies in 1785. It Is not known whether he succeeded in avenging his mother's death.

1769
George III issues a Royal Proclamation prohibiting the molestation of the Beothuk.

1770, June
Another Beothuk child is captured, and is given the name Tom June. He is allowed to visit his people, whose language he still speaks, but he refuses to teach the Beothuk language to the English settlers. He works as a boatmaster in the cod fishery, and is found drowned in the harbour at Fogo Island in 1790.

1800, August 25
John Bland writes a dramatic piece based on an exchange of letters about the Beothuk.

1803, September 17
William Cull captures a Beothuk woman near Gander and is given a reward for not killing her. At a formal ball she is exhibited to the island's upper-class inhabitants, who admire her light hair and pale skin. She prefers the company of children, with whom she plays.

1804, September 27
The captive woman becomes sick, and Cull is ordered to return her to the place where she was captured: James Howley states that she was taken to the mouth of the Exploits River, although she had been captured near Gander. Rather than staying to care for the woman, Cull abandons her on the beach.

1807, July 30
A second Royal Proclamation is issued to protect the Beothuk.

1807
Nonviolent contact in Bonavista Bay.

1808, June 8
Governor Holloway decides to send an expedition to make contact with the Beothuk.

1809
Lieutenant Spratt is ordered to establish contact. He draws up a list of useful items to give to the Beothuk, but makes contact with no one.

1810, January 1.
William and John Cull make an expedition up the River of Exploits, with two Mi'kmaq guides. As companions, they take John Waddy, Thomas Lewis, James Foster, and someone named Joseph.

After four days, they find a structure fifty feet long within which are more than one hundred caribou, skinned and neatly packed in boxes made of birchbark. Each box contains the tongue, liver, and heart of the animal. They also encounter some Beothuk, who quickly make off. The Newfoundlanders steal all the furs they find and leave utensils and other objects in exchange.

1810, August
Royal Navy Lieutenant David Buchan, aboard HMS *Adonis*, sails up the Bay of Exploits without seeing any Savages. He decides to spend the winter at either Ship Cove or Borwood.

1811, January 12
Buchan goes back up the River of Exploits with William Cull, Matthew Hughster, Thomas Taylor, and twenty-three men from the *Adonis*. On the twenty-fourth he discovers three mamateeks, surprising their occupants. An attempt to exchange gifts goes badly and two of his men, James Butler and Thomas Bouthland, are killed. On January 28 Buchan and his men retreat to the bay and their ship.

1811, August 10
A third Royal Proclamation is issued to protect the Beothuk.

1819, March 10
Demasduit is captured. She gives her name as Wonaoktaé, but is called Mary March by her captors. She is captured along with her husband, and taken from her son, who is still nursing. Her husband is killed before her eyes, and the child is left to starve.

1820
The ailing Mary March is returned to her people, many of whom have already died. She dies on January 8. Her body is taken to Red Indian Lake, where it is placed beside the graves of her husband and child.

1823

In the spring, in Viewbay on the shores of Notre Dame Bay, a group of trappers meet a Beothuk couple who are obviously starving. When the Beothuk ask for food, they are beaten to death.

1823, June 10

Three women are found huddled in a mamateek and brought back to the nearest settlement. They are nearly dead of starvation. One dies on the way back. Then the oldest one dies. The third, Shanawdithit, lives in captivity for the rest of her life. She had been wounded three times by musket balls, in her breast, her calf, and her side. She tells about the massacre of four hundred Beothuk on a point of rock: no one had ever admitted to knowing about the incident.

1829, June 5

Shanawdithit dies of tuberculosis.

A BEOTHUK LEXICON

*(based on the lexicon provided by Ou-bee,
in captivity in England c. 1760)*

BEOTHUK	ENGLISH
Abdobish	Rope, cable
Abemite	Fish net
Abideshhook	Lynx, wild cat
Abidish	Marten
Abobidwess	Eagle feather
Abodoneek	Hat
Adadimite	Fishing lure, bait
Adadimiute	Spoon, ladle
Adamadwet	Musket
Addaboutik	Literally, "We are red" (the name the Beothuk gave themselves).
Addizabad-Zéa	White woman
Adenishit	Star
Aduth	Harpoon
Adijith	To sneeze
Adoltkhtek	Vessel, boat
Adosook	Eight
Adothook	Fish hook
Aduse	Leg
Adyouth	Foot
A-Enamin	Bone (thin person)
A-eshimut	A kind of fish
A-E-U-Chee	Snail
Agamet	Button, silver
Aguathoonet	Whetstone
Ahune	Stone

Akushtibit	To kneel down
Amet	To wake up
Amina	Spear, lance
Amshut	To get up
Anadrik	Sore throat
Anawasut	Halibut
Anin	Comet
Annawhadya	A kind of bread
Annoo-ee	Tree, forest
Anwoydin	Spouse
Anyemen	Bow
A-Oseedwith	I am going to sleep
Aoujet	Ptarmigan
Appawet	Seal
Aschautch	Meat
Asha-Bu-Ut	Blood
Ashei	Thin, meagre, sick
Ashmudyim	The Evil One, wicked
Ashwameet	Red Ochre
Ashwogin	Arrow
Asson	Gull
Ass-soyt	To anger
Aszik-dtounouk	Twenty
Athess	To sit down
Awoodet	To sing
Baasothnut	Gunpowder
Baashooditte	To walk
Badisut	Dancer, to dance
Baétha	Home
Basdic	Smoke
Bashoodité	Owl, wood-owl
Bashubet	To scrape
Bassik	Collar
Bathuk	Rainwater
Bawoodisik	Thunderbird
Bebadwook	Blackflies, mosquitoes
Beedeejamish	May flowers
Beothuk	The true men

Berroïk	Cloud
Bethoeote	Good night
Bibidegemedic	Berries, fruit
Bidissoni	Stick, sword
Bitoweit	To lie down
Boad	Thumb
Boagadoret	Chest, breasts
Bobbidish	Guillemot
Bobbidishumet	Guillemot oil
Bobusowet	Cod
Bogodoret	Heart
Boobishat	Fire
Botchmouth	Buttocks
Botowait	To spread or lay (something) out
Boubashan	(It's) hot
Boubishat	Fire
Bouboushats	Fish
Boudowit	Duck
Bougatowishi	To kill
Bouguishaman	White men
Bouguishamesh	Strangers, foreigners
Boushauwith	To be hungry
Bousik	Right away
Boutonet	Teeth
Bouzawet	To sleep
Boyish	Birchbark
Buh-Bosha-Yesh	Boy, son, male
Bukashaman	Man
Buterweyeh	Tea
By-yeetch	Birch
Camtac	To speak, he speaks, speaker
Dabseek	Four
Dabsook	Fourteen
Dattomesh	Trout
Datyun	Don't shoot
Debimé	Duck eggs
Debiné	Eggs

Dedduweet	To cut, to saw
Dee-cradou	Very large boat
Deed-rashow	To be red, to redden
Dee-Hemin	To give
Delood	Come
Demasduit	The flower that grows by the lakes
Deschudodoïck	To breathe
Deyn-yad	Birds (in general)
Dingiam	Loincloth
Dogajavik	Red fox (a Viking word)
Dogermaït	Long arrow
Doothun	Forehead
Dosomite	Pine
Drakkar	Small Viking boat
Drona	Fur, hair
D'toonanven	Small axe (a Viking word)
E-adzik	Twelve
Ebantook	Drinking water
Ebantou	Water
Edath	Fishing line
Edruh	Otter
Eedshoo	To see, to see again
Eenohaja	Cold
E-ènoodjah	To hear
Eeseebouin	Helmet, cap
Eewa-en	Knife
Eguibididwish	Kerchief
Ehege	Animal grease
Ejahbtook	Ship's sail
Emeothuk	Trembling aspen
Emet	Oil
Emmamoos	Woman
Emmamooset	Young girl
Eshang	Sky blue
Ethenwith	Fork
E-U-Anau	Outside, to go outside
Ewinon	(My) father

Gaboweete	Breath
Gashu-Uwith	Bear
Gasook	It is dry (weather)
Gausep	(He's) dead, breath
Geokabooseet	To be not afraid
Geonet	Tern
Ge-oun	Jaw
Geswat	Fear, panic
Gidyathuk	The wind
Gigarimanet	Fishing line, fish net
Gobidin	Eagle
Godaboniègh	The ptarmigan moon (October)
Godaboniesh	The freezing moon (November)
Godawik	Shovel
Godet (or Gotheyet)	Puffin
Goosheben	Lead (metal)
Gower	Scallop
Guashawith	Murre
Gunguiwet	Solid ground
Hadalaet	Ice
Haddabothik	Body
Hadowadet	Ice pick
Hanawasut	Halibut
Hanyees	Fingers
Haoot	Mind, spirit
Hodamishit	(My) knees
Homedish	(It is) good
Ibadinnam	To run
Iwish	Hammer
Jewmetchem	Soon
Jiggamint	Currents
Kaassussa-boon	Snow
Kaesinguinyeet	Blind (person)
Kannabush	Long (time)

Kawin-Jemish	To give one's hand (or fist)
Keathuts	Head
Kingguiaguit	To remain standing
Kobshuneesamut	The Creator, Spirit, God, January
Kooseebeet	Louse, nit
Koshet	To fall (to the ground)
Kostabonong	The cold moon (February)
Kosweet	Caribou
Koweaseek	The warm moon (July)
Kuis	Sun
Lathun	Trapping
Macoushan	A general feast (an Innu word)
Madabooch	Breast milk
Maduch	Tomorrow
Madyrut	Hiccough
Maemet	Hand
Magaragois	My son
Mamadponit	Harlequin duck
Mamasheek	Islands
Mamateek	Habitation
Mamatrabet	Song
Mamchet	Beaver
Mameshook	Mouth
Mamisheet	Living, alive
Manamiss	The thawing moon (March)
Mandee	(It is) muddy
Mandoweesch	Brushwood, underbrush
Mandzey	Black (colour)
Manegemeton	Shoulders
Mangawoonish	Sunlight
Manneetash	Pitcher plant
Manune	Cup (carved from a tree knot)
Manus	Wild fruit
Mapet	To feel, to suffer
Marmazing	A kind of boat
Marmeuk	Eyelids
Mathik	To stink

Mazook	Saltwater
Memasuk	Tongue
Memayet	Arm
Meroobish	Thread made from animal intestines
Meseeliguet	Baby
Metabeet	Horse
Moeshwadit	To draw
Mogaseech	Young man
Moisamadruk	Wolf
Mondikuet	Lantern, lamp
Moogaguinit	Metal, iron
Mookus	Elbow
Moosin	Moccasins
Moosingei	(My) ankle
Mootamuk	Thread
Mootdiman	Ear
Mowead	Trousers, leggings
Moydebshu	Comb
Myaoth	To steal, to take
Neechwa	Tobacco
Newin	No! (negation)
Nonosabasut	Handsome
Obosheen	One who warms, to warm
Obseedeek	Gloves, mittens
Obseet	Cormorant
Odaswitishamut	The cold moon (December)
Odemen	Red earth
Odishuik	To cut (oneself)
Odjet	Lobster
Odoït	To eat
Odusweet	Rabbit
Ooadjumit	To boil (water)
Ooish	Lips
Podebeek	Paddle, oar
Poochowhat	Bed
Pugatoït	To throw

Shamut	Caplin
Shapok	Candle
Shéashit	Grumbler, to grumble, to be grouchy
Shébin	River
Shébon	Stream, creek
Shégamit	To sneeze
Shosheet	Stick, branch
Shootak	Sharpener
Shumana	Birchbark pail
Tapatook	Birchbark canoe
Tedesheek	Neck
Teehonee	Star
Thing	Thank you
Toowidgee	To swim
Wadahwehg	The fruit moon (August)
Washgeesh	Moon
Washi-Weuth	The night spirit (also to become dark, to darken)
Washoodiet	Archer
Washumesh	Herring
Wasimouk	Salmon
Wasumaweeseek	Three moons
Wedumite	One who embraces, to embrace
Wenouin	Cheeks
Whitig	Arm
Whooch	Crow
Woadtoowin	Spider
Woasut	A Beothuk woman
Wobee	The White Man
Wobeesheet	Sleeve (of a shirt)
Woodamashi	Messenger, to run away
Woodum	Pond
Zoozoot	Hare

The Five Beothuk Seasons

The season of snow and cold
The season of new growth
The season of abundance
The season of falling leaves
The season of dead leaves

The Thirteen Beothuk Moons

January	The cold moon
February	The moon when the ice cracks with cold
March	The windy moon
March–April	The frosty moon
May	The moon when the snow melts
June	The moon when the seabirds lay eggs
July	The moon when birds hatch
August	The wild fruit moon
September	The moon of changing colours
October	The moon of dried grass
November	The freezing moon
December	The moon of the longest night

BIBLIOGRAPHY

Assiniwi, Bernard. *Histoire des Indiens du Haut et du Bas Canada.* 3 vol. Montréal: Leméac, 1974.

Barron, Bob. *Newfoundland and St. Pierre.* St. John's: Atlantic Divers, 1988.

Carignan, Paul. *Béothuk Archaeology in Bonavista Bay.* Mercury Series Paper no. 69. Ottawa: National Museum of Canada, 1977.

Fardy, B. D. *Desmasduit (Native Newfoundlander).* St. John's: Creative Publishers.

Howley, James. *The Beothucks or Red Indians (The Aboriginal Inhabitants of Newfoundland).* Coles Publishing Co., 1980. Reprinted from 1915, Cambridge University Press.

Marshall, Ingeborg. *A History and Ethnography of the Beothuk.* Montreal & Kingston: McGill-Queen's University Press, 1996.

————. *The Red Ochre People.* Vancouver: J. J. Douglas Ltd., 1977.

————. *Beothuk Bark Canoes (An Analysis and Comparative Study).* Mercury Series. Ottawa: National Museum of Man, 1985.

————. "Beothuk and Micmac (Re-Examining Relationship.)" *Acadiensis, Journal of the History of the Atlantic Region,* September 1988.

Morandière, Ch. de la. *Histoire de la pêche française de la morue dans l'Amérique septentrionale, des origines à 1789.* Paris: Maisonneuve et Larose, 1962.

O'Neill, Paul. *Legends of a Lost Tribe.* Toronto: McClelland & Stewart, 1976.

Oxenstierna, Éric. *Les Vikings*. Paris: Petite Bibliothèque Payot, 1976.

Pastore, Ralph. *Fisherman, Furriers and Beothuks, The Economy of Extinction*. St. John's: Memorial University, 1987.

Peyton, Amy Louise. *River Lords (Father and Son)*. St. John's: Jesperson Press.

Powers, Bob. *Shanawdithit (Last of the Beothuck)*, St. John's: Harry Cuff Publications, 1987.

Robbins, Douglas T. "Regards archéologiques sur les Béothuks de Terre-Neuve." *Recherches amérindiennes au Québec*, vol. XIX, numbers 2,3.

Rowe, Frederick W. *Extinction (The Beothuks of Newfoundland)*. Toronto: McGraw-Hill Ryerson, 1977.

———. *A History of Newfoundland and Labrador*. Toronto: McGraw-Hill Ryerson, 1980.

Seaman, Stewart S. *The Western Hemisphere Before 1492*. Portland, Ontario: Nordljo's Publishers, 1975.

Speck, Frank G. *Indian Notes and Monographs*. New York: Museum of American Indians, Heys Foundation.

Such, Peter. *Riverrun*. Toronto: Clark, Irwin & Co. Ltd., 1973.

———. *Vanished Peoples: The Archaic Dorset and Beothuk People of Newfoundland*. Toronto: NC Press, 1978.

Tuck, James A. *The Newfoundland and Labrador Prehistory*. Toronto: Van Nostrand Reinhold Ltd., 1976.

Weber-Podolinski, Alika. *The Red and the Circle (as told to the author)*. Buckland, 1984.

Whitehead-Holmes, Ruth. *Micmac, Maliseet and Beothuk Collections in Europe and the Pacific*. Halifax: Nova Scotia Museum, 1989.

———. *Micmac, Maliseet, Beothuk Collections in Great Britain*. Halifax: Nova Scotia Museum, 1988.